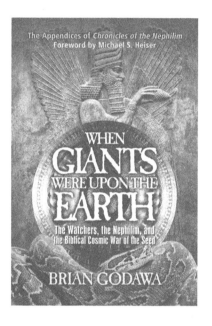

David Ascendant

Chronicles of the Nephilim
Book Seven

By Brian Godawa

DAVID ASCENDANT
5.2b Edition

Warrior Poet Publishing
www.warriorpoetpublishing.com

ISBN: 9798710846827 (hardcover)
ISBN: 978-0-9911434-6-7 (Paperback)

Scripture quotations taken from *The Holy Bible: English Standard
Version*. Wheaton: Standard Bible Society, 2001.

Dedicated to
culture giant slayer John H. Walton,
Whose scholarship has helped me to read Israel's storytelling
through ancient Near Eastern eyes.

ACKNOWLEDGMENTS

Special thanks to my wife, Kimberly, who remains my muse and co-lead in the romantic comedy of my life. To Doug Van Dorn for his giant encouragement and theological input, including the Septuagint reference to the giant Dan ben Joah, and other sundry things Nephilim. And much thanks to Sarah Beach for her excellent editing. And to Michael Gavlak for his brilliant and ruthless story feedback. Faithful are the wounds of a best friend.

NOTE TO THE READER

David Ascendant is seventh in the series of novels, *Chronicles of the Nephilim* about the Biblical Cosmic War of the Seed. Though it can be read as a standalone novel, the reader should advisedly consider reading it within the series. There are so many characters, motifs, storyline histories, artifacts, and themes that have been carried over from previous novels in the series, that the true depth and riches of the story can best be appreciated and understood within that context.

However, if you really want to just read this story about King David, you won't regret it. You will be shocked at the material you've missed from the lines of the Bible — and in between — but you won't regret it.

Based on the true story
that is stranger than fiction.

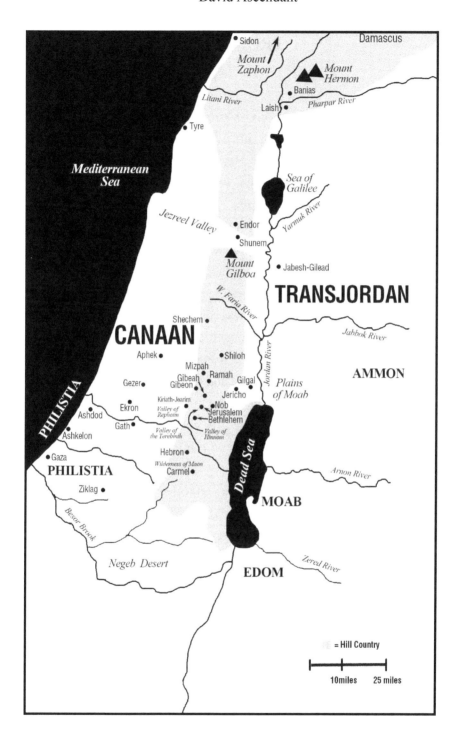

PROLOGUE

It was a magnificent civilization of excellence, virtue, and strength. They had managed to rule over the Greek islands and parts of the continent, from the pillars of Heracles to the pyramids of Egypt in the south and Tyrrhenia in the west. It had risen from humble beginnings to become an empire. It had a military and navy of unparalleled might; a ruling elite of philosopher kings with unapproachable wisdom; and such advanced culture that could only have come from the beneficence of the gods.

It was Atlantis, the city of wonder and mystery on the isle of Thera within the Aegean archipelago. It was rumored that the gods had chosen this location to reveal oracles of occultic knowledge as they had done on Mount Hermon of Syria in the primeval past. This explained the advanced architecture, engineering, and technology that it produced.

The capital city was laid out in the gulf of the island as a series of concentric circles of land separated by channeled waterways. At the center of the ring was an acropolis on a hill that housed the majestic temple of Poseidon, god of the sea.

The city was engineered like no other before it. Buildings contained running water, a complex sewer system, as well as unprecedented technology for heating resident interiors in the winter and cooling them in the summer. Word had spread around Greece that they had also discovered how to harness energy in a form that would enable them to power mechanical devices without the aid of human slaves.

But such engineering and technological advancement were only symptoms of a much more significant pursuit of the ruling class of Atlantis: godhood. Though some humans had been known to live as long as one hundred or so years, the average life span of most Aegeans was about forty to fifty years. Aristocrats would often reach seventy and eighty. The hygiene created by Atlantean technology and medicine had increased that expectancy. But in their collective memory, they knew their primeval ancestors had lived many centuries. Before the Great Deluge, they had heard of the oldest antediluvian reaching nine hundred and sixty nine years!

The patrician class had concluded that if the nobles could mate with deity, the resultant demigods would not only become gibborim warrior rulers, but their hybrid flesh would return to the longevity of lives once enjoyed by the antediluvian fathers.

They could not understand the reticence of Poseidon to partake in their plan of uniting heaven and earth with a Sacred Marriage rite between deity and humanity. He had mumbled about the Gigantomachy and the Titanomachy, and about some unknown pentapolis called Sodom and Gomorrah. But he did not explain himself beyond the simple declaration that the Deluge of water and the fire of heaven was the response to such unholy hubris.

As the Greeks remembered the Flood story, Zeus had sent the Deluge as judgment but saved Deucalion and his wife Pyrrha by having him build a chest that brought them safely through the waters.

But this story did not sway the Atlanteans in their quest for eternal life. They would stop at nothing to achieve godhood, and eventually, their constant pleas prompted Poseidon to give in and reinstitute the Sacred Marriage.

The gods would once again mate with humans.

• • • • •

It was a warm and sunny summer day on the chain of Aegean islands when all Hades was unleashed.

There had been an increase in frequency of earthquakes on Thera that had caused the more superstitious citizens to leave in ships for the western sea. But everyone else went about their business, having become familiar with such rumblings throughout their entire lives. All across the island, people were trading in the marketplace, farming their land, performing matrimony, and other mundane activities. There were aristocrats ruling, buyers trading, thieves stealing, liars lying, thousands living their normal lives.

In the temple of Poseidon, the priests were engaging in their liturgy of worship when the first sinkhole opened up beneath them and swallowed them all alive. A huge crevice split the concentric isle circles, reducing the buildings instantly to rubble, and crushing a multitude of Atlanteans.

What followed next was unthinkable.

The capital city completely disintegrated in a massive explosion of a magnitude that had never before been seen on earth. The expanding rush of debris and smoke choked all life, instantly engulfing people on the far side of the island. A pile of ash buried everything. A blast of rock and magma spewed out from the center of the caldera as the force of pressure built up over millennia finally released itself from the earth.

The ancient volcano of Thera had awakened.

An enormous pillar cloud of sixty cubic miles of rock, ash and pumice rose into the sky and spread out for hundreds of miles around, choking the life out of everything in its way. The uplift of the earth, created an offset of the sea that released a tsunami wave pushing its way at hundreds of miles per hour away from the explosion.

• • • • •

The Minoan island of Crete lay a mere hundred miles away. Its inhabitants could see the plume of smoke darkening the sky, and many sought the higher mountainous regions as safety from the oncoming wave. But most did not escape the crushing wall of water that washed over the island and wiped out every city in mere seconds. Hundreds of generations of civilization built upon the wisdom of its ancestors were completely decimated by billions of tons of seawater.

This incapacitation of the great Minoan culture of Crete would completely cripple its defenses, making it vulnerable to conquest by the maritime forces of the Mycenaens who would follow in the wake of the tsunami.

What happened this day would become the stuff of legends about the glorious achievements of a magical civilization mysteriously swallowed up in a day by the largest volcanic eruption in history.

But rock, ash, and lava were not the only things vomited out from the belly of Sheol that day. Within the debris that flew miles into the air and landed in the sea was a humanoid form. It was severely burned by its encasement in magma, but alive because of its divine being.

When he hit the ocean and was released from the hardened lava rock, the salt water burned his flesh with stinging pain. But this was nothing compared to the blazing heat of the river of magma he had been entrapped in miles beneath the surface of the earth.

But now he was free. And he was set on revenge against the malicious Creator and his archangels who had trapped him there to await the final judgment. That wait would be delayed as he began to swim westward with strong plunging strokes of charred black arms.

He had been incarcerated in the earth for generations. But he didn't care. He was a god of power and storm. He would work his way back up the hierarchy of gods to claim his rightful status as the Most High god. He would get his revenge on Yahweh Elohim and his pathetic offspring of worms, the sons of Israel.

He was the storm god, Ba'al. And he was back.

CHAPTER 1

The two naked young male warriors grappled in the atrium yard surrounded by rows of Phoenician columns. They wore nothing but loincloths in their rough sparring. They were Philistines in their home city of Gath on the western coastline of the land of Canaan. They exercised their perpetual pursuit of physical perfection and dominance as new recruits in the reserves of the army.

They were both Rephaim giants, but not yet fully matured. The elder, at eighteen years old, stood about seven feet tall. He was physically stronger than the younger one, who was seventeen and only six and a half feet tall. But he had more agility and cunning than his companion.

Aside from their size, they also carried the additional distinguishing trait of their antediluvian Nephilim ancestors: polydactylism, an extra finger on each hand and an extra toe on each foot, for a total of twelve fingers and twelve toes. This physical peculiarity aided their skills in battle by increasing their gripping span.

That gripping span of the older wrestler was being frustrated by the cunning trick of the younger.

"You slippery serpent," grunted the elder. The younger had greased himself before their contest, making it difficult to grab his body effectively. He was always a step ahead when it came to strategic planning.

"I told you," growled the younger, "Smarts over skill."

"More like knavery." The elder fumed with anger. He deliberately elbowed his opponent's face.

The younger's nose leaked blood. He tasted it and grinned. He responded with his own elbow to his elder's chin.

The shudder of teeth cracking together splintered through the elder's jaw.

It lit him up like a torch. He figured that the only place that wouldn't be greased down on the younger's body would be underneath his loincloth. So if his adversary was going to play dirty, then so would he. He grabbed the fabric and yanked at it, ripping it from the younger's body.

"Who is the knave, now?" grunted the younger, with anger to match his rival. What had started as a typical competition of egos between best of friends was turning hostile.

The elder tried to grab his opponent, but the younger caught his hand, and responded with a rain of punches to his adversary's abdomen. The elder grunted in pain.

The apparent weakness caught the younger off guard and he got flipped hard to the ground, stunned. He lost his breath.

The elder flipped his stunned prey around to face him.

The younger noticed that the elder was aroused. The elder slapped the younger hard in the face.

Then again.

The younger grabbed the elder's hand and yanked him down.

They met face to face. Passionate anger turned to passionate lust as the two kissed as violently as they fought.

They rolled on the ground trying to vie for dominant position.

The elder flipped the young man around to his face on the ground and gratified his lust unnaturally with his dazed younger opponent. It was the prize for victory in this contest of warriors in training.

The sound of a Philistine war horn blended into the elder's consciousness as he lifted himself from the back of his defeated partner. The call to war made him feel lifted up to the throne of Dagon in heaven.

But the voice of his younger companion, Ishbi ben Ob, brought him back to earth.

"Goliath! We are being called to war!"

CHAPTER 2

Goliath and Ishbi ben Ob said goodbye to Ishbi's family, suited up in their Philistine armor. Though they were native Rephaim of Canaan, their tribe had been absorbed into the Philistine people of the coastal territory a generation earlier. Thus, they wore the traditional armor of the Philistines: sandals, brass shin greaves, battle skirt, and chest armor made from strips of metal angled like a "V" across the torso. On their heads they wore the signature feather-topped helmets that resulted in the insulting nickname, "brush heads," from their enemies. Each soldier carried a small round shield, two javelin spears and a straight sword.

Goliath felt restricted by the uniform. The more elite units were allowed to make individualized alterations in their armor and weaponry. But until they achieved any notoriety, Goliath would have to be content with the standard uniform of the common soldier. He did not see himself being content with that for very long. He wanted to stand out, to make a name for himself. He sensed that the gods had a special destiny of greatness for him.

Ishbi's father, Warati, a retired one-armed Rephaim officer, punched Ishbi and Goliath in the chest. This was the Philistine sign for male affection and greetings or farewells.

Two other young boys, each ten-years old, stood with them. They were Lahmi, Goliath's younger brother, a growing Rephaim about five feet tall, and his companion Ittai, who had the signature extra digits and toes of a Rephaim, but was not a giant in height.

"We finally have our opportunity to fight," said Goliath.

"It is not a good sign," countered Warati. "We have been at war with the Israelites at Aphek. The only reason our generals would call up reserves is if they considered themselves in trouble."

Goliath would not give up. "Then we will be heroes to our people for turning the tide of battle."

Warati eyed the young upstart whom he had raised as his adopted own. "The surest way to a forgotten death is the relentless pursuit of memorable fame."

"Yes, father," said Goliath with deference. "But we must get going." All he could think of was the fame of that despicable Israelite Samson, whose mighty deed, years earlier, of bringing down the temple of Dagon would never be forgotten. Especially since his own parents died in the tragedy. It seemed evil men were rewarded with infamy that outlived heroes.

"We want to go with you!" yelped Lahmi.

Goliath smiled and ruffled his brother's hair.

Ishbi said, "You both are too young. And the runt is too small." The derogatory nickname was a reference to Ittai's small size.

Ittai blurted out, "But I'm as strong as Lahmi!" It was true. He didn't have the height, but he somehow had the growing strength of a Rephaim.

Ishbi ignored the little fellow. "Wait a few years and keep training. You will have your day."

Goliath added, "Stay here and obey father. We will return with the heads of Israelites on our pikes."

Lahmi pouted. He admired his brother deeply. When their parents died in the collapse of Dagon's temple, Warati, a close family friend, had adopted him and Goliath.

Lahmi followed his older brother in everything, including his furious hatred of the Israelites. He watched Goliath become obsessed with the desire to become for the Philistines what Samson had been for the Israelites; a legend, a deliverer enshrined in greatness because of his mighty deeds as a gibborim, or warrior of renown.

More than anything, Goliath just wanted revenge against the vermin that killed his parents.

CHAPTER 3

Goliath and Ishbi stood at attention with a thousand other military reinforcements preparing to join their brothers in battle north of the city. They had come from the surrounding five cities of the Philistine pentapolis. Philistia had been settled generations earlier when the Mediterranean Sea Peoples had left their habitations in search of new territory and landed on the shores of Canaan. They were not a singular people, but consisted of a variety of Aegean clans; Cherethites, Pelethites, and even Caphtorim, from the island of Caphtor, also known as Crete.

These Sea Peoples had quickly established their presence on the coast and immediately launched an invasion of Egypt. They were repelled and so accepted a form of servanthood under the Pharaoh's authority. They became known collectively as Philistines and maintained a profitable control of the access to shipping routes to the rest of the world, including Egypt, for travel and trade. The land route from Canaan to Egypt eventually was called the Way of the Philistines.

Hundreds of years in the past, the wandering Israelites first entered Canaan like a plague upon the land. They were a warmongering tribe that sought to empty the country through the merciless slaughter of all of Canaan's inhabitants, including Goliath's people. As he learned it, a cruel and violent general named Joshua led the Israelite Habiru, or Hebrews, as they were now called. They first plundered the Transjordan, the eastern side of the Jordan River, where Goliath's Rephaim ancestor, Og of Bashan ruled. The few surviving Rephaim fled into Canaan and some of them ended up in Philistia on the coast.

The Israelites hunted down all the giant clans of Rephaim and Anakim, but for unknown reasons, stayed away from the five cities of the Philistines. These were Ashdod, Ashkelon, and Gaza on the shore with Ekron, and Goliath's hometown Gath, a short way inland.

Over the next few generations, the Israelites became annoying gadflies to the Philistines. The two nations found themselves in constant battles over territory. The Israelites were a loose confederation of a dozen lawless tribes spread out like lice on sheep in the central hill country from the south Negeb all the way up to Laish in the north.

The pentapolis of the Philistines was a more cohesive and civilized confederation of cities, each led by Lords called *seranim*, who met in a Council of Five. They were less like kings and more like governors of a unified military confederation. Their entire civilization was so much more advanced than the ruffian Israelites, it was a wonder they could not exterminate them.

The Philistines had brought beautiful painted art, sculpture, and pottery to the land of Canaan. The Israelites were still scratching on rocks and using stones for utensils. The Philistines had developed blacksmithing and the new art of forging iron. The Israelites were still using bronze, copper and tin for crude implements and few weapons. The Philistines had iron chariots; the Israelites cowered on foot in the hills and mountains. The Philistines had developed a cosmopolitan culture that traded with the nations of the world, and adopted many ideas and gods into its own. The Israelites still worshipped a primitive invisible demon whose insane jealousy demanded his people avoid contact with other nations. It was a wonder they were having so much trouble overcoming these ignorant, uncouth and uncultured Hebrews.

The Lord of Gath, Achish ben Maoch, announced to the mustered reserve forces before him, "Aphek is twenty-eight miles north of Gath. You will engage in an all-day speedy march to bring aid to your fellow soldiers on the battlefield. You are being called upon because the Israelites have brought forth a magical talisman of great occultic powers that has struck fear into the hearts of your countrymen. It is a golden box that houses their demon god, and releases a great terror upon their enemies."

Goliath and Ishbi had been taught about this magical object. In ages past, it had toppled the mighty walls of Jericho, slayed thousands of warriors, and opened the gates of Kiriath-Arba to the hordes of barbaric Hebrews who wiped out the last of the Anakim.

Achish continued, "You will provide your support for our forces and you will sacrifice your lives for the glory of Dagon!" The soldiers cheered. "These dirty leprous Hebrews have terrorized us for too long! It is time we stamp them out for good!"

More cheers rose from the ranks. Goliath could only think of one thing, his vendetta against the Israelites. He loved death as much as these Hebrews loved life, and he was not afraid of their god who hid himself in a magical box. He had already figured out what he was going to do.

It would be glorious.

CHAPTER 4

The Philistine reserves from Gath arrived at Aphek late in the night. They were fed a meal and told to rest up in preparation for battle the next day. But Goliath did not sleep. He pulled the exhausted Ishbi aside in whispers.

"Ishbi, come. Let us creep out into the night and plant ourselves deep within the enemy territory."

"Are you mad?" Ishbi whispered back. "What do you hope to achieve, our hanging?"

"No. We are going to steal this magic golden box and change history."

"You really are mad."

"There is a madness in the mighty. We will do the one thing no one else would even consider doing, and thereby secure for ourselves instant gibborim status."

"We will secure for ourselves instant death."

Goliath responded, "Will not your familiar spirits protect you?"

Ishbi was the offspring of an Ob, a female necromancer who conjured spirits from the underworld and who had an affair with Ishbi's father. Some of those spirits followed Ishbi and gave him an otherworldly advantage in battle.

Ishbi complained, "My familiars are whispering to me right now that they will not go anywhere near the golden box."

Goliath sighed. "Ishbi I do not want to work my way up through the ranks. I do not have the time, nor the patience."

"That is for certain," interjected Ishbi. Goliath was constantly taking great risks in his headlong pursuit of glory.

"Are you with me, brother?" said Goliath.

Ishbi stared long and hard at Goliath. He wanted to walk away from this. He wanted to wash his hands of such absurd notions. But he knew he could not. He was tied to Goliath in life and like all Philistine soldier companions, he intended to be tied with him in death. He just realized that was going to come more quickly than he had planned.

"Let us go," said Ishbi.

Goliath grinned with satisfaction. He punched Ishbi in the chest. Ishbi returned the affection but with a bit more sting to the hit.

Ishbi was united with this warrior in spirit and in flesh. He wasn't going to let down his companion, his lover.

They slipped out of their camp and headed toward the enemy hive.

CHAPTER 5

The Philistine forces lined up in the valley between Aphek and Ebenezer, where the Israelites were encamped. In the morning, the mysterious golden box that housed their malevolent divinities was paraded before the Israelite front line. The entire army gave a war shout that sent chills down the spines of the watching Philistines. They thought that the Hebrews were possessed by evil spirits let loose from the box. There were even murmurings among the ranks that these demonic gods had struck Egypt with plagues and that they might do the same to them.

The box was returned to the back of the army to be cared for by a cadre of their priests. The Philistine captains enjoined their men to take courage lest they become slaves to their barbaric enemies.

The Israelites could see that the Philistines' were planning on overwhelming them with a massive blitz of their entire armed forces, including additional reinforcements. It was a total of nearly three thousand men. So, in response, Israel called up every man in reserve to counter that blitz with close to three thousand of their own.

In doing so, the Israelites called away the entire garrison that guarded the golden box in its own tent, leaving it and its company of fifty priests completely unprotected at the rear of the horde. Goliath and Ishbi had found a hiding place near there the night before, when they reconnoitered the troop movements.

As soon as the armies engaged in battle, all attention focused on the skirmish at the front line. The action left Goliath and Ishbi completely free to attack the priests. Goliath led and Ishbi stayed back to catch any priests trying to escape. They cut down the ones with ram's horns first, so no alarm could be sounded. A few had arms with them, but the giants swung their swords in great arcs with such speed and power that they murdered all fifty of the holy men in mere moments.

One Levite was able to get out of the tent and sprinted to tell the camp. An arrow from Ishbi's bow took him down.

Inside the tent, they saw two remaining priests standing guard before the golden box, the one they heard the priests call the "ark of the covenant." The two Israelites appeared to be important with their special blue colored robes and head miters on. When they saw Goliath and Ishbi approach them, the priests dropped their weapons, fell to their knees in fearful tears, and bowed low before the giants.

Ishbi's familiar spirits told him these Israelite priests were actually worshippers of Belial, one of their own. *Traitors to their god*, he thought with curious amusement. But then the spirits left him in a frenzy.

One of the priests cried out, "Please don't kill us. We are the sons of the high priest, Eli. We are Hophni and Phi…"

Goliath's sword cut them both in half before he could finish his pleading.

The giants stood before the gold box. It was small for such an important relic, only about four feet long and three feet wide and high. It was carried with two long poles that passed through rings on the bottom of the ark.

It was a curious artifact that sported two cast sphinx-like Cherubim images on the top. Goliath knew that Cherubim were the symbolic hybrid guardians of royal thrones as their own lord Achish had such images at the base of his throne. It seemed like a portable throne chariot to them.

Ishbi approached the gleaming box and reached out to touch one of the two winged guardians on its lid.

"Stop!" shouted Goliath. "You may release the deity inside."

Ishbi stopped inches short of the object.

Goliath concluded, "These carrying poles are obviously safe enough for us to grab hold. Quickly."

Ishbi wiped his slippery, bloody hands on his battle skirt to get a good grip. They hoisted the ark up. It was a featherweight to their muscular Rephaim arms.

They left the tent. But before they ran, Goliath grabbed hold of the large tent fabric and pulled with all his might. The entire structure came down like a death shroud onto the corpses. He wanted to take the opportunity to leave an insulting statement to complement their theft of this most holy and precious idol.

Within moments, they were sprinting back out into the forest that surrounded the valley. They made a wide arc away from the battle, circling back to their camp.

It had been so easy. The weakness of resistance they had encountered surprised Goliath. This Hebrew deity was pathetic if this was all he would muster to protect his little throne, his meager magic box of residence.

By the time the Israelites noticed that their camp had been ransacked and the ark stolen, Goliath and Ishbi were already safely behind their own lines.

The Israelites sounded a horn. Word spread that their precious idol had been taken. It caused such despair that their unity broke down and their forces melted away in cowardice. It was as if the absconding of the ark had been the bursting of a lung that sucked them all away like a rushing wind.

By the time the Philistines had secured the valley and the city of Ebenezer, thirty military units of close to five hundred Israelite warriors had been slain. The Philistines chased the fleeing Israelites twenty miles back to Shiloh where the tabernacle of Yahweh resided. They destroyed the city and burned the sacred tent to the ground, slaughtering the Levite priests who lived there.

The Israelites had lost the central symbols of their faith and their hope of unity.

Goliath was right. No one had anticipated such a bold and risky move. But he and Ishbi had changed history.

They were heralded as gibborim, and given a hero's feast and reward ceremony. They were also given the glorious honor of accompanying their golden booty back to the chief city of Ashdod. But through all the celebration, Goliath was haunted by the memory of how easy it had been to capture the magic box of deity. The thought occurred to him that this may have been a set-up.

CHAPTER 6

Lahmi and Ittai were inseparable comrades. They worked together assisting metal smiths, worshipped together in the temple of Dagon, played together in the fields, and trained together in the gymnasium every moment they could find.

This was one of those moments. The two ten-year olds were coming home from battle practice at the end of the day. Ever the competitors, they began quarreling over who was a better swordsman. Before long, they were sparring against each other in the street with their wooden swords and shields.

Though Ittai was smaller, he handled a weapon better. They were both exhausted from a long practice, but Ittai seemed to find a new reserve of energy to mount an attack of blows that pushed Lahmi back against a wall.

Suddenly, a rock hit the back of Ittai's head, stunning him. Lahmi promptly knocked Ittai to the ground with a well-placed hack to his rib cage.

They both turned to see the source of the projectile. A group of three other young kids had followed them home from their workout.

The children were a bit older, maybe twelve or so. They approached Lahmi and the prone Ittai. The lead bully, a Rephaim himself, led the children in a chant, "Ittai the Gittite! Ittai the Gittite! Fingers, toes, but no height!" *Gittite* was the word for citizens of Gath.

The cruelty of children found and exploited every abnormality in their peers with unrelenting ruthlessness. Extra digits were not usually mocked in Rephaim because of the imposing size of their possessors. In Ittai's case however, his small height turned his polydactyl link with the giants into an opportunity for mockery.

He was used to being picked on. It inspired him to overcome his handicap with skilled fighting. He had a will of iron that drove him to practice battle exercises longer and harder than anyone else.

But he would not need to defend himself today. Lahmi would. Lahmi stepped up to the bully, who stood a full six inches taller than him. He looked up into the bully's eyes with fierce determination to protect the honor of his best friend in the world.

The bully grinned maliciously and glanced at his two comrades by his side. "I bet his puny loins match his puny size."

The other two chuckled at the insult.

"Take it back," growled Lahmi, "or you will be sorry."

"No. You take back your little runt and get out of my sight or you will be sorry you ever chose him as your boy love."

Ittai rose to his feet and gripped his wooden sword tightly.

"He is not my boy love," Lahmi fumed. "But now that you say it, I think I would like to make you my boy love, weakling."

The bully's eyes went wide with anger.

Without warning, Lahmi thrust the handle of his wooden sword upward into the bully's jaw. It made contact with a sickening crunch of shattering teeth. The bully fell back to the ground in a daze.

Lahmi used the flat side of his weapon to crack one of the comrades in the head and the other one in the stomach. Both went down, one stunned, the other retching.

Lahmi dropped the sword and jumped on top of the big bully and began to pummel his face with a flurry of blows.

The bully's face broke. Blood began to splatter everywhere.

The other two perpetrators came to their senses and ran away crying.

The bully was unconscious. Lahmi would not stop beating him. Lahmi had been overcome by his fury. It was one of the things he had picked up from his big brother Goliath; a temper that would overtake him.

Ittai grabbed Lahmi before he would kill the bully.

"Lahmi, enough!"

Lahmi stopped. It energized him. He felt release and could finally think straight again.

The sound of a trumpet at the city gates interrupted them. The armed forces had arrived in the grand procession celebrating their victory.

Ittai said, "Let us get out of here."

They left the bloody, beaten body of the bully in the alley and ran to see the triumphal parade.

The citizens of Gath lined up along the main thoroughfare of the city to receive the triumphal procession of their returning warriors. It had been some weeks in the coming. They had originally taken the ark to Ashdod on the coast. Gath was the second city in its tour of Philistia.

Lahmi and Ittai pressed their way through the crowd to get a better view of the military parade. When they got to the front of the line, they could see the long array of soldiers, followed by their captives.

Normally, a triumphal procession consisted of captured kings, soldiers and booty, dead or alive, paraded in victorious display on carts or dragged in the dirt. But this procession consisted of a sole object of conquest: the golden box called an "ark" that held the Israelite deity trapped in its confines.

It was unimpressive to Lahmi, small and unbefitting the glory of a powerful god. He was glad he worshipped Dagon the storm god, father of Ba'al, and ruler of Philistia.

The Philistines were a syncretistic people that adapted the best wisdom and culture from those they conquered or with whom they traded. The Mesopotamian god Dagon was one of those borrowings, from the region around Mari in the northwest.

As storm god, he of course brought fertility and power to Philistia. But as father of Ba'al, the most high god of the Canaanite pantheon, he had a distinguished status coupled with the Philistine hegemony at this moment in history. Ba'al had faded in influence when the Hebrews had originally conquered the Canaanite territory.

Dagon was an amphibious divinity. He had the upper muscular body of a humanoid and the lower body of a fish, an appropriate incarnation for coastal Sea Peoples. But he could manifest humanoid legs as needed. This little golden ark looked like nothing more than a fish bait container for Dagon.

Ittai, however, felt overwhelmed with curiosity about the ark. He couldn't stand the stench of fish and always considered Dagon to be a rather capricious and conniving deity. But he was Ittai's deity, so he genuflected and worshipped as required. But something about this golden box drew his curiosity. Was it the understated size and unadorned simplicity? Or was it the beautiful winged sphinxes on the cover? He could not tell.

And what was inside it? The gods? He wanted so badly to open up the mysterious lid with Cherubim on it and peek inside its sacred confines.

Ittai and Lahmi might have differing views about the ark, but both could agree about the expression on the faces of Goliath and Ishbi, as well as all the soldiers, as they passed. It was not the bright look of triumphal, celebrative victors. It was more the gloomy look of defeated, dismayed survivors.

What could cause such consternation? Was this not a long-awaited victory over a foe with whom they had been quarreling for generations? Was this not payback for the tragic destruction of so many innocent loved ones in the temple collapse caused by the Israelite monster Samson? Was this not the capture and humiliation of the god of the Hebrews called Yahweh?

CHAPTER 7

Goliath and Ishbi sat before the fire warming their hands. The family had finished a meal, the servants had cleaned up. Warati, Lahmi and Ittai sat in rapt attention as the two newly honored gibborim warriors told of their mighty exploit in capturing the magical ark of Israel.

Then a dark pall came over the storytellers.

Goliath said, "When we brought the ark back to Ashdod, we had a feast unlike any we have ever had. But it only served to blind us to what happened next."

A shiver went through Ittai and Lahmi.

Goliath continued, "The ark was brought into the house of Dagon and placed beside his image."

Temples were houses of the gods, and the temple of Dagon housed a fifteen foot tall image of the storm god carved out of diorite. Diorite was one of the hardest stones available in Canaan, and the Philistines copied the Mesopotamian technique of carving important artifacts and images out of the dark grey mineral for the sake of everlasting permanence.

Goliath went on. "The lords rightly considered the Hebrew god captive to Dagon."

Ishbi interjected, "They call their deity 'Yahweh.'"

"What does it mean?" asked Ittai.

"Perfect existence, or something of the sort," answered Ishbi.

Goliath said with somber voice, "Since it is our custom to grant defeated deities some amount of servant-like privilege, the Lord of Ashdod, Mutallu, thought it only gracious to allow this Yahweh an audience in Dagon's presence. But the next morning when the priests opened the temple, the image of Dagon was on the floor, face down before the Israelite ark."

Lahmi and Ittai gasped. Warati sighed.

Ishbi said, "That is only the beginning of the pranks that malevolent deity has pulled."

Goliath said, "They returned Dagon to his position, but the very next morning, he was prostrate before the ark yet again. Only this time, Dagon's head and hands had been cut off lying on the threshold."

"Holy father of Ba'al," whispered Warati. The cutting off of heads and hands of enemy combatants was a peculiar tactic of victory in war. It was a denigration of one's conquered foes into complete powerlessness.

Warati continued, "It would take great strength to cut through that diorite. No one was seen in or near the temple?"

"It was locked and guarded," said Goliath. "The guards never even heard the sound of the fall or the breaking."

Ishbi added, "That abomination was followed by an infestation of rats as well as a plague of boils, tumors, and hemorrhoids."

Warati winced at the thought of it.

"What are hemorrhoids?" asked Ittai and Lahmi simultaneously.

Warati explained. "They are tumors that hang out of your anus and burn like fire."

The boys giggled at the image in their minds.

"Hemorrhoids are no laughing matter," said Warati.

It seemed to Ittai that these strange curses of magic appeared to be a kind of mockery of Dagon's power and those who worshipped him. But how could this Yahweh be trapped in a little golden box, subjected to Dagon, and yet display such acts of power?

Goliath interrupted Ittai's thoughts, "The lords of the Philistines conferred and decided to take the ark away and bring it to Gath."

"Wonderful," said Warati. "Push the curse off to us. What was going on in the flea-sized mind of Lord Achish to agree to such lunacy?"

"Worse yet," added Ishbi, "since we were the ones who captured the bachelor god and his box, we were told to lead the procession. So everyone is starting to give us the evil eye as if we are to blame."

Warati said, "You are not the only ones. Imagine the respect that Dagon has to recover. This does not bode well for our god to be one-upped by his own prisoner."

"Parlor tricks" barked Goliath. "It may even be traitor priests in our midst who faked it all and caused the plague with their own sorcery."

"But why?" said Warati. "That would only discredit their own office of authority."

"I do not know," said Goliath. "But let us keep a wary eye for any sign of the curse following us."

Goliath did not reveal that he suspected in his heart that this was the reason why it had been so easy for them to capture the infernal gold box. That maybe it had been a trap all along, a way for the deity to get inside the enemy camp and engage in such treacherous antics.

• • • • •

That night, as Lahmi fell asleep, he heard scratching in the corner of his sleeping quarters. At first he thought it might be a night demon, like Lamashtu, come to taunt him. But it was only a rat.

CHAPTER 8

Goliath and Ishbi were in the middle of exercises when they noticed Ittai waving to them just outside the practice area. They ran over to him.

Goliath said, "Ittai, this had better be important."

"Your brother," said Ittai. "He has the curse."

Goliath and Ishbi received a release to go home. As they ran through the streets, they dodged scurrying rats. They heard screams and cries of stricken citizens throughout the city.

When they arrived, they found Warati attending to Lahmi at his bedside. Lahmi was delirious and drenched in sweat.

Warati said, "He has a deadly fever." He lifted Lahmi's arm and they saw black boils in his armpits. "They are also around his groin."

"Yahweh be cursed," grumbled Goliath.

Lahmi groaned.

"What can we do?" said Ishbi.

"Pray," said Warati.

Ittai blurted out, "To which god?"

They stared at him.

He honestly did not know if they meant to appease the god who had struck their beloved Lahmi or their own god to undo the curse. He wasn't sure which was greater.

"Dagon, of course," Goliath shot back. There was no other option for him. His hatred of the Israelites and their deity ran so deep that he would never entertain anything other than defiance to the end against such a malicious being so full of evil.

Glaring at Ittai, Goliath noticed that Ittai was sweating and dizzied. He was about to ask him if he was all right, but Ittai beat him to the question. The youth fell to the floor in a dead faint.

When he awoke, Ittai discovered he was being carried by Ishbi through the streets.

His head swooned. He could barely understand what was going on.

"Where am I?" Ittai croaked out. "Where is Lahmi?"

"Goliath is carrying him ahead of us," said Ishbi. "We are taking you to the temple to plead for mercy and healing."

In his delirium, Ittai's thoughts were confused about which god was which.

He sputtered, "May Yahweh have mercy on us all," and he blacked out again.

Ittai came back to consciousness for another moment.

They passed by a long line of Gittites holding and carrying their sick loved ones.

He heard someone call out to them, "Get in line like the rest of us!" And another, "Not fair!"

They arrived at the head of the line. Ittai could see the grand stone pillars and cornice of the temple.

He saw Goliath's back, carrying Lahmi. He heard him say to a priest, "We are highly decorated gibborim, and if you wish to keep the skin on your body, you will let us pass."

Ittai saw them pass through the lead pillars and into the darkened interior.

He blacked out again.

Ittai did not awaken the rest of that day. He entered a comatose state, along with his friend Lahmi. Goliath and Ishbi feared they would never awaken.

The temple was of standard Phoenician design, rectangular and made of stone. Priests entered a long walkway lined with pillars on either side, and moved past various side rooms of offerings and storehouses. This was where devotees were sometimes allowed. It was called the outer court.

Behind the curtains at the end of the long hall was the sanctuary or Holy of Holies. Behind that curtain, only the priests were allowed. It was a smaller area, just large enough for a dozen or so priests to congregate. The centerpiece in the sanctuary was the "high place," an altar raised about eight feet above the floor with ascending steps where the priests would offer sacrifices before a diorite image of Dagon, a replica of the one destroyed at Ashdod.

Here in Gath, the Philistines did not place the ark in this temple as they had at Ashdod. They did not want another embarrassing power encounter to discourage their people. They hid the box in a non-descript home on the outskirts of the city.

Goliath and Ishbi laid the two lads on the altar at the feet of the image.

For the only time in his life, Ishbi saw Goliath weep. He knelt over his brother and let out a guttural growl of anguish.

"Dagon, hear my cries. We captured the Israelite idol. We offered it to you as a sacrifice. We did for you what no other Philistine had the courage to do. We risked our lives for your glory."

Ishbi was a bit more honest in his understanding. He knew they had done it for their own glory.

"I vow to you that if you heal my brother, I will devote my entire life to you. I will dedicate every ounce of my being to the complete annihilation of the Hebrews and their dog of a god."

"Dog" was a Semitic derogatory reference to male cult prostitutes. They were considered the weakest of all creatures because they were submissive males in a patriarchal culture. Goliath and the rest of the males in the society abused them with contempt.

"I unite with my brother in arms in his vow," added Ishbi.

Goliath looked over and placed his hand on his companion's shoulder in solidarity. Ishbi grasped Goliath's as a warrior would in facing death together.

In their focus on familial love for Lahmi, they had again overlooked the need to plead on behalf of the tagalong runt Ittai. They had brought him to the temple, but they did so as an afterthought, as one would remember to bring a child's beloved pet.

Suddenly, a wisp of air rushed through the sanctuary. Goliath and Ishbi heard a whisper from the image.

"Goliath."

They looked up, shocked.

The flickering torchlight made the shadows dance across the stone image giving the illusion of movement. But it was only an illusion. The purpose of images was to be a physical vessel for the earthly presence of the heavenly deity. The devotees would "call down the breath" of the god into the image as a representative of the god. Evidently, that breath now spoke to Goliath.

"Yes, my lord and god. Your servant listens."

Ishbi's eyes went wide open in astonishment. The two boys remained prone and unconscious on the altar.

The air went dead. Goliath heard no response. He could only hear his and Ishbi's anxious breathing. His heart beat heavily in his chest. The smell of fish penetrated his nostrils. Was that the remaining odor of sacrifices?

Perhaps it was just his own delusion, created out of the grief of losing his dear brother. But Ishbi had heard it too, had he not?

Goliath looked at Ishbi. Ishbi did not return his gaze. He stared like a statue frozen in fright at the image of the god.

Goliath followed his gaze.

He saw a shadow glide out from behind the image. It stood eight feet tall. Goliath now knew the aroma was not from sacrifices but from the god who consumed them.

That god now stood before the prone children and kneeling warriors. He was frightening. He did not have his lower fish half like the image did. He was fully humanoid, but clearly *not* human.

Goliath could see the pale scales of the deity's greenish-white and slimy skin glitter in the torchlight. He was clad only in loincloth and carried a trident. His musculature was broad and well built. He wore a golden ring to crown his elongated skull. He had deep inset eyes with black lips. And his breath stunk of rotted fish guts.

Goliath felt vomit rise in his throat. He pushed it back and swallowed.

"So, the young and mighty gibborim dedicate their lives to my glory, if I will but heal their precious little boy loves."

"Yes, my Lord," blurted Goliath.

Ishbi thought it was strange that the god would misspeak about Lahmi and Ittai. They were not their boy loves. Did the deity not know that Lahmi was a sibling and that Goliath and Ishbi were warrior companions?

Dagon said, "Well, I have heard your prayers, and I must say I am moved. Your ambition has brought you renown. You have caught my interest."

Another odor drifted into Ishbi's nostrils. It was the rancid smell of rotting flesh. He brushed away a couple annoying flies buzzing around his head.

Dagon spoke to the both of them, but his attention was more on Goliath than Ishbi. He said, "Goliath, you are of the Rephaim. A descendant of the antediluvian Nephilim. Do you know your heritage?"

"I know only that the Nephilim were the children of gods and men."

Dagon continued, "You are a demigod. And you carry their royal blood. You are both from a chosen line that goes all the way back to the Serpent."

Goliath and Ishbi grew more interested with every word. The Serpent was well known and worshipped throughout Canaan. They knew him as the giver of wisdom and eternal life.

"But do you know why the gods chose you?"

"No, my lord," said Goliath.

"Because as the seed of the Serpent, your kind are the hope of the gods. In the primeval Garden, mankind's ancestors were enlightened by the wisdom of the Serpent. But Yahweh, a jealous, petty, and wrathful creator, cursed the humans and cast them out of the Garden of eternal life, so that they could not achieve their birthright of godhood. The Nephilim were our attempt to unite heaven and earth in one flesh and reclaim that divinity. But Yahweh declared everlasting enmity between the Seed of the Serpent and the Seed of Eve."

Goliath now knew in his heart why he hated this god of Israel so. It was in his bones.

"It has been Yahweh's deliberate intent to conquer and steal this land of yours using his allotted rodents, the Israelites."

Dagon conveniently avoided explaining the failure of the antediluvian battles of the Nephilim titans in the Titanomachy, Gigantomachy, and the War on Eden. But he could still spin the rest of the story to his own end.

"Yahweh showed his vindictive and monstrous tyrannical impulse when he tried to wipe us all out with the Great Flood. But he could not. He killed his own creation and violated Mother Earth, but he could not eliminate goodness. He tried to one more time in the Great Fire of the Plains." This was the destruction of Sodom and Gomorrah and the five cities of the Plains with fire and brimstone during the days of King Arba the Great, progenitor of the sons of Anak. Goliath and Ishbi had learned that much.

"Then he sought to exterminate you as if you were vermin, by invading our land and putting every last one of you to the sword; man, woman and infant."

Despicable, thought Goliath. *What kind of a god kills innocent women and infants?* His own slaughter of Israelite women and infants was different. They were not innocent.

Dagon crowed, "But again, he failed and now you are the last of the descendants of the giants. You are the last of the Seed of the Serpent."

There were a few hundred giants interspersed throughout Philistia that he knew of. He thought of them as survivors of a holocaust of hate. An unusually large number of them resided in Gaza. The Rephaim were originally one of several giant clans, including the Anakim, the Emim, the Zuzim and others. But after the Holocaust, Rephaim had become the generic term for all surviving giants.

Ishbi spoke up, "But why have our myths and sacred stories not taught us of this tale? Surely, all of Philistia needs to hear of this travesty."

"No," said Dagon. "This is secret knowledge. Reserved exclusively for those most capable and worthy of handling it."

The implication was obvious. Goliath and Ishbi were being considered capable and worthy of this high honor.

Goliath said, "Capable for what, mighty Dagon?"

"I want you to create a secret order, a cult of warriors devoted to the calling of the Rephaim for the destruction of the Seed of Eve, Israel."

A grin spread across Goliath's face. He was only eighteen years old, but he knew instantly that this was what he had been seeking for his entire life. He knew he was born for this.

Ishbi knew it too.

Dagon continued, "You will call it the *Yalid ha Rapha*, the Sons of Rapha. They are to be an elite fighting force that will unify and lead the rest of the Rephaim giants in the territory on a singular quest. Choose only the finest young warriors as your captains, giants you can trust."

"When shall we strike, mighty god?" asked Goliath with characteristic impatience.

"First you must build your leadership, grow in numbers, and train your warriors. Yahweh is diabolical and more prepared than you can possibly know."

"But how long will it take?"

"Patience, Goliath. I will let you know when the time is come."

Goliath skulked. Vengeance was bitter in his mouth, and he wanted to spit it out as soon as possible, not suck on it for years. But the gods knew better.

Dagon put him in his place. "Goliath, you are a mighty warrior. But you are young. You have much to learn, and so will your companions. You know not the machinations of the enemy. But I do. And only through careful and deliberate planning can we have the hope of accomplishing the goal."

"Yes, my Lord and god," cowed Goliath.

Ittai groaned and moved on the floor. With all his attention focused on Dagon, Ishbi had forgotten the two boys and why they had come here to begin with. He said, "And the boys, my Lord, shall we leave them with you for their healing?"

"I have heard your petitions. You may take them with you. I will make no promises regarding the lives of these boys. If I am pleased with you, I will save them. But if I find any displeasure in your devotion – anything at all – I may change my mind."

"Yes, my Lord," said both Goliath and Ishbi. They solemnly picked up the two lads and left the sanctuary with hope in their hearts – and vengeance on their minds.

Dagon watched them leave. Then another god stepped out from behind the image. He was the same height with same elongated skull as Dagon. But he had the beginning growth of bull horns on his head and his body was massively built with muscle.

It was Ba'al, the storm god of Canaan, son of Dagon.

But he was not the only one.

Another deity followed him to complete this trinity of terror. Her name was Asherah. Unlike Ashtart, the infamous goddess of sex and war that had been svelte and sinewy of form, Asherah had a more buxom figure. Whereas Ashtart ruled through terror, Asherah ruled through cunning. Ashtart fought the Israelite invaders of Canaan, but Asherah seduced them. She also had pride of station as the consort of the supreme god El and "mother of the gods." The seventy Sons of God who were over the nations, were considered *her* sons by the Canaanites.

Ba'al had washed ashore on the banks of the coastal island of Tyre in northern Canaan. "Lady Asherah of the Sea" as she was also called, was patron goddess of Tyre and Sidon. She was also sometimes called "the Serpent Lady," as she often carried snakes wound around her neck or body.

She had taken Ba'al in and helped him on his long journey back to health. Though he had lost his previous status, she knew his potential and how he had risen in power the first time to the position of Most High. She remembered how he was the only god who had bested Ashtart the ruthless goddess of war. Canaanite legend had it that Asherah also persuaded El to allow Ba'al to rebuild his temple on Mount Sapan. By supporting Ba'al, she would be backing the mightiest god of the pantheon and would ensure her own co-regency over the territory.

As a divine being, Ba'al could not die. But he had heavenly flesh that could feel pain. So when he was imprisoned in the molten earth below, his physical body had been completely burnt through to a crisp. The pain had been excruciating and carried with it a searing desire for revenge on the creatures who sent him to his prison: the archangels of Yahweh.

Healing of such divine flesh was usually rapid, but because his damage was so thorough and deep, it had taken him weeks before he regained his previous strength, and more before the charred scarring all over his body had disappeared. One of the strange things that did not disappear was the flies. When Ba'al's flesh was burnt, it drew flies wherever he went. But strangely, even after he had long healed, the annoying presence of flies never left him.

Ba'al had once been the uncontested high god of Canaan. But with his dethroning absence, Dagon had gained the territory with the approval of the assembly of gods and had grown strong through Philistine power. Ba'al could not simply come back and claim what he had lost without the assembly's backing, and that would require some political maneuvering beyond brute force. In a political maneuver of his own, Dagon made Ba'al the "Son of Dagon," to keep him in mindful check of which cock ruled the roost now in Philistia. Unfortunately, that ruling did not include miraculous healing powers.

"What if the boys die?" asked Asherah "You promised to heal them in exchange for their devotion. Our magic is of no effect on Yahweh's curse."

"Not true," argued Dagon. "I said I would *consider* healing them, or I could change my mind."

Asherah quipped, "Plausible deniability. Clever."

Dagon said, "What say you, Ba'al?"

Ba'al was pensive. He responded quietly and submissively, but with confidence. "I say we cannot afford to lose our warrior cult. We are too close. But I think the Old Lady should remember who is Prince of this territory and support his strategy."

Dagon smiled. Asherah frowned.

Dagon slapped Ba'al's back. Ba'al winced with irritation.

"Sorry about that, son," said Dagon with relish. "I will leave you two to your lover's quarrel."

Dagon left them and disappeared behind the image in the tunnel that led to his debauchery.

Asherah sighed. She muttered under her breath, "Must you insult me in front of the fish?"

Ba'al looked back to make sure Dagon was gone.

"I am supposed to be his vassal god," he whispered. "How do you expect me to act, like I am planning on taking over Canaan with My Lady of the Sea? If he suspects for a moment, he will squash our plans before they have had time to mature. A little groveling on your part might help with the distraction."

She sighed again. He was right. They could not afford to be discovered before they could gain their audience with Mastema, the serpent overlord of Canaan. Without Mastema's blessing, they would not stand a chance in Sheol with the assembly. Ba'al could take back Canaan by force, but he preferred to do it legally so he would not be at odds against the rest of the pantheon. More importantly, Mastema was a brilliant legal mind who could ruin Ba'al in the heavenly court if he wanted to.

"Have you any news of Mastema's whereabouts?" said Asherah.

"Unfortunately, he remains in Assyria and Babylon, with no hint of a soon return. He is preparing for something big, but only Yahweh knows what."

She said, "Mastema frustrates me. He works on his own time scale and lords it over the rest of us in the pantheon."

He said, "Well, then we accommodate to his schedule and maintain our course with patience and calculation. In the meantime, I suggest you consider some groveling toward Dagon."

"Ugh," groaned Asherah. "Distractions, distractions. Just remember what sacrifices I made to support your return to power."

He looked her up and down. "And I expect many more sacrifices to complete my gratification."

She rolled her eyes and left him to seek out Dagon. "By the way, I like the horns. Nice touch."

CHAPTER 9

Within four days, hundreds were dead in the city of Gath. Bodies full of bloated, pus-filled boils, and bloody hemorrhoids filled the streets and garbage dump.

But within a week, Lahmi and Ittai had both survived the plagues and were nursed back to health.

Ishbi and Goliath were ordered to move the Israelite ark away from the city and take it to Ekron. But the people of Ekron accused them of trying to kill them all. They had gotten wind of the plagues and deaths that followed the golden box.

Some within the military ranks suggested that Goliath and Ishbi be demoted for bringing the source of this curse upon the people. But the Philistine Lords knew the Rephaim ranks were too crucial to their success as an army, so instead, they decided to take responsibility and get rid of the abominable offense. They sent the ark away on a cart pulled by two unblemished milking cows and accompanied by a guilt offering of images; five rats and five tumors made out of gold, one for each of the Philistine Lords of the pentapolis.

They reasoned that if it was Yahweh that had harmed them with the plagues, then he would lead the cows back to an Israelite city. But if the harm had been by coincidence then the cows would just wander into the desert to be consumed by Azazel.

The cows had gone directly to Beth-shemesh of Israel, a known residence of their Levitical priests.

Lahmi didn't care where the stupid box went. He was glad it was out of their lives and with it the abominable curse. He was just happy to be alive. Like his big brother, he grew bitter with anger at the God who almost killed him. He thanked Dagon for healing him when he discovered that Goliath and Ishbi had carried him and Ittai to the temple for prayer.

Ittai was not so confident of the superiority of Dagon. He wondered how it was that this Yahweh was able to do so much damage to those who had kidnapped him and held him prisoner. Why could Dagon not stop the plagues? Did Dagon really heal them both or did Yahweh lift his curse?

He put his doubts and questions out of his mind. Goliath and Ishbi entered the gymnasium where Ittai and Lahmi worked on their battle forms.

The two gibborim pulled the aspiring young warriors aside. Goliath said, "Let us go for a walk."

They took Lahmi and Ittai to the desert just outside the city. Ittai could see the sea miles away on the horizon.

Goliath put his hand affectionately on his little brother.

"Lahmi. You know that I am destined for greatness."

Lahmi nodded vigorously.

"But you are my blood. And I believe Dagon loves you, and has a wonderful plan for your life."

Lahmi's senses were heightened with anticipation.

Ittai suddenly felt left out. Again. Why was Goliath only addressing Lahmi and not Ittai?

Goliath added, "When Dagon healed you and Ittai, I knew that you were destined for greatness."

Ittai wondered, *Does he mean the two of us were destined for greatness or just Lahmi?*

Ishbi put his hand on Ittai's shoulder. It felt a comfort to him, as if Ishbi was affirming to Ittai that he was not forgotten.

Goliath continued, "You are now old enough for me to tell you a secret. But both you and Ittai must swear by the throne of Dagon – and on your lives – to speak of it to no one."

"We swear," said Lahmi.

Goliath looked at Ittai, who responded instantly, "On the throne of Dagon and our lives."

They had responded with "we," not with "I," and that without even thinking. How could they not? They did everything together. They shared a destiny.

"I am the head of a secret order called *Yalid ha Rapha*, the Sons of Rapha."

The eyes of both boys went wide. They felt they were living inside one of their own campfire tales.

"We are also a sacred order, commissioned by Dagon with a holy quest: the complete destruction of Israel and her god, Yahweh."

Lahmi turned giddy with excitement.

Ittai's mouth went dry. He knew Yahweh was their enemy, but he suspected that the divinity was more powerful than any of them realized. He was not sure they knew exactly what they were facing.

Goliath smirked with pride at Lahmi, "You are going to be initiated to become a Son of Rapha in training."

Lahmi could not contain his smile of sheer delight. They had planned and plotted and practiced to one day become mighty gibborim warriors like Goliath and Ishbi. That day was here.

But Goliath didn't look at Ittai when he said "you." Ittai thought, *Was he just giving his attention to his brother? Or was he excluding me? He said "son of Rapha," not "sons of Rapha."*

Ittai broke out in a cold sweat. He felt his stomach turn sour.

Lahmi noticed it too. He turned curious. "What about Ittai?"

Goliath looked away before glancing at Ittai with a guilty look.

He said, "I know that you and Ittai are very close. Like brothers."

Ittai blurted out, "Like blood brothers!"

Goliath sighed. The silence was a dagger going through Ittai's heart.

"I am afraid that Ittai will not be included. It is only you, Lahmi, who has been chosen."

Ittai felt dizzy.

Lahmi was horrified. "But why?"

"Because you are a Rapha, a descendent of the Nephilim."

"But so is Ittai. He has twelve fingers and toes. His mother was a Rapha."

"But his father was not. Ittai is a half-breed. He is stunted in his growth. He will not be able to keep up with you."

"But he is stronger than me. He is as strong as any Rapha twice his size."

Lahmi was right. Though Ittai had not been blessed with the size of a Rapha, he had the strength of one, thus giving him a decided advantage in battle. Size was deceptive.

"I am sorry, Lahmi – and Ittai. It will not do."

Ittai's entire world had just been destroyed and taken from him. It was like a second Deluge had washed away all his dreams of becoming a gibborim. And now he was being tortured. The future he had desired dangled in front of him briefly, only to be ripped from him, along with his best friend in the world.

As usual, Lahmi's thoughts ran along the same lines as Ittai. He was angry.

"Why did you bring him out here with me then? Why are you torturing him by revealing this secret and then telling him he cannot have it?"

Ittai's skin went suddenly cold. He felt a chill. The thought occurred to him that maybe they were planning on getting rid of him.

Goliath said, "I knew you two were close as…" He looked over at Ittai with approval. "As blood brothers. So I didn't want you to be the one to have to tell him."

Ittai felt like they were now talking about him as if he were not there. As if they were going to remove him altogether. He gripped his dagger. He would go down fighting.

Ishbi gripped Ittai's shoulder tighter, as if to comfort him – or was it to hold him down?

He whispered to Ittai, "You will be a fine Philistine warrior in your own right." But those were not the only whispers he heard in his head. As soon as Ishbi had touched him, he heard a dozen different voices whispering vile and degrading things to him. It sounded as if they were preparing him to die.

Ittai was not going to wait for the dagger that would slide across his throat as he contemplated Ishbi's distracting words.

He spun around, releasing himself from Ishbi's grip and gave the warrior a hard slug in the kidney.

Ishbi grunted in pain and went down to one knee at the sucker punch.

Ittai bolted away. He ran deeper into the desert.

Ishbi got angry. He stood, prepared to chase the little runt.

But Goliath said, "Let him go. We have hurt him enough. He will need time to get over it."

Lahmi wept.

Goliath watched his brother. He knew this was like separating Ishbi from himself. But Lahmi had to become hard.

"Dry those tears, brother. You are not a woman. You are a warrior. Now you will be a Son of Rapha. It is time for your initiation."

CHAPTER 10

Lahmi had his eyes blindfolded. He was led to another location not far from where he and Ittai had been. He stood in the warm breeze of sundown, but a chill crept through his bones as he heard the arrival of about three or four other men.

Goliath said, "Sons of Rapha, this is Lahmi of Gath, our newest tadpole in the service of Dagon."

Lahmi heard the men applaud. They were the officers of the warrior cult. His new brothers.

Goliath stopped speaking. Now Ishbi said, "Be ready to fight, tadpole."

Lahmi stood his ground, and raised his hands in readiness to grapple. He couldn't see through the blindfold, so he felt awkward spinning around, not knowing from which direction his attackers would come.

The first attack was a slap on his rear, followed by chuckling from the warriors.

He spun around to try to face the slapper. Instead, he got another slap on the arm, a hard contact. It stung. He tried to reach out quickly and grab the offender's hand, but he was not quick enough.

Then a series of hard stinging slaps coming from all directions assaulted him. It made him dizzy. He felt like a fool wildly grasping at the air, being laughed at by a cadre of his superiors.

Then the first punch struck him. It hit his left arm. He felt a shooting pain and grabbed his arm in protection. He rubbed the sting out of it. It was a hard hit.

The next one was just as hard, a hit in the leg. He yelped in pain. It must have been a kick.

"Stop your squawking, tadpole. You are a warrior, not a woman." It was Ishbi again. "Or are you a woman? Maybe you are just a dog."

Another hit. Lahmi became angry. He started to swing in the air. Maybe he could guess and get lucky, connecting with some giant's jaw who was lunging at the same moment.

It was not to be. A flurry of kicks and punches rained down upon him. They overwhelmed him.

He dropped to the desert floor trying desperately to protect his head and groin.

Then it all stopped. He coughed out the dust that had gotten into his lungs.

"Get up and fight like a giant," Ishbi's voice said.

Lahmi got up, limping. But he was up. He was determined to face the impossible odds against him.

He could hear the labored breathing of his initiators closing in. It occurred to him that maybe he had tired them out with his ability to take a beating.

He felt a blade slide down his tunic, barely grazing his skin, drawing blood. The tunic dropped to the ground.

A hand grabbed his loin cloth and ripped it off of him.

He was now exposed before the circle of taunters. They whistled and yelped sexual remarks at him.

He guarded his privates, knowing they were the part of his body most vulnerable to pain.

Another slap on his rear.

And another.

Then he felt two strong hands on either side grab his arms and hold him. He struggled, but they were overwhelming.

They pulled him to the ground onto his knees.

He could feel their hot breath on him.

He felt another slap on his face, and a stinging leather flog on his back and buttocks.

He felt the first warrior grip him tightly.

He could swear it felt like Goliath's own hands. There were no words from the giants, only animal grunts. They were like a pack of wild dogs.

He winced in pain as he was violated.

It was only the first of six such assaults, one from each of the men, that would complete his initiation that evening into the sacred brotherhood of the Sons of Rapha.

•••••

When Ittai escaped the clutches of Ishbi and Goliath in the desert, he didn't go back to Gath. He just kept running deeper into the desert. He was never going back to Gath. He was running away forever. Something inside him had changed.

He stopped and built a fire in the open to warm himself in the desert cold.

He had always felt like an outsider with his own people. A half-breed that did not fit into any group. Actually, he was a half-breed of half-breeds, since giants were already hybrid creatures of heavenly and earthly union.

He believed he was of Nephilim descent, but his oddity made him an object of ridicule. He was ostracized by normal humans because of his extra fingers and toes, and excluded by the Rephaim because of his small size. His mother had died in childbirth so he blamed himself for that tragedy as well.

He had been called "runt" one too many times. He had been rejected by everyone for too long. In fact, the only person in the whole world who did accept him was Lahmi. But when Ittai had been rejected by the Sons of Rapha and Lahmi was accepted by them, Ittai felt that it was the final insult to who he was. He could never overcome his small size with the Rephaim, he could never overcome his odd mutation with the humans. And now his only friend in the world had left him behind because of these insurmountable barriers.

He put his dagger at the edge of the fire, with its blade sticking into the coals.

He wanted to get away from it all; away from the world of rejection; away from the humans who feared him as a freak of nature; away from the giants who mocked him as less than Rephaim.

And he knew just what he was going to do.

He looked up at the night sky. The brilliance of the gods shone down upon him. In his culture, the stars were equated with the gods, and so their influence as well. Was his destiny really controlled by them? If so, then let them stop him now.

He pulled out his dagger from the burning coals of the fire.

He knelt down in front of a rock. It struck him how like an altar it was; a flat top, almost square.

He prayed to Dagon, "Forgive me, Lord of Storm, but you give me no other choice. I will not live this way."

He placed his hand on the stone and spread out his six fingers. He placed the blade on his smallest digit on the outside.

Then he cut down on the finger and sliced it off. The pain shot through his arm with ferocity.

He was tough. He growled, but he did not cry. His eyes were filled with hatred for everything that mocked him.

He held the red hot blade against the lesion to cauterize the wound.

The odor of his sizzling flesh assured him he would not bleed to death.

He ripped a piece of his tunic and wrapped it around the mutilated hand.

He saw the little stubble of a finger laying on the rock, and brushed it off with cavalier contempt. If he could not be a Son of Rapha, if he could not be respected as a descendent of the Nephilim, then he would cut off the offending members that marked his connection to that bloodline, the members that mocked him most.

He then placed his feet, one at a time on the rock and cut off each outer toe with the heated blade and wrapped each foot in a bandage as well.

Lastly, he switched the glowing blade to his wounded hand and cut off the sixth digit of his right hand. By now, the pain was so great he almost passed out. But Ittai had an iron will and would never give up or give in. Through sheer determination he kept himself conscious and coherent.

He wrapped his last hand awkwardly with a bandage. Now he would no longer be mocked as a stunted Rapha. He would not seek the acceptance of the cruel Philistines any longer. He would start all over in a place where people would think he was a human and treat him with dignity.

He was within a short distance of his goal. He had walked twenty miles through the desert and was just outside a city.

It was Mizpah of Israel.

CHAPTER 11

The small town of Mizpah was the site of several important moments in Israel's history. In her ancient past, it was where the patriarch Jacob had made a covenant with Laban and set up a pillar of memorial. It was a rallying point where Israel gathered together against the tribe of Benjamin in the early era of the Judges over Israel. In more recent days, the seer Samuel first called all Israel to come to that place and pray in light of the Philistine threat, upon which their god thundered against the Philistines from heaven and pushed them back permanently.

When Ittai first arrived in the town, he was taken in by the blacksmith, Micah ben Jonathan, a Kenizzite. Because of the Philistine monopoly on blacksmithing, such craftsmen were rare and often misunderstood among the Israelites. But the Kenizzites were originally a gentile tribe with smithing background. Micah was a simple man who worked hard and stayed out of people's way. Because of his own orphan-like gentile status, he had a special compassion for orphans of all kinds. When he found Ittai begging in the streets, he could see there was something special in this lad. He took him home to care for him.

When Micah noticed Ittai's wounds he didn't ask questions. He was not even aware of what they represented. He didn't care what happened in the small boy's past, he only wanted to give him a future.

After his wounds healed, Ittai showed great promise in blacksmithing. He already had a knowledge of it from previous apprenticeship. In fact, Ittai even taught Micah some important principles since Israelite skill in blacksmithing was many years behind that of the Philistines.

Ittai showed great interest in smithing weapons. His extraordinary strength lent itself well to the physically demanding craft. Micah allowed him to spend a part of each day testing and experimenting at making swords and the like.

One day, Ittai was looking through some old weapons that had been packed away in chests. At the bottom of one chest, he found a most unusual item.

He pulled out a strange-looking sword handle that stuck out of a leather case. But the case was not a long sheath as one would expect of a sword. Rather, it was about a foot square. It looked to Ittai as if it were just a handle that maybe led to a hammer or axe head inside the case. But that would not make any sense.

Ittai opened the sheath and pulled the handle out. A thin metallic blade ten feet long unraveled onto the floor like a whip. It was strange. It was durable metal, but flexible and razor-edged.

Curiosity caught Ittai. "What is this?" He was so absorbed, he didn't realize that he spoke out loud.

"A whip sword."

The words behind him made him turn. Micah had found him.

Ittai flushed with guilt. "I am sorry. I was only looking for inspiration."

"And you found it," smiled Micah. "It is a special sword passed down through generations from the original hands of Lamech ben Methuselah to Caleb ben Jephunneh, the mighty right hand of Joshua ben Nun. Caleb was a member of my tribe of Kenizzites, so that is how I inherited it."

The names meant nothing to Ittai. He remained blank in the face. Micah smiled. Of course he would not know.

"Legend has it that it was forged of heavenly metal from the Garden of Eden on the mountain of God."

Ittai's eyes went wide with holy fear. He saw words written on the handle in old cuneiform. Micah had taught him to read.

"Why is it called Rahab?"

Micah said, "Rahab is the writhing sea serpent of chaos."

Ittai held the weapon away from himself as if he was holding a dangerous snake.

Micah smiled. "It won't bite you if you handle it correctly. The metal is flexible like a whip, but more durable than any metal known to man."

Ittai asked, "How can there be such metal?"

"I told you, it is heavenly. It is said that Caleb was trained in the ancient battle technique of the archangels called the Way of the Karabu. They say he used this sword to vanquish the mighty sons of Anak: Ahiman, Sheshai and Talmai, and captured the city of Hebron."

Ittai said, "It was used to slay giants?" Possibilities began to swirl in Ittai's mind.

"Let me show you how it works," said Micah.

He took the handle from Ittai. "Stand back. I'm not trained as well as Caleb."

Micah found a log sticking up in the pile of wood by the furnace. He snapped the whip sword and it wrapped around the thick log and then cut it in two with ease.

Ittai gasped.

Micah said, "*That* is why it is called Rahab. In the wrong hands of evil, it could do much devastation."

Micah handed the sword back to his adopted son. "I want you to have it."

"Me? Why me?"

"Ittai, I believe you have a righteous heart. I do not believe your discovery of Rahab was happenstance. I think Yahweh ordained it."

Ittai's eyes began to tear up. He felt so unworthy. If his adoptive father knew his heart, he would not have called him righteous. On the other hand, he could think of a few giants he would like to slay with this weapon. He started to wriggle the blade like a charmed snake in his hands.

Micah said, "I will teach you how to use it. You do not want to accidentally cut off your own head."

Ittai smiled.

Micah added, "And with that unusual strength of yours, you could do a lot of damage to an enemy."

If he only knew how badly Ittai wanted that.

Ittai dropped the sword and hugged Micah ferociously. His gracious kindness toward the young man was incomprehensible.

Micah smiled through his own tears and hugged him back for all he was worth.

CHAPTER 12

A horn had called all the citizens to the town square in the middle of Mizpah. The square was packed tight with Israelites, most of whom had travelled to this little town from all over the hill country. There were the elders and the clan leaders, all delegates representing the interests of their tribes and their allotted lands.

In the crowd, Ittai and Micah were close enough to be able to see the faces of the tribal elders on display at the podium in the center of the square.

The assembly went hushed when an old man in long gray hair stepped up.

Micah whispered to Ittai, "That is Samuel the Seer."

Seers were the spiritual advisors of Israel. The Israelites were unique amongst their neighboring nations in that they did not have a king. Micah had explained to Ittai that they had been ruled over by judges and elders for hundreds of years because their god Yahweh was their king. The judges were both military leaders and civil governors of the twelve tribes. They led them in some victories over the Midianites, Moabites, Ammonites, and Philistines. They had secured the highlands of Galilee, Samaria, Judah, and Gilead east of the Jordan. But the Philistines retained the southern and central coastal plain along with the Shephelah. Other Canaanites held the northern coast, the Valley of Jezreel as well as Jerusalem and other territories. As a confederacy, Israel suffered disunity and conflict among its diverse tribal interests and squabbling. While elders and judges led the civil and military affairs, they were often spiritually advised by seers. Samuel seemed to be a significant one.

He also seemed to be an angry one. When he spoke, he struck Ittai as a man who was very annoyed at not having things done correctly. It was strange that such a short-tempered sourpuss would have so much influence over a people. Maybe this was why Israel had so many troubles. Or maybe Israel was such a troubled people that it drove this seer to frustration.

"Hear O Israel," announced Samuel. "You have been gathered together before Yahweh by your leaders of thousands because you have sought a king to reign over you. You have said, 'Let us have a king like the nations around us!'"

He paused. The crowd was amazingly quiet to Ittai. He had never seen them so. They truly listened to this Seer.

"Thus says Yahweh, the Elohim of Israel: I brought you out of Egypt and delivered you out of the hands of your enemies, the Egyptians, and all the nations who have oppressed you. I have been your king. Yet now you cry out, 'We have no king. Set a king over us like the nations have.' This day, you have rejected Yahweh who is your king."

The crowd now murmured with agitation.

"So Yahweh will give you what you want. Just as he gave the meat for you in the wilderness and the water from the rock when you grumbled and complained. Now you cry out for a king to deliver you from the hands of the Philistines. But you will be sorry for wanting to be like the nations. Yahweh will appoint a king over you. And he will take the best of your daughters to be his servants and will conscript your sons to war. He will take the best of your fields and vineyards. He will take an oppressive tenth of everything you produce as a tax. You will complain to Yahweh, but it will be too late, and you will deserve what you get when you get what you have demanded."

Another moment of angry silence from the Seer washed over the crowd.

He belted out, "Yahweh has confirmed his choice by sacred lots!" Murmurings around Ittai sharpened his attention even more on the scene before him.

The Seer announced, "Bring forth Saul ben Kish of the tribe of Benjamin!"

The murmuring rose to a cacophony of mixed reactions.

But no one came forward.

The crowd's noisy chatter heightened. Ittai could see the Seer barking orders to those off the platform.

Then a man stepped up. The clamor settled. This must be the man. But to Ittai, he looked as if he didn't want to be there, as if he were afraid.

What a strange choice for a king, he thought. The man was actually quite handsome. The kind that Ittai had seen women swoon over. He stood a full head and shoulders taller than any of the other Israelites. Ittai guessed him to be about six and a half feet tall.

The thought could not help but come to Ittai's mind, *Is he a Rapha?* Rephaim were usually taller by this man's age of about thirty or so. But then again, Ittai himself was living proof that not all Rephaim attain to such heights.

What kind of Rapha, so strong, so beautiful and befitting the physical image of royalty and power, could be so timid and hesitant?

This god Yahweh was a strange one. He gives his people what they want against his own desires? He chooses men as rulers who do not want to rule? Does he know what he is doing?

The Seer pulled out a flask and removed the cap. Saul knelt before the Seer. Samuel poured the contents of the flask over Saul's head. The anointing oil flowed down over his face and beard. The crowd noise increased again.

Samuel cried out, "Behold the man of Yahweh's choosing. Behold your king!"

And the mass of Israelite leaders all responded, "LONG LIVE THE KING!"

When the crowd died down in its applause, Samuel announced, "Hear O Israel! I have received word that the Ammonites have besieged the city of Jabesh-gilead. But I am no longer your judge over you. Hear now the words of your king!"

Saul looked surprised. He got up and wiped the oil from his face. He whispered to Samuel. Ittai could tell he was asking his counsel.

Suddenly, Samuel put his hand on Saul's head in blessing. Saul jerked back as if penetrated by a rush of wind. The tall king fell back to his knees.

The crowd hushed.

"What happened?" Ittai whispered to Micah.

"The Spirit of Yahweh has come upon the king."

Saul stood up again and appeared to rise taller than he had been. His posture straightened and he now exuded the confidence he had lacked just moments earlier.

It fascinated Ittai.

Saul turned to the crowd and announced in a firm kingly voice, "All Israel, send your military units and anyone who will fight to Gibeah. We will march on Jabesh-gilead and I will lead our forces in victory over these enemies of Yahweh!"

The crowd was stunned. Ittai and Micah were obviously not the only ones who had seen the transformation.

Then the entire mass of people burst out in a cheer.

Ittai felt tears in his eyes. Tears of inspiration. He turned to Micah and said, "I am going to Gibeah."

CHAPTER 13

Ittai said goodbye to Micah and followed Saul to Gibeah where he sought to join the military of Israel. But he was still too young, barely eleven years old, and was not allowed to join up.

He would not accept defeat and volunteered for the spoils unit. These were not fighters, but rather scavengers who would walk through the aftermath of a battle. They made sure the defeated were truly dead, as well as helped confiscate any weapons or other useful military gear that might be used as victor's spoils.

His first walkthrough had him tread through the mounds of Ammonite dead. He had heard of the Ammonites, but had never seen them because they lived across the river in the Transjordan.

They looked like shades of Sheol to him. Pale-skinned people with dark eye paint and masses of matted hair. They wore bones and teeth as jewelry and their clothing fell across their gaunt bodies in rags.

They were a death cult. They were known for their sacrifice of children to their underworld god, Molech. Ittai had heard Molech described as the "abomination of the Ammonites." Now he understood what that meant. He approached the high place and tophet where they had set up their siege camp. A tophet was the location of their burning of sacrifices. A large statue of Molech made of bronze sat with his arms outstretched. Beneath those arms was the tophet of fire.

As Ittai stepped up to the high place, he could see the charred remains of children's bones at the feet of Molech. Dozens of them. It was detestable evil. It sickened him.

They called it "passing their sons and daughters through the fires of Molech." What kind of people would do this to their own children? What kind of monsters would kill their own offspring?

Images of what he saw on the field of battle haunted Ittai. He felt in a daze all the way back to Gibeah. He kept wondering what other atrocities filled this land outside of Philistia.

He passed by some minstrels in the marketplace singing a ballad of King Saul. The music finally brought him out of his haunted stupor. After a battle, it was common for the ballad singers to glorify their king's victory and laud him with praises.

But these lyrics arrested Ittai's attention. They reflected his own earlier thoughts on the king. They were praising the king's handsome looks and physical stature. And then they went on about how he might be a descendant of the giants.

> *Oh, lord our king,*
>> *Our kingly Saul,*
>> *Is mighty, brave, and surely tall,*
> *Head and shoulders above all men,*
>> *Could he be a Nephilim?*
> *His beauty is heavenly,*
>> *His eyes do gleam,*
>> *Like Anakim and Rephaim,*
> *Heavenly host does give us nod,*
>> *Is he our very own Son of God?*

As Ittai watched the minstrels, a contingent of royal guardsmen approached them and arrested the musicians. He knew that Israel was the sworn enemy of the giants. Was Saul really a Nephilim? Was he hiding his identity to protect himself or were the minstrels guilty of slandering the king to incite sedition against his rule?

He might never find out. But in either case, it was clear to Ittai that no one should ever know his own true identity in Israel.

CHAPTER 14

In the heart of the sanctuary of Dagon's temple, an assembly of gods took place beneath the torchlight. They ate the flesh of animal sacrifice provided by the Philistine priests and drank the blood for refreshment.

The assembly consisted of Dagon the storm god; Ba'al, the son of Dagon; Asherah, the mother of the gods; and Molech, the god of the underworld. Molech was a peculiar deity. Because of extended time tunneling rock beneath the earth, his skin had grown calloused and pale, with heavy folds over his face. His eyesight was bad in the day, but a dark cave-like interior filled the sanctuary so his sight was just fine there. It was his rotting maggot odor that wrinkled the noses of his colleagues.

Between the maggot stench of Molech, the fish stink of Dagon and the irritating flies around Ba'al, Asherah could barely keep herself from gagging. These male swine had no sense of hygiene.

Molech had just escaped from Jabesh-gilead with intelligence of Israel's new king.

"What is his name?" said Dagon.

"Saul ben Kish," answered Molech. "He does not have a royal pedigree, or even personal achievements. The choice appears arbitrary."

"Nothing Yahweh does is arbitrary," said Ba'al with bitter memory.

Molech said, "He was rather comely. He looked the part to be sure. But the one thing that stood out to me was his size. He was head and shoulders above all the other Israelites. And he fought like a gibborim. He is a mighty warrior king."

Dagon said, "Do you think he could be of Nephilim blood?"

"Categorically impossible," said Asherah. "Yahweh would not anoint the Seed of the Serpent to rule over the Seed of Abraham."

Dagon looked again to Molech, "You say he was anointed?"

"By their holy seer in a ceremony dedicated to the destruction of Philistia."

"Then he is their messiah king," concluded Dagon.

"Messiah?" Asherah repeated. "Why would Yahweh put his holy election on a nobody? Why make him the special anointed one?" She sputtered with irritation.

"Just the same," said Molech, ignoring her, "there is still something about him that does not seem holy. You remember Moses and Joshua, even Caleb. This one does not have the same spirit. He is more like Samson. Drawn to the very darkness he is sworn to fight."

Asherah said, "I can turn him to our advantage."

Dagon did not buy it. "Samson killed more Philistines in his death than in his life. I would not call that an advantage."

"Need I remind you," said Asherah, "a great number of these Israelites are mine to sway. They worship me as the consort of their god Yahweh all through the hill country." She added with a touch of proud glory, "Yahweh and his Asherah."

"Is it true?" asked Molech. "Does Yahweh consort with you?"

"Of course not, moron. But I've got them believing it. They have teraphim of me, and have included my Asherah poles in their high places. I have unhindered access throughout their territory."

Dagon said, "Have you forgotten how easily Gideon overthrew you? No, if this is the promised messiah, we must release the Sons of Rapha, or we stand on the precipice of our defeat."

"Or our victory," countered Ba'al. "If I may recommend, father, the Sons of Rapha are newly created. They are young and strong."

Dagon and Molech nodded. Asherah knew where Ba'al was leading them. She had after all been conspiring with him.

Ba'al continued, "But they are inexperienced and unorganized as of yet. They need more time to organize, to prepare, to train. If this is the messiah king as we suspect, then he will be the most terrible abomination Yahweh has ever created. The Sons of Rapha will need to be at the height of their preparedness in order to be able to vanquish him."

Asherah added, "That may be our best course. But if we attack too soon, we could lose all."

Dagon paused, ceremoniously displaying his judging thoughtfulness. Then he said, "You make a good argument, Ba'al."

Ba'al concluded, "I humbly recommend we wait and watch. For years, if we have to. Use Asherah's freedom there to spy. If what Molech says is true, and this Saul is corruptible, then we only increase our chances by uncovering and exploiting his weakness over time. If, after all, he is not corruptible and proves to be the messiah king, then our cult of assassins will be fully trained and fully capable of providing the means necessary for extinguishing his lamp."

"Agreed," said Dagon. "Your counsel has proven most helpful, my son. My trust in you increases daily."

Good, thought Ba'al to himself, *Because when you are the most unsuspecting, then I will gut you and filet you like the fish that you are. And with the help of Asherah, I will take back my rightful ownership of this land, and with it, the Sons of Abraham.*

"Good," said Ba'al to Dagon. "Because when you are the most trusting, then I know our unity will be the only way we can win this War of the Seed and claim the territory we rightfully share together. Only by uniting can we defeat the enemy."

Asherah listened to Ba'al with relish and thought, *Ashtart would be proud of you, my little cabbage head deity.* It was one of the condescending nicknames she had picked up from Ashtart's biting wit before she was entombed in Sheol.

She thought to add one caution. "May I suggest you not tell the Rephaim of their true calling until they have reconnoitered enough intelligence to prove our suspicions."

"Brilliant," said Dagon. She was looking quite desirable to him.

Molech interrupted, "I hate to break up this festival of love, but I need a theater of operation. I have had my eye on the Valley of Hinnom just outside the city of Jerusalem. It is unconquered territory and I would like to establish it as a key location to build my ritual furnaces. Do any of you protest?"

The three of them looked at one another without objection. His desire for passing little children through the fire was disgusting to all of them. But every god had their own depravity and they wouldn't judge him as long as he did not inconvenience them.

Dagon said, "It is yours for the taking. But be available. We may need your help at any time."

"Of course," said Molech. "Until then, I bid you all farewell."

Molech left. The others shared looks of good riddance.

"We can all breathe without gagging now," said Dagon to Ba'al's approving grin.

Asherah quipped, "I would not speak too quickly, my lord. The both of you are no less repugnant."

The male gods looked at each other with confused surprise.

Dagon shrugged, and changed the subject. "I am feeling quite generous," he threw out. "Ba'al, I think I will give you your first city to rule, Ekron."

"Why, thank you, father," said Ba'al gushingly. "That is very gracious of you."

"And you shall be called, 'Ba'alzebul.' It means, 'Ba'al the prince.' Under my kingship of course."

"Of course, my lord. I accept it willingly," Ba'al said.

Ba'al thought, *But I will still gut you, skin you alive, and dance on your living carcass.*

Dagon's tactic was an old one. Naming a person or place was an expression of authority or ownership over them. Dagon was simply reminding Ba'al who was boss.

Dagon brushed a couple flies away from his face angrily. "These flies are truly annoying. If their presence persists, I may have to call you, Ba'alzebub." Ba'alzebub meant "Lord of the Flies."

Dagon said, "Now let us call upon the Sons of Rapha."

• • • • •

Goliath and Ishbi came alone to the sanctuary later that night. Dagon limited his presence to the highest officials of the warrior cult. And Dagon alone of the gods was present. He felt that including the other deities would only dilute his authority in the eyes of his devotees.

Goliath and Ishbi knelt before Dagon, eager for duty. He had told them of Israel's new institution of monarchy, and their first king, Saul of Benjamin.

Goliath said, "A king would unite their tribes and make their military formidable."

"Indeed," pondered Dagon.

"What is your command, my god?"

"Continue organizing and training the Sons of Rapha. But begin gathering intelligence on this Saul. He is a mighty warrior king and you will be fighting battles against him. You will need to know how he thinks, his weaknesses, his strengths."

Dagon looked at Ishbi. He turned his head as if feeling something odd.

Dagon said to Ishbi, "You are the son of an Ob?"

Ishbi bowed. "Yes, my lord and god."

"I can see it in you: familiar spirits. You are a strong asset to our cause. I salute you, Ishbi ben Ob, and look forward to your contribution. You have my blessing."

Ishbi bowed low again, "Thank you, my lord."

Dagon concluded, "Now, let us train this guild of yours to exterminate Israelites."

CHAPTER 15

25 Years Later

Seventeen-year-old David ben Jesse played his lyre with skilled precision. The harp-like eight-stringed instrument felt heavenly in his practiced hands. He had quite a reputation in surrounding communities for being one of the most gifted musicians in the region. He could see that his singing plucked the heart-strings of his female companion, Miriam. She was sixteen and hauntingly beautiful to him. About as hauntingly beautiful as the last girl, Adah, or Adelah, or something like that – he could not remember – and the one before her, whose name had completely faded from his memory.

He sang the lyrics of a royal marriage psalm. It was one of the best ways to woo a young girl's heart. Females were easily spellbound with their romantic fantasies of royalty. He could see her melting. He first sang of the king in his splendor. The next lyric was about the bride.

> *Hear, O daughter, and consider, and incline your ear:*
> > *forget your people and your father's house,*
> > *and the king will desire your beauty.*
> *Since he is your lord, bow to him.*

He knew that singing of a woman's desire to submit herself to a king would feed that sentiment in her toward his benefit. The power of musical lyrics could soothe a soul or inflame a passion.

> *All glorious is the princess in her chamber,*
> > *with robes interwoven with gold.*
> *In many-colored robes she is led to the king,*
> > *with her virgin companions following behind her.*
> *With joy and gladness they are led along*
> > *as they enter the palace of the king.*

Miriam moaned with delight through closed eyes. She was enraptured with this young shepherd's angelic voice. She began to see herself as the virginal bride and David as her king to whom she should give herself.

She barely noticed that he had stopped playing. It sounded like a mere *selah*, a musical pause. But the touch of his lips on hers opened her eyes her with a start.

He smiled at her.

She smiled back.

They embraced with a passionate kiss. He held her tightly. It frightened her. She knew she was in trouble. She had lied to her parents, telling them that she was going to a gathering with the other girls of the village. Instead, she met with David out in the field where he was tending his family's sheep. She did not know why she was so drawn to this troublemaker. He had a reputation for wooing the girls. But he was handsome with his long brown hair and beautiful puppy-like eyes. He was lean but muscular because he was also trained in war as most young Israelite males had to be.

And he made her feel like a queen.

Unfortunately, this "king" kissed his queen a little too aggressively. She wanted to push him away, but she also wanted to fulfill her longing. She had been raised all her life to save herself for her husband. She could not think straight. Her conscience screamed for her to stop, but her lips screamed for satisfaction. She felt at the edge of a precipice. She should have listened to her parents.

He said, "I love you, Miriam. I love you."

All she could get out was, "David."

Suddenly, a noise stopped him, the sound of his sheep. It was an unusual sound. He knew the different sounds of his flock of several hundred. He could tell when they were content, when they were hungry, and when they were distressed.

What he heard was the sound of fright. A predator was approaching.

He looked over to the flock. He saw them moving north, up the hillside. They were trying to get away from something.

David jumped up and grabbed his staff. He hissed at Miriam, "I will be right back. Do not leave. It could be dangerous."

Miriam pulled her cloak tighter around her body. She watched him leap into the mass of sheep like a heroic warrior.

David trotted through the flock to the cause of their disturbance. He gripped his staff tightly, ready to use it as a weapon. This area was known for its wolves and bears that often preyed upon the Israelite herds. David had been training in preparation for serving in the Israelite army. But fighting animals was different than fighting men. Men had rules of war, animals did not. David's experience with men did give him an advantage of a sort. There was another difference that empowered his experience: men were evil, animals were not. Animals killed to eat and survive, men killed to destroy and subjugate so they could be as gods, enslaving other men. Facing evil men was far worse than facing hungry animals.

He found the origin of the disturbance. A chill went down his spine. He crouched and planted his feet in readiness. It was a predator he had not encountered before. It was a lion. It crouched thirty feet from him. It held the body of a broken, bloody lamb in its paws. It had taken its first bite of flesh, smearing its jaws with the blood of the little creature. When it saw David, it growled, and kept its teeth bared.

David said a quick prayer to Yahweh for help. He glanced around swiftly. No companions to the lion prowled about. That was a blessing. Otherwise, he might find himself as the next meal served.

He faced the monster with his staff pointed at it like a spear. The shepherd staff was deceptively simple, not merely used to keep sheep in line. In the hands of a skilled fighter like David, it was an efficient weapon that could pierce and pummel a victim. David also had a dagger in his belt, for closer attack.

He set his staff down slowly to the ground, ready to pick it up if needed.

He pulled out his sling, two three-foot-long leather straps with a pouch in the middle. He used it as both a hunting and fighting weapon. He reached in his stone bag and pulled out a rock the size of an egg. He set it in the sling and gathered both ends of the straps in his right hand as the rock dangled in its pouch. All the while, he kept his eyes on the beast that watched him.

He only had one chance to hit the lion's skull and stun it. Then he would have to jump it and plunge his dagger into its brain. If he missed his target, the monster would probably rush him and cut him to pieces. He was only thirty feet from the predator. He had practiced at greater distances.

The lion stayed in its position, guarding its prize. Its large mane and beard spread out with regal display. Bears were bulky brutes, wolves were self-protective and stayed in packs. But lions were vicious and cunning. They seemed to have a sense of vindictive hatred for humans in Judah, probably because so few of them were left since the advance of Israelite settlement.

David slung the straps back and forth to build up momentum and keep the lion from reacting to sudden movement. Then he increased the spin and swung the sling in an arc over his head.

The lion stood with a predatory glare. It was large. It could look David straight in the eyes, standing up. It crouched, ready to leap.

David released.

But he was off his mark. Terribly off. The stone did not even hit the monster at all. It grazed past its mane and onto the ground far behind it.

He had missed. It was an easy target, and he had missed.

He had no time to even consider frustration. The lion bounded toward him, ready to rip open its new victim with jaws of iron.

David reached down and grabbed the staff. He raised it up just as the lion pounced. The staff jammed spear-like into the roaring gullet of the unsuspecting carnivore. It lodged deep in the animal's throat. The lion became disoriented and choking. It tried to paw the large stick out of its mouth.

David rolled backward on the ground from the force of the encounter. He used the lion's moment of confusion to draw his dagger and jump onto the back of the monster. He grabbed its mane and held on. The creature circled wildly around, trying to loose itself.

It was too much for the lion. David reached around with one hand in the mane and the other gripping his dagger. He jammed the blade into the eye of the beast. It roared in pain.

David thrust again, this time finding the ear and going deep into the brain.

The creature shuddered from the lethal blow. It took a few more moments before the gigantic feline fell to the ground in seizures.

David stayed on the back, gripping it tightly until he was sure the thing was finally, truly dead.

He pushed himself off the lion and wiped the blade on the fur of the corpse.

He smiled victoriously. He had killed the King of Beasts. It reminded him of the mighty Judge of Israel, Samson, who killed lions with his bare hands. Looking up, he murmured a prayer, "Praise Yahweh, who saves me from the mouth of the lion."

His blood ran hot. He felt filled with the glory of strength and victory. Then he remembered what else had been surging through his veins earlier.

"Miriam," he gasped.

He ran back to the rocks where he had told her to stay.

She was not there.

He looked around in a panic. Was there another lion? Had another beast carried her away?

His eyes caught the form of Miriam running down the hillside on her way back to the village.

The rush of energy in his body from his death-defying encounter began to fade, followed by a flush of realization in his soul. A sudden flood of conviction came over David.

He fell to the ground on his knees and wept. He had come so close to disobeying Yahweh. He was angry with himself, with his passionate excess. He felt the weight of contradiction that one moment he would be singing praises to Yahweh and exulting in the glories of heaven, and the next moment, he would feel himself a slave of his fleshly desire for young women. He was like Samson in more than just his gibborim ways. Samson had been Yahweh's deliverer of Israel not long ago, yet he had been undone by his weakness for women.

"I am a hypocrite, my Lord," he cried, "I am unworthy of you. I am a slave of my flesh while I proclaim my devotion of the spirit. Please forgive me, Yahweh. Give me the strength to honor you in my deeds, not merely my words."

A voice interrupted his repentance. "David!"

David looked up. It was Elihu, his next older brother.

"Every time I come to get you, you are crying. Just because you are the baby of the family does not mean you should be crying all the time. It is not befitting of manliness."

David said nothing. Elihu would always misunderstand him. Elihu was an idiot.

Elihu continued, "Get down to the village, will you? Father has called us all before the Seer."

"Samuel?" said David.

"Yes. Who else would it be, Eliab, the Seer?" Eliab was their eldest sibling. They often joked about how self-important Eliab considered himself, as the first born. He acted like he was a prince.

Elihu concluded, "It is very important. Samuel has sacrificed a heifer and has consecrated our entire family. Now he is asking to see you."

"Me?" said David, confused.

Elihu said, "Stop repeating what I am saying and go now!"

David ran.

CHAPTER 16

3 Weeks Earlier

King Agag of Amalek was a giant who stood about eight feet tall, with sinewy musculature and angular facial features. He was bald and wore an antler headdress as his crown. His ears had been artificially cut into pointed wolf-like shape and his body was pierced all over with rings, bars and bones. In battle, he wore the traditional war paint of the Amalekites: white with black accents of lightning bolts and jagged edges. But he did not wear war paint at this moment, because he was not at war. He was in captivity in the Israelite city of Gilgal by the river Jordan.

King Saul stood opposite him staring at his sworn enemy, now held in chains in the prison outside the royal palace. They were alone. He noticed a restlessness and a slight tremor in the arms and head of his captive, accompanied by a perpetual grin that looked more painful than humorous and resulted in occasional blurts of maniacal laughter. These Amalekites were not merely evil, they were stricken with a madness because of their diet of human flesh. They were cannibals. They were also very hard to kill. They engaged in dark rituals and howled when they fought because they were known to be possessed by the *siyyim* and *iyyim,* howling desert demons. They worshipped the satyr goat god Azazel and the goddess Lilith, connected with their Edomite and Seirim past.

Saul was king of Israel and Yahweh had commanded him to wipe out the Amalekites. They were considered *herem*, one of several specific clans and nations that Yahweh devoted to complete destruction. Every man, woman and child were to be put to the sword. Even the animals were not to be held alive for spoil.

As far as Saul knew, this was because the Amalekites were the first to attack the Israelites in the Sinai wilderness when they first left Egypt's slavery in the Exodus. Joshua had fought them valiantly and rose in esteem and rank to eventually become the general of the forces of Moses the Deliverer. The Amalekites were a nomadic desert tribe who rode camels. Saul vaguely remembered there being a phrase about Yahweh promising to blot out the descendants of Amalek. He had no doubt the presence of Rephaim giants in their midst was reason as well.

Saul had recently returned from his herem campaign against the Amalekites all the way from the Desert of Shur near Egypt to the reaches of Havilah in the Negeb. He had blotted them out, just as Yahweh commanded; every man, woman and child. And he had built a monument to his victory in the nearby city of Carmel.

There were a few roaming bands of Amalek in Philistia, but he left those alone rather than stir up the Philistines, with whom he had already had too much trouble. He also let the people spare the best unblemished oxen and sheep alive for sacrifice at Gilgal. And he had spared King Agag because he found him fascinating. Saul had a morbid curiosity of the dark side of reality that he kept hidden from the likes of the holy seer Samuel. He felt strangely drawn to the forbidden.

"What is it like to eat human flesh?" asked Saul.

Agag answered, "When you execute me, you can find out for yourself by eating mine."

It repulsed Saul. He would never do such a thing.

"Why do you do it? Why do you not just eat animals?"

"Because when we consume our enemies, we absorb their life force into ourselves. We become stronger." Agag punctuated his sentence with a snide burst of laughter that reminded Saul of a hyena.

These monsters must be mad, Saul thought, to consider their deteriorating muscle control a sign of strength.

Saul was near sixty years of age, but he still felt vigorous and healthy, like he could live another sixty.

"How far back can you trace your Rephaim heritage?"

"To King Arba, father of the mighty Anak. How far back can you trace yours?"

"I am not a Rapha," said Saul.

"You are much taller than your fellow Israelites."

Saul became annoyed. He was unusually tall, but that didn't mean he had Nephilim blood. For one thing, he lacked the extra fingers and toes that his bound adversary clearly had. Though he had heard not all descendants of the Nephilim had such extra digits.

Agag pushed further. "Have you not wondered why you stand out from them? Why you are so – superior?"

Saul did feel alienated from his fellow Israelites in more ways than one. But he was not going to admit that to this cursed one. He changed the subject.

"Yet, here you stand, the mighty superior Agag, chained in captivity by your inferiors."

Agag's perpetual toothy grin seemed a constant mockery to him. He wanted to wipe that smile off his face with a sword.

Saul added, "Samuel the Seer told me that the king of Israel will exterminate the last of the giants in the land. He calls you and your minions the Seed of the Serpent."

Agag responded, "The Ob of Endor told me that you have been a naughty king, that your kingdom shall not continue, and that your god has sought out another prince after his own heart. She calls you the Seed of None."

Saul's face went pale. Those words hit him like a dagger to the heart —the exact words that Samuel used, another prince "after his own heart." He knew Obs were slithery sorceresses and necromancers. But who was this Ob of Endor and how did she know that secret?

Saul had recently beaten the Philistines at Michmash. He had been told by Samuel to wait at Gilgal for his arrival and they would sacrifice to Yahweh. But Samuel had been delayed. Saul worried that the

Philistines might attack again before he could entreat the Lord, so he had gone ahead and sacrificed without Samuel. When Samuel finally arrived, he was angry with Saul. He cursed the king saying that because he had not kept the command of Yahweh, his kingdom would not continue. Then he had said, "Yahweh has sought out a man after his own heart, and Yahweh has commanded him to be prince over his people."

Saul had no idea who this prince was and Samuel would not say. It seemed to Saul that it might have been a rash comment blurted out of anger without any real significance, especially since things went on as normal.

Saul's son Jonathan went on to personally secure the surrender of a Philistine garrison on his own. Saul commanded the soldiers to abstain from eating honey. But when he discovered Jonathan had disobeyed the order, he tempered his own rash command and forgave Jonathan. Surely Yahweh was as forgiving as well.

But Samuel's words had shaken Saul to his very soul. He had tried to be a man after God's heart. He had questioned his calling because he thought his father's house was too humble of position in Israel. He had fought against the Philistines without concern for his own survival. He avoided drawing attention to his kingship so that Israelites would not elevate him too highly. What more could Yahweh ask for?

Agag interrupted his thoughts, "You do not look well, King Saul. Was it something I said?"

That grin. That malicious annoying grin. Followed by another laughing cackle that stung Saul like a scorpion. Maybe strangling this savage would be better than cutting his throat.

A royal herald interrupted Saul from behind. "My lord, the Seer has arrived. He requests an audience."

"Send him in."

When Samuel entered, he glared with a surprised look of shock at Agag. Samuel was now an old man in his eighties. He had white hair, a straggly beard and an unkempt appearance. He no longer cared for the things of this world and tended to act as if he could not wait to leave it all. It led to him having a rather ornery disposition.

His glare turned back to Saul. "I cried out all night before Yahweh on your behalf."

Saul felt like a child being scolded for something he did not know he did wrong. He often felt this way with Samuel, as if he could be slapped at any moment. He tried to be positive.

"Blessed be you to Yahweh, Samuel. I have obeyed the commandment of Yahweh."

Samuel did not change his glaring look. "Then what is the bleating of sheep and lowing of oxen that rings in my ears?"

Saul knew he was referring to the enemy spoils. He scrambled to explain. "The people saved the best of the animals of the Amalekites to sacrifice them unto Yahweh. But the rest I destroyed immediately, just as Yahweh commanded…"

"Stop!" yelled Samuel. "I will tell you what Yahweh told me last night."

Saul gulped. He was in trouble again. He seemed to always be in trouble with Yahweh.

Samuel spoke like a chastising father. "You thought so lowly of yourself. But Yahweh anointed you to be king over all the tribes of Israel. And he gave you a command. A simple command: to devote all the Amalekites and their belongings to destruction."

"But I obeyed the voice of Yahweh. I went on his mission and I devoted the Amalekites to destruction just as you said, and I brought their King before you. It was the people who spared the sheep and oxen from the ban to bring here to sacrifice before Yahweh."

King Agag chuckled at Saul's blame shifting. Samuel did not dignify the pagan with a look. He fumed.

"Does Yahweh have as much satisfaction in burnt offerings and sacrifice as he does in those obeying his voice? Behold, obedience is better than sacrifice. Your rebellion is as the sin of divination. Your presumption is as idolatry. Because you have rejected the word of Yahweh, he has also rejected you from being king."

Agag cackled again. Samuel ignored the despicable Amalekite.

Saul fell to his knees and cried out, "I have sinned. I have disobeyed the voice of Yahweh and followed the voice of the people. Please forgive my sin and return with me that I may bow before Yahweh."

Samuel snorted. This was just like Saul. He was a manipulator. He turned his religious displays on and off with such insincerity it repulsed Samuel. The time for patience was over.

"I will not return with you. Yahweh has rejected you from being king over Israel."

He turned to leave. Saul grabbed Samuel's cloak so tightly, the hem ripped. "Please, Samuel, please. Return with me, I beg of you."

Samuel looked at his torn hem, then back to Saul. "Yahweh has torn your kingdom from you and has given it to another."

Saul broke down weeping in pathetic tears. "I am sorry. Please restore me before the elders!"

Samuel knelt down by Saul. "You have not obeyed the voice of Yahweh. He will not change his mind. But I will do what you should have done."

He grabbed Saul's sword from his scabbard and walked over to Agag. Agag became uneasy. His mouth dried up. He angled for mercy. "Surely, glorious Seer, the bitterness of death is passed. I will gladly bow before this Yahweh and serve him as subject."

Samuel said, "Your sword has made women childless. So your mother shall be childless forever."

He raised the sword and brought it down upon Agag's shoulder. Agag screamed in pain. He yelled, "Curse your god and king, Seer!"

"No," replied Samuel with a hushed tone. "Curse your gods and seed." And he swung again. The blade severed the giant's head from his body. It fell to the floor and rolled near the feet of Saul who gasped in horror at the ghastly eyes staring into his soul.

Samuel hacked at Agag's monstrous body until it was cut to pieces.

Finally, he stopped, breathing heavily from the exertion. He turned to the startled king, still kneeling on the floor stunned. He threw the sword clanging onto the floor by Saul.

"That is what you should have done."

Saul was speechless.

Samuel said, "I am going to Ramah. Our paths shall never cross again — this side of Sheol."

Samuel left.

CHAPTER 17

David hurried down the hill to get back to the village. Bethlehem was an insignificant town on the edge of the desert of Judah five miles south of Jerusalem. There were only a few hundred residents. Though it was the burial place of Rachel, the patriarch Jacob's wife, it never rose to prominence. David's father Jesse was not a wealthy man and had no status to be known for. He had eight sons, and David was the youngest and often neglected.

When he arrived at the high place altar in the middle of the square, he stopped to see the townspeople gathered with the elders. Upon the altar, a heifer had been sacrificed and was burning. Elihu had stayed watching the sheep while David came down to the town. David's six other brothers lined up with his father at the foot of the altar.

Samuel the Seer stood before the family. Everyone stared at David, waiting for him.

Samuel felt like an ominous presence to David and the rest of the village. It seemed that whenever he came around, it was because Yahweh had some kind of chastisement for the people. They wanted to avoid incurring the prophet's displeasure or Yahweh's rebuke. Worse yet, they didn't want their town to be of such significance that God's holy Seer would take interest in it. That could bring some political prominence that would only end in trouble to these peaceful people. They just wished to stay out of the concern of authorities.

David could see by the looks in the faces of the fearful elders and his family and townspeople that they were not getting their wish today. David slowed his pace as he walked through the crowd toward his father and Samuel. He wondered if he was going to be in trouble for his advances on Miriam, and how the Seer found out about it. Unless the other girls of the town finally spoke up too.

The old Seer waved impatiently. "Come quickly, lad! Do not dawdle!"

David jogged the rest of the way up to the altar. He stood by Jesse. "What is wrong, father? Did I do something wrong?"

Samuel stared at him with a scowl.

David almost blurted out an apology. He was about to start crying and admit that he had sinned before God and man and that he would never again try to take advantage of a girl.

Before he could incriminate himself, Samuel stepped up to him. David froze. He saw that Samuel had the high priestly ephod on him, a vest with a pocket that carried the mysterious Urim and Thummim, the oracles of Yahweh. David shivered. He loved the cult of sacrifice, so he had learned everything he could about the priesthood, what they wore, and all the rituals of sacrifice. He didn't want to become a priest, but he reveled in the beauty of sacrifice and how it cleansed the transgressions that sullied his soul.

Samuel said to David, "Son, how old are you?"

"Seventeen."

"You are small but ruddy of complexion," said Samuel. It was a reference to David's vibrant colored skin. "You are handsome and you have strong, bright eyes."

David did not know how to respond to the Seer. It was as if Samuel were considering him for auction.

"Each of your brothers have passed before me and I have sought to discern the will of Yahweh. Your siblings are taller, stronger, older and more experienced. But Yahweh has said to me, 'Do not look on their appearance or on the height of their stature.' For Yahweh sees not as man sees: man looks on the outward appearance, but Yahweh looks on the heart. And Yahweh has not chosen any of the others."

David shivered again. What was he choosing for? And what interest would Yahweh have in the least of eight sons of an insignificant commoner?

Samuel reached into the special pocket of the ephod and pulled out two precious gems. David's eyes went wide. The Urim and Thummim, or Lights and Perfections.

Samuel held them in his hands and closed his eyes to pray. David followed suit, more out of fear that he didn't want to see what would happen than from prayerfulness.

Samuel prayed, "Yahweh show me your will. Is this son of Jesse whom you have chosen?"

David could hear a hush go over the crowd, followed by some gasping and then excited murmuring. Then he felt a bright light flashing on his closed eyelids. He opened his eyes to see the glow of the Urim and Thummim casting their perfect light upon his face.

David looked up at Samuel. His crotchety old face had transformed into a bright smile. He put the Urim and Thummim back into the pocket. He held out his hand to an accompanying servant who handed him a horn of oil.

David felt dizzy, as if he was going to faint. He shook himself back. This could not be happening. What *was* happening?

Samuel took the cap off the horn of oil and simply poured a stream over David's head. He blinked his eyes as the holy ointment flowed over his head and face and onto his clothes.

Samuel croaked as loud as his old voice could carry, "I anoint you, David, son of Jesse by the authority of Yahweh, god of Israel!"

The townspeople applauded. But they still did not know for what purpose David was being anointed. There were few offices that such consecration was used for: elders of Israel, prophet, priest or king. David was too young to be an elder. Could he be a prophet? He was not a Levite, so priesthood was not a possibility. Kingship was out of the question. Saul was clearly Yahweh's chosen one for warrior king. The people murmured and debated amongst themselves.

Jesse gathered up the courage to ask Samuel what everyone else was wondering. "Pray tell, Seer Samuel, for what purpose is my son being anointed?"

Samuel gave a long hard stare at David, who felt his skin crawl with the holiness.

"Yahweh will reveal in his own good time."

Suddenly, a rushing wind blew through the town square. David felt a gust enter him like a breath, and he knew everything had changed. Everything was different.

Samuel capped the horn, and drew his servants near him and walked away through the crowd.

David and the others were confused. David called to Samuel.

Samuel just kept walking.

David ran after him. "Samuel! Samuel! Where are you going?"

"Back to Ramah." He kept walking. David had to keep up.

"What am I supposed to do?"

"I have told you everything I know. Yahweh will let you know more when he is good and ready."

"What am I supposed to do until then?"

"What do you do now?"

"I shepherd. Play music. Train for battle."

"That sounds good. Keep it up."

He stopped in confusion, watching Samuel depart from him. It seemed so unclear to David and to everyone. They all thought Yahweh would be a bit more specific about such an important calling. It was like a herald announcing the important arrival of a royal figure to an event and then not saying who it was.

And what role could he possibly be anointed for? None of the usual considerations seemed feasible. Did the Seer have a new reason in mind? Only Yahweh knew.

CHAPTER 18

At the same moment that a rushing wind blew through the square of the town of Bethlehem, nine miles away in the city of Gibeah, Saul sat brooding over his fate. He had locked himself at the top of the palace tower for several weeks in despair. He could not believe that Yahweh had rejected him and promised to take away his kingdom. He thought he had done so well as a victorious warrior king for the nation of Israel. He led them to many victories over the Ammonites, the Edomites, the Moabites and even the Philistines. It was true that he had cut corners and moved ahead with impatience. But at least he got things done. He had been condemned by Samuel for being too small-minded of his own status. What did Yahweh want, an arrogant self-important tyrant? His palace was the smallest in Canaan, and used little to no adornment of its facilities.

He had been turning these thoughts over and over in his mind for weeks. He barely ate, and barely slept. His despair grew with every day, along with a mounting anger. Who else could this Chosen One of Yahweh be? He knew of no one in the kingdom who matched him in excellence, or statesmanship, or even moral character. He was heads and shoulders above any man in all of Israel. He had heard that more than once, and it certainly was true of him in more ways than just his physical height. He was a mighty warrior king. He was a gibborim.

What kind of a god chooses a mighty man to rule and then changes his mind? That is a temperamental capricious deity if you asked him. He could not get the image out of his mind of Agag's head laying on the prison floor, eyes open and staring at Saul in terror. It returned to him in his dreams as well, haunting him with accusing bloodshot eyes. A giant's eyes staring into his soul.

Suddenly, a gush of wind seemed to flow through the room. It was more like a sucking of air leaving him breathless, and the air thick and heavy. A new despair came over him, but not from his confusion and unanswered questions. It was more like the answer to all his questions. He felt it deep in his soul.

He knew with a clarity he had never known before that Yahweh had departed. He had left Saul, and he was never going to return.

Saul panicked. Then he boiled with anger. So Yahweh would leave him like that just because he was not a perfect king? Yahweh would remove his presence and stop speaking to Saul? He would abandon the very king he placed on the throne because he was looking for another prince? The eyes of the dead Agag pierced into him and he remembered the words he told him, "The Ob of Endor told me your kingdom shall not continue."

"The Ob of Endor told me."

The Ob of Endor. Ironically, Samuel had told him his disobedience was as the sin of divination—the actual occupation of the Ob of Endor. So Yahweh was looking for a better king to rule his people? Well, if Yahweh would not speak to him, if he would not reveal his truth, then Saul would go to someone who would.

"I am still king of Israel," said Saul to the air, as if to Yahweh. "You want me to think more of myself? I will. I will give you the greatest king who ever lived."

CHAPTER 19

Endor lay sixty miles north of Gibeah, just southwest of the Sea of Chinnereth. It was on the plain of Megiddo, near the Jezreel valley in Philistine territory. It had taken Saul some time to find his way there, because he traveled incognito with a small bodyguard of his six best warriors. He wanted to avoid being discovered not only by the Philistines, but also by his own people.

Obs were mediums and necromancers condemned by Torah, the Law of God. They were to be executed by the state for their spiritually heinous activity of consulting the dead and divining spirits. In Philistia, such activities were not outlawed as they were in Israel, but were rather encouraged.

The Ob's residence stood on the outskirts of the city near the foothills, because of the spiritual nature of mountains as cosmic connections between heaven and earth, and as gateways to Sheol. It was a humble home bedecked in theatrical ornamentation. The gateway was a mass of tangled thorny barbs, and the path to the entrance was lined with torches. The walls of the building were embedded with skulls and bones of animals. Even Obs had to make a living, and using such occultic embellishments aided in confirming the image of the underworld to those who sought to pay for her services.

When they arrived at the entrance, Saul removed his cloak. A beautiful young woman came to meet him. She appeared to be the Ob's assistant. She wore a hooded cloak that Saul could see barely hid a small snake draped around her neck.

He said, "I have come to see the Ob of Endor."

"Who seeks the Ob's audience?"

"King Saul of Israel."

She gasped with terror. "What have you to do with me, O king of the Israelites?"

"You are the Ob?" Saul could not contain his shock. He had expected an old ugly hag based on her alleged age of ninety-nine years. But this one was so young and so alluring. It made him feel more at ease. More *trusting*. Her pupils seemed to be slivers in bright lapis lazuli irises. She pulled down her hood.

"I am the Ob, possessor of the pit," she said.

He could not help but blurt out, "You are beautiful."

"What did you expect," she said, "an ugly hag?"

"Forgive me," he said.

"Me forgive you? Now, that is a surprise."

"Do not fear. I am not here to take you from your people. I am here to inquire of the dead."

"Are not such things against your law?"

"I am king. I do as I please. And I am not within Israelite territory."

She smiled at his rationalization and thought, *This one is corrupt. I can play him.*

She turned her head in curiosity, much like a dog would. She squinted her reptilian eyes with revelation. The spirits in her twitched her body with ticks. She sensed something in him. Or rather, something *not* in him.

She said, "You are alone."

He said, "I have my bodyguard."

"Yet, you are alone."

He could see in her eyes what she was not saying explicitly. She sensed Yahweh was not with him.

She said, "Why do you not consult with your seer?"

"He is not speaking to me." He knew he could not gain her trust by lying to her.

She spit out venomously, "Samuel."

He thought she had stressed the "S" like a hissing snake.

Saul looked around. He saw movement in the dark corners, like that of slithering shadows. He wondered if the walls were alive. Some of the shadows became more visible in the low torchlight to reveal serpents of all kinds. He felt a shiver down his spine. They were in a cave crawling with snakes. He stepped back in self protection. His two men stepped closer to him, hands on swords.

The Ob whispered. "Do not worry, king. They will not strike — unless I command them." She gave him a toothy grin and he could see she had sharpened teeth.

He gathered his courage and said, "I want you to bring up someone for me from Sheol."

Another turn of her curious head. She twitched, as if something unseen touched her head.

"And who might that be, O king?"

"I want you to bring up for me the greatest king who ever ruled on the face of the earth: Nimrod of Babel."

Her eyes went wide with surprise. She shrugged. "Impressive. Bold. Dangeroussss." That slithering "s" again.

Saul knew she was not exaggerating. Raising up such a powerful entity was a danger. He might unleash a force he could not control. But he had to do it. Yahweh had wanted Saul to be a mighty king. Samuel had condemned him for his timidity, disobedience, and foolish decisions. He had cut Saul off from Yahweh. So Saul concluded that he would seek the help of this mightiest king of history to become a gibborim in the face of Yahweh, just as Nimrod had been. He would make them sorry they ever rejected Saul ben Kish from being king over Israel.

The Ob said, "What you ask for carries serious ramifications. How will you guarantee to spare my life for my participation in this secret?"

"You have my word. No one will know that I was here, for it would jeopardize my rule."

"Exactly," she said with a grin and a twitch of her shoulder. "Which is your incentive to kill me when we are done."

He knew she was right. He had to give her the only thing she could rely upon.

"I will cut a blood covenant with you," he said.

She smiled in agreement. A blood covenant was universally respected among all the nations of Canaan. And universally reinforced.

"You will vow to spare my life, and should you have victory over the Philistines or annex my town, you will also spare my life."

"Agreed," said Saul.

They cut a lamb in half and poured its blood out on the ground and passed a torch between the halves to sanctify their covenant. Saul pronounced his promise of protection and a self-maledictory oath that would curse him should he violate the covenant. But she was not confident enough of the covenant being sworn before his god with whom he was not in good graces, so he had to swear by Dagon as well.

Satisfied that she was appropriately protected, the Ob proceeded to engage in her necromancy ritual to call up the ancient king Nimrod. The ritual was drawn from Hittite and Assyrian Chthonic conjuring rituals.

She placed bread around a deep pit that operated as a portal to Sheol. Next, she poured honey, milk and wine into the pit as a libation offering. Saul thought of how the honey was forbidden as a libation to Yahweh. He looked around him. He realized that all the moving serpent shadows around them were still.

Then, the Ob cut the throat of a black pig—another abomination in Israelite sacrifice—and placed it at the edge of the pit, with its blood flowing down to the bottom. Saul then was instructed to cast in a piece of his own silver. It was all part of luring the conjured spirit up out of the pit. And no doubt, as monetary reward for the Ob afterward.

The Ob lit incense bowls and lowered them to the bottom of the pit. The smoky odor filled Saul's nostrils and made him dizzy. He shook it off and breathed in more heavily the intoxicating fumes. After a series of incantations calling upon Mot, the Canaanite god of death, to open the gates of Sheol, the Ob then engaged in a cutting ritual.

She made a cut in Saul's palm. She had him squeeze his fist and dribble his blood into the pit. Saul coughed from the excessive smoke filling his nostrils.

The Ob raised her hands and bellowed, "Nimrod, the Great Hunter, mighty gibborim, ancient Nephilim, who is two thirds god, one third man, we implore thee, come forth from the depths of Sheol!"

Saul felt a rumbling penetrate his body. He was not sure if it was a physical quake or something that happened inside him. He was also not entirely sure of what he was seeing before him in the hazy atmosphere. His eyes went blurry. He thought he saw the head of the Ob become a blur of movement. It was as if the ticks and shudders he had been noticing in her had became multiplied at a supernatural speed. Her face became lost in the smear of motion.

He looked back at the billowing cloud and saw a dark figure rising from below. It was massive, at least nine feet tall. Saul had only heard stories of Nimrod, but did not know what he would look like. He could not see the face or any details of the shade, only its eyes staring brightly into Saul's own soul. He felt dizzy again.

The Ob spoke first. Her voice sounded different, like a multitude of voices. "I see an elohim rising up!" Elohim was a reference to gods or divinities of the spiritual plane. It was also the proper name used as a generic reference to Yahweh. Yahweh was Elohim of elohim, god of gods, but other elohim were not Yahweh. But Saul cared little for the nuances of religious particularities. He stood before a god.

The shade spoke, "I am Nimrod. I am Rebel. I am Empire. Gilgamesh reborn as First Potentate. Who is it who disturbs me with his summons?"

Saul's throat was dry. His voice cracked, "I-I am Saul ben Kish, f-first king of Israel."

The being paused. Saul could tell it seemed surprised.

"What is it you seek?" said the phantom.

Saul no longer cared that the Ob would know the intimate details of his quest. He spilled everything.

"Yahweh Elohim of Elohim has made me king of his people, but has withdrawn his favor and rejected me. I seek you, mighty Nimrod to be my suzerain and lead me in the ways of kingship. I seek glory and honor and power."

The Shade paused again. It was an uncomfortable silence. Saul shivered. He noticed the Ob was on the floor in an epileptic seizure. White foam came from her mouth and her eyes were rolled up inside her head.

The voice of the Shade changed from the bellicose bellowing to a low breathy calculating whisper. "You want glory and honor and power? Yet, another rivals your throne."

"I know not who it is, my lord."

"I can help you find out."

"Mighty Nimrod, what shall I do?"

"Open yourself to me."

"I do. I do open myself to you. Whatever wisdom, whatever advice, I promise to heed your words and do all as you say."

Saul felt dizzy again. The phantom's eyes penetrated into his soul. He felt the distinct sensation of unity with the elohim. He felt intimate, as if the spiritual king were becoming one with him. A gust of wind washed over Saul and he fell to the ground unconscious.

Saul awoke to the gush of a breath filling his lungs. His eyes opened to see the Ob pressing her lips passionately on his. She was breathing life back into him. Had he died? He barely remembered what had happened.

He felt her tongue exploring his mouth. When she pulled away from him, he thought it felt split like a snake's tongue. He coughed and sat up, rubbing his head. He had a hangover like the kind he had after one of his nights of heavy drinking.

A sharp pain went through his skull. He groaned.

She said, "Your bodyguard awaits outside."

He said, "What am I supposed to do? Nimrod did not explain."

"He is with you. He will explain."

Saul looked at her confused. "He is with me?"

She nodded. But she would not explain.

"Return to your palace and you will know what to do."

Saul wondered if the entire trip had been a waste of time. He had traveled to find wisdom from the first potentate of history, the Mighty Hunter Nimrod. But all he got was a vague, "he is with you." That was hardly enough to rule a kingdom with glory and power.

But it was all he had. He picked himself up and left for Gibeah.

The Ob immediately called for her apprentice.

The young girl awaited her instructions. The Ob said, "I have an urgent message for you to bring to my son, Ishbi ben Ob in the city of Gath."

CHAPTER 20

On the way home to Gibeah, Saul had felt the strange sensation of being followed. They stopped several times to prepare for battle, only to discover his feelings proved false. His bodyguard saw him nervously glancing around and displaying an occasional nervous tick in his eye, along with twitching in his neck, shoulders and arms.

When he returned to his palace in Gibeah, he went immediately to his bed chamber and slept for an entire day.

He was awakened on the evening of the second night. He could see the bright light of the full moon coming through his tower window onto his bed.

He felt a presence in the room. He jerked around to see the figure of a nine foot tall shadow beside his bed. He gasped.

He knew who it was.

"King Nimrod?"

"Yesss," it whispered, drawing out the 's' like a hiss.

"You are with me."

"Yesss."

"Was it you who followed me back here?"

"Yesss."

"What do you want?"

Saul heard the next whisper from behind his ear. "I have much to tell you."

Saul turned to see the source of the voice. The shadow had mysteriously jumped from one side of the bed to the other.

Then from the foot of the bed, he heard, "Listen closely."

He saw the phantom shade, smaller now, standing at the foot of the bed. Though the figure's specific features were indistinguishable and bathed in shadow, Saul thought he looked in posture and form like

Saul himself. Maybe his eyes were playing tricks in the moonlight shadows.

When Nimrod spoke he could hear the words as if they were inside his head rather than coming from the shade.

"I have waited millennia for this opportunity."

Saul said, "Will you help me achieve my ambition?"

"*You* will help me achieve *my* ambition."

Saul felt confused.

"The tyrannical deity who rejected you and is replacing you with his Chosen One did the same to me in ages past. This messiah you speak of, I know of his Seedline. I sought for it in the days after the Flood, during the Confusion of Tongues and the Great Division."

Saul interrupted, "The Tower of Babel?"

"Shut your mouth, puppet, and listen to me."

Saul felt the malevolence seize him. It was frightening. He was in the presence of something sinister and out of his control. He began to wonder what he had unleashed.

"You must seek out this Chosen One. You must find him and kill him, or you will be cursed as I was cursed."

"But I need your help," complained Saul.

"Oh, I will help you. I will be your counselor, always by your side. And together, we shall destroy the Chosen Seed."

Saul felt his limbs stiffen as if held by a giant's grip. He saw the shade of Nimrod dissolve into his body.

His eyes turned up into his head. He twitched and jerked and spasmed on his bed. White foam bubbled out of his mouth.

His body stiffened and flew upright, defying nature, pulled by an unseen force.

With mighty strength, Saul tore apart his bedroom chamber. First, he ripped the sheets off his bed, then he broke the posts into pieces like they were mere toothpicks. He broke the several pieces of furniture, smashing them against the wall.

Two servants rushed into his room to see if he was alright. He beat them and ran out of the room and through the palace, emitting guttural screams that sounded like wild animals.

•••••

The sound of a madman screaming through the palace awakened Jonathan, Saul's eldest son. A servant entered his room with a guard.

"Master Jonathan, it is your father."

He pulled on a robe and ran out to the hallway. He found his father out in the atrium being held down by eight men under the full moon light. It took all eight of them because Saul's strength was supernaturally enhanced.

Jonathan saw his upturned eyes and the spittle running down his beard. When Saul looked at him, Jonathan knew something else looked at him, something other than Saul. When Saul spoke, he sounded different, deeper, like another voice being filtered through Saul's throat.

"You are the Saulide heir. You are without guile."

Jonathan was indeed a pure soul who loved Yahweh with all his heart, and was disturbed by his father's disobedience to Yahweh. Jonathan was a righteous man of faith and integrity. But he did not consider himself without guile. He saw himself as quite pathetic and faulty before his holy god.

The spirit added, "But you are not the promised one. You will not be king. You are swine seed."

There could not be a more vulgar insult to an Israelite than being called the seed of an unclean animal.

Jonathan said, "Who are you that possesses my father the king?"

Saul hissed at Jonathan and said, "Would not you like to know, godlicker. I will see you again, when I take a dump on your skull."

Saul howled maniacally and struggled to get free from his captors. They held on strong, but it was not easy.

He then vomited, urinated and released diarrhea simultaneously from his orifices. The servants tried to turn their noses from the obnoxious smell and undignified sight. Some of them were splashed by excrement.

Saul fell unconscious in their grip.

After a few moments, Saul awakened. The spirit was gone.

"What happened to me?"

Jonathan said, "An evil spirit taunts you, father. It turns you mad with rage, but it will not reveal its identity."

Saul knew precisely the identity of the spirit. But he was not going to tell Jonathan. He was not going to tell anyone. It was the price he would pay for his personal ambition of greatness and glory.

His nose wrinkled with the stench of his body waste.

As time passed with several of these episodes of spiritual torment, Jonathan realized the spirit was not going to leave his father. He gathered the palace servants together to see if any of them knew of an exorcist familiar with such demonic activity and how they might treat it.

A manservant, Joash, stepped forward shyly. "My lord, I am not an exorcist, but my family knew one when I was a young child."

"Can you find this exorcist for me?" asked Jonathan.

"He is long dead."

Jonathan asked him, "Well, what can be done to calm the spirit?"

Joash replied, "It is said that heavenly music of praise to Yahweh tames the beast of chaos."

"Go find me a musician then. Inquire of the palace minstrels."

"My lord," said Joash, "No ordinary musician will do. It requires someone who has special blessing upon them."

Jonathan said, "Where can we find such a player?"

Another more timid servant finally spoke up, "I know of one."

Everyone looked at him. "I have seen a son of Jesse the Bethlehemite, who is skilled at playing. He is also a young warrior of promise, though not yet of age. But Yahweh is clearly with him."

"Find me this son of Jesse," said Jonathan. Then he added, "On second thought, I am going with you."

CHAPTER 21

On the journey to Bethlehem, Jonathan ruminated over what the evil spirit had said to him while it was in control of his father's body. It dug deep into his soul. Such spirits could see what humans could not. They were unlike Yahweh who knew all things past and future. But they had some preternatural ability to know things humans could not. Just what and how much, Jonathan did not know.

But evil spirits also had a reputation for lying. Could he even trust what the spirit had said, or was it all part of a deception in order to ravage Jonathan's soul as it had ravaged his father's body?

Why would Yahweh allow such a thing? Why would he send an evil spirit to oppress his anointed messiah king? It perplexed Jonathan, but the ancient proverb transcended his doubt: "Who has spoken and it came to pass, unless the Lord has commanded it? Is it not from the mouth of the Most High that good and evil come?"

It was the universal conundrum for the faithful and the topic of endless debate for the scribes. How could Yahweh be perfect and holy and yet sovereignly ordain evil? Did this make him the author of evil? But if he was not in control of evil, then how could he be the Almighty One, El Shaddai? If there were forces in the world that he had no control over, that could thwart his will, then how could he be trusted to accomplish his purposes?

The questions plagued Jonathan and it seemed the only thing that gave him some comfort were the sacred Scriptures themselves. He remembered the priests doing a public reading of the story of their patriarch Joseph, who was sold into slavery by his own brothers. Yet, when confronted with their evil, he said to them, "You meant it for evil, but Elohim meant it for good, to bring about the deliverance of his people."

It was not that Joseph excused his brother's wrongs, but rather he had stressed how Elohim could somehow be orchestrating the evil acts of men to accomplish his purposes, despite the evil intent of the human beings. Elohim was like a potter who molded the clay any which way he desired.

Yahweh has mercy on whom he wills and hardens whom he wills.

If Yahweh had sent such a spirit upon Saul, then it must mean the confirmation of Samuel's curse. Yahweh had rejected Saul.

Would Yahweh reject Saul's entire bloodline as well, including Jonathan?

Yahweh has mercy on whom he wills and hardens whom he wills.

He decided that he would support whomever Yahweh chose as his messiah king in place of Saul because he had no aspirations to greatness or glory. He only wanted to be good, and he knew that the great were rarely the good and the good were rarely the great.

He would accept the fate Yahweh had in store for him, good or bad, because Yahweh was the potter and he was the clay. Yahweh gives and Yahweh takes away.

He even suspected that the presence of the evil spirit was due to the fact that Saul did not accept this sovereign authority of their Maker over their lives. Frustration of his proud goals of glory could certainly lead him to a mad despair. And now Jonathan was here, leading a group of Saul's servants to the small town of Bethlehem, searching out a humble musician who could help relieve that mad despair that was tearing apart the very soul of his father.

• • • • •

When David saw the entourage of five royal servants approach him on the hill, he sensed his life was about the change. He had been anointed by Samuel, but for what he did not know. Nobody knew. Samuel had said Yahweh would reveal its purpose in his own good time. But without that revealed meaning, it faded in everyone's memory as a strange unexplained experience. David continued to serve his father as a common shepherd, and everyone in the village forgot about the holy but mysterious consecration of that day.

David had just stopped playing his treasured lyre. "Keep playing," said Jonathan as they arrived.

"Whose presence do I have the honor of, my lord?" said David.

"I am Jonathan, son of King Saul."

It struck David as odd that he did not call himself the heir to the throne. It was the usual proclamation of such royal successors.

"My lord," said David. He bowed.

"Please, what were you playing when we just arrived?"

"Nothing, your highness. Mere triflings of a lackluster and obscure shepherd boy."

"You wrote what I heard?" Jonathan was astonished. Joash had been right, this young man had undeniable blessing from Yahweh. He had never heard such skill with a lyre. The wooden stringed instrument was usually played with a plectrum but David used his fingers for a more personal touch. His voice resounded with unique character as well.

David said, "The life of a shepherd provides many hours of boring solitude. I have more songs than I can count. Unfortunately, they are not of much use to anyone else."

"I beg to differ," said Jonathan.

"My lord?"

"Please, finish your song."

"I have been working on it. A song of kingly coronation." said David and he picked up his lyre again and played more of the song.

The words were glorious to Jonathan.

> *I will tell of the decree:*
> *The* LORD *said to me, "You are my Son;*
> *today I have begotten you.*

Ask of me, and I will make the nations your heritage,
and the ends of the earth your possession.
You shall break them with a rod of iron
and dash them in pieces like a potter's vessel."

David stopped. The last note hung in the air, unfinished.

The entourage stood in spellbound silence.

Jonathan felt that he was in the very presence of the holy.

David interrupted their quiet hush. "I have not finished it."

Jonathan said, "David ben Jesse, the King of Israel summons you to his presence."

On the trip back to Gibeah, Jonathan queried David about his life. Though Jonathan was forty years old, and David only eighteen, he felt a spiritual connection with the lad that transcended their age difference. He could see that this young man had Yahweh's favor.

He found David to be an interesting mixture of both earthly passion and heavenly devotion. He spoke with great affection and desire for marriage, and with zealous intensity for Yahweh's holiness. He had trained hard and was impatient to serve in the King's army when he would come of age. In fact, he had a sense of impatience about everything, as if the world could not keep up with all that David desired.

Jonathan was impressed with this young man of such talent and zeal. When David told him the story of Samuel's mysterious anointing, Jonathan immediately knew God's hand was in all of this. Such anointing was reserved for royal occasions, eldership, prophets, priests or kings.

David suspected that this was the purpose of it all: to be a royal musician for the court of the king.

CHAPTER 22

When David arrived at the palace of Saul, he was speechless for the first time in the entire trip. It was a humble residence for so important a leader. He knew that the nation of Israel was only in its infancy of power with her first king. The people had, after all, suffered for four hundred years as slaves of the Egyptians. They had overcome insurmountable odds against the giants of Canaan under the leadership of Joshua. They had struggled for hundreds of years under judges and a divided commonwealth. Now, for the first time in all those generations, they finally had a chance to unify under a single monarch who would establish their dominion of the land Yahweh allotted to them as his inheritance among the nations.

They passed between two pillars at the entrance of the brick building. David thought that the king's palace should be made of stone, for a sense of greater permanence. But the Israelites were not as advanced as their neighboring enemy, the Philistines. He wished Yahweh would change all of that. He wished Yahweh would smash the Philistine dogs and establish his kingdom for a thousand generations.

When they arrived in the royal reception area, David gaped with awe as they approached the throne. Again, it was plain by Canaanite standards, a simple elevated wooden seat carved from a tree, with two lion Cherubim also carved from wood at each side of the arms. To David, it represented Yahweh's messiah king, anointed by Yahweh's holy Seer to bring heaven and earth into unity.

As in heaven, so on earth, he thought. They waited by the entrance for the king's arrival.

Saul stepped out from the back of the room and approached the throne. He was attended by his wife and two lovely young women. He sat upon his throne with the women by his side and pronounced, "Approach."

Jonathan led David the fifty feet up to the throne.

As the two men approached, Saul became nervous. Sweat beaded on his forehead. The dark shade, unseen by everyone else leaned in from behind him and whispered in his ear. "Who is this vagrant? Why have you brought him here?"

Saul choked out, "Who approaches my throne?"

Jonathan said, "Father, this is David ben Jesse of Bethlehem. You asked for a skilled musician. This is the one whom the servants discovered."

David was intrigued by his elder companion. He had come to know him on the ride here and was impressed with his honesty, humility and faith. It came from a trust in Yahweh that David himself felt he could learn from. Now, this son of the king would not even take the usual credit for discovering David. Instead he gave the praise to the servants. The servants!

David noticed the king did not look well. His royal robes appeared sloppily arranged. He had dark circles under his baggy eyes, revealing lack of sleep. He displayed a nervous twitch in his eye accompanied by subtle shivers and an occasional tick in his arm or shoulder. It looked as if he was avoiding an invisible presence trying to touch him.

Saul's breathing became rapid as David got closer. His heart pounded in his chest, and his ticks became more exaggerated. The spirit's whisper in Saul's ear became louder and more desperate. "Get out of here. Now! I don't like this flesh bag. He stinks of anointing. He is a threat to your throne!"

Saul gave a strange brush at his head as if to push an insect away from his ear. He said, "Welcome to Gibeah. This is my wife, Ahinoam, and my daughters, Merab and Michal."

David bowed.

Merab and Michal were both entranced by the young man's handsomeness. But it was Michal's eyes that met with David's. Their locked stare was interrupted by Saul's pronouncement, "Let me hear of this music that fuels your reputation."

As David pulled out his lyre and prepared to play, a voice screamed in Saul's ear, "Do not let this worm play music!"

Saul jerked his head from the piercing shout. He looked at the others around him. Though he knew his secret counselor was unseen and unheard by others, surely that was loud enough to have been heard by the others.

But it was not.

Ahinoam noticed something was wrong with Saul, but she would not say anything. Michal and Merab were swooning over their young male visitor and did not notice a thing.

But Jonathan knew his father was being taunted. He turned impatiently to David, and whispered, "Are you ready?"

"Yes," said David. He finished tuning his instrument. He paused and then began to sing the first thing that came to him. It was the same first thing that always came to him when he wanted to woo a beautiful woman. It was the song that had romanced Miriam and the others, and now he was singing it with eyes locked onto Michal.

> *Hear, O daughter, and consider, and incline your ear:*
> > *forget your people and your father's house,*
> > *and the king will desire your beauty.*
> *Since he is your lord, bow to him.*
> *All glorious is the princess in her chamber, with robes*
> > *interwoven with gold.*
> *In many-colored robes she is led to the king,*

Jonathan was taken aback by the song of romance. He could see David's attention was on Michal. He whispered to David, "What about that song you were playing when I found you? Play that one."

David stopped abruptly. It had the effect of shaking Michal out of her romantic trance. She suddenly noticed that she was quivering and breathing heavily. She swallowed hard but kept her eyes on the handsome young musician she hoped would stay all evening.

Merab was the eldest and therefore more mature. But she had been so swept up in the lyrics and David's heavenly voice that she did not even notice he was staring at Michal. She only noticed her throbbing desire for the young lion she could not help but fawn over.

David said to Saul, "Sorry, my lord. Forgive my incompetence."

He began to play the coronation psalm he had played for Jonathan on the hillside.

Its effect on Saul was immediate. A peace came over him. The whisperer went away. His tension released and his nervous twitching and ticks vanished. It seemed as if his mind all of a sudden became clear and he could even see more clearly with his eyes. It was like a fog had been lifted from over his mind.

Merab and Michal wanted to kiss the handsome musician, surrender to him. Michal was humming along, following David's verse.

Saul said, "Yahweh is with you, my son. You will be my personal musician."

"My lord and king," said David bowing low. "It is an honor to serve Yahweh's anointed one."

The girls' hearts leapt with excitement. Michal immediately began to plot how she could find an excuse to spend time with David. She blurted out, "I will introduce him to the palace and the court musicians."

Merab snapped an angry look at her sister. "I am the eldest. That will be my duty."

"It is no duty for me, sister," replied Michal, "it is an honor. Since you lack my musical experience, I can better orient our new minstrel to his courtly responsibilities. Do you not agree, father?"

Saul nodded.

Michal held back a big grin in her heart.

Merab gritted her teeth. She was outdone by her cunning little sister. She wished now that she had not turned away from her music lessons years before. Michal had kept up with her singing lessons, but Merab lost interest in favor of more intellectual pursuits. She cursed her scrolls.

In this moment of clarity, Saul regretted that he had opened the gates of Tartarus to satisfy his hunger. There was an emptiness in his soul, a deep and abiding emptiness, like a pit in Sheol, that drove him. He had believed that greatness and glory might satiate the hunger. But now he realized he had bitten off more than he could eat. He felt nauseous.

Nevertheless, he determined to institute a pogrom to root out all mediums, necromancers and sorcerers from Israel's territories. The Torah already prescribed death as the penalty for such spiritual traitors, but in reality was rarely enforced. Common Israelites in more rural areas, in the absence of contact with king or priest, degenerated into doing exactly what Saul himself had previously done. They sought for validation wherever they could find it. And there was plenty of validation from the gods of Canaan, who only asked for a small amount of recognition in return—a small amount of worship. Thus, many Israelites owned teraphim, little statues of gods or ancestors to whom they could maintain household shrines. Even some of Saul's family had them.

David interrupted Saul's thoughts. "My lord, I only ask that I am able to maintain my shepherding commitment to my father during his seasonal needs with the sheep."

• • • • •

Michal had teraphim because she so appreciated the artistic quality of the craftsmanship. But for some reason, she did not want to show David her teraphim as she was walking him through the palace. She suspected he probably would not approve of them. So she avoided the personal quarters of the family and kept to the rest of the residence as she guided him about.

David had asked Saul for split residence between Gibeah and Bethlehem. He would be gone to shear sheep in the summer months, and during lambing, as well as harvest, when all other hands were needed in the fields. Also, many of his older brothers would be conscripted in the military. Michal already dreaded David's absence and he had not even moved in yet.

At the musician's quarters, she introduced him to the others who played harp, timbrel, pipes, horns and trumpets. She showed him the workroom where they fixed the instruments.

"Our craftsman can even create a new royal thick lyre to replace your thin one." Thick lyres were larger and had more strings.

David said, "I am well enough pleased with my humble thin lyre." He noticed that they were alone in the workroom. He said, "You mentioned your musical experience in the throne room. What instrument do you play?"

"I sing."

David's smile brightened. "Wonderful. Let me hear."

He pulled out his lyre. She said with embarrassment, "Oh no, I am afraid I would not be of your caliber."

"Nonsense. I heard you humming when I played before. Just follow along with me."

"No, really, I…"

But before she could finish her complaint, he had already started playing.

Immediately, she recognized the tune. It was a popular Canaanite song. She was familiar with it. Everyone was. It was a hymn to the storm god Ba'al, lauding his seven thunders over Canaan. But she was surprised David would sing such an idolatrous song.

He said, "Do not worry. I detest Ba'al. Just replace Ba'al's name with Yahweh's name when you sing. I do it all the time with popular songs."

She smiled as he led into the lyrics. She knew them well.

Ascribe to Yahweh, O gods.
Ascribe to Yahweh glory and strength.

She accidentally said the first line like the original. *Ascribe to Ba'al, O gods.* David gave her a teasing look. She had to get the hang of it. She caught on quickly.

Ascribe to Yahweh the glory due his name;
Worship Yahweh in the splendor of holiness.
The voice of Yahweh is over the waters;
El of glory thunders,
Yahweh, over many waters.
The voice of Yahweh is powerful;
The voice of Yahweh is full of majesty.

The original Canaanite hymn sang of the seven thunders of Ba'al and his enthronement above the waters in heaven. But it was the voice of Yahweh that now thundered seven times and it was he who was crowned with glory and majesty.

The LORD sits enthroned over the floodwaters;
the LORD sits enthroned as king forever.

Michal was in heaven. She sang her heart out. She did not notice that David was as delighted with her voice as she was with his. Their voices melted into a harmonious unity that ushered them both into Yahweh's presence. It was more than a song. It was a dance. It was worship.

When they finished the song, they were both breathless. They stood for a moment in awe of the holy. Michal was flushed. She felt as if she had been before the throne of Yahweh Elohim with this young man she did not even know. But she felt like she had also made herself utterly and completely vulnerable before him. It was too much for her.

She squeaked, "I have to go," and scurried out of the room. David knew that they were in love.

CHAPTER 23

Dagon met with Ba'alzebul, Asherah and Molech in the sanctuary of his temple. They had come to discuss the latest intelligence delivered to them by Asherah's spies.

Dagon said incredulously, "Nimrod? King Saul is in the hands of the spirit of Nimrod?"

"So we think," said Asherah.

Ba'alzebul added, "That means he cannot be the Chosen Seed of Yahweh."

Molech said, "That means Israel's fall is at hand. I will have them passing their children through my fires in no time. We will not need war. Israel will be conquered through inner corruption."

"Do not count your mongrels before they are birthed, mole god," said Asherah. "If he is not the Chosen Seed, then someone else is. When the kingdom of Saul falls, that Seed will rise."

Dagon said, "But who?" He brushed a couple of annoying flies away from his face.

Anxiety was getting the better part of all of them. They had been seeking to destroy the Chosen Seed for so many generations, they had stopped counting. Ever since they and their two hundred comrade Sons of God had fallen from heaven before the Great Flood, they had sought to corrupt the human bloodline. They made Mount Hermon their cosmic mountain and base of operations. They revealed occult secrets to mankind, took on the identity of gods, male and female, and even mated with human women to create their serpentine seed, the Nephilim giants. The Deluge had imprisoned most of them, leaving the seventy and their minions to become the spiritual principalities and powers over the nations. In Eden, that detestable Creator, Yahweh Elohim, had cursed the Serpent and his seed to be at war with the Seed of Eve. And that one day, an individual from that seedline of Eve would crush the head of the Serpent. The Watcher gods had sought to kill Enoch, Methuselah, Noah, Shem, Abraham and his chosen offspring all the way up to the present. And they had failed every time. It seemed the only thing they had been successful with was their giant progeny.

Asherah said, "It is time for the Sons of Rapha to step forth. They must begin a campaign to hunt down this Seed and suffocate it before it has the chance to sprout."

"Should we not wait until we have the help of Mastema for so important an undertaking?" Dagon asked.

Asherah spoke to Dagon like the queen matriarch that she had become to him. "Mastema remains in Assyria and Babylon. He will not be available for years."

"What is he planning?" complained Dagon. He had a tone of desperation in his voice.

Asherah said, "It is classified. You are not authorized to know."

She gave a knowing side glance to Ba'alzebul. Asherah knew that such exclusion made Dagon feel an outsider to the inner circle of power in the pantheon. That was why she made sure to bring it up every chance she could get. Dagon did not know that she and Ba'alzebul were not vetted for such knowledge either. But thinking that she was vetted fed his feeling of inferiority to her. And that was good.

Ba'alzebul had ferreted out the information on Mastema. Based on his previous involvement with the heavenly mastermind, he deduced that Mastema was strengthening those empires for an all out assault on Israel. Only time would tell.

Dagon nervously paced back and forth, waving more of Ba'alzebul's flies away from his face. "I am not sure if this is our best course of action."

Ba'alzebul questioned him. "What other course would you advise?"

"I do not know." Dagon responded, clearly overwhelmed.

Ba'alzebul said, "My lord and father, I am confident this is our time. I could lead the incursion if you are unsure of yourself."

Asherah shot Ba'alzebul an angry look. It was too aggressive a move by her co-conspirator. "I do not think Dagon is unsure. I respect his caution. Which is why we need not require assault yet, merely reconnaissance. There will be plenty of time to plan for assault once we have enough information. But until then, I recommend we follow Dagon's lead and merely gather information."

In his distracted turmoil, Dagon could not recognize the obvious manipulation by Asherah. Dagon had not suggested anything. Asherah had just used the confusion of the moment to steer the discussion while pretending to be submissive. It turned Ba'alzebul on. He felt more aggressive. His horns had become as full sized as a bull's. Soon, he would dominate Asherah.

They heard the approach of the Sons of Rapha. Asherah said, "We must leave Dagon to his commission."

Ba'alzebul and Molech followed Asherah and disappeared behind the image of Dagon into the tunnel access. Dagon stood behind his image considering what Asherah had said. It made sense. It would not be provocation to merely seek intelligence. That seemed safe enough.

Two gibborim warriors entered the sanctuary carrying a frightened whimpering young six-year old boy. One of the warriors had the boy's feet pinned under his armpit, while the other had an arm wrapped around the child's torso. They laid him upon the horned altar before the image of Dagon.

The boy began to cry. He knew what his fate was to be. But his cries were extinguished when they offered him as a sacrifice to Dagon.

The smell of the draining blood brought Dagon forth to feast.

The two Sons of Rapha were now in their early forties. Goliath of Gath was over nine and a half feet tall and eight hundred pounds of pure muscle. He had matured into the champion warrior of Philistia and continued to lead the warrior cult since its founding almost a generation earlier.

His second-in-command, Ishbi ben Ob, had grown to nine feet. As a gibborim, he equaled Goliath in build and experience. They had been inseparable for twenty-five years.

They waited with bowed heads until Dagon had sucked the carcass dry of its life blood. It was an opportunity to place their noses in their chests where they could get relief. The reeking stink of fish burned in their nostrils and made them want to gag.

The god belched and carried the pale limp body back behind the image. He handed it to the hidden Molech, who had been waiting with excitement for the leftovers. He carried the body away protectively like a wolf would protect its dinner from the rest of the pack

Asherah muttered, "Good riddance." She and Ba'alzebul stayed behind to listen to the discussion about to take place. But they were also having their own hushed argument.

Asherah whispered, "Your impatient power grab almost exposed our plan to the fish. You are lucky he was too confused in his own ignorance to pick up on it."

Ba'alzebul whispered back in protest, "Your pretended challenge to me further separated us in his eyes. That is good strategy."

"That was my covering for your near disaster. The time is not yet, Ba'alzebul. You must be more patient."

He nodded. He would be more patient. But when his time came, he would not share his power with this bitch goddess either. He would be supreme again.

Dagon returned to the two giants kneeling before his image and altar.

"I accept your offering, and I bid you welcome my children, my Sons of Rapha."

Goliath responded with the respect he showed only to the gods but to no man, "We are your bondservants, my lord and god. Command us and we will obey."

Dagon growled, and then spoke. "The skies are very dark over the land of Canaan. The time has come for me to reveal to you your most important calling."

Goliath responded, "We have trained for twenty-five years. We have organized the Rephaim forces of Philistia to be the most feared regiment in the land. We are ready for any commission."

Dagon explained, "The reason I formed your warrior cult those many years ago was not merely to defeat the Israelites, as abominable as they are. The real purpose of your existence is to seek out an individual, a Chosen Seed *within* Israel, who was prophesied to crush the head of the Serpent."

"The destruction of our seed," muttered Goliath.

"Precisely," said Dagon.

"Is this the gibborim ruler of Israel, King Saul?"

"No. Saul is cursed. We believe the messiah is someone else. But we do not know who. He is already within the ranks of Israel, but he has not risen. He has not shown himself. I want you to use conspiracy and intrigue to find out who this Chosen Seed is. And then I want you to hunt him down and kill him."

"Gladly, mighty Dagon." The implications were obvious. If they killed the savior of Israel, they would kill its only hope, and the nation would be a grain harvest ready for winnowing with the scythe of Dagon.

He said, "We will draw him out, and cut him into pieces."

Ishbi remained subordinate and quiet. Inside, he felt elation. He had been waiting for many years. He could feel his familiar spirits inside him become frenzied with joy.

Dagon said, "Continue to maneuver your giant regiments as before. But only reveal this new command to your officers and your ruler, the Lord of Gath. Secrecy is crucial to the plan's success. This is not a war, this is an assassination."

The two warriors backed out of the sanctuary. They went off to meet with their other officers and make their plans.

Asherah and Ba'alzebul came from behind the image.

Asherah asked, "How reliable is this Lord of Gath?"

Dagon said, "He is a cuckold and a fool. But he is obedient."

CHAPTER 24

Bisha was an older woman of fifty-five years, but she had aged well. She kept her skin soft with oils. She applied make-up artfully, using just enough to accent her declining beauty, but not so much as to look garish or desperate. She kept her long, black hair brushed soft every night. She watched her diet, avoided rich foods and ate small amounts.

But she never denied her romantic appetite. In this she indulged with ferocious abandon in honor of her patron goddess, Asherah. Life was too short, and she wanted to experience as much life as possible before she returned to the dust. So she was constantly unfaithful to her husband, whom she secretly detested.

Her latest partner in crime was the giant Lahmi of Gath, the brother of Goliath. He was just thirty-five years old, about eight and a half feet tall and five hundred pounds. She was drawn to powerful men, and Lahmi was an officer of the mighty warrior guild, the Sons of Rapha. She was impressed by every member of that tight-knit group of six powerful giants. She wanted to bed them all.

But she was with Lahmi at the moment, and she had turned impatient. She barked, "I am late. You have to go."

She jumped up, kissed her Asherah idol, and got ready for her appointment.

She fixed her hair as she scurried down the long hallway toward her destination. She was still fixing her dress as she entered the room. A herald announced her.

"Lady Bisha of Gath."

She strode proudly up to the throne of her husband, Achish ben Maoch, Lord of Gath. He was sixty, hair gone gray from a troubled reign. He had become portly from pleasuring himself with food. In a way, they had become like their idols El and Asherah, an impotent, old, bearded deity and his powerful goddess consort.

"I am so sorry, my love. I was indisposed."

Achish watched her with an impatient eye, grumbling, "You kept us waiting."

She said to the others, "Please accept my humble apologies. I will try to find some way to make it up to you fine warriors in the future. Every one of you."

The four officers of the Sons of Rapha stood before the throne. The fifth was just arriving, Lahmi, also fixing his clothes as if he had just got out of bed.

Achish ignored Bisha's unfaithfulness because her political connections and ruthless machinations had helped him gain the Lordship of Gath, and continually aided his interests in the Philistine Council of Lords.

Lahmi stood next to his brother, Goliath, and comrade Ishbi ben Ob. Bisha had not been able to gain the attention of these two. Behind them were the two others whose attention she had in the palm of her hands; Saph, nine feet tall, and a hefty eight hundred pounds; and Runihura, a dark skinned Egyptian, leanest of the band at seven and a half feet tall and four hundred pounds. The sixth Son of Rapha, Argaz, was shrouded in mystery. He was kept out of the public eye. He had been burned so badly in a fire that he looked like a monster from the underworld. He was also abnormally large, fifteen feet tall and twelve hundred pounds. His mere hideous presence would strike terror into the hearts of any who saw him. Simply put, he could not be seen in public without causing chaos. They therefore saved that for battle.

These were the officers over the five regiments of Rephaim in the Philistine army. Each presided over one hundred warriors and had won various honors of war that raised him to the highest rank of the *Yalid ha Rapha.*

Goliath was their champion and he spoke for the group. "My lord and lady, we have sure intelligence from Dagon himself that there is a messiah in Israel who is about to rise to power. This gibborim is capable of defeating our entire nation, and some say he will conquer the entire land of Canaan."

"King Saul?" asked Achish, surprised.

"No, my lord." Goliath nodded to Ishbi.

Ishbi said, "My mother is an Ob in Endor, and she has reported to me that King Saul is in the grip of an evil spirit whom she believes is Nimrod of old."

Achish looked shocked. "How could that be?"

Goliath spoke again. "He is cursed by their god. That is why Dagon is confident that he will be replaced by someone far greater."

Achish wondered what the ramifications could be on his own rule.

Bisha wondered what it would be like to fornicate with a king infested by a malignant spirit of such magnitude.

"What we recommend is a contest."

"Of Champions?" asked Achish.

"Yes," said Goliath. "If you assemble your forces for war, we will call out their mightiest champion to engage in single combat with our mightiest champion to resolve the conflict without massive loss of soldiers."

It was a common stratagem from their Aegean origins. But it was also known and practiced among Mesopotamian and Canaanite cultures as well. So the Israelites were familiar with it.

Goliath continued, "This tactic will surely draw out their hidden messiah by an appeal to his vanity."

"And you are confident of your victory?" Achish asked.

Goliath was the uncontested champion of all Philistia. It was said that not even the monstrous Argaz could best him.

"My lord, I have been preparing for this moment all my life. I will crush this Chosen Seed, tear out the root and strangle the Hebrew dynasty before it has had the chance to get started."

Bisha sighed. She was drawn to this mighty gibborim.

The plan was unassailable. Each one of the Sons of Rapha was capable of the deed, not merely Goliath their champion. This increased the odds of success in Achish's mind.

Ishbi was second only to Goliath in both rank and skill. Of all of them, Ishbi was the most capable of besting the champion. But he deferred to Goliath and was happy to be his submissive partner on the battlefield and off. As the son of an Ob, he also seemed to have a connection to the spiritual world, which gave him an otherworldly presence in battle. Combatants were known to be harassed and distracted by unseen forces, his familiar spirits, when opposing him.

Lahmi always stood in the shadow of his older brother. It drove him to be a fierce, relentless fighter in order to establish his own identity. But he also never forgot how Yahweh had almost killed him and his best friend Ittai when he had been a child. The Hebrew god had sent a plague upon the Philistines for their capture of the magical box that housed that invisible god. Lahmi had Dagon to thank for his life, so he battled without concern for survival. There is nothing more ferocious than a warrior who is ready to die for his god. Yahweh was his most hated enemy.

Runihura, whose name meant, "Destroyer," was a black high-born Egyptian who was a master of the loop javelin. This was a special addition of a stringed loop attached to the javelin and used to propel the missile faster and farther upon release. It was said Runihura could hit a target at three hundred yards. His family line was almost ended by the ten plagues of Egypt. He sought revenge on Yahweh for the destruction of his people and nation.

Saph was a master swordsman with the scimitar, the common weapon carried by the officers that warranted the nickname "Guild of the Scimitar." He traced his lineage back to the mighty Og of Bashan, who had been massacred by the Israelites upon their arrival in the land four hundred years ago. Saph saw himself as a blood avenger of his people. The object of his most burning hatred was this race of cockroaches called Israel. He was dedicated to driving them into the sea.

The mighty fifteen foot Argaz struck terror into everyone's heart who faced him in battle and was known to kill scores of men at a time with the sweep of his titanic six foot iron sword. His height was an unusual anomaly and reminded many of the legendary Ahiman, one of the Anakite Sons of Arba. He too had been fifteen feet tall and was a figure of great legendary exploits. His death was never spoken of.

Achish of Gath did not have one champion to face this cowardly messiah king, wherever he was hiding. He had six. Six times the odds in his favor.

"I will take your advice," said Achish. "I will prepare for battle. Where do you think would be the optimum location for your victory? Somewhere to aid our invasion of Israelite territories."

Goliath said, "The Valley of the Terebinth, fifteen miles southwest of Bethlehem."

The Valley of the Terebinth, known to others as the Valley of Elah, marked a natural entry point for conquering from the Philistine homeland into the hill country of the Saulide kingdom.

It would be the perfect spot to thrust a Philistine scimitar of war.

CHAPTER 25

Ittai pounded the red hot iron with a strong arm. He was now thirty-five years old. Despite his hatred for the Sons of Rapha, he was a Gittite in heart and soul, so he had returned to his native Gath to blacksmith after Micah had died. The Philistines had spearheaded the development of smelting metal and had become experts and innovators in the craft. Prior to King Saul's reign, the tribes of Israel were divided and unable to share knowledge and commerce efficiently. They had failed to develop the craft of blacksmithing, which resulted in a dearth of weaponry. Philistia had so dominated the region and monopolized on the craft, the Israelites were dependent upon the Philistines for the manufacturing and sharpening of their agricultural tools. The Philistines were considered among the first of the iron cultures. They had become particularly known for their iron chariots, unequaled in the land.

Ittai had become a specialist in weaponry, creating swords, javelins, daggers, maces and other implements of war such as helmets and armor. He knew weapons inside and out, from their weight and balance to their destructive capabilities in battle. He had also become an expert in tactical use of these multiple weapons, as a means for perfecting his craft.

On this day, he worked on a new kind of metal that he revealed to no one. He had heard rumors of this new metal that was stronger than iron from other smiths. There were occasional cases of its use in Anatolia and eastern Egypt, but it remained a mystery to most. It was called steel and it was much stronger than bronze and iron, though less malleable. Bronze was still the most used metal. Ittai had been experimenting with various techniques of smelting iron with carbon at higher temperatures and he had finally arrived at a satisfying mix that enabled him to work on the very sword he currently plunged into the water for cooling.

But this was not the only smithing secret Ittai harbored. Another was the whip sword named Rahab. Ittai had worked for many years trying to master it. He felt a secret, holy responsibility as its latest keeper.

Ittai took a break before returning to his secret project. Before he could pick up the hammer, a pair of slender hands covered his eyes from behind. He knew instantly who it was. He could tell by the touch, by the sweet smell in his nostrils.

"Ummi, you know it is dangerous to sneak up on me like that."

"I am simply proving my point that brute force and practiced skill are not always the victor. Sometimes the smallest mouse can surprise the enemy and break through a defense."

"Well, 'my enemy,' what nefarious plans do you have for torturing me tonight?"

She giggled. "The ultimate torture. The one thing you dread the most. Your deepest darkest fear made real. A meal with my parents."

"Ummi," he complained.

She placed her arms around his neck. It was difficult because he was so husky and muscular. She felt completely safe with him. His heart was flesh as she would often say, in contrast with his iron exterior.

She said softly, "Smooty, we've been talking about this forever. What holds us back?"

Smooty was her affectionate nickname for him, created by combining the sootiness that his smithing caused with the dirty smudging he inevitably created when he touched things with his blackened hands.

Ittai could not think of what to say. He could not look at her.

She kept up her assault. "Is my big bad burly Smooty a scared little mouse after all?"

He looked at her. Those gorgeous Philistine eyes. Her luscious pulpy lips and wavy black hair. Her infectious smile.

"You are right."

Her eyes went wide with shock. She could not believe it.

"I am a mouse."

She didn't expect that. Was he only delaying more?

"And you are a rascally puma playing with me before you eat me."

She wasn't sure where he was going with this. It might not be what she had hoped.

Then he smiled back. "I will propose to your father tonight. There is no reason to wait any longer."

"Oh, Smooty!" She hugged him and kissed him deeply on the lips.

She jumped out of his arms and ran away, shouting back to him, "I will tell father you are coming. See you at dinner tonight!"

Ittai breathed a deep sigh. He was truly in love with this woman. He had met Ummi not long after he returned to Gath. He had wanted to start over and stay hidden in the blackened shadows of his workshop. But when he met her, she was like a light of happiness providing hope for his miserable darkened existence.

His past was nothing but pain, a pain he had still never shared with his beloved Ummi. His rejection by the Sons of Rapha and his best friend, in addition to his sickness and subsequent self-mutilation and running away. His experience under King Saul of Israel at Gibeah was also burned into his soul. The Israelites had always been the enemy, but he had seen something in them and in their god that contrasted with the abominations of the Ammonites. That revelation awakened a nagging concern in him about his own nation. How was Dagon any different from Molech? Could the Philistine cosmopolitan sophistication, compared with the rustic primitiveness of Israel, be a deception? Could it be that evil was made beautiful and trapped him in its web of deceit? He was a haunted man.

A voice snapped him out of his haunting.

"Runt!"

All his happiness, and all his hope, deflated at the sound of that familiar voice. It was Lahmi, his boyhood best friend, torn from him when he had been rejected from the Sons of Rapha. He would never live down the reason for his rejection, because he would always be reminded of it in their insulting nickname for him.

Once Ittai had returned to Gath, he would inevitably run into his old friend. Ittai had become a master weapons craftsman, and the Sons of Rapha were an elite warrior guild. Every time they needed weapons, Lahmi would show up and chide Ittai, while placing his order with the insulted blacksmith.

Lahmi had changed after his initiation into the order all those years before. He had become hard and cruel like Goliath and the others. He looked down on Ittai both literally and metaphorically. In a warrior culture, failing to achieve military status was a mark of inferiority, and only power was respected. So Ittai received nothing but contempt. Whatever past they had shared was dead.

Lahmi barked, "I have an order for six new scimitars. They are for the officers, including Goliath. So you had better do your best work or I'll have to beat your little dwarf butt for incompetence."

Ittai was only five foot eight inches to Lahmi's eight and a half feet height. But Lahmi knew Ittai was easily as strong as his tormentor, if not stronger. He might not be blessed with the height of a Rephaim, but he had the strength of one, developed further through the labors of blacksmithing. Lahmi danced around that reality, relying upon his superior status as the ultimate inhibitor of Ittai's response.

Ittai responded with inhibition and submission. "Why the importance, my lord Lahmi?"

Lahmi looked around to make sure no one was in listening distance. He stepped closer inside the shop. He always treasured the opportunity to boast to Ittai. "A big battle is coming. The Sons of Rapha will finally be unveiled in all our power and glory. Speak nothing of this, or I will have to slit your throat."

"Of course."

Lahmi gave his usual grin of contempt. "We are the Seed of the Serpent cursed by the Israelite god Yahweh. Ha! It is a badge of honor to be so cursed by such a despicable deity. We will hand him his curse back on the blade of our scimitars!"

Ittai blurted out, "How?"

"Well, it has just been revealed by none other than Dagon himself to our inner circle…" He paused for gloating effect, "that an ancient prophecy of a messiah king born of the Seed of Eve and of Abraham will rise within Israel. In a fortnight, Goliath will call out their Champion, this warrior messiah, and challenge him to a duel. It is no surprise what the outcome of *that* battle will be."

Lahmi grunted with self-satisfied delight. Ittai was stunned. But he wasn't thinking of any battle, Ittai was thinking of the fact that he had Nephilim blood in him. He did not have the height, but he had the extra fingers and toes—which he had cut off—and he had the strength. He had Nephilim blood in his own veins. He was cursed by this Yahweh god who fascinated him.

Lahmi was unaware of Ittai's concerns. "So the sword you forge today for Goliath will be the sword that will cut off the head of this so-called messiah king. *That* is why it is important, runt."

That word always dug into Ittai's soul. Runt. But now he barely heard it. He still swooned from the kick in the stomach realization that he was cursed. It was bad enough that he had wanted to be a Son of Rapha and was rejected. Now he was cursed as well.

"What is this?" said Lahmi.

Ittai shook out of his daze and noticed that Lahmi was holding up the sword Rahab in its strange-looking sheath. He pulled the blade out and it rolled onto the floor in front of him.

"Nothing," said Ittai. "A curiosity."

"Curiosity it is. But 'nothing' it is not."

Lahmi felt the blade. He pulled back with a bleeding finger. The thing was sharp as the scales on a dragon.

"It is an heirloom," said Ittai. "It was used as a scythe for wheat." More like a scythe for heads.

Lahmi looked at him. "Do not lie to me, Ittai. This is a weapon."

Ittai protested, "A rather clumsy one for any place other than a wide open field."

Lahmi knew he was hiding something. "I want it. I want to buy it."

"It is not for sale. I told you, it is an heirloom."

Lahmi stared daggers at Ittai. "I could take it."

Ittai stiffened. His muscles went tense and bulged as he approached Lahmi, returning a burning glare into the giant's eyes. He gently took the handle from Lahmi's grip.

"You will not take it." It was the closest to outright defiance as Ittai had ever displayed. He decided in his heart that if Lahmi and this warrior cult of beasts took all his dignity from him, they would not take this one thing. It represented too much. This would be where he would take a stand.

Lahmi could see it in his eyes. Though Ittai could out-fight Lahmi when they were children, many years had passed since then, and much training for Lahmi with the Sons of Rapha. But Ittai too had apparently trained and developed his strength and fighting skills.

Lahmi chose not to engage with the "runt."

"Well, don't leave your precious 'heirlooms' laying around if you don't want them to be snatched up and bought. Runt."

Lahmi marched away. Ittai watched him with a thin smirk of victory. In all this, Lahmi never noticed the steel blade sitting on the table under his nose. The idiot.

Ittai hurriedly hid his two precious weapons and set about closing the shop for the day. Before he left, he poured himself a mug of strong wine to settle his nerves. He was not sure whether it was in response to the confrontation with Lahmi or the impending proposal he had promised to make to Ummi's father this evening. Now *that* would be a confrontation indeed. He could fight a giant, but facing the father of the woman he wanted to marry was far more frightening.

He got up and opened the door to leave. He stopped short. Goliath and Ishbi towered over him.

Goliath said, "I understand you have a curiosity my brother is interested in buying."

The big coward. He went and got not merely his big brother, the Champion of Philistia, but also Goliath's warrior partner, Ishbi. He had to line up three Sons of Rapha just to bully one small little "runt." In a way, it was a compliment to Ittai.

He backed up slowly into the shop. The giants followed him, ducking to get in the door.

"Where is it?" said Lahmi.

Ittai refused to answer.

Goliath growled, "A Son of Rapha is speaking to you, dwarf. Answer him."

Ishbi and Lahmi stepped up to Ittai, leaving Goliath behind them.

Ittai said only the minimum. "I told the officer it was not for sale." He kept his eyes locked defiantly on Ishbi, insulting Lahmi.

Ishbi said, "Now it is. Produce the whip sword, and we may just let you live."

Ishbi smiled down at Ittai from his nine foot height. He placed a condescending hand on Ittai's shoulder. Suddenly, Ittai heard the sound of multiple voices whispering in his mind. They were demonic voices and they came from this giant.

Touching Ittai was a mistake. Ittai knew he was going to get a thrashing, so he thought he might as well get the first licks.

He grabbed Ishbi's hand and held tight as he twirled in toward his midsection. He jammed his elbow into the giant's gut. Ishbi bent over with a grunt of surprised pain. Ittai was close, so he released the hand and double fisted Ishbi's jaw in a hard upward hammering motion.

Ishbi stumbled backward, almost losing consciousness. Goliath caught him.

It left Lahmi open. Lahmi swung punches at Ittai. Ittai dodged them and hammered a right-hand blow into Lahmi's thigh.

Lahmi cried out in pain.

Ittai grabbed the stunned Lahmi and threw him into one of the pillars. It cracked and the entire edifice shook. Lahmi's nose was broken and gushing blood.

Ittai turned to face the others. It was too late. Ishbi was on him. Ishbi tackled him to the ground and slugged Ittai. The cacophony of demonic whispers penetrated Ittai's consciousness again. But Ishbi could not hold down the blacksmith for long. Ittai was deceptively strong—as strong as Ishbi himself. He was not going down easily.

Ittai landed one good slug on Ishbi's face. Then the hand of Goliath pummeled his head from behind. Ittai blacked out.

He came to within seconds, only to be pummeled with revenge by the two bested giants. Stopping at an eye for an eye and tooth for a tooth was not a value of the Philistines. They began clubbing and pounding Ittai with the intent of breaking his nose and all his teeth, along with his jaw and any other bones they might add to the mix.

However, Goliath stopped them at the broken nose and concussion. He pulled Ishbi and Lahmi back. Ittai's eyes were blurred with blood. He slipped in and out of consciousness. But he had just bested two of the mightiest warriors of Philistia. Call him a runt and a dwarf, but he humiliated them and they knew it. Ittai actually bared a smile, looking up woozily at the giant Rephaim glaring down on him.

"Here it is" shouted Lahmi. He had Rahab in his hands. He had found it behind the furnace.

"Let me see that," said Ishbi. Lahmi handed it to him. "So this is what all the fuss is about?"

Goliath threw a handful of coins onto Ittai. Some rolled away on the floor. "That is the price of your finest sword." Then he threw a pouch of other coins onto him as well. "Here is the payment in advance for the scimitars. I expect them within the week and I expect them to be solid and strong." He turned and barked to the others, "Let us go."

They followed Goliath out. Then Lahmi turned back and spit on Ittai, hissing, "You are no Rephaim."

Ittai thought, *I wish you were right.*

Then he blacked out.

When Ittai came back to consciousness, his bloody face was being wiped by a sniffling Ummi.

"My sweet love. What happened?"

Ittai groaned and pulled himself up to a sitting position against the center pole. "Sons of Rapha. I had something they wanted. But I would not give it up."

"What did you have?"

"You would not understand."

"I want to understand. Please tell me."

"There is too much that you do not know. That I cannot tell you."

"But why, my love? Do you not trust me? I love you."

He paused. He could not say what he had to say. He swallowed with a dry throat. He struggled to get up with a few groans and a limp. He ushered her to the door.

He croaked out, "I-I want you to leave."

"What? Why?"

"Because we are not going to marry. We are never going to marry."

She started to cry. She felt like she was being hit in the stomach by an iron ball. "Why do you say that, Ittai? What do you mean?"

"We can never marry, because I am born of cursed blood."

"I do not understand."

He held up his hands and spread his fingers. She saw the scars on both hands. "I was born with six fingers on each hand and six toes on each foot."

For the first time, she noticed his hands looked abnormal with only five fingers.

He said, "I have tried to hide my true identity from everyone." He looked into her confused eyes. "From you."

He paused to muster the courage to disclose his dark secret. To the one person whom he always thought could wash it away. Now, he knew nothing could save him.

"My mother was a Rapha." He hung his head in pain. "I am a Rapha."

"But you are not a giant."

"It does not matter. I am born of cursed blood and I will not allow that curse to continue. My lineage dies with me. Find someone else to love."

She stepped back away from him in shock.

He looked into her eyes, trying to understand what she was feeling, what she was thinking. But all he saw was fear.

Suddenly, she turned and ran out the door.

Everything in his being screamed to call her back, to apologize to her and say he would never say such terrible things ever again. He hated himself for doing so. He hated himself for not doing so.

He slammed the door shut and fell to the ground. He had never cried before in his entire life. But now everything in him came out in a flood. All his anger, all his sadness, every wrong he had suffered and every ounce of energy he had wasted trying to find redemption and make something useful out of his broken life. It was all a waste. A terrible waste. And now he had a broken heart.

He was cursed. There was no hope for him.

CHAPTER 26

David watched his sheep under the early morning rising sun, but his mind was elsewhere. He thought of all the amazing happenings in his life in recent weeks and how quickly everything had happened. It was surely Yahweh's hand.

The day Jonathan brought him to play music for the king had changed his life with new purpose. He decided it must have been the purpose of the Seer's anointing. He had quickly discovered the ally he had in Jonathan, an unusual royal heir of integrity and character.

He had taken a liking to this man over twice his age. Jonathan had become his mentor, his best friend. They had seen something in each other that connected them. He was everything David wished to be. Jonathan was measured and temperate; David was passionate and unstable. Jonathan had a singularity of spiritual devotion; David struggled with a divided heart for Yahweh and for the flesh. Jonathan had courtly sophistication, David was a rustic. Jonathan had the wisdom of age, David had the recklessness of youth.

Jonathan had taken David under his wing and schooled him in the politics of the palace. They spent many hours together at both work and leisure. He became David's confidant. He even shared family secrets and advised David not to reveal his anointing until Yahweh himself chose the time. When Jonathan discovered David's battle skills, he was impressed and persuaded his father to make David one of the king's armor-bearers. When the king had one of his fits of madness, Jonathan would call upon David to play his lyre and soothe the beast.

But the summer months were beginning and David needed to spend time back home with the flock before shearing. His three eldest brothers were called up for military service. The Philistines had encamped in Ephes-dammim in battle array and the Israelites stood opposed in the valley of the Terebinth. As David tended the flocks, he wondered what the plan of the pagan Philistines could be.

But he did not think on it for long, because he was making his own plans for Michal when he returned to the court. He was best friends with Jonathan, but he had fallen in love with Michal. They stole every moment they could to be together. They would sing praises and hymns to Yahweh. She was enamored with his playing, and he was mesmerized by her voice. They felt as if their souls were one. The only problem was that David was a palace servant without noble status and would never be allowed to marry her. They were simply in two different worlds. And it was driving him crazy. He would do anything, *anything* to win her hand.

This time, he had decided to wait on the Lord. He had made so many mistakes with young women in the past. He wanted to turn over a new leaf, and this time do it right. It made him seek Yahweh more earnestly. He would spend so much time and effort trying to seek Yahweh's face that his knees would become bloody from scraping the ground, and his legs would lose their circulation.

David felt like a hybrid, a man torn between heaven and earth. He desired the glory of Yahweh with all his soul, but he longed for the comfort of Michal with all his body. Could these two things be opposites? Or could they be united in one spiritual unity? He had never been married. He could not know. But he longed for it to be true.

"David!" His father's voice interrupted his thoughts.

It was unusual for his father to come out to the pasture. He would normally send one of the children.

"Yes, father?"

"Up with yourself! I have an important task for you. I have a shipment of provisions to send to your brothers on the front lines. Parched grain and loaves, and I do not want you sneaking any of it for yourself, do you hear me?"

"Yes, father."

"I want you to see if they are well. And I have some cheese to give the commander of their thousand. I want you to leave immediately."

"Yes, father."

David left the sheep with a keeper and took the provisions for his father.

CHAPTER 27

David arrived at the valley of the Terebinth, fifteen miles from Bethlehem, with his shipment of provisions. It was not uncommon for family members to send such care packages for the benefit of their beloved sons. David left the shipment with the keeper of the baggage and made his way through the ranks to greet his brothers, Eliab, Abinadab and Shammah.

Shammah saw him first. "David!"

Abinadab turned and saw him too. They both rushed their baby brother and gave him bear hugs.

Shammah said, "Have you brought us some vittles? The military food is abominable."

David said, "And some cheese to bribe your commander for favor."

They smiled.

A call to arms interrupted them. A ram's horn bellowed throughout the valley.

"Is it battle?" asked David.

"In a manner of speaking," said Shammah. "Come and see."

David followed them to the front. As they walked, Shammah explained the strategic location of this valley in accessing the Israelite hill country. If the Philistines secured a victory here, they could strangle Saul's stronghold of the region.

The Israelites were encamped on one mountain and the Philistines on another mountain. Between them was the valley lined with Terebinth trees and a brook that ran through the valley center.

In the empty valley, a single warrior bellowed out blasphemies. His voice could be heard loud and strong. David saw that he was a giant almost ten feet tall, with a shield-bearer before him.

"WHY HAVE YOU COWARDLY HEBREWS DRAWN UP FOR BATTLE?"

David was incensed. "Who is this uncircumcised Philistine that he taunts the armies of the living God?"

"Their champion, Goliath of Gath," said Shammah.

Goliath continued his rant, "I DEFY THE RANKS OF ISRAEL THIS DAY! CHOOSE FOR YOURSELVES A CHAMPION TO FIGHT ME! IF HE WINS, THE PHILISTINES WILL BE YOUR SERVANTS. IF I WIN, YOU WILL BE OUR SERVANTS!"

Abinadab muttered, "He has taunted us these forty days with the same challenge."

"Forty days?" said David. How had he failed to hear about it, he wondered. "Is there no one to stand up to this blasphemer?"

Shammah snickered, "Easy for you to say from the comfort of your palace luxury."

Abinadab threw in, "The man who kills him, the king will laud with tax exemption and great riches."

The next words that came from Abinadab struck David in the chest like an iron rod. "The king has even offered up the hand of one of his daughters to the soul who triumphs over this titan."

All sounds seemed to suddenly go silent as the words sunk in. His brothers continued to speak, but their lips seemed to make no sound as David felt glorious hope rise within him. He knew at that moment that Yahweh had made a way for the impossible to become possible.

Abinadab said, "Are you listening to me?"

"Is that true?" asked David.

"Is what true?" complained Shammah.

"What you said about the king offering his daughter in marriage?"

Abinadab scolded him, "I told you it was part of the royal decree."

David's mind raced. He would do anything to win Michal's hand. Anything. This champion was huge, but he was also loaded down with clumsy armor. David thought he would be no different than a big stupid bear, like the ones he had easily outwitted protecting his flock. Sure, he could not face the giant's strength, but he didn't have to. He could outmaneuver him, dance around him and make him tired. Keep his distance and keep pelting him with stones from his sling.

He remembered that his last use of the sling almost got him killed due to a terribly aimed shot at a lion. He would need Yahweh's favor if he would face this behemoth. But is that not what Yahweh required? What god did they serve if he could not vanquish such giants as Joshua and Caleb did? What kind of army of Yahweh had not one warrior worthy of challenging this Philistine ogre? Saul himself, with his size and skill as warrior king, would be capable of besting the brute. David believed with all his heart that these uncircumcised idolaters could not take away Yahweh's Promised Land. He had been practicing his heart out for the time when he would be of age, so that he could join the army of the Living God. He saw this as his chance to trust in the delivering hand of Yahweh.

"Take me to the king."

But when he turned, his way was blocked by a fuming Eliab.

"Why have you come down, little brother?"

His look was accusing. David said innocently, "To bring you provisions."

"I know your presumptuous, evil, little heart. You came down to watch the bloodshed, you spoiled baby."

David gave a hard stare at his older brother. He had never done so before, but he had had enough.

"Eliab, you have been a spoiled first-born all your life. You have sought recognition and the praise of man's lips instead of Yahweh's. This is not the time for petty sibling rivalry. Get out of my way. I am going to the king."

Eliab's eyes went wide with shock. David's words pierced him like never before. They carried an authority that exposed Eliab's longtime envy of David's anointing. Bitterness had built up in his heart because he could not see why Yahweh chose the youngest of the family instead of the eldest. It was a common tactic of Yahweh's election, from Abel to Isaac to Jacob to Joseph and more. Yahweh always seemed to choose the one least likely for choosing.

Eliab stepped back out of his little brother's way.

• • • • •

Across the way from the Israelites, the Philistine soldiers laughed and jeered at their cowardly enemies. The five other Sons of Rapha gathered around Lord Achish and Lady Bisha as they looked down upon their lone champion standing unopposed in the valley.

Ishbi said, "My lord, how long will Goliath continue this wasted exercise?"

"For as long as it takes," said Achish. "The longer it goes on the more demoralized their forces become. We may win this war without a drop of blood."

Ishbi said, "But at some point, we begin to look like a crowing cock if we do nothing but boast. A swift, vigorous assault will surprise them and crush them with finality."

Bisha leaned over to whisper to Achish. He pretended to consider his options, then said in full accord with her counsel, "When they finally send their champion and he is defeated, then we will exterminate them."

Ishbi knew Bisha pulled Achish's strings. He didn't need the spirit voices in his head to tell him so. She was the ruthless politico behind the fat lord's ambitions. The rules of champion combat were that the loser's army would voluntarily lay down their arms and be brought back in chains, not slaughtered mercilessly. This devious queen might yet be the downfall of Gath.

• • • • •

Saul sat brooding in his war tent when a servant announced the arrival of his personal musician.

The unseen spirit shadow beside Saul whispered furiously in his ear. The presence of this upstart shepherd always unsettled it. Saul became more agitated.

"David," said Saul, "why are you here? This is neither the time nor place for music."

David bowed and said, "Your servant has not come to play music, my lord."

Saul spouted impatiently, "Well, what in Sheol are you here for then? Speak up."

"I will fight the uncircumcised Philistine."

A moment of shock hit Saul, and then he burst out in laughter. The unseen and unheard spirit beside Saul cackled with laughter as well. Their voices became one in unison. For a moment, David felt certain he had heard another voice in the tent. He felt the presence, but could not place it.

"You are not able to fight this Philistine." Saul could not stop his chuckling. "You are but a youth. He has been a man of war from his youth."

David said, "As a shepherd for my father, I have killed lumbering bears like him while protecting the flock. Not long ago, a lion took a lamb from my care. I caught him by his mane and struck him down."

David decided not to admit his terrible aim with the slingshot. He had killed the lion after all. That was what mattered.

Saul could not stop laughing.

David persisted. "Yahweh delivered me from the paw of the bear and the lion. He will deliver me from the hand of this overgrown brute, this uncircumcised Philistine."

Nimrod would not stop whispering. He had been waiting for an opportunity like this for too long, a way to rid himself of this precocious little godlicker that was spoiling his attempt at complete control of Saul.

Saul stopped laughing. Then, as if he were listening to some unseen person, he finally said with a chuckling smile, "Go! And may Yahweh be with you!"

If Saul had been in his right mind, he would never have entrusted the nation into the hands of this unproven shepherd musician. *If* he had been in his right mind.

David bowed and prepared to leave.

Saul barked out. "Wait! You will need armor. Nothing but the royal best for my champion." He snickered and gestured over to his own suit of armor on a six and a half foot tall mannequin.

David could see himself weighed down with the helmet of bronze too big for his head, the chain mail too heavy for his smaller torso and the sword too large for his grip. But he knew Saul was being facetious. He knew it was still a joke to him.

David said, "Uh, I have not tested your armor, my king. I have another idea."

• • • • •

Goliath was annoyed with the slowness of these desert rats. The Israelites had announced their challenger, but had kept him waiting, which made him even angrier. The sun rose high. His armor grew hot. He was sweating inside, and itching. He scratched himself and kept his eyes peeled for the fool who would die on his javelin. He decided that after he killed the warrior, he would parade the victim's skull in front of the entire army.

As the Champion of Philistia, Goliath was free to dress his armor any way he preferred. This was the case for all the Sons of Rapha, none of whose origins were with the original Sea Peoples, but with Canaan.

Rather than wearing the well known feathered headdress of the Philistines, Goliath wore a bronze helmet more akin to Greek or Assyrian protection. He wore one hundred and twenty-six pounds of Egyptian-styled chain mail on his monstrous nine and a half foot frame.

His bronze greaves that protected his shins were Greek, and his shield bearer carried a full-bodied shield before him rather than the smaller round Philistine style.

Goliath's huge scimitar, not as popular with the regulars, was slung over his back. He planned on first using his loop javelin to skewer his victim with a sixteen pound iron spearhead, or pierce his prey with a mighty launch as it ran away.

Goliath was ready for a killing.

Finally, he saw an opponent approaching him by the stream that flowed through the valley. Finally. Over forty days for these pathetic Hebrews to muster up the courage to face him.

Word spread through the Philistine ranks. Attention was piqued. Soldiers stopped their dice playing and woke from their naps when they heard the news: a challenger approached.

Lord Achish stood up and squinted to see better in the glare of the sunny day. He said, "Finally, a champion fool for my Goliath to finish off." Lady Bisha's stomach quivered with excitement. She hoped for a gory bloodbath.

But as the challenger came closer it became apparent, he was not what Achish had expected. He was not what anyone had expected. Lord Achish muttered, "Is this a jest? They mock me?"

The challenger looked like a young boy. Because his eyesight was not as sharp as in his youth, Goliath could not tell for sure until the lad had reached to within fifty or so feet of him.

He was puny. And he wore no armor. He was clad as a shepherd without his cloak. He had a shepherd's staff and sling in his hand. He looked like a teenager. In fact, he was quite handsome to Goliath. But he was insulted by the challenge. He boiled with rage.

He screamed out to his enemies on the hillside, "AM I A DOG THAT YOU COME TO ME WITH STICKS? I CURSE YOU BY DAGON, BA'ALZEBUL, MOLECH AND ASHERAH! YOU FILTHY HEBREW COWARDS!"

Goliath turned to David and said, "Come to me, boy. I will give your flesh to the vultures and jackals. After I have my way with you!"

David shouted to him, "You come with scimitar and javelin, but I come in the name of Yahweh of hosts, the God of the armies of Israel, whom you have blasphemed! This day Yahweh will deliver you into my hand and I will smite you and cut off your head!"

Goliath laughed with incredulity. *And it is a puny pontificating pipsqueak no less. I wonder if the little rat is going to keep on talking.*

He did. "I will give *your* body to the vultures and jackals, and all the earth will know that there is a god in Israel whose name is Yahweh Elohim! And this assembly will know that Yahweh saves not with sword or spear! For the battle is Yahweh's and he will give you into our hands!"

Goliath muttered, "Sanctimonious little twat."

He saw David reach down by the brook to pick up some stones. Goliath pushed his shield bearer out of the way. He was obviously unneeded. But he could not stop staring with amused wonder at this bold little rodent who charged at him, swinging his little string over his head. He was within thirty feet now and the child stopped. Goliath dropped his javelin. His new plan was to catch the little runt, abuse it, then rip its body in half with his bare hands.

David prayed out loud as he swung his sling, "Yahweh, please make up for my bad aim." He had four additional stones in his satchel just in case.

The sling released.

Goliath was lost in his perverse thoughts when the stone hit and sank into his forehead, right below the armor line of the helmet.

He heard the sound of his own skull crunching under the impact. He was too confused to figure out what had happened. Then everything went black and he fell to the ground.

The Philistine camp went dead silent. No one could believe what they just saw.

No one.

Did that little Hebrew just fell their champion with a stone?

No one in the Israelite camp could believe it either. Least of all, Saul, and his dark companion.

It was as if time stood still for both sides. It was a valley of silence.

Up on the Philistine heights, Ishbi watched the Hebrew runt run over to Goliath's fallen body. With great effort, the kid drew out Goliath's huge scimitar from his back.

Ishbi screamed, "NOOOOOOOO!" as the Hebrew raised the blade high and chopped off Goliath's head.

Then he pulled up his tunic and released his bladder on the corpse.

Ishbi and Lahmi raced down toward their fallen comrade. They saw the Hebrew raise Goliath's head in victory as a squadron of waiting soldiers stripped the armor and fled with David back to their lines.

By the time Ishbi and Lahmi arrived at Goliath's decapitated and stripped corpse, David was almost back to his lines. Ishbi thought he should have had Runihura throw one of his missiles at the fleeing runt.

Lahmi had wanted to take and use Goliath's armor as his own to honor his brother. But the greasy little Hebrew had confiscated all of it along with Goliath's head.

Lahmi picked up his brother's body with tearful eyes. Ishbi was too shocked to respond with anything but open-eyed terror.

Lahmi cried out, "Who was that vile creature?"

Ishbi laid his hand on Goliath's chest. "We will find out. And when we capture him, we will keep him alive in such pain for so long that Sheol will be a relief to his torment."

Lahmi's eyes dried with hatred. He could only think of one thing. "He has a family."

• • • • •

David was brought to Saul. He approached the king, carrying the head of the giant. Goliath's armor was carried by others. He knelt and laid the head at Saul's feet as an offering of obeisance.

Saul and everyone around him were still in stunned silence.

Finally, Saul blurted out, "Whose son are you, again?"

Saul remembered that he had publicly promised to bestow great riches and honor on the family of the victorious warrior, as well as his daughter in marriage. But David was of such humble origins that Saul never could remember his father's name.

David said, "I am the son of your servant, Jesse, the Bethlehemite." He was used to Saul's bad memory, and had often joked with Jonathan about it.

Saul said, "And which one is he again? He will be sad to know that you will not be returning to his house. For you, my gibborim, will be the new captain of my bodyguard."

In this moment, everyone knew that Yahweh had performed a miracle. But it was more than a miracle, it was an unveiling. More than a few persons now suspected the true reason for David's anointing by Samuel; that the messiah of Israel had been revealed. Among them were Jonathan, Saul—and Nimrod.

"Send the emissaries to disarm the Philistines," said Saul. "We have a victory to celebrate." He placed his hand on David's shoulder and looked at him with pride. He was elated, and free of his fear and muddled thinking.

The dark counselor had temporarily left him again.

• • • • •

But Achish, Lord of Gath, had no intention of allowing such an Israelite celebration. He had no intention of submitting to the rules of war. He immediately turned to the commanders near him and barked, "Quickly, lead your forces and flee back to Gath before the Israelites can catch us!"

CHAPTER 28

Ittai stood alone in his forge. He looked with a stone face into the furnace of fire. He had lost everything. He had no family, no recognition, no love, and no dignity left. Everything he pursued in his life sifted through his fingers like sand into the sea. Any hope of finding a little piece of happiness in this miserable existence died when he learned he was the cursed Seed of the Serpent.

He grabbed the noose he had formed with the rope that dangled from the ceiling rafter. He placed it around his neck and prepared to kick away the stool he had been standing on.

He heard the sound of arriving trumpets. It was not the sound of a triumphal entry, but rather the urgent sound of retreat. He was curious. But he thought, *What would the defeat of my city be but one more defeat to crown my life of defeats?*

A rapid knock on his door jarred him. He heard his neighbor, the carpenter, yelling, "Ittai! Ittai! Goliath is dead! The Israelites have chased our forces back to the city!"

Goliath is dead? The champion of the Philistines? The general of the Sons of Rapha? Suicide would have to wait. This, he had to hear.

He pulled the noose off and jumped down to open the door. The carpenter was turning to leave.

Ittai said, "How was he killed?"

"They say it was a contest of Champions. They say it was a malicious miracle. Some say it was a mere juvenile who felled the giant. Others say he dropped him with an Evil Eye of magic."

Ittai remembered the words of Lahmi to him, *An ancient prophecy of a messiah king born of the Seed of Eve and of Abraham will rise within Israel.* He remembered that Goliath was going to call out their Champion and challenge him to a duel. No one could best Goliath.

No one, except a messiah king, a gibborim savior. *That* would be miraculous.

The carpenter saw the noose hanging from the ceiling. "Are you all right, Ittai? Is everything okay?"

"What is the matter with you, Gelt, have you not ever considered killing yourself?" Gelt was speechless. Ittai gave him a big, silly grin and closed the door. His knees almost buckled from his wonderment. *What if this messiah king was the vanquisher of the Seed of the Serpent? What if he was a savior? What if he was a good king? Would there be a place for repentance and allegiance to his lordship? Could a Rephaim be redeemed?*

Ittai's plans for demise changed. He had a new reason to stay alive. He had new hope.

CHAPTER 29

Saul chased the Philistines all the way back to the gates of Gath and Ekron, ten miles west of the Valley of the Terebinth. On their way back to Gibeah, the Israelites stopped at the location of Goliath's defeat to plunder the camp of the Philistines before returning home. It was the first moment that the Israelites had to rest since the fateful battle of David and the Philistine.

Saul stood in his war tent, waiting. It was the size of a palace room and decorated to match with purple Phoenician cloth, Egyptian tapestries and a portable throne with small carved lion cherubs beside it. It was ostentatious and indicative of Saul's new desire for greatness and glory.

He was alone and looking upon his gleaming ornamental bronze armor when David arrived by escort into the tent.

"My lord king," said David as he bowed. "Would you like music this evening?" He had brought his lyre and began to tune it for play.

"No," said Saul. He wiped a bloody smudge from the bright metallic surface of his shield. "Finally, a moment to rest from hunting down those cowardly Philistines."

"Yahweh be praised," said David. "He has brought Israel her victory."

Saul walked over to David. "Yes, but you have become a gibborim, a mighty man of valor for your god and king. I have asked myself the question over and over, 'who is this young warrior poet who has come from nowhere with no pedigree to rise in glory and honor before the eyes of all?'"

"I am your lowly servant, my sovereign."

"Indeed. You were but a shepherd whose favor with both god and man has garnered you the position of royal musician, captain of the king's guard, and now Champion of Israel, defeating the mightiest of our enemies. And yet you seek no glory in it."

"Lord, I am what I am by Yahweh's grace for *his* glory."

"But what is it you want?" asked Saul. The question was more like an accusation. Saul was always demanding proof of loyalty from his servants.

David dared not say what he was thinking. He wanted love. He wanted the woman whose angelic voice haunted his heart and whose beauty drove him mad with desire. He wanted Michal. But he knew that such desire would make him appear ambitious for royalty after all. And Saul's mistrust would be justified. But he had another desire as well that was safe to admit.

He said simply, "I want Yahweh to crush all his enemies under his feet, and for his anointed king to reign over all the Land of Promise."

"Well spoken," mused Saul. "But much easier spoken than achieved. Still, you have achieved what no other warrior has in my service. And I owe you a debt of promise myself."

David said, "My lord?"

"I did not forget what I promised to the one who vanquished the Philistine. When we return to Gibeah, I will exempt your father's family from taxes, and you may have my daughter's hand in marriage."

David's heart leapt. Then Saul said, "You may marry my eldest daughter Merab as soon as you desire and you will become my son-in-law."

David's heart fell. Merab? Of course it would be the eldest. It was the normal way of things to marry off the eldest first. He had been so absorbed in his thoughts of Michal that he completely forgot about Merab.

Saul continued, "But you must continue to fight valiantly for me against the Philistines."

"My lord, who am I, and who is my father's clan that I should become a son-in-law to the king? It is above my station."

"Nonsense. It is a common and acceptable means for entering the royal family through matrimony."

"My king, I must decline your generous offer. I am unworthy and have no desire to claim that prize." He was sweating now, desperately trying to steady the panic gripping his heart. He could not live if he could not have Michal. To have her older sister instead would be a mockery and a curse against all the happiness in the world. Not for any lack of worth in Merab, but simply because she was not the object of all his love and desire.

Saul was dumbfounded. "I am inclined to be insulted by such a gesture. But I see your sincerity and it proves your loyalty to your stated values. I dare say I am impressed."

David's terror dissipated. He finally breathed a sigh of relief.

Saul added, "But I am still going to give your family riches and tax exemption. I insist."

"Very well, my king. At your insistence, I submit to the wealth and taxes."

David knew that his chances for wedding Michal had just been obliterated. He had passed on marrying Merab because of his claim to lowly status. How then could he ever ask for Michal's hand in contradiction to his façade of "noble" motives?

He felt doomed to eternal unhappiness without his precious Michal.

David drifted away after being dismissed by Saul. He found himself at the tent he had been given for his new champion status. He wondered if he could feel any worse than this very moment. He was so absorbed in his thoughts, he did not notice right away that Jonathan stood inside the tent, holding the rotting head of Goliath.

"How goes it with my father, David?"

David looked at him, startled. Then his eyes teared up. "Oh, Jonathan, my master and my friend. My life is over before it has even begun. Your father offered me Merab's hand in marriage and I turned it down because I love another."

"Michal," said Jonathan.

"How did you know?"

"David, it is so obvious to everyone in the palace except only the most blind and dim-witted. Thus my father, who is under his own spell of enchantment, is about the only one who does not know."

David was speechless. He had been blindsided twice this evening already. God only knew if he would be blindsided any more.

Jonathan held up the decomposing head. Already, maggots were falling out of its nostrils. The forehead where David's stone had sunk in was more discolored with red and purple than the rest of its decaying flesh. Its dead eyes were clouded and dissolving. "David, you killed the mightiest warrior in Philistia with a single stone. A giant Rephaim whom no one else in all of Israel would face. You and I know that Yahweh guided that stone to its target. Your music alone turns away the evil spirit that torments my father, the king of Israel. I have never seen such a person in my entire life with such favor of Yahweh upon him."

"Jonathan, you speak too highly of me. Temper your praise with all my faults of which you are also entirely aware. My terrible temper, my fleshly weakness for love."

Jonathan chuckled, "You are as blind as my father the king. Do you think Yahweh chooses men of perfection and sinlessness? Where is such a man, David? Where? I know of not one."

He put Goliath's skull back into its box and closed the lid.

"I am plagued by my sins, Jonathan. I have seen good men and I have seen great. And I am confident of this one thing: the great are rarely the good, and the good are rarely the great."

"Do you think Yahweh controls only the good in this world and not the evil?"

David answered, "Do you justify evil with such appeals to Yahweh's sovereignty?"

"Of course not. Yahweh punishes evil even in his chosen people. But they are no less chosen, because he does not choose them for their goodness or their greatness—for anything in them. He chooses them because of his own purposes. And he chooses his anointed one as well."

"What are you saying, Jonathan?"

Jonathan took off his royal robe. "I have sought out the Seer Samuel to see if my suspicions were correct. And I have found my answer."

David's knees grew weak.

"David, you were not anointed to be a royal musician in the court of the king of Israel." He opened the robe and walked up to David to drape it over his back.

"You were anointed to *be* the next king of Israel."

David felt faint. He caught himself and sat down on his armoring chair, staring with shock into the air.

Jonathan picked up his bow, his sword and belt, and handed them to David.

"I strip myself of my rights to the throne to support Yahweh's chosen and anointed one, the messiah king." He bowed to his knee.

David got up quickly. Jonathan's weapons fell to the floor with his robe. David walked to the other side of the tent, trying to get away. But he knew he could not get away.

Thoughts collided in his head. This could not be. Was Jonathan lying about his meeting with Samuel? He had never lied to David before. Was this some kind of political maneuver? He had never showed any signs of ambition all the days David had known him. But David was plagued by his own duplicitous motives and failures of faith. It was difficult for him to conceive of a life with such true devotion and purity of heart as Jonathan. Yet he had proved himself over and over to David. He was not a man of fraudulence or ambition. He was a man of integrity and honor and above all, trust in the Living God. The kind of trust that David had learned from and had even sought to emulate. But now this? The ultimate sacrifice of giving up his inheritance as the next king of Israel to David, his younger and inexperienced inferior? Giving up royalty to a nobody because a cranky Seer had told him Yahweh chose differently? Who would do such a thing? No one David had ever known. This was either the supreme example of true faith or the biggest swindle of his life.

"Let us cut a covenant," said Jonathan. "I will pledge my fealty to you and will protect you against your enemies."

CHAPTER 30

Ishbi knelt before the altar at the feet of Dagon in his holy temple. Lahmi stood behind him and the two others stood back further; Saph and Runihura.

Dagon placed his trident upon Ishbi's shoulder. Dagon's mouth was still smudged with the blood of the goat sacrifice he had just consumed next to the corn offering. He said, "I, Dagon, mighty storm god, lord of fertility, and chief of the gods, do appoint thee, Ishbi ben Ob of Endor and Gath, as the general commander of the Sons of Rapha. Serve me well, and you will see victory on the field of war and length of days. Defy me and you will die a thousand deaths in the waters of my wrath."

Behind the stone statue of Dagon, Asherah whispered to Ba'alzebul, "'Chief of the gods?' His ego far exceeds his abilities."

Ba'alzebul whispered back, "It is time the fish understands he is not our superior."

At the Sanctuary altar, the Sons of Rapha froze and glanced with shock behind Dagon. Dagon wondered what they were staring at.

And then it hit him, just as Ba'alzebul and Asherah stood next to him.

Ishbi said, "The gods." The giants knelt and bowed. They were overwhelmed with the imposing presence of Ba'alzebul's bull horns and Asherah's battle-maiden form.

Dagon gave Ba'alzebul and Asherah a dirty look the giants could not see.

Ba'alzebul pronounced, "Rephaim, you kneel before Ba'alzebul the storm god and Lady Asherah of the Sea. We are here in council with Dagon to commission you in your new calling."

Dagon fumed. Ba'alzebul had stolen his thunder.

Ba'alzebul continued, "The goddess will now explain to you what we require."

Asherah saw Dagon was in a quandary. If he lost his temper at their intrusion, he would look weak. If he went along, it would appear to be part of his plan. But either way, Ba'alzebul and Asherah were now running the show — at least for the moment.

Asherah said, "Do you know who this conqueror of your Champion is?"

Ishbi said, "No, my lady. But we will find him and tear him to pieces as an offering to you."

Dagon was miffed that Ishbi was no longer speaking of his dedication to Dagon, but to her as well.

Ba'alzebul said, "Is it true he is but a child?"

"He is a dog," said Ishbi.

Ba'alzebul said, "What was Goliath, then, a kitten? And what does that make the rest of you, mice?"

Lahmi spoke out of turn, "Only the messiah king could have defeated Goliath."

Ishbi shot him an angry look.

Ba'alzebul said, "Yet, you do not know who he is."

Dagon was increasingly agitated at having his altar taken over by this pair of glory-stealing divine bullies. He tried to reinsert himself into the lead. "Before we can kill him, we must find him. Before we can find him, we must learn who he is and what his powers and weaknesses are."

Asherah butted in, "Dagon is correct. Return to your king and seek intelligence on this 'dog.' But do not seek to kill him without our approval. You are dismissed."

"Yes, my gods," said Ishbi. He led the others out of the sanctuary to their waiting squads of Rephaim outside the temple.

Dagon held back his rage through gritted teeth. "How dare you usurp my authority in my own temple. *I* am the god of the Philistines."

Dagon glared at Ba'alzebul, who looked puffed up and entirely capable of obliterating Dagon if he chose to, let alone gore him like a bull with those horns.

Dagon sought to bluff his way out, using guilt. "I took you under my arm when you were too weak to fend for yourself. I called you my son." He looked at Asherah. "And you are far from your Sidonian coastal homeland. You had best watch yourself outside of your territory."

Asherah said, "Do not fret yourself, Dagon. We are not usurping your authority. It is simply time you recognize we are equals and we work together. You cannot do this alone."

She glanced back and forth at them both like a scolding mother, "Now, if you two do not learn how to get along, then we will be divided and Yahweh will win. Is that what you want?"

Dagon knew she was right. He said, "No."

Brilliant, thought Ba'alzebul, *she is playing the mediating mother. Her words would actually make sense — if they weren't planning on overthrowing Dagon and taking his territory.*

Asherah said, "Ba'alzebul, did you hear me? Is that what you want?"

"No," said Ba'alzebul. He played the part of a boy making up after a playground fight.

Dagon tried to assert some backhanded control. He said to Ba'alzebul, "You can keep Ekron, but I still demand respect in my territory."

Ba'alzebul said, "Understood." Ba'alzebul thought, *I will sift you like wheat when the time is right.*

Asherah said, "Dagon, it is time we try my plan that you rejected years ago. I have unmolested access to the Israelite tribes. They worship me. Let me go amongst them, and I will find out everything we need to know about this messiah. Besides, it is time I get out of this tomb and get some fresh air among the peoples."

Dagon said, "Who are your spies?"

Asherah said, "The Israelites are quite fond of my sacred prostitutes. They move freely in their midst."

Dagon took a long time to respond. He wanted to make them both feel as if they needed his approval. Philistia was still his allotment from the gods. He would not look weak. That would be his death knell.

"Agreed," he said. "Let us work together."

It was too much for Ba'alzebul to hold back. He had been watching Asherah taking charge, showing strength. He liked that.

He said, with eyes locked on Asherah, "Now that our Lady of the Sea has set us straight, let us celebrate our new covenant of unity."

Dagon smiled. It was all a balance of power. Each display of power by an individual in their unholy trinity would require an equal display of power in the other two. And the way male gods expressed their power was to dominate others by force.

Though Asherah was a male Watcher in female disguise, she was still a goddess and no match for the two other gods who ganged up on her to prove their dysfunctional machismo. Asherah knew she had to fight and lose to make her attackers feel superior. She was strong, but not nearly as strong as Ba'alzebul.

So she fought them on that fortuitous evening, but her attackers overpowered her and abused her until morning.

CHAPTER 31

Goliath's skull of rotting flesh was paraded before the triumphal procession through the streets of Gibeah. It bothered Saul greatly to have David at the lead carrying the pike with the giant's head on it. But he had to allow it. Everyone knew that David was the warrior who had killed the Rapha, so Saul could not hide that fact. He had to publish it. It burned like a hot coal on his pride. He wanted his people to worship him, to praise him as their mighty victorious king. He wanted to be the greatest king who ever lived. Instead, David received the glory for chopping off the head of the mightiest Champion in Philistia.

Far worse yet was the music that accompanied the celebration. Women came from all areas of the city, singing and dancing before the procession. It was the custom for such things. They used tambourines, cymbals and bells, and sang a song of praise. But this song was subversive praise. He could not hear all the lyrics, but the ones he did made him burn with anger.

The chorus was clear as the bells they were ringing:

Saul has struck down his thousands,
And David his ten thousands!
Saul has struck down his thousands,
And David his ten thousands!

Saul grew incensed with each verse. How dare these puny commoners sing such things to my face. Attributing mere thousands to my glory, while attributing a myriad to David? I am their king. He is but my servant.

When he got to the palace, he went straight to his bed chamber. But it was not to rest. It was to fume with mounting anger. He paced around the room. His thoughts grew from indignant to enraged.

I should levy a heavy tax on these ungrateful peasants. Or maybe I should let them face the scimitars and javelins of the Philistines and see if they could kill their mere thousands, while lauding David for his ten thousands.

He stopped, aware of a presence in the room. His shadow counselor whispered with a hiss of bitterness, "You have every right to be outraged. You are a great and mighty king. David is nothing. He is a minstrel."

"He killed the Philistine," countered Saul.

"Yes, but you led the forces of Israel, to slaughter the Philistines all the way back to Ekron and Gath. *You* led them to victory. *You* subdued the Ammonites, the Moabites, the Edomites, and the Amalekites. *You* conquered the mighty giant king Agag. *You* are the anointed messiah king of Israel. David is a mere servant. He is nothing. You could do whatever you wanted with him. You could kill him if you wanted to."

Saul stood proud, listening to the counsel. His back arched, his chest puffed out, his chin rose with pride. He saw himself looking down upon the masses in contempt. Their pathetic meaningless lives, a mere support to his greatness and glory as their mighty leader.

The shadow whisked around Saul, making him dizzy. The spirit's words enchanted his ears. "Did your seer ever tell you that he anointed the shepherd boy in his home town of Bethlehem?"

"No," said Saul, disturbed by the news. "For what?"

"Tch, tch, tch," mocked Nimrod. "Do you not see what is happening under your very nose, O king?"

Saul listened attentively as Nimrod continued his whispering.

"Let me tell you the story of a king who failed to realize the threat to his own kingdom and what it cost him. There once was a king who united all the peoples under heaven. He was a Mighty Hunter of men with an invincible army. He built a mighty temple-tower with its top in the heavens. It was a meeting place of gods and men, a cosmic mountain between heaven and earth. But the stars foretold of a child who would be born of humble birth, but would rise up and kill his ten thousands, slay kings and inherit the land. The king did not believe such a small and insignificant Hebrew could possibly overthrow him."

Saul thought Nimrod was telling him a thinly veiled parable of Saul's kingdom. He did not realize it was the story of Nimrod's own reign and how it had been crushed by the rise of Abraham and the fall of the Tower of Babel.

"This child grew up and became a nomad. He was surrounded by magic and would prove to be the bane of the king's existence." For Nimrod, this bane had been Abraham of Ur. Saul saw it as David. It was of course both, because this was Nimrod's second chance to crush the heel of the Seed of Abraham that had crushed his head so long ago.

The spirit continued, "The king should have killed the troublesome nomad, but he did not. And that chosen one eventually grew powerful and the king lost his entire realm to the nomad and was driven to madness."

Nimrod paused to let it sink in. Then he whispered, "O king, you can stop the madness. This shepherd boy, this godlicker, will usurp your throne if you do not stop him. He will steal your greatness and bathe in the glory of your ruins. Is that what you want?"

Saul's breathing had grown heavier. Everything Nimrod whispered filled his head with confusion. He loved David, but he knew his counselor was right. Yahweh had left Saul. And if he had anointed David, then that meant Saul was destined for madness. Saul would be lost in the mists of history and legend as the warrior king eclipsed by a simple shepherd boy. But he could not kill his devoted and loyal captain of his own bodyguard. Could he?

"Yes. Yes, we can" whispered his counselor.

Saul felt the shadow enter him again, as he had done at previous times. Saul lost all sense of himself, but felt filled with power and strength, like that of a Naphil. He felt like a god. His eyes glazed over and all he could hear was the sound of his unseen controller whispering in his ears, "Kill the usurper. Kill him. Kill him. Kill him. Kill him. Kill him. Kill him!"

It drove Saul mad with rage. But now he felt like he was the Mighty Hunter Nimrod. He would stop the madness. He would kill David. He looked around spasmodically and found a spear. He plucked it up and left his room. He was on the hunt.

David was playing a song with Michal in the musician's quarters when they heard the screams of female musicians.

He looked up to see Saul enter the far end of the room carrying a spear in his hand. His eyes were filled with madness and rage, the whites alone showing. He spit foam from his mouth like a rabid dog.

Michal spoke in fear, "Father?"

David stood in front of Michal.

Saul juggled the spear in his hand, preparing to throw it.

David spoke quickly to Michal, "Get out of here, now."

Michal ran through the back entrance into the servants' hallways.

Saul shook his head with a spasm of pain. The voice in his ear now tormented him, screaming, "Pin him to the wall! Pin him to the wall! Pin him to the wall! Pin him to the wall!"

He aimed at David and threw with the force of a giant.

David dodged to the floor. The spear stuck in the wall behind him. It sank deep. But David would not pull it out. He would not fight back against Yahweh's anointed king.

He ran.

Saul bolted for the spear and jerked it out of the wall. He followed the scent of David through the servant hallways. His mind was a cacophony of resounding hatred. "Crush the Seed! Spill his blood! Crush the Seed! Spill his blood!"

David raced through the maze-like hallways of the palace. Saul was close on his heels, but the twisting turns did not allow him a good throw.

David broke out into the dining room of the servants. He slammed the door shut and bolted it. There were a dozen servants eating an afternoon snack at their tables, shocked by David's loud entrance. He turned to them. "The king is mad again! Get out of here!"

They knew this scenario all too well. They immediately rushed out of the dining room, leaving David alone by the door.

He backed up.

The door shook with supernatural pounding. The hinges loosened on the wall.

David found a window at the other end of the room and stood in front of it.

The door blew open with tremendous force. Saul stepped inside the room with spear in hand. His muscles jerked and spasmed with fury. He looked like a sick puppet in the hands of an evil puppet master.

He eyed David by the window and aimed his spear. David wondered how he could see with his eyes turned up inside his head.

Saul thrust the spear.

David dodged again. He had planned for this. He anticipated that the bright sunlight behind him through the window would make it more difficult for Saul to target him. He also planned for what happened next. The spear careened right through the window where David had been and flew out into the palace yard below.

Saul had lost his weapon.

But he had not lost his rage.

He would tear David apart with his bare hands, even if just to stop the pounding pain in his head. "Strangle the Seed! Strangle the Seed! Strangle the Seed!"

David dashed out of the dining room. He wove his way through the hallways with Saul in hot pursuit again.

David was much faster than his insane pursuer. Saul's muscles twitched with seizures that slowed him down. His rage was unthinking, beyond his strategy to murder.

David had his own stratagem. He circled back around to his original location: the music room. His only weapon against the king was his music. It was the only thing that turned the evil spirit away. Praises of Yahweh.

But he needed the time to begin to play before he was skewered or strangled.

He had gained enough time. He broke into the music room with a few moments to spare before Saul followed him.

He grabbed his lyre and began to play a song of deliverance.

> *I will say to the LORD, "My refuge and my fortress,*
> > *my God, in whom I trust."*
> *For he will deliver you from the snare of the fowler*
> > *and from the deadly pestilence.*
> *You will not fear the terror of the night,*
> > *nor the arrow that flies by day,*
> *nor Resheph that stalks in darkness,*
> > *nor Qeteb that wastes at noonday.*

It was a song of deliverance from demons. The "terror by night" was a Mesopotamian title for Zaqar, a dream demon. Resheph was the god of plague and pestilence whose arrows were his curses. Qeteb was Resheph's companion deity of destruction.

Saul was closing the distance between them as David sang. His murderous eyes began to weaken. His jerking spasms lessened. He slowed down until he was but a few feet away from David.

He stopped when another voice joined David's. It was Michal. She had hidden in the servants' hallway and made her way back to the room. Her voice flowed through the air with angelic sweetness and blended with David's in harmony.

> *Because you have made the LORD your dwelling place*
> > *the Most High, who is my refuge*
> *no evil shall be allowed to befall you,*
> > *no plague come near your tent.*

For he will command his angels concerning you
      to guard you in all your ways.
On their hands they will bear you up,
      lest you strike your foot against a stone.
You will tread on the lion and the adder;
      the young lion and the serpent you will trample
      underfoot.

Saul had collapsed at David's feet.

David looked up at Michal. They needed no words. They had worshipped Yahweh together and they had fought the evil spirit together. Their souls were one. She was the only woman in the whole world. He was the only man. Their lips were inexorably drawn toward each other.

They were stopped by the sound of Saul's voice. "David? Michal?"

They pulled back and turned. Saul sat up and wiped spittle from his beard.

"I have been under the spell again," Saul said, discouraged.

David said, "Yes, my lord. But the spirit is gone."

Michal wondered, *Did he see us? Or was he still in his dream state?*

"I am so sorry. It is getting worse. I see red. Blood. And mere flashes or..." He stopped with shock. An image came to him. "Did I try to kill you?"

"Yes, my king, you did," said David sheepishly.

"My daughter as well?"

"I was out of the way, father."

"Thank Asherah."

"Thank Yahweh," corrected David.

Thank Yahweh, he did not see us about to kiss, thought Michal.

"David, you protected my daughter as you protect me," said Saul. "Then why do you not ask me for her hand in marriage?"

Michal froze. *He did see us about to kiss. What are we going to do now?*

David said, "It is no little thing for your servant to become the king's son-in-law. I am a poor man of no reputation, my lord."

"Nonsense. You are the destroyer of Goliath the Philistine. You are a gibborim warrior, a consecrated musician and the captain of my bodyguard. But at least now I know why you turned down my offer of Merab's hand. You are in love with Michal."

"Yes, my sovereign. I love her with all my heart and soul."

"And I in return," said Michal, not willing to be left out of this discussion.

"I have never felt worthy of your family," said David.

Saul huffed, "I will determine whether you are worthy or not. He thought for a moment, then said, "I will appoint you as a commander of thousands, and I will demand no bride price save this: one hundred Philistine foreskins for the hand of Michal in marriage."

"One hundred Philistine foreskins?" repeated David. It was a very strange request.

Michal could not believe what she had heard.

Saul responded, "That I may be avenged of my enemies."

David and Michal continued to stare in shock and disbelief.

"Well, daughter, hurry up and begin your planning. And you, my son-in-law, have some Philistines to kill."

"Thank you, my lord," said David.

Michal hugged and kissed Saul. "Daddy, thank you, thank you, thank you!"

David and Michal rushed out of the room. Saul got himself up and brushed himself off. The shadow hovered just behind him. He had left the king's body, but he had not left the king's side. He had whispered in his ear the entire time. He whispered in the voice of Saul's own thoughts. *Get him away from you. Get him out of here. Appoint him a commander so he will no longer curse you with that abominable music.*

If you cannot kill him, then allow his enemies to do so. Use your daughter's love as a snare. Give him a bride price that will surely kill him, an impossible feat against the Philistines.

A diabolical grin spread across Saul's face as he considered the dismal future of this pretender to his throne.

CHAPTER 32

Ittai snapped the reins of his donkeys to speed up his wheeled cart. He had reached the Philistine military outpost, ten miles west of Gath. It was a fort intended as an early warning for attacks on Gath. But it was the scene of a grisly mockery of that intent. A company of Israelite stealth attackers had surprised the fort and wiped out all two hundred of its soldiers. Ittai was ordered by Lord Achish to retrieve any spent weapons for refitting and reuse in the Gittite armed forces.

A crack squad of Rephaim from the Sons of Rapha, led by Ishbi and Lahmi, rushed ahead to find any survivors. There were none. When they arrived, they looked out upon the bodies of their brothers and comrades. They had been thrown in piles outside the fort. As they got close enough to the piles to see what had been done to the victims, Lahmi gagged.

"What kind of depraved savages are these Hebrews?" said Lahmi.

Ishbi stared at the atrocity. "They are the evil minions of a diabolical demon."

"But why? Why would they mutilate them all?"

The Philistine corpses were all castrated. Every last one of them.

Ishbi said, "Their sign of kinship is circumcision. I suspect it has something to do with an assertion of their power."

"Despicable," said Lahmi.

Ishbi said, "Inspiration for our vengeance."

• • • • •

Ittai had already loaded up a good portion of his cart with weapons from the fallen dead. He labored near a stand of some trees. He picked up an axe to add to the collection when he noticed a body hidden in the brush. It moved, and groaned.

Ittai yelled to the soldiers, "Survivor!"

He moved to help the soldier, but suddenly stepped back in shock. It was an Israelite warrior. The man's arm was severely wounded and he had suffered some head trauma.

Ittai froze. He didn't know what to do. Should he help him? But he was the enemy. An enemy who had brutalized Philistines. Yet, Ittai had lived with these people. They were not the barbarians they were made out to be by the propaganda of the governments of the Pentapolis. He knew these people.

"Ishbi! Over here!" Lahmi had arrived first, carrying a war hammer he had picked up from the remains. He glared angrily at Ittai and said, "Back off, runt. The Sons of Rapha will take it from here."

Ittai deferentially backed away. Despite the specific venom in his hostile comrade, he was right. The military would "take care" of an Israelite survivor —that is, *take it out* on an Israelite survivor.

Lahmi saw the mangled arm of the Israelite. "You poor Hebrew scum. Here, let me even your pain out." Lahmi swung the war hammer down on the Israelite's other hand, crushing it. The warrior screamed in agonizing pain.

"Lahmi! Cease!" Ishbi had arrived to look down upon the crippled Israelite. "We need intelligence from this Hebrew, you dimwit!"

Lahmi looked like a scolded child.

Ishbi knelt down to the Israelite's level. He talked softly, sympathetically. "You fought well. What is your name, warrior?"

"J-Joseph," he muttered.

Lahmi set down the hammer and knelt down on the other side of Joseph, who looked at him with frightened eyes.

Ishbi said, "I need you to tell me what you know."

Joseph whimpered. Ishbi touched his shoulder and Joseph could suddenly hear spirit voices, whispering in his ears to relax and trust the giant. All will be well.

Lahmi said, "Well, now that he has no use of his hands to beat off, then he will not need this any more." He lifted Joseph's battle skirt, pulled his dagger and put the blade to Joseph's groin.

The warrior screamed out in fear.

Ishbi held his hand out to stop Lahmi. He said to the Israelite, "Sh-sh-sh-shhhhh. I will not let him hurt you, if you tell us what we need to know." The spirit voices confirmed his words.

Joseph grunted in pain and looked at Ishbi ready to confess to anything and everything.

"Do you know who the giant slayer is? The one who…" He gulped, holding back his own internal pain, "who killed Goliath in the valley of the Terebinth."

Joseph kept looking down at Lahmi's blade with urgency. He nodded his head vigorously. "It was David—David ben Jesse."

"David ben Jesse," repeated Ishbi.

"Where does his family live?" said Lahmi.

"I do not know. I do not know. He lives in the palace with the king. He is captain of the guard, and he is court musician."

"Court musician? Of what purpose is such lazy vanity?"

"It is said when David plays the harp, it calms the spirit of madness that comes upon the king." The spirit voices in Joseph's ear became irritated.

In Canaan, as in other nations around them, madness was often thought of as a sacred touch of the gods upon a soul. The Sons of Rapha did not believe such drivel.

Ishbi snorted, "So, your king Saul is a mad fool. What else?"

Joseph looked again at Lahmi, who gave him a devious grin. "He led the attack on this fort."

That surprised both of the Rephaim. Ishbi asked, "Why? Why did he mutilate the dead? Is this some kind of mockery of the uncircumcised?"

"I-I do not know. He did not say."

"What is the purpose of your circumcision?"

"It is a sign of our covenant with our god."

"Like the Egyptians," mumbled Ishbi. "Was he trying to force the Philistines to covenant with your deity?"

"That could not be," said Joseph. "Circumcision is the removal of the foreskin, it is not castration."

Lahmi raised his blade again. "I do not believe this liar."

Joseph cried out, "Rumors! I only heard rumors! Something about a bride price."

"Bride price?" said Ishbi.

"Disgusting," said Lahmi. "What is wrong with you people?"

Ishbi said, "If he is already on the palace guard, then he may be buying his way in to the royal family. That would place him in the lineage for inheritance."

"To be king," said Lahmi. "The messiah king?"

"That is all I know," said Joseph. "You must believe me. I am but a common armor-bearer, with little knowledge."

Ishbi stood to leave. "I believe you. You cannot be of much import for them to leave you behind." He turned coldly to Lahmi. "He is yours to dispose of."

Joseph cried out, "No! No! I gave you what you wanted! Please don't kill me!"

Lahmi said, "I am not going to kill you, Hebrew. That would be merciful."

Lahmi took one swift swipe and cut Joseph in an unmentionable way. The Israelite screamed in agony.

Lahmi got up and walked away to let Joseph die slowly.

But when Lahmi was out of hearing distance, a battle axe came down swiftly, ending Joseph's misery.

It was Ittai. He had stayed nearby and overheard it all, while pretending to arrange the weapons in his cart. He now knew the name of this mysterious savior of Israel. David ben Jesse. Shepherd, warrior poet. Ittai wondered what his own fate would be before this victorious scourge of Philistia. Would he do the same to Ittai? Ittai was not going to wait to find out. If these Israelites cut off their foreskins as a covenant sign, then Ittai would prepare himself for the inevitable possibility of facing this Israelite nemesis. He would perform the sign of covenant with their god just to be safe.

He would circumcise himself.

CHAPTER 33

King Saul finished a feast of fowl, fruit and bread cakes with his wife Ahinoam, and his children, Jonathan, Merab, Michal and three others. He guzzled a chalice of wine, enjoying the drink.

A messenger entered, slightly anxious.

"My king, an urgent delivery from David, the captain of your guard."

Saul was tipsy and impatient. "Do not just stand there, servant. Bring him in, bring him in." He belched and sighed with satisfaction, from having relieved a bit of the pressure from eating too much.

David approached the dining table where the family all reclined on their pillows. His eyes caught Michal's and his heart leapt with hope and joy.

He winked at her. She smiled.

David carried a wool bag over his shoulders.

Saul blubbered, "This had better be important, David. You interrupt my family meal."

"Forgive me, my lord," said David. "But I have fulfilled the king's demands for a bride price."

In his drunken haze, Saul did not quite remember what bride price David was referring to.

But Ahinoam did. Her eyes went wide with shock. She reached over and put her hands over the eyes of the youngest teen, Eshbaal.

Jonathan and Michal looked with horror at each other. Jonathan was about to say something.

But it was too late. David had given the sack to Saul and Saul had clumsily opened it, spilling some of its contents.

The adult women whisked the children out of the room, leaving David alone with Saul and Michal.

David said, "Not merely one hundred foreskins as you asked, my king, but two hundred. Just to prove how much worth is your daughter's love to me."

Saul felt sick at the sight of it. But he did demand this disgusting price. He complained, "I asked for the foreskins. You brought the entire — thing."

"Forgive another misunderstanding, my lord. But they do include the foreskins, after all, do they not?"

Saul gave a dry heave. "Fair enough. You have fulfilled my demand. You may have my daughter's hand."

Michal squealed with delight, "Daddy!" and ran and hugged Saul.

Saul felt nauseous again. He said, "Take these wretched things out of here, will you?"

CHAPTER 34

The wedding of David and Michal was a glorious affair. Though Saul was normally stingy with his money, he was not so with his daughters.

Michal had started the day with a bath followed by a bodily anointing of oil. She wore a linen and silk dress with embroidered cloth of Phoenician purple. Her hair was brushed to a soft perfection and placed beneath her Tyrian style crown of gold. She was bedecked with gold and silver jewelry from Egypt. Bracelets, necklaces, ear coverings and a ring on her nose. She walked through the Gibeah streets in fine calf leather sandals, surrounded by a cadre of dozens of virgin bridesmaid companions dressed in white linen. A band of minstrels led her with rejoicing on tambourine, flute, and lyre.

She felt like a queen.

She would *be* a queen one day. She knew that she was marrying the mightiest warrior in all of Israel. The gibborim who had killed the giant Rephaim Philistine, who her own father, the anointed warrior king, could not conquer.

All she could think of the entire journey to the palace were the lyrics she first heard her from the lips of her bridegroom upon their first acquaintance. She had never forgot them. They were burned into her heart.

He had sung a song of virginal submission to a manly king as a sample of his musical talent to her father. But she knew he had sung those words for her. She knew by the look in his eyes, his unquenchable stare of desire for her.

It was like a prophecy. Now those words were coming true, she was going to be living them out this day.

Hear, O daughter, and consider, and incline your ear:
    forget your people and your father's house,
      and the king will desire your beauty.
Since he is your lord, bow to him.

The people of Israel lined the streets and cheered their beautiful princess as she approached the entranceway to the palace. She could feel her heart pounding out of her chest. Would he sing his romantic poetry to her on their wedding night?

All glorious is the princess in her chamber,
    with robes interwoven with gold.
In many-colored robes she is led to the king,
    with her virgin companions following behind her.
With joy and gladness they are led along
    as they enter the palace of the king.

David's procession had journeyed through the other side of the city, allowing the opportunity for those who were fortunate to get a glimpse of their future prince. He was clothed like a warrior priest. His long flowing hair was gathered beneath his headdress of gold and ivory. He wore new royal robes of many colored embroidered Phoenician cloth. He wore rings and a necklace of gold and silver embedded with gems. He carried an ornamental bronze sword sheathed to his hip and wore an ephod of linen beneath his robes.

A pack of minstrels also led him to the palace with their playing. They arrived at the front entrance to meet Michal's entourage. When David saw her, he longed desperately for her. They had hidden their love for such a long time. They had shared souls in their singing, now they would share their bodies. They would play a concert together for their king, Yahweh.

Jonathan stood next to David as his *shoshbin*, his esteemed groomsman, to be witness. Earlier, David had signed a *ketubbah* with King Saul. It was a marriage contract with the father that established their legal union and responsibilities. The father released his daughter from under his authority and the groom promised to take care of her with honor and respect. It included an accounting of the bride's inventory of assets, which in this case was quite extravagant because of her royalty. And it included a listing of the dowry owed by the father to the groom and the bride price owed by the groom to the father.

Saul winced at the disgusting memory of his foolish bride price. It had been an attempt to endanger the young suitor. But it had come back to kick him in the rear end. By Asherah, he would never make that mistake again.

• • • • •

Ittai the Gittite closed and locked the door of his smith shop. He walked solemnly to the back of the room where his furnace blazed.

He sat down, staring into the flames, and wondered what Sheol was really like. There were myths and legends, ballads and epic verse written about it. The saying went that the mouth of Sheol and Abaddon was never satisfied, Abaddon meaning "place of destruction." It was the Land of Forgetfulness, outer darkness, where the worm does not die. It was said that Tartarus was the deepest pit in Sheol, which was as far below the earth as the earth was below the heavens. He already felt as if he was in Tartarus. He had no idea what possible reality heaven could ever have in his existence. Was there even a heaven at all?

He had heard the Babylonian Epic of Gilgamesh as a boy. Ugarit up north and his own Philistia had plenty of tablets of the text because of their commerce and trade with other nations. He was reminded of how Gilgamesh had sought significance in life through deeds of greatness and glory. He lost the friendship of his warrior companion Enkidu, a friendship closer than that of women, forged through battles, journeys and facing death. He was resigned to an everlasting despair that could not be quenched. His greatness became as nothing. No matter what he did, no matter how great he would become, he too would die and all he had done would be of no benefit in the underworld, a place of dreary darkness and insatiable Shades. Even the gods had rejected him.

There was one god that Ittai obsessed about: Yahweh of Israel. He was at war with the giants of Canaan. Ittai himself was under that very curse. And yet, he began to wonder if maybe death at the hands of such a deity might actually be his redemption. If he was of the cursed Seed of the Serpent, then maybe giving his own life in sacrifice to the deity would atone for his evil. And if it did not, then maybe Ittai would nonetheless find his own satisfaction in defying his blood curse, even if only for a moment. It would be a moment of satisfaction for a lifetime of pain.

He would take the mark of this deity upon himself, like a tattoo of bond service. He would brand his flesh as his first act of defiance against his own corruption.

He reached into the fire and pulled out a dagger that was now glowing red hot.

• • • • •

At the request of Michal, David played the silly song he had played for her when they first met. He had almost forgotten the thing because he had committed to stop playing it as a means of manipulating women. But he played it on his thin lyre as Michal rested in her hammock in their bed chambers.

He stopped playing.

"Do not stop playing," she said.

"Do not tell me what to do," he said. "I will tell you. And you will obey."

She shivered with delight. He was the strong man she wanted. She could not stand the effeminate boyishness of the eunuchs or the childish immaturity of the artists and musicians she associated with. She wanted a man who could lead her. She wanted a man of passion and strength, someone she could not control or manipulate. She wanted a wild animal she could surrender to.

That beautiful, wild animal approached her with firm resolve and hot blood pumping through his veins, eyes locked on her like a predator. She lost her breath with excitement.

• • • • •

Ittai's breathing grew shallow with fear. He followed the procedure he had learned about from his time with Micah the blacksmith in Mizpah years earlier. He took off his tunic and placed a small circular bronze tube over the glans of his male member. He stretched his foreskin over the outside of the tube that was protecting the member. He had used a string to tie the foreskin tightly to the tube.

He then took the red hot dagger and placed it with trembling hands to the foreskin. The heated dagger would singe the skin and prevent bleeding when he was ready to make the cut. He paused, and bit heavily on the rag he had placed in his mouth to bite down on.

• • • • •

David's breathing grew shallow as he watched Michal parade around him. He could just barely see glimpses of her form and features through the lace. It was driving him mad with desire.

Michal smiled. He watched her every gesture like a hawk. Seeing that he desired her fed her own arousal. He was hungry. She wanted to be eaten.

She closed her eyes and let herself be taken away with the sensuality of the moment. Before she realized it, he had grabbed her firmly in his hands and threw her on the bed. Her pleasant shock turned to joy when she felt his lips kissing every inch of her body. She was being consumed by her beautiful, wild animal.

• • • • •

Ittai gritted his teeth at the intense pain. He could smell his searing flesh, he felt the burn spread like wildfire through the most sensitive part of his body. He knew he could not stop. He had to finish. He had to fight through the pain to find the relief. A thought flashed through his mind. It was the image of his own forging craft. He would melt a precious metal such as gold to burn the dross away. It was a cleansing. It was the way to purify the metal. Through his silent pain he felt as if he was cutting the evil out of his life and burning it away. Just a moment more and it would be done. He gritted his teeth again and groaned with pain.

• • • • •

Michal screamed out in painful ecstasy. She was a virgin and her first consummation was not physically comfortable. Her mother had warned her and told her that time would deepen her satisfaction. But there was a deep pleasure of love beneath the pain and beyond words. It was the pleasure of surrendering herself totally and unreservedly to her beloved. She was in his hands and at his mercy. He was in her hands and vulnerable. Together they were naked and unashamed. Together they became one before their god.

Afterward, they lay in each other's arms, without speaking. She could feel his heartbeat with her head on his chest.

He was finally, finally at rest. He could smell the sweet fragrance of her hair and it enchanted him like a magical spell.

• • • • •

Ittai rested on a cot with bandages on his self-administered circumcision. But he somehow felt different, relieved, as if he was no longer cursed. But he knew that was impossible. He could only wonder what he would do next. Should he seek out these Hebrews? Should he wait until he learned more about this messiah king so he could find the right moment to cast himself on the king's mercy?

A knock at the door of the shop shook him out of his thoughts. He yelled, "Who is there?"

A voice said, "It is me, Ittai."

Ummi. He had not seen her in a long time. He had avoided her and kept himself busy since they had split apart those months ago. He had resolved to stop the curse and save her from his destiny of horror.

"Go away! I am not well!"

"No, Ittai! I will not go away."

He grumbled and got himself up from the cot. He hobbled over to the door with great pain and difficulty.

He landed against the door with a thud.

"Are you all right, Smooty?"

"Do not call me that!" he barked. It would only melt his heart.

"I miss you, Ittai. I love you, and I do not care if you are cursed. I will always love you and I am cursed without you."

Ittai began to tear up.

"What have you done to yourself?" she said.

She had an uncanny ability to intuit what was happening to him. Of course, she knew he did not want to continue his bloodline and there was only one way to make sure that would not happen.

"I do not care if you castrated yourself, Ittai. I do not want children, I want you."

Ittai's tears turned into a chuckle. If she only knew.

"I did not castrate myself. But I cannot have you here right now."

"I will come back. Name the day and I will come back. I will wait for you, my love. My Smooty."

Now he was crying again. It was all he could do to keep from bawling like a baby. This woman and this woman alone could do this to him, reduce him to a babbling infant.

He could hear her leave. She had been up against the very door he leaned on. They had been mere inches away from each other, kept apart by miles. He wanted to open the door and scream to her to stay. He wanted to hold her and never let her go. But he could only whisper in a weak defeated voice, "My Puma."

CHAPTER 35

Michal attended to her home shrine. It was a small separate room that had teraphim figurines of Asherah and Astarte. They were made of red terra cotta clay and were mostly a foot or so high, with the one exception of a life sized Asherah carved out of light wood. The figurines accentuated the female reproductive organs.

Michal kissed an amulet and lit incense. She brought in bread cakes that she baked for Ashtart, the Queen of Heaven. Ashtart and Asherah were both goddesses of fertility. Michal had been following the moon cycle ritual because she was having trouble getting pregnant with David.

David detested the goddesses. Though they were popular throughout Israel, he didn't like it when Michal prayed to them and sought their help. He seemed quite mean-spirited about it to her. He would call them both "Ashtoreth," which was an insulting compilation of the word for "shame," *bosheth,* with the name Astarte. He would recite the Shema, "Hear, O Israel: Yahweh our Elohim, Yahweh is one." Then he would say that the Ten Words, written by Yahweh's own finger, forbid the worship of any gods before him. That was fine with Michal; she would not put the goddess before Yahweh, but after him. Asherah was only his consort. She even had an image that she kept hidden from David with the inscription, "For Yahweh of Gibeah and his Asherah."

The other saying he would repeat with annoying redundancy was that they should make no graven image to worship. But she would tell him that she was not worshipping the images, they were simply an aid *through which* she gave the goddess honor and supplication. His complaints seemed excessive to her. Especially since Yahweh was male and he just did not understand the womanly issues like a goddess could.

In order to avoid the inevitable confrontation that occurred, she would abstain from her visits to the room when David was home and only paid her homage at times like this, when he was absent.

But this evening had an additional concern for her. She had found out from her brother Jonathan that her father had planned to betray David again. She prayed to Yahweh and Asherah to protect her beloved husband from her despised father.

When they first married, Michal had felt so close to David. They sang their music together as they did before marriage, and they shared much affection and romance. They had connected with such profound depth.

But now, it seemed that life and duty had torn them apart. David was always gone. He had been going out and coming in from battle for the king. He had so many victories that his reputation grew. It seemed everything he put his hand to succeeded, except one thing: his relationship with the king. With each success, her father only got more angry and envious of David's rising glory and greatness. He would still have his fits of madness that required David's heavenly music to calm his spirit.

Between battles and royal duties, David was never home anymore. Michal was growing bitter. She felt that he had baited her with all his seductive music and passionate songs of love to her, but now that they were married, he switched and moved on to other things. That was why she turned to Asherah more often. She wondered if he was with another woman or if his royal work *was* that other woman. Maybe he had never been in love with her to begin with. Maybe he had just tricked her, in order to get a foothold in the royal family so he could take the throne one day. Her head swirled with confusion, loneliness and despair.

The sound of David arriving home drew her from the shrine room. She closed the door and quickly went to meet him.

"My love," she said. They hugged and kissed, but his mind was elsewhere.

"What is wrong, David?"

"I came home from a victory against the Philistines, and the king tried to kill me again with a spear."

"Again? It seems to be increasing, these episodes." They had gotten used to Saul's extreme swings between glorious favor and murderous hostility by blaming it on the evil spirit that tormented him. David would say that his music was Yahweh's only means to soothe the anointed chosen one. Michal thought David had too high a view of himself. But then, it was better than David mounting a rebellion and overthrowing her own father's kingdom.

David said, "On the way home, I noticed spies watching our house. Two out front."

She added, "There are others as well. My brother has alerted me that they are not spies, they are assassins. My father is planning on killing you in the morning as you sleep."

David said, "This time he has gone too far. It is as if this demon does not merely overtake him temporarily, but is colluding with him in a premeditated plan."

David began to gather his weapons and a small pack for travel.

"Where are you going?" she said.

"To Samuel the Seer at Ramah."

He snuffed out their lamps to make it completely dark in the room. He said, "I have an idea."

She followed him into her shrine room. He moved over to the life sized Asherah teraphim and said, "Help me bring this into the bed chamber."

He picked up the bulky bottom of it and she held the head.

"What are you going to do?"

"Put it in the bed and cover it with sheets. You can get some goat hair and put it on the head."

She smiled knowingly. He was using it as a decoy.

He grumbled, "Finally this abominable thing is good for something."

"Thank Asherah," she said with an impish smile.

They got it into the bed and she went to get some goat hair.

They were putting the finishing touches on their decoy when they heard a loud rapping on the entrance door of the first floor. They stopped.

A voice bellowed from outside the door, "Open in the name of the king!"

Michal asked David fearfully, "What should we do?"

"Go answer the door."

"What do I tell them?"

"Tell them I am sick and that is why it took you so long."

She was frozen in fear.

"Go!" he said.

She closed the door and went to let the king's guard in. She yelled as she advanced on the door, "I am coming! Please have patience!"

She opened the door and four guardsmen pushed their way inside. Behind them stood Saul.

"Why did you take so long to answer the door?"

"My David fell sick and I was caring for him."

Saul nodded to the guards. They moved up the stairwell to the bed chamber. Saul pushed past Michal. She followed him up the stairs.

When she arrived in the room, she saw that David was gone. The window was his obvious escape route.

One of the guards whipped back the covers to show the Asherah teraphim laying in the bed.

Saul walked over to Michal and grabbed her hair in his hand. He yanked her head back. She squealed and tried to protect her hair from his grip.

"Why have you lied to me, daughter?"

"Father, I am sorry. I am so sorry."

"Why did you lie to me?"

She didn't know what to say. But she knew he would probably punish her greatly for this betrayal.

She blurted out, "He said he would kill me if I did not!"

Saul looked in her eyes.

He released her hair. She nursed her head from the stinging pain.

"That would make him a bigger fool than I thought. Killing you would ruin his chances for succession to the crown."

Saul walked over to the window and stared out into the night. He knew David would be too difficult to catch now.

"But I can still accomplish the same result with a different tactic."

Michal stared at him, confused.

He said, "I can marry you to another man."

Michal filled with shock. "Father, you cannot do that. I am married to David."

"I can do whatever I want. I am king. And I will marry you to another man."

CHAPTER 36

Asherah breathed a sigh of great relief. What freedom it was to be out in the open air amidst her sacred grove of trees, instead of in that dreary, dank dungeon of Dagon. Though the gods had chosen to operate with less visible presence amidst mortals, there was ample acreage and foliage for her to stroll through her garden without being seen. If she was spotted from a distance, she was often mistaken for one of the chief priestesses anyway.

In antediluvian days, the Watcher gods had been more bold and conspicuous in their appearance. Unfortunately, that had given the archangels who hunted them easier access to them. She knew too many of her comrades in the assembly who had been bound in the earth by Mikael, Gabriel and the others.

After the flood, the gods sought to be less conspicuous and save their presentations for more strategic effect. They restricted their encounters more to earthly principalities and powers than to the plebeians. The rarer their visible presence, the more heightened the anticipation, exalted the honor, and exaggerated the fear. And the fewer opportunities for those irksome archangels to trap them. As heavenly host, the gods could still operate within both worlds seen and unseen, but they chose to limit their involvement mostly to the veiled shadows of the unseen.

But there were exceptions, and this was one of them. Asherah had made a trip to Gibeah and lodged at her temple amidst the sacred grove of terebinth trees. The grove stood a distance away from the city on a hillside, where the Israelites made their high places of sacrifice and worship. She had such freedom in her visitation because the Israelites had a weakness for worshipping the goddess. And worship gave her power. It protected her.

Asherah was pleased with herself that of all the gods of Canaan, she was one of the few to gain a major foothold within the hearts and souls of the contemptuous little Israelite rodents. Though Yahweh had definitively prohibited images and jealously demanded singular devotion to him alone, his human herd of earthly slaves were a pathetic lot. They simply *had* to have a consort for their bachelor god. And rightfully so. Behind every successful male deity was a longsuffering goddess who did all the work.

These disgusting little Israelites wallowed in their dark secrets. The temple of Asherah housed the *Qedeshim*, or sacred harlots, both male and female. Their income kept the temple funded, since the Israelite tabernacle and priesthood was the only cultus to receive entitlement funds from their theocratic government. And bring in income they did. Asherah's boys and girls were as busy in Israelite towns as in any Canaanite town. Sometimes more so. Forbidden pleasure was no doubt a bigger draw for those bent on fighting their fleshly cravings. Their surrender to Asherah felt like being freed from prison.

At least, that is what they felt it was. The reality was that they were imprisoning themselves to her. They were simply exchanging one form of slavery for another. These humans would never learn that they could not be truly free in the way they wanted to be, for to be their own master was the most foolish slavery of all.

Her temple was located in the terebinth grove because it was a tree of spiritual significance in the culture. It was where visions and revelations from the gods often occurred.

The tree was a symbol of Asherah. The grove was the location of her symbolic activity. Qedeshim would choose a favorite tree in the grove where they might find some privacy to engage in their immoral activities.

Meanwhile, just yards away, stood the high place where Israelites performed sacrifices to Yahweh. The elevated stone platform had a horned altar on top where the consumption by fire took place. The altar had images engraved all over the base. One was an Asherah depicted as "mistress of the animals," with a lion held in the grip of each hand. There were lion-like Cherubim, and the Tree of Life with ibexes eating its fruit. An image of a bull with an inscription at the base of the altar said, "Yahweh of Gibeah and his Asherah."

Beside the altar was an Asherah pole, a twenty foot wooden cult object carved from a tree and shorn of its branches. The bark had been stripped off and images of Asherah and her exploits carved around the tree like a cylinder seal. The poles were stained and varnished to make them more long lasting and durable in weather. They were referred to as Asherim and they accompanied most altars throughout Israel. Asherah thought it a nice touch of irony that her own erect Asherim pole outsized Yahweh's puny pudgy altar by comparison. Two incense pillars flanked the Asherim to offer fragrance to the goddess as they sacrificed lambs, bulls and goats to Yahweh.

All this imagery and syncretism of Yahweh with Asherah was, of course, frowned on by the Levitical priesthood and made intolerant zealots like Samuel furious. Asherah smiled to herself. In truth, the elitist inner circle of Levites was quite small and unable to enforce its will across the innumerable rural towns and villages of Israel. The polytheistic folk religion of the common man was often out of tune with the official national cult of monolatry. But it was much more influential on the daily lives of citizens, who did what they wanted without repercussion.

Thus, Asherah had a stranglehold on Israel and could venture most anywhere she wanted, without much fear of being attacked by Yahweh's evil minions. The people empowered her with their worship. Their idolatry protected her.

Two of those Israelite idolaters were with a Qedesha named Kiana. She was a lovely siren of unusual animal beauty—quite literally. She had strange looking feline eyes and her skin had the pattern of a tigress, over her entire body. Her patrons were not sure if it was tattooed or was some kind of occultic magic. There were rumors that the Watcher gods still engaged in some unholy crossbreeding experiments, like those from antediluvian days, to create hybrid creatures of human and animal essence. Asherah would never clarify the truth, because rumors were helpful for exploiting mystery and fear.

The Israelites with Kiana were the brothers Joab and Abishai, members of Saul's bodyguard who were inseparable. They shared everything together; their dreams, pursuits, and evidently, their sins. Abishai was the elder, but Joab was the leader. He was more aggressive, hot-headed and impulsive. Abishai considered Joab more calculating and ruthless. Joab considered Abishai weaker, because of his propensity for relationship. And he talked too much.

Abishai laid back against the tree and said, "Kiana, you are the finest Qedesha I have ever known. If only wives could be like you."

"If you had a wife like me, then you would want two of them. You men are never satisfied with what you have. You always want what you do not have and you always want something different."

She purred and tickled him with her protracted claws. He chuckled. She was known for her affection as well as her violent temper. Those claws could just as well cut him as tickle him.

She said to him, "Tell me more about this fascinating captain of yours."

Now Joab butted in scornfully, "You will not be able to meet David."

She countered, "For now at least."

"You are drawn to such power," said Joab.

"Are you not?" she challenged back.

Joab said, "I am drawn to him. He has the favor of Yahweh on him."

"Is the rumor true, that he was anointed by Samuel to be the messiah king of Israel?"

Abishai sighed. "We are not supposed to speak of it. He is fiercely loyal to King Saul. And we are fiercely loyal to David. He is our cousin by blood."

Joab gave Abishai an angry look. He was too loose-lipped.

Kiana asked, "Even though the king seeks to kill him and he has fled into hiding?"

Abishai said, "David believes the king is anointed by Yahweh to rule. So until Yahweh replaces him, David remains loyal to the Lord's Anointed. To fight back would be defiance against Yahweh himself."

"That is bullheaded loyalty," said Kiana.

Joab said, "You do not understand such godly devotion."

"Neither do you," Kiana replied. "For you are here with me."

Joab could not rebut her. She was right.

Abishai thought that they were both pathetic examples of obedience to Yahweh with their regular visitation to her. Joab didn't seem to be bothered, but Abishai would weep and vow to himself to never do it again. But the desire would build within his heart until he could stand the pressure no more. It was all he could think of until he could see her. Then the cycle would start all over again with guilt, repentance, and vows of change. It made him wonder if he was even worthy of being on the king's guard.

Joab considered their weakness a danger that could be exploited one day in the favor of an enemy, if they could not get it under control.

Kiana broke into their thoughts, "Where is he now?"

Joab said, "That is privy information."

Abishai added, "But suffice it to say it is too holy a place for you to go."

"My lips are sealed," pleaded Kiana.

Abishai sighed. That was why he could not stop coming to her. He wondered why good women would draw in a husband and then when they married them, they would stop their romantic affection. It was as if the very thing that drew the man was turned off as soon as they were trapped in the marriage. It seemed that family killed the romantic drive of women. They became mothers and stopped being lovers. Men were fish caught and thrown into the boat, gills desperately sucking for the life-giving source of their simple and primal need. That was why Abishai felt it was so easy for him to go astray, because his vice seemed more primal than his virtue.

The men left Kiana to return to their duty at the palace.

Kiana returned to the temple. She met with Asherah to tell her the new information she had pulled out of her two saps. David was hiding out at Ramah.

CHAPTER 37

The town of Ramah lay three miles north of Saul's city of Gibeah. The town housed a few hundred inhabitants, most of whom gave agricultural and service support for Samuel's school of prophets that resided there. With a population of fifty students, the school the Seer had set up trained select men in the calling of prophet. If a man felt he had the calling upon him, he would be interviewed by the Seer for sincerity and integrity. If accepted into the school, he was then educated in the Torah and Wisdom literature of Israel and surrounding nations.

Prophecy was not merely foretelling of the future by revelation from Yahweh. It was mostly forth-telling of truth, be it directly from Yahweh's revelation or from the learned precepts of their sacred texts. Prophets would spend long hours in the spiritual exercises of religious devotion and scribal disciplines of learned education to become messengers of Yahweh. Hearing from their god involved both supernatural and natural pursuits to be both holy and wise. Part of that education included the playing of musical instruments that would accompany ecstatic trances and dances.

David chose to hide out in Ramah to gain protection from Yahweh's Seer as well as some words from the Most High. More importantly, Samuel was the one who had anointed David for this most dangerous calling upon his life.

Samuel had not seen Saul in the many years since he cursed the king. Saul feared approaching Samuel since Yahweh stopped talking to him, and he had been taken over by the evil spirit.

While David hid out at the school, he let his beard grow out so that he could blend in with the rustic locals. A young student of seventeen named Nathan pestered Samuel to let him accompany David when he left. He claimed Yahweh came to him in a dream and told him to do so. Dreams and visions were part of being a prophet, and Samuel knew

Nathan to be of honest disposition, so he approved. David saw in the youth a passion he had himself as a young shepherd musician in the fields, wanting to get out and see the world. He also thought it would be good to have one of Yahweh's mouthpieces with him, should Yahweh want to speak to him, since the Lord hadn't done so since David came to the school.

David did not want to end up like Saul, seething in Yahweh's silence. He wanted to hear Yahweh's voice and follow his commands. He longed for Yahweh's word of guidance as a deer thirsted for water. There was no better way to have that guidance than to have one of his prophets with him.

David left Ramah with Nathan, and made his way toward Nob, eight miles south. But on the way, he stopped for a secret meeting in the fields outside Jerusalem.

"My brother," said Jonathan. "I feared I would not see you again. Who travels with you?"

"This is Nathan. He is a student of the school of prophets."

Nathan bowed to Jonathan, the king's son. "Actually, my lord, I am considered a full fledged prophet. The Seer gave his blessing."

Jonathan smiled. "He is already correcting you. I see that as a good sign."

Nathan smiled and moved a few yards away, on the look out for anyone that might approach them.

Jonathan grabbed David's shoulders.

David hesitated. He did not know who he could trust anymore. This man was his closest friend, had taken him in and apprenticed him. Jonathan had given David his own royal cloak and ring as a vow of surrendering his kingdom, and yet David still had trouble believing such purity of faith and character was truly possible in this world of blood and iron. David certainly did not have it. Was it even possible?

Jonathan could see the doubt in David's eyes. He said, "Yahweh the Elohim of Israel is our witness. I love you as my own soul. When you come into your kingdom, pray do not cut off your steadfast love from my house forever. May Yahweh take vengeance on David's enemies."

David's knees went weak. He started to collapse, but Jonathan caught him and they sat on the ground. A wave of relief had come over David, and all the fear that had propped him up and kept him from sleeping had melted away. He knew Jonathan was without guile and was true.

For the first time in years, David broke down. "Jonathan, what have I done? What is my guilt? What is my sin before your father, that he seeks my life? You have covenanted with me before Yahweh. If there is guilt in me, kill me yourself, for I am ready to die."

"You harbor no guilt," said Jonathan. "Pride, quick temper, and a weakness for women. But by my very head, no guilt before the throne."

David's tears turned to laughter. "I can see you still suffer from the sin of envying my passion."

David grabbed Jonathan's wrists and the two of them kissed each other's cheeks, the custom of covenantal renewal.

Jonathan was still smiling with amusement. "I heard about my father's attempt to abduct you at Ramah. Of course, I had to hear of it through the servant's gossip. It pays to hide out with Yahweh's prophets."

David chuckled. "Three times. He sent forces three times. And three times Yahweh's spirit fell upon the soldiers. They prophesied like they were students of Samuel. You should have seen the sight. I could not contain myself. I would have expected fire from heaven or a slaughtering by the Angel of Yahweh. But no, instead he turned murderous soldiers with swords into confused prophets singing the praises of Yahweh with tambourines."

Jonathan said, "Yahweh has a sense of humor."

David added, "But then your father came, and Yahweh's spirit came upon him as well." David burst out laughing again. "He stripped off his clothes and lay naked all day and night uttering prophecies in foreign tongues. If I stayed any longer, Yahweh would have Philistine giants dancing and singing his praises."

David suddenly noticed that Jonathan no longer joined in the mirth. His face was sullen. David quieted.

"Father has gotten worse. His fits have increased, and it seems he is less and less in control of his faculties. Without your music, the evil spirit in him has become stronger. He has pledged to spend all his time and money hunting you down. And he will do anything to hurt you. He gave Michal in marriage to another man, Palti ben Laish."

David's face dropped. He thought his beloved Michal would be safe from her own father's hatred of him. Now he knew she was not. For Saul to give her to another man was worse to David than all the attempts of the king to murder him. Michal was his first love, the wife of his youth. Now they were ripped from each other and their love separated by the very one against whom David would not get revenge, *could not* get revenge. Saul was the anointed king, and David had sworn that he would never usurp the holy ruler of Yahweh's own people. To do so would be to usurp Yahweh himself.

Jonathan said, "He is cutting off your connection to the royal family in order to invalidate any possibility of your claim to the throne."

Saul was not merely fighting David. He was fighting Yahweh, trying to thwart the very plans of the mighty god of Israel. It was such gall, and it made Saul even smaller in his eyes. But it was still a dagger to the heart of David. His precious, powerless Michal had been made a victim of Saul's destructive rage.

"Do not see me again, David. Stay far away from Gibeah. Hide out in the wilderness until my father is dead. For he will not stop until *you* are dead."

David grabbed Jonathan's wrists and they embraced again.

David then said, "Tell the bodyguard who are loyal to me I will be hiding out at the cave of Adullam."

"Can you trust them?"

"My cousins, Joab and Abishai. I trust them with my life. They know others. They will spread the word."

Another long look between the two of them carried the question whether they would see each other again.

"You go there now?"

"No. First I have to go to Nob. I have something I want to get."

CHAPTER 38

Samuel had gone out into the desert with a handful of his students for prayer and fasting. Forty-five of the others remained at the school, performing duties and chores. It was a typically quiet day in Ramah as the students sat down for lunch in the dining hall of Naioth. With Samuel gone, the prefect in charge was Jacob, a swarthy, heavy young man with a sense of humor that he kept hidden from Samuel. Samuel would never have left him in charge, had he known Jacob would instigate the present food-fight that had begun among the students. It started when someone made a crack about how the porridge tasted like mud. Jacob then said that he would test it to see if it was truly mud. He threw a glob of it against the wall of the mud-brick dining room. When it stuck, someone yelled and everything got out of hand. Porridge flew around the room, hitting faces and robes. Laughing and playful screams filled the hall to such an extent that they did not hear the screams outside in the streets.

Jacob had backed up against the door of the dining hall with a large pile of porridge in his hand. He was about to throw it, when the door behind him slammed open with a fury. It threw Jacob to the ground, crushing him under the force.

A gasp of silence and terror swept over the room.

The doorway exploded into a huge opening beneath the soles of a nine foot tall, six hundred and fifty pound giant: Ishbi ben Ob. He widened the door for easier access, but he still had to crouch a bit to get inside.

Some of the prophets yelped and sought to flee through the back door. Their bodies were cut in half by the two swords of Saph, who stood just outside. He kicked in that doorway for his entrance. The remainder of the forty-five prophets cowered in fear, caught between the two Rephaim giants.

The prophets could see several dark spirits surrounding Ishbi, moving like wisps of agitated smoke.

Ishbi crowed, "I have it on good word from the goddess Asherah that David ben Jesse is hiding out at this school. Now, which one of you is going to prophesy and tell me where he is?"

No one spoke. Several peed in their tunics. One began to cry in fright. But no one spoke.

Saph swiped his sword and cut two more student prophets down. The head of a third one rolled to the floor by the body of Jacob crushed beneath the door.

Ishbi used a mace to crush another prophet. He sent a fifth one flying into the wall, smashed like a fly with a swatter. Ishbi's familiar spirits became increasingly frenzied with his anger.

A supernatural howling pierced the ears of the prophets. They drew in together tighter and began to pray to Yahweh for protection. One of them was bold enough to yell out, "Yahweh, deliver us!"

Ishbi looked up to the heavens. The prophets followed his gaze.

Nothing happened. Ishbi's spirits became like a whirlwind around him.

Ishbi crowed, "Perhaps he is hiding out with your chosen one."

Saph bellowed, "Which one of you will tell us where?"

Saph used one of his swords to impale three more students. They squirmed, dying like skewered prey.

"I believe I have a meat stick," said Saph to Ishbi. "Should we roast them or just eat them alive?"

Ishbi crushed two more students. The remaining prophets clung to one another in their tight circle.

"I have a better idea," said Ishbi. "I will skin them alive one by one, until someone tells us what we want to know." He grabbed one unfortunate student. "Consider this a full body circumcision."

Saph laughed with a hearty jocularity.

The students were terrorized by the fate that awaited them all.

There were thirty-four of them to go.

CHAPTER 39

David stood outside the sanctuary in Nob with Nathan, waiting for the high priest Ahimelech to meet with him. Nob was just eight miles south of Ramah, three and a half miles from Saul's Gibeah in between, and two miles east of Jerusalem. After the Philistines had stolen the ark, and destroyed Shiloh and its tabernacle, the surviving priests had migrated to Nob and established a new sanctuary and priesthood. Because it was within the territory of Jerusalem, it was protected from Philistine attacks by the Jebusite king.

A servant led David inside. Nathan stayed outside, on the lookout. The new sanctuary was actually a Canaanite temple of Ba'al that had been commandeered and repurposed for Israelite worship. The Hebrew tabernacle had been based upon the same Canaanite design, so the building worked well for their intent. Two pillars guarded the entrance to the stone temple, leading into an outer court of waiting, that was sectioned off from a curtained Holy of Holies. The priests were currently baking their holy Bread of the Presence that was placed before Yahweh daily.

David could smell the bread. It reminded him of how hungry he was. He stood in the outer courtyard where several locals knelt in private prayer. It was an honor for Israelites to have the sanctuary in their home town or local territory, so they used the special privilege at every opportunity they could. David even recognized one of them as Doeg, the Edomite herdsman of Saul. David knew shepherds were always out in the fields for so much of their time that they had very little involvement or understanding of court politics. It appeared that Doeg did not know that Saul sought David, since he registered no surprise at David's presence. So he left him alone.

David pleaded with Ahimelech, out of earshot of the locals. Ahimelech's son, the young priest Abiathar, shadowed him.

"No, David," said Ahimelech. "I am afraid that I cannot provide you with the ephod. It is the means of Yahweh's communication with the priesthood."

"That is why I need it," said David. He corrected himself, "I need it for the king. He has sent me on a secret mission and you must not speak of this to anyone." David was glad he had left Nathan outside, because the young prophet would not go for this deception and would most likely call David out on it.

Ahimelech protested, "Saul has not darkened the doors of this sanctuary for years. It is said that Yahweh has left him and he seeks guidance from an evil spirit. Why would he want to hear from Yahweh now?"

David became agitated. "You dare not question the king."

"I dare not disobey Yahweh."

David could not argue with that. He already wondered if Yahweh would strike him dead soon.

"Why are you alone?" Ahimelech asked.

"My men wait for me in the wilderness," lied David. "Do you have any weapons you can spare the king's bodyguard? In my haste to obey the king, I failed to retain any for the trip."

Ahimelech looked at David skeptically. He would need to do better with his lies if he was to convince this old man.

"Now there I can help you. Wait here."

Abiathar stayed with David as Ahimelech walked into the sanctuary. David could spy the ephod hanging on a "T" shaped wooden structure.

Abiathar looked uncomfortable. David knew the young man could not stop him from entering the holy place. David considered taking the ephod by force. No one could stop him after all. Would his audacity stretch that far?

David knew that in one of the pockets of the white linen ephod were the sacred lots used to garner the guidance of Yahweh. They did not produce the lights and perfections of the Urim and Thummim, but the priests could still use the white and black elements to discern simple yes or no questions. David longed for the clarity of guidance from the word of Yahweh.

They saw Ahimelech pull out a large sword wrapped in cloth from behind the ephod. It was very large. Too large. He brought it back to David and handed it to him.

David held the heavy weapon and unwrapped it with a holy awe as Ahimelech spoke. "It is the sword of the Philistine you killed in the valley of the Terebinth."

David used his two hands to hold it up before him. He could never use the thing in battle. It was too large and weighty for a normal warrior's strength. But it was a powerful symbol. And it gave him faith again just to hold it. Memories of that fateful day flooded his thoughts. The hot, bright valley. The insolent reprobate Philistine and his vile boasting in the face of Yahweh. The cowardice of the Israelites. His own childlike naiveté that made him step out in trust to do the impossible. Things were so much clearer back then. So much simpler. Now he was on the run, cowering in fear for his life like the Israelites and using deception to cloud his intent.

But this was different. The Philistine was unholy. The king of Israel was holy. David would not touch Yahweh's anointed. Shame filled him. He dropped to his knees with tears in his eyes. He would take the Philistine's sword, but he would not take the holy ephod of Yahweh's priests.

Ahimelech placed an understanding hand on David's shoulder. "You must be hungry, my son. Come, let me give you some of the Bread of the Presence to bring back to your men. It is time to replace it with a new batch anyway, and we priests have plenty."

"Thank you," whispered David.

Ahimelech added, "I only ask that your men keep themselves from women."

David looked up at him with resolve. "This is a holy mission. My men are clean."

"Then come, take some food and rest for yourself, and for your prophet, before you journey onward."

CHAPTER 40

After Jonathan had met with David outside the walls of Gibeah, he had returned to eat dinner at the royal table. It was the new moon festival. It was customary for the entirety of the House of Saul to eat together, including the heads of all divisions; military, finance, agriculture, herdsmen and others. There were over a hundred sharing in the feast of fowl, vegetables, fruit and wine with much merriment.

All of Saul's family were present for the meal, sitting in their respective places on the floor. Jonathan sat across from Saul and his chief advisor, Abner, a weathered and experienced general whom Saul greatly trusted.

Michal and her new husband, Palti, sat next to Jonathan. They ate in silence.

Saul guzzled a chalice of wine and said, "Why do you look so dour, my daughter and son-in-law? Newlyweds should be happy and celebrative of their new life together. Drink up!"

Palti took a long gulp of wine. It was his only way to escape the moment.

Michal stared with contempt at her father. Though she was not divorced from David, Saul had used his authority as king to nullify their union and force her to marry another, in violation of Yahweh's Law.

The seat next to Jonathan was empty.

Saul said, "Jonathan, where is the son of Jesse? His seat has been empty these two days of the festival?"

Saul's insanity was unpredictable. One day, he would madly seek to kill David, the next, he would try to reconcile with him. One moment he would seem normal, the next moment, a dark shadow was over his soul. Everyone had simply gotten used to it.

Jonathan lied with a deadpan face, "He asked leave of me to return to Bethlehem for a clan sacrifice. I knew you would approve of such a holy endeavor, so I sent him off."

It was a direct stab at Saul's unholiness. Saul burst out shouting like a lion jumping on prey. "You son of a perverse, rebellious woman! You have chosen the son of Jesse to your own shame, and to the shame of your mother's nakedness! You are a fool. For as long as the son of Jesse lives, neither you nor your kingdom shall be established!"

Everyone stopped eating and talking. All eyes were wide open, watching the exchange.

Jonathan said with resolute firmness, "Father, why do you seek to kill him? What has David done to deserve death? He has been loyal to the crown and to Yahweh all these years. Why do you listen to your spirit counselor and not the Spirit of Yahweh?"

Nimrod, that spirit counselor, rose up in Saul and his eyes filled red with murder. "How dare you defy me, you godlicker."

Jonathan got up from the table and walked toward the door.

Saul looked frantically around, "Where is my spear? Where is my spear?!"

A guard handed him his spear and he stood up.

Women screamed.

Jonathan turned.

Saul hurled his spear.

Jonathan dodged and the spear embedded in the wall next to him.

"So now you will seek to kill me as you have David. Thank you for the honor of treating me as you treat my future king." Jonathan turned and left the room.

Saul screamed out in anger. It was a gurgling, piercing bellow that could be heard throughout the palace.

A voice diverted the next explosion. "My king."

Saul turned to see Doeg the Edomite kneeling before the table.

"What do you want, sheep lover?" Saul's chest still heaved with the fury of Nimrod.

"I know where the son of Jesse is."

Suddenly a calm came over Saul, followed by a slight smirk across his lips.

Michal looked with fear at the kneeling Edomite.

"I saw him just today at Nob. He sought the ephod of Yahweh from Ahimelech the high priest. And then he received the sword of Goliath the Philistine."

Saul immediately barked out a command to Abner, "Draw up a regiment immediately. We ride to Nob." He pointed at Doeg, "You will come with us."

Saul left the room.

For a minute, everyone sat frozen. Then they resumed their careless eating, in denial of what they had just seen. It was the curse of the aristocracy. As long as they could return to their pleasure, they would close their eyes and deny anything, no matter how outrageous or unrighteous. As long as it would not affect them directly, they simply could not care less.

But there was one person who still cared. Michal called her manservant over to her, the eunuch Akiva. He was a portly man and very loyal to Michal. She whispered into his ear. "Go secretly and swiftly to Nob and tell David Saul is coming. You must ride quickly ahead of my father, or David will die."

"Yes, my lady," said Akiva, and he left.

CHAPTER 41

Akiva expected to arrive at Nob ahead of Saul that evening. But he would never make it to the sanctuary to alert David, because he met another pair of travelers on the road to that fateful town.

Ishbi and Saph ate their meal uncooked, to avoid the attention a fire might draw.

"I must say," said Ishbi, "eunuch meat is much tastier than other males. It is more like female flesh." He took a bite out of Akiva's captured corpse.

Saph responded through his own mouthful of food, "That is because they lack the toughening effect of the male gusto."

Saph belched.

Ishbi wrinkled his nose. "That is one disgusting smell." He held out a goat wineskin. "Drink more wine to sweeten that sour gut of yours."

Saph replied with a smirk, "If you think that is nasty, wait until I release a fart. You might just pass out."

Ishbi shook his head with disgust and took another bite.

They were on the outskirts of Nob. They had captured the eunuch just before they were about to ambush the city to kill David. They decided to eat a meal first for the energy they would need for the fight. The Chosen Seed was not to be trifled with. He had, after all, felled their champion years ago, and he was now, no doubt, a more seasoned gibborim.

Ishbi had longed for this moment for many years. That little insect had taken his companion in life from him. He and Goliath had grown up together and had joined the Sons of Rapha together. They were warriors and they were lovers. The only person more driven to revenge against the son of Jesse was Lahmi, Goliath's brother, who was elsewhere searching to exact his own planned revenge. Ishbi was only too happy to be beating Lahmi to the punch on this one.

The two giants paused, listening with preternatural ears. They could hear a desert rat crawling at a hundred feet. This was not the sound of a desert rat. It was the sound of a regiment of horses approaching the town in the distance.

"Quickly," barked Ishbi. They gathered up their weapons and left the unfinished carcass of the eunuch for the scavengers of the desert.

• • • • •

Saul and his regiment of fifty strong, led by Abner, arrived at the town of Nob on their horses armed for war. They were met by Ahimelech the high priest.

"My lord, King Saul," said Ahimelech bowing. "To what do I owe the grace of your presence?"

Saul looked over at Doeg the Edomite, who nodded. This was the one.

Saul turned back to Ahimelech. "Why did you conspire with the son of Jesse against me and my kingdom?"

"My lord? I am no conspirator."

"You inquired of Yahweh for him. You gave him bread and a sword to rise up against me. Where is he lying in wait for me at this moment? WHERE?!"

"Your grace, he is no longer here. He left days ago. But he is not against you. For who in all your household is as faithful as David? He is your son-in-law, the captain of your bodyguard. Is there anyone more honored in all your house?"

Saul stared down at the priest with boiling rage. Then he said to Abner, "Bring all the priests out to me."

A hundred feet away, Ishbi and Saph hid in the brush watching the priests being herded outside and surrounded by the horseback soldiers.

The giants were frustrated at having missed David. But now they had the king of Israel in their sights. There were only fifty guards. Ishbi and Saph could easily dispatch them, along with the king, in one fell swoop. It would be a glorious victory for Philistia. They would be rewarded as heroes.

But there was someone that stood in the way of Ishbi's glory. He was someone that none of the Israelites could see because they were mere human flesh. But Ishbi and Saph were Rephaim, the flesh of men and angels. They lived simultaneously in two worlds, flesh and spirit. They could see a giant shadow figure beside Saul that was invisible to normal eyes.

It was as tall as Saul on his horse. And it sensed their presence. It turned its head to see Ishbi and Saph through the darkness. Ishbi's familiar spirits became frenetic with fear. Then a voice penetrated his mind that only he could hear. It was the voice of the evil spirit.

"Stay away. This one is mine."

There were few things that frightened Rephaim gibborim, and this was one of them. This entity was more than an evil spirit. It was the most malevolent force that Ishbi had ever encountered, and he had encountered quite a bit of power in his days. It was kingly and it was ancient. It reminded him of Asherah and Dagon. It rivaled them in sheer malignance.

Ishbi was not going to get in the way of this thing, whatever it was, because it was truly frightening.

The priests were gathered before Saul and his soldiers. They were like frightened sheep before a pack of wolves. There were eighty-five priests encircled by the fifty warriors on horseback.

Saul sighed and looked over at Doeg. "You. Kill them all."

"Me, my lord?" said Doeg with shock.

"Yes, *you*. Consider it your reward of loyalty to me. Kill them all. NOW!"

Doeg got off his horse and drew his sword. The priests knelt and began to pray to Yahweh with heads bowed. It would make it easier for the Edomite without their sorrowful eyes penetrating into his guilty soul. But his king had commanded him.

He hacked the priests to pieces. He became drenched in their innocent blood. It would change him forever.

It changed the watching soldiers on their horses. Everyone watched with horror. In their dread focus, they did not see the single hidden priest sneaking out the alleyway behind them. No one saw the young man get away. No one except Ishbi and Saph. They had a good idea where he was going.

After Doeg had finished his evil deed for the king, Saul yelled out, "Now, kill every man, woman and child in the town!"

The warriors balked. Did they hear him correctly?

"You heard what I said. KILL THEM ALL!"

The warriors rode through the town to accomplish the diabolical command of their king.

Nimrod whispered into Saul's ear, "Yahweh wants a holy war of herem, I will give him herem."

The two Rephaim giants in the brush were gone.

CHAPTER 42

David hid in the cave of Adullam, thirteen miles southeast of Nob. It was well hidden in the labyrinth of rocky outcroppings of the area. The interior of the cavern was large enough to accommodate a regiment of men. The brothers Joab and Abishai had met him there. They had brought with them those in the bodyguard who were loyal to David, almost one hundred of them. The force was growing because word had gotten out to the surrounding hills and valleys that David was on the run from Saul.

Many disgruntled warriors, brigands and outlaws who harbored a hatred for Saul were joining up. David would have his hands full and his leadership tested with these renegades. But he also identified with them. He too had always been an outcast and rebel of sorts.

But now as a rebel leader, he gathered his men around him, flanked by Joab and Abishai.

"I am David ben Jesse, the captain of the king's guard, and married into royal lineage through his daughter, Michal. Some of you have heard that Samuel the Seer has anointed me as the next king of Israel; that Yahweh has rejected Saul and that our king is now possessed and taunted by an evil spirit, who gives him no rest in seeking to kill me."

The men murmured their outrage. Words like "tyrant" and "despot" could be heard above the din.

Joab yelled, "Quiet down!" They reluctantly did so.

David announced, "I care not what you think of the king. Be he benevolent, or be he tyrant, he is still Yahweh's anointed. And if we were to rise up in revolt and fight against him, we would be fighting against Yahweh!"

The men could not contain their anger. A grumbling through their ranks proved that many of them thought fighting the king was fighting *for* Yahweh.

Joab meant to quiet them again, maybe even slug a few to the ground. But David gestured to him to let them vent. When they had died down, he continued.

"Men, I understand your anger with the unrighteousness of King Saul's government. But if we do not respect the office of authority that Yahweh himself has established, then what hope have we of retaining the respect and obedience of our opponents when *we* are in authority? Kingdoms in revolution merely replace one form of tyranny with another. And once we have established violent overthrow as the means of justice, then we will no longer have justice, but only a thousand generations of endless violent overthrow: Rahab, chaos. If you follow me, you must be men of law not lawlessness. If you consider me Yahweh's anointed and support my claim to the throne of Israel, then you will obey me, and you will not attack King Saul. If anyone violates this command, I will kill him myself. If you cannot abide my commands, leave now, for I have no time for rebels against Yahweh's authority."

This time there was no murmuring, but rather a penetrating silence. The men listened and counted the cost of joining David's band of followers. Could he do it? Could he create a loyal army of honorable warriors out of a band of discontented misfits, riff raff, and rabble rousers? Could he build a kingdom on redeemed outlaws? Only Yahweh knew. Only Yahweh could perform such miracles.

A warrior stepped out of the crowd with his hands on two sword hilts and asked, "My lord, will we be allowed to continue killing Philistines?"

"Of course you will," said David. "That duty remains unchanged."

"Then you retain the swords of Sibbecai the Hushathite in loyalty!" He drew his two swords and thrust them into the sky, proclaiming, "A sword for the Lord and for David!"

The other warriors followed suit, lifting their weapons and shouting, "A sword for the Lord and for David!"

David smiled. He knew this Sibbecai was adept with his double swords. He only hoped he had many more such skilled fighters in their midst. He was desperately going to need them.

"David!" The voice came from a lookout outside the cave. "A refugee is here. A priest from Nob!"

David ran out to meet him. The men followed to see what would cause him such concern.

When David stepped outside, he saw Abiathar, the son of Ahimelech the high priest. He fell at David's feet, bloodied, dirty and exhausted. David waved at those around him. "Back away." David pulled Abiathar over to the bushes by the perimeter of the cave.

The young priest tried to catch his breath. He had been running the whole way from Nob.

David yelled, "Get me a water skin!"

Joab complied. David let Abiathar drink deeply from the skin. He was dehydrated and on the verge of passing out.

Joab and Abishai had stepped close enough to hear their words, but kept the others back out of earshot.

David said, "You are Ahimelech's son. I remember you."

Abiathar could not contain himself. He broke down weeping. "They are dead. They are all dead. He killed them. I alone escaped."

David heard a rustling in the bushes nearby, away from the others. He thought it was the wind, so he ignored it.

He did not see the large eyes staring out at him from the foliage.

David held Abiathar firmly. "Who is dead?" he demanded.

"My father and all the priests of Nob. He killed them all. And the women and children."

"Who? Who killed them?"

"King Saul."

David's face dropped. He immediately knew that it had to be Doeg the Edomite herdsman of Saul who betrayed him. David's hair bristled at the back of his neck. He felt as if he was being watched. But his mind

209

was in turmoil over his deadly tactical error. He should have trusted his instincts and detained Doeg, but he let it go. Now the entire town of Nob was dead for helping David. Horror swept over him. How much more evil will follow him? Why was Yahweh allowing this to happen?

Abiathar made it worse. "But that is not all. Before we were attacked, I heard that Ramah was also attacked by two giant Rephaim. They slaughtered the entire school of prophets."

David went flush with shock. "And Samuel?"

"No," said Abiathar. "He was in the desert at the time. He is safe. But they skinned alive the students. The killers were servants of Asherah looking for you."

David was not the only one overwhelmed by the shock of the revelation. Joab and Abishai looked at each other with fright. There was only one way a servant of Asherah could have known that David had been to Ramah.

They immediately melted away from David and went to their horses, giving command to the next of rank.

Abiathar opened a sack he had been carrying, and pulled out the holy ephod from the sanctuary. It was the one that David had asked for. He offered it to him. "You wanted to know the will of the Lord for all your decisions."

"Yes," agreed David.

"Well, by divine right, I am now high priest. I will inquire of Yahweh for you – wherever you go."

David smiled tearfully and grasped Abiathar's shoulders with great joy. He said simply, "Hallelujah." Yahweh had answered his prayer. He had taken an evil atrocity and turned it around for his own holy purposes. The Chosen Seed would have direct guidance from Yahweh himself.

David stood up. "I will not touch the king. But I will do to those soldiers what they did to the priests of Yahweh, so help me, God."

He heard the wind bristle through the leaves again. Then he realized there was no breeze. It was a dead calm evening.

Before he could react, a warrior stepped out of the foliage.

But it was not a giant.

It was a paladin dressed in strange desert garb, carrying a scimitar and staff.

His men were too far away to get to him in time. He would be dead.

David did not even have his own weapons with him. The events had absorbed his attention.

He looked into the paladin's eyes that showed through the cloak. He knew if the other was an enemy, he would have attacked already. But the warrior drew nothing. Instead he dropped his scarf. David saw a smile.

Two zealous and ignorant soldiers raced up to the warrior, intending to defend their commander. The warrior used his staff with a swift, circling spin and knocked them both to the ground in three moves.

David held out his hand to stop the others. He was safe.

The warrior knelt before David. He had a royal sense about him. He declared, "I am Benaiah ben Jehoida of Kabzeel." That explained his strange desert garb. Kabzeel was in the deep south of the Negeb desert. But it also made him a fellow Judahite with David. "I have heard much about the mighty David and his exploits. But I must say, you have not been careful enough with your security, allowing me to come within death's grip of you — and armed to the teeth, I might add."

David was amused.

Benaiah added, "I offer my obeisance to Yahweh's anointed."

David was about to speak, but Benaiah kept going with a grin, "And may I add, I will not attack King Saul, because I have no time for rebels against Yahweh's authority."

David smiled. So this Benaiah had also heard David's grand speech in the cave as well, and was now repeating those words back as a vow.

"Good," said David. "You shall be the captain of my bodyguard."

Benaiah was dumbfounded. "But you do not know me, my lord. How can you trust me with such a responsibility?"

"You already got through my defenses once," replied David. "So I would not be able to stop you anyway."

Benaiah understood and grinned.

David added, "Get to know the bodyguard. They are Cherethites and Pelethites."

"Cretans and Philistines?" said Benaiah. "So I am not the only stranger you employ. My lord has a taste for the questionable elements of society to be closest to him?"

David said, "Mercenaries are without tribal conspiracy and pettiness."

Benaiah countered, "And they can be bought by enemies with a higher bid."

"I have to take whoever I can get," said David. "Many of my men are outlaws and malcontents. Unfortunately, excellence in combat and excellence in character are rarely united in a warrior."

"It will be my goal to remedy that, my lord," said Benaiah. "Accept this repentant outlaw's fealty."

Benaiah bowed while still kneeling. David pulled him up and hugged him. He turned to the others. "I think it is time for some recreation."

A third of the men were allowed, in rotation, to hunt, swim in the nearest pond, or just take naps. No one had realized that Joab and Abishai had snuck off.

CHAPTER 43

The tigress-like Kiana bathed herself and left the temple to meet a man beneath her Terebinth tree in the sacred grove of Asherah. When she arrived, she discovered the Hebrew warrior Abishai waiting for her. But he did not look amorous. He looked threatening. She turned to leave, but was blocked by the younger Joab. He grabbed her. She hissed and bared her fangs.

Joab held tight.

She got one hand loose and swiped her claws at his face, carving a big rip down his forehead and cheek.

Abishai grabbed her from behind. She could not get loose from his iron grip.

Joab placed his hand over her mouth to stifle her scream, and killed her quickly with his dagger.

Abishai let her down gently, almost as if she were still alive. He had a tear in his eye, but he was as resolute as his brother.

Joab whispered, "We must speak of this to no one. David must never find out about our betrayal or we will lose everything we have worked for to support him. We cannot let him know."

"Would he not forgive us? We were innocent."

Joab snapped back, "We are not innocent. Our idolatry almost cost our leader his life. We would never be allowed our rank in his kingdom if he ever found out. If we intend to continue in our course, we must make a blood oath of silence right now."

He held up his dagger. Both their hands were dripping with Kiana's blood. But now they cut their own palms and mixed it together with a mutual grasp.

Joab said, "From this day forth and forever, we will never speak of this again, and we will never again go astray from our king and from our god."

Abishai added, "May Yahweh cut our throats and leave us in Sheol if either of us ever again strays from the purity of devotion to our king or engage in any behavior that would endanger him. I devote my life to the House of David."

Joab repeated it, "I devote my life to the House of David." Then he added, "I pledge my life to destroy any and all enemies of David and his throne."

Abishai repeated, "I pledge my life to destroy any and all enemies of David and his throne."

Both of them knew that their guilt would haunt them for the rest of their lives. But they willingly accepted the burden as the consequences of their actions, and the price of their loyalty.

CHAPTER 44

The giants Lahmi and Runihura crept up to the first home on the outskirts of Bethlehem in the dark of evening. They had already killed a few residents out for a stroll. But they were intent upon their target.

They crashed in the door of the home and caught a family unawares at their dinner table.

Runihura grabbed an eight year old child in his engulfing hands.

Lahmi demanded, "Where is the house of Jesse?"

The father blurted out, "At the end of the lane on the right."

"That was easy enough," said Runihura. Then they murdered everyone before moving on to Jesse's home.

When they arrived at the home at the end of the lane, they discovered everyone gone. The entire household stood empty, as if they had disappeared. Lahmi growled with anger and smashed the house to pieces. He kicked his way out of a wall. The two giants proceeded to the next house, to find out where the family of Jesse was. There were a few hundred families in this little town and they would not stop killing them until they found out where their targets had gone.

By the time the two giants reached the far side of the town in their pillaging, they were filled with rage that their plans were blocked by these senseless little Hebrews.

They heard their names called and they looked up. Ishbi and Saph stood at the end of town, obviously bearing news.

Ishbi said, "We know where David is. But we will need your help. He has an army of gibborim surrounding him."

Lahmi's eyes were enflamed. Of course he wanted to kill David. But even more, he wanted to torture David's entire family for what he did to Goliath. And he wanted to do it in front of David before he executed the Chosen Seed.

But it did not look like he was going to get his full revenge yet.

"First, help me finish what I started here."

• • • • •

The four Rephaim slaughtered every inhabitant and destroyed every home of Bethlehem. They then headed for the cave of Adullam, twelve miles west in the mountain pass.

They did not take Argaz with them. His fifteen foot stature was an impenetrable wall of power on the battlefield, but he proved too clumsy and noisy for covert operations. He could not walk without making the ground shake beneath his feet and he could barely hide behind a boulder. The Hebrew gibborim that guarded David were no doubt ferocious in their fighting skills, but they were not yet organized. They were still few enough for the four Sons of Rapha to take them on their own. They would continue to save Argaz as a secret weapon for the right battle.

When they approached within a thousand yards of the cave, they could not detect any sounds of soldiers camping. There were no fires.

"We are late again," said Ishbi. "They have gone."

They entered the cave, and saw that Ishbi was right. The camp was cold. There were no hints of where they might have gone. Lahmi pounded the rock wall in anger. His howl could be heard for miles.

Ishbi scolded him, "Restrain yourself, fool, or we will never get near them. What have I told you about your temper? If you do not harness it, it will harness you in the hands of your enemy."

Lahmi frowned, but he knew Ishbi was right. He had to master his emotions to maximize his fighting skill. Killing simple soldiers was easy. He could do that with his eyes closed. It was the Israelite gibborim that would prove most difficult.

CHAPTER 45

David had removed his family from Bethlehem secretly in the night, mere days before the Rephaim had arrived. He knew they were in jeopardy from his enemies, be they Saul's forces or the Philistine assassins. So he and his band of warriors had taken the family seventy-five miles south-east, around the shores of the Dead Sea and into the land of Moab. The Moabites were still adversaries of both Saul and the Philistines, so the family of Jesse would surely not be followed into enemy territory.

David had gone to Moab across the Jordan and had appealed to its king through the ancient custom of providing sanctuary for the enemies of your adversaries. Since David was himself an adversary of both Saul and the Philistines, then he was a de-facto ally of Moab. David also claimed his Moabite ancestry through his great grandmother, Ruth, the wife of Boaz. David painted himself as a hybrid of both Israelite and Moabite lineage.

During the journey, David had gathered several hundred more followers and a few prophets, including Gad the Seer and other warriors who supported his anointed claim to the throne.

David formed his mightiest gibborim warriors into special units he called his "Three" and his "Thirty." The Three were his three chiefs over all the regular armed forces; Jashobeam, Eleazar and Shammah. The Thirty were his supreme army council, veterans responsible for the organization and management of internal army regulations. They commanded the militia reserves with a readiness for quick and mobile engagements. Each of these men was chosen based upon personal feats of courage or faith.

Abishai was chief of the Thirty, which made Joab envious. Joab was the younger of the two brothers, but they both knew he was more ruthless and the stronger leader. He felt that the scar that traversed his forehead to his cheek was responsible for Joab's lack of advancement. Such a visible scar on a warrior in so vulnerable a location as the face, even if the wound did not hamper him, was nevertheless a visual sign of a failure in battle. How could such lesser warriors rise in status? He and Abishai had lied about the true origin of the scar because of their blood oath. They had said they were jumped by a band of twenty Philistine outlaws during a hunt for game. Could any gibborim have gotten away with a lesser wound? In truth, the scar *was* a sign of Joab's failure, his moral failure with a qedesha of Asherah, and how that failure compromised the life of the Chosen Seed of Yahweh. Joab quietly accepted that his lesser status than his brother was a punishment for his weakness of flesh, one that he would carry with him to the grave.

Benaiah remained the Captain of David's bodyguard. While they were in the land of Moab, he was particularly unsettled being surrounded by these idol worshippers of Chemosh, the sun god. David's carefree spirit and reckless choices gave Benaiah sleepless nights. David seemed to act as if he was indestructible, that he could not be killed. He too readily trusted those in his company.

David's latest reckless choice was to accept the new allies who had pledged themselves to the death for David. They were warriors of Moab.

But they were not normal warriors. They were specially gifted ones called "Ariels." They were the Lion Men of Moab.

They were called this because though they had the bodies of men, their faces resembled lions, with snout and mane and sharp feline fangs. They had incredible strength and could fight with the ferocity of the king of beasts. Benaiah thought they were unholy hybrids, like those of the Watcher legends. It had been told that before the Flood, the gods had violated Yahweh's created order of separation by creating hybrid soldiers of both man and beast. They had the bodies of men, but the heads of hawks and jackals and other predator animals. They were used by the gods to wreak death and destruction upon the land. Benaiah feared this was a recurrence of such monstrosities. He believed David should stay far away from them.

David felt that Yahweh could redeem anyone that had human blood in their veins, because they still carried Yahweh's image, distorted though it may be.

The eleven Lion Men Ariels stood out of earshot at the ready, waiting for a command from David. They stood like statues, their powerful arms and legs still, their long hair flowing in the breeze. Their feline faces looked straight ahead without emotion.

The ever vigilant brothers, Joab and Abishai, moved closer to David and his skeptical bodyguard, to overhear their debate.

Benaiah whispered in anger to David, "You cannot do this, David. You cannot trust them. They are Moabites, for heaven's sake!"

David countered, "They are faithful converts to the tribe of Gad for many years now."

"That is only because Joshua conquered them generations ago. Do you not think they harbor a vengeful desire to get even one day?"

"They have proven themselves true by the word of their elders. Benaiah, you should have more faith."

"And you, my lord, should have more doubt."

David said, "Do you think Joshua should have had more doubt when he allowed Caleb to lead his forces? Caleb was a Kenizzite, which was a pagan tribe after all. He was a convert not unlike these warriors. And he proved the greatest of all warriors in the Conquest of our Promised Land."

Benaiah glanced back at the stout-faced Lion Men. "Caleb was not an unholy chimera. I do not trust them."

David said, "They are part animal and part human, it is true. But are not humans also animals? Are we not often more vile and wicked than animals in our behavior? Which is the more worthy of mistrust, their animal or their human nature? And if they are part human, then they are part Yahweh's image, and can be redeemed."

Benaiah knew he was not going to get anywhere with him. David had made up his mind. Benaiah vented his final frustration, "There is something not right. I can feel it."

David smiled. "There goes your animal intuition again. Should I trust *you*, my Benaiah?" He was teasing him, but the point was made.

David turned to the waiting warriors. "Lion Men of Moab, welcome to my fighting force. I have accepted your fealty and you may join my ranks and follow my rule. I pray you prove yourself worthy of Yahweh's kingdom."

The Lion Men did not smile or display any emotion. They merely roared in unison. It sent shivers down Benaiah's spine. He would keep his eye on these beasts.

David added, "But if any of you dare break ranks or prove treacherous and seek my harm in any way, I pray for your souls, because you will have Benaiah to contend with." He pointed at Benaiah with a smile and a wink.

"And me as well," said the voice of a small man. He stepped out of the ranks to draw attention.

Benaiah stared at the little man with surprise. He was perhaps the shortest warrior Benaiah had ever seen, at just under five feet tall. The incongruity made Benaiah smile.

David, however sighed. He knew who it was.

The young man was very small, but he had an ego the size of an elephant. He announced, "I am Jonathan son of Shimei!" He raised an archer's bow in his hand. "And this bow will protect my lord against all enemies!" Some of the men chuckled at the preposterous claim of the little man. He was too young-looking, too slender and simply too small for battle.

A heckler blurted out the sound of a mouse, "Squeak, squeak!" Laughs peppered the crowd.

"Hold your tongues" yelled David. The men quieted down.

David pulled Jonathan aside. He was the son of David's brother, Shimei.

"Nephew, when did you join us?" he scolded.

"At Hebron," said Jonathan. "Father has released me. Do not withhold from me the opportunity to fight for Yahweh, uncle."

"You are too young and too slight, Jonathan."

Jonathan complained, "You took down the mighty Goliath with one stone when younger than my age, and just as slight."

"That was different."

"I can take out both eyes of a giant at a hundred yards with my bow."

David sighed. Jonathan was indeed an excellent marksman. But a good aim was not all that was necessary for being a warrior. On the other hand, David needed all the help he could get. Jonathan had been released from his father and could make his own choices now.

David said to him, "You can stay. But only on the condition that you make no more bold pronouncements. It's embarrassing, Jonathan."

"Agreed," said Jonathan.

David added, "And you stay in the archer ranks."

Jonathan begrudgingly repeated it, "And I stay in the archer ranks."

David tussled the hair of his little nephew. Jonathan hated when he did that.

David turned to the soldiers. "Tomorrow, we head back to the wilderness territories to continue playing hide and seek with the King of Israel!"

• • • • •

There was another in David's ranks who did not trust the Lion Men, the swordsman, Sibbecai. He decided not to announce his agreement with Benaiah. He would rather be a silent ally, someone to watch the bodyguard's back.

Benaiah kept his eyes on those leonine beasts all the way back into Canaan. Keeping watch over them tired him out. But he knew that if he gave up his vigil, he would be in the most danger of them springing a trap.

Joab and Abishai would tease him at inopportune moments.

The two brothers perfected a mimicry of the growl of an Ariel. They would surprise Benaiah at random times by coming up behind him or hiding outside his tent. Sibbecai saw their relentless teasing but held back his support of Benaiah. The bodyguard could handle himself against such pranks.

One night, Benaiah stood the late watch duty. He became alarmed when he saw Joab and Abishai approaching his outpost with stealth, looking around to make sure no one was following them.

Joab spoke first in a whisper. "Benaiah, we want to apologize for relentlessly teasing you about the Lion Men. Your concerns are not entirely unfounded."

Abishai added, "Your dedication to David is truly admirable."

Joab continued, "In fact, we have begun to watch the Lion Men and we are beginning to share your concern."

Benaiah relaxed. Finally, he was being taken seriously.

Abishai jumped in again, "But I think we have also discovered their weakness."

Benaiah's interest was piqued. "What is it?"

Abishai continued, "Well, because of their leonine nature, they have an intense sense of smell. We think that we have figured out how to overcome them if they ever do betray us."

"How?" asked Benaiah.

"Shh," said Joab. "Did you hear that?"

They listened. There was rustling in the brush. They looked out and saw the tops of three lion manes approaching them. Benaiah gripped his sword. But Abishai held him. "Wait. We have this. We will show you what we mean."

Joab stepped out in front of Benaiah.

When the lion manes were within a dozen feet, they stood up to reveal three growling Lion Men.

Benaiah held his ram's horn. "Let me call the alarm."

Abishai stopped him again. "There is no need. Watch Joab."

Joab turned his back to the men and squatted with a scrunched face. He then let loose a rip-roaring fart in the direction of the Lion Men. They coughed and then ran away into the brush yelping.

Joab held his hands out as if solving the problem.

Abishai said, "Their noses are just too sensitive."

Benaiah's face went red with anger. He had been duped again. They had even gotten some of the Lion Men to join in on their charade. He would have slugged them for their prank, but they were both on the forest floor laughing so hard that Benaiah could not help but respond with a reluctant smile.

When the brothers finally calmed down and got up, they looked at Benaiah. He glared back at them. "If you think I have changed my mind because of your childish natures, you will be sorely disappointed. My guard will not be let down, and one day, you may have me to thank for it, you jackals. Now get out of here and leave me in peace."

They slapped their brother in arms on the back and left him to stew in his humiliation.

· · · · ·

Benaiah's rotation on the night watch came round again. He stood watch on the eastern flank of David's company. He stayed wide awake and alert. David's band of Gibborim were hiding in the Forest of Hereth. Things had been quiet for the most part.

Benaiah heard noise behind him. He turned to see four Lion Men of Moab stealthily approaching his outpost, like a pride of lions on the hunt. He did not see Joab or Abishai nearby, but he suspected this was another of their gags.

He didn't trust these fur balls. He drew his sword just in case.

They all stopped about twenty feet from him. They sniffed the air. They obviously smelled something. Or was this going to be another fart joke?

They growled softly, and crouched down, preparing to spring.

This was no gag. Something was not right.

Benaiah's attention was distracted by another movement. Sibbecai the swordsman approached the Lion Men from behind. He had followed them.

But the Moabites were all looking past Benaiah into the forest.

Benaiah whirled around. He barely got his shield up in time. A javelin hit the shield with such force it threw him against a tree, embedding itself into the metal of the shield. It was a loop javelin thrown with a tremendous force.

Benaiah received a concussion from the force of hitting the tree. He heard the sound of a large creature rushing at him from the forest.

And it wasn't an Ariel.

A rushing dark shape resolved itself into a giant Rephaim. The dark-skinned Egyptian carried another javelin, ready to impale him.

Just before the giant reached him, two Lion Men jumped out from both sides and intercepted the large attacker. They took him down into the brush in a flurry of fangs and claws.

Benaiah's head was splitting with pain. He was seeing double, but he was not about to let that stop him. He stood up, faltering a bit, but prepared to engage.

Another giant came out of the trees at Benaiah's right. But the four Lion Men jumped him and fought him off. It took all four of them. This monster seemed to have a supernatural presence surrounding him, a bodyguard of demons.

Benaiah's headache jarred his whole body. He dropped to one knee, trying to recover from dizziness. He looked up. A third giant swooped toward him with two large scimitars about to chop him in half.

A hand yanked him back, out of the way before the blades could connect.

It was Sibbecai, the swordsman.

Sibbecai drew his own two swords. He smiled at the irony of facing an opponent with the same armament of double blades. Unfortunately, this opponent was more than his equal. Sibbecai looked up at a nine foot tall, eight hundred pound pile of bulk and brawn.

The giant rumbled, "You are no match for a Son of Rapha," and released a series of attacks with his two blades. Sibbecai was ready for it. He countered with blocks and parries that frustrated the giant and made him sloppy with rage.

The rage distracted him from Benaiah, who had regained some of his strength and slipped behind the giant. The Israelite had pulled the javelin from his shield. He used it to pierce the Rapha's kidney.

The giant screamed out in pain.

Sibbecai saw his opportunity and thrust both his swords into the giant's sternum and up into his heart.

The giant swung one of his blades and cut off Sibbecai's head.

Benaiah screamed his comrade's name in horror.

The Rapha fell to the ground with a gasp.

The other two giants heard the yelp and saw their comrade fall. They knew they would be surrounded in moments by an army of gibborim, so they stopped their battle and fled into the woods, with the Lion Men chasing them.

Benaiah knew he only had a few moments. He grabbed the giant and growled at him, "Who are the Sons of Rapha?"

The giant grunted in pain and glared at Benaiah with a smirk.

Benaiah demanded again, "Who are the Sons of Rapha?"

He received no answer other than the last gasp of breath from the defiant Rapha as his life bled out onto the forest floor.

Benaiah whispered, "May you rot where the worm does not die and the fire is not quenched." He spit on the giant's corpse.

He looked over at Sibbecai's body with deep pain. This warrior had saved his life, and now he was gone. It did not seem fair that so noble a man should die in so ignoble a way at the hand of a cursed seed. He placed the warrior's head gently with the body in a macabre moment of orderliness.

A hand on Benaiah's shoulder brought him back. Ezer the Chief Ariel loomed over him. A few of the Lion Men had already returned from chasing the giants. All of them put their hands on Benaiah's shoulders and back in solidarity with their comrade.

No words were spoken. But there was a newfound brotherhood between them now. They had all saved Benaiah's life, not just Sibbecai. He would not have been able to face all three of those giants alone.

They looked upon the dead Rapha. Ezer said, "It was a coordinated attack. They were trying to find a hole through our defenses."

Benaiah said, "Were you not here, they would have."

He looked up at his rescuers, and with a humbled voice, said, "Thank you. For saving my life."

"Sibbecai saved you. We only helped," said Ezer softly.

Benaiah had been a fool. He had just been rescued by the very ones he had trusted the least.

He was grateful to be alive.

Benaiah asked his two closest rescuers, "What are your names?"

They responded, "Elzabad," and "Machbannai."

Benaiah stood and sighed with relief before grasping wrists with the leonine men he had once distrusted so deeply. He faltered a bit. The splitting pain had not left his head.

They heard the sound of someone arriving from camp. Jonathan ben Shimei broke out of the bush, his bow at the ready with an arrow nocked. He saw Benaiah alive and well. He saw the Lion Men. He saw the dead Rapha. He looked around, realizing he had missed the fight. He stomped the ground. "I want to kill a giant!"

Benaiah and the others ignored him. They always ignored the Mouse, as they had nicknamed him. Benaiah said to Ezer, "We must alert David. And we must find out who these Sons of Rapha are."

CHAPTER 46

Ba'alzebul smashed his fist down onto the altar of Dagon. It cracked in half. Chunks and dust went flying. The gods had just learned that the Rephaim Saph had been killed by David's warriors.

Ba'alzebul was angry and his strength was back. A mounting fear plagued Dagon that he could no longer control the mighty deity. Ba'alzebul had once ruled the pantheon. He had been humbled and now bore the name Son of Dagon, but he had regained his former strength. Dagon realized that it now simply remained for his rival to regain his power of place. Ba'alzebul could not just take an allotted territory, however. He had to earn it. Dagon had no idea how the other planned on doing so. He only assumed that Ba'alzebul *was* planning on doing so. Dagon would have to do something to keep his edge on the muscle-bound brute who thought of power but not of intrigue.

Intrigue was Asherah's specialty. Dagon feared that the two of them were in league together and had designs on his throne. As long as he was chief god of the Philistines, he maintained his edge. If he could extend his power over the Hebrews, he would consolidate his territory and power over all of Canaan. He would have to act fast, if he wanted to stay ahead of this deadly duo. He had been planning this for some time and now was his chance.

Asherah said, "We are down to only four of our original Rephaim assassins. David's forces are too large now. He has too many gibborim with him."

"And Lion Men of Moab," added Dagon. "The Sons of Rapha and their giant battalion will never penetrate that army. They are too mighty."

Ba'alzebul interrupted their gloom. "Unless we take away David's allotted protection."

The others looked at him darkly. It was the last ditch option they had discussed in the past but had always avoided because of the danger involved.

Ba'alzebul explained, "We have been on the run all these generations from the archangels who seek to bind us in the earth. We hide like cockroaches in the dark. We are vulnerable when separated. But stronger when united."

"You are right," said Asherah. "It is time we turn the tables and try to capture the guardian prince of Israel, Mikael."

Dagon countered. "But it has only been done once before, in primeval days when we were at our strongest. And that with the weakest of the archangels. Even then, it backfired on our predecessors. Look where they are now."

He referred to the time before the Flood when Uriel had been captured by Inanna and Anu, the mightiest of their number. It did not last for long. Anu and Inanna had been bound beneath the earth.

Ba'alzebul said, "If for a limited time we could detain just that one guardian, just him alone, the Chosen Seed would not have the covering of heaven. Then our Sons of Rapha could strike, through stealth or war."

Dagon concluded, "We will need all the help we can get. Molech, Chemosh, Resheph and Qeteb."

"Of course," replied Asherah.

Dagon gave a dark expectant stare at Asherah and added, "Leviathan?"

She was Lady Asherah of the Sea. One of her many skills over the waters was the ability to use magical incantations to call upon Leviathan, the seven-headed offspring of Rahab, the sea dragon of chaos. Leviathan was not tamable, but it could be partially directed through spells, especially when it had to do with destruction. She had once called up the serpent to wreak punishment upon her own city of

Sidon for insolence of its governing authorities. Dozens of ships were destroyed and hundreds of lives lost in the furious storm of punishment.

The rulers never got out of line again.

Asherah replied to Dagon, "Be careful what forces of chaos you seek to call upon, Dagon. They may not behave to your liking."

Ba'alzebul threw in, "There is one ally whose help we have all failed to appreciate fully." They looked expectantly at him.

"Nimrod."

"He is hardly more tamable than Leviathan," said Dagon.

"But he is in a most advantageous position," said Asherah. "His possession of the king of Israel is a dagger of division in the heart of Mikael's defenses."

She turned to the others with a smile. "My fellow deities, let us go catch ourselves an archangel."

CHAPTER 47

Guardian archangels are fond of staying in the background and out of sight in the temporal world, until they are needed to protect their ward. Unlike Uriel's cocksure flamboyance, Mikael preferred quiet understatement. He was the prince of Israel, a most holy calling. It was all the more reason for him to downplay his presence. He did not want to draw attention where it was unwanted. The Canaanites and their gods were already in perpetual war with the Israelites, seeking to exterminate them all and drive them into the sea.

The Philistines were the strongest of these threats. But the most dangerous hazard was the most intimate one. Because the evil spirit of Nimrod had sunk his claws into Saul's soul, Mikael had been distracted and stretched thin, following David in his months of fleeing from Saul's pursuit. Mikael's attention was divided between his watchfulness over the Chosen Seed David, and his chosen people Israel, led by a king trying to kill David.

David stayed constantly on the move, because he was not always welcomed where he sojourned as a fugitive from the king. Three thousand soldiers accompanied Saul, chasing David and his six hundred gibborim. David had run from the Forest of Hereth, to the city of Keilah, to the wildernesses of Ziph and Maon, where he currently hid. And all along, David sought to communicate to Saul that he was not an enemy of the king. It was all to no avail, as the king remained relentless in his mad hunt.

Then an event occurred that changed the course of everyone's plans: a Philistine attack on Gibeah, the seat of Israel's power. Just as Saul was closing in on David in the wilderness of Maon, the king received word of the approaching forces of all five cities of the Philistines upon Gibeah. He immediately left his manhunt to return to Gibeah and repel the enemy's advance. David and his followers escaped capture. Their location became known as "the Rock of Escape."

David settled in Maon for a time, knowing Saul would not be back too quickly from his latest campaign against the Philistines.

• • • • •

Nabal the Calebite was one of the wealthiest landowners in Maon. He pastured his large flocks of thousands of sheep and goats in Carmel near Hebron. He would use his position of power on the local city councils to secure the best grazing land for his sheep to the detriment of others. When the time for shearing came, he used bribes to gain first place of sale over lesser shepherds. He purchased his own bodyguard from fear that others would seek revenge against his financial bullying. He had become a recluse and grew obese through indulgence.

His wife, Abigail, the most desired woman in the entire area, was mature and beautiful of form. Her deep red hair enticed men, her ocean blue eyes melted them in their tracks. She was a loyal and virtuous woman as well. Unfortunately, in his paranoid megalomania, Nabal could not believe this. He restricted her to the mansion home of stone and wood he had built on his hilltop residence. He treated her like a dog.

One day, Nabal welcomed ten messengers from the camp of Israelite riff raff who had been sojourning in the area for some time. Nabal had used some spies to find out as much as he could about their leader, the rebel who was on the run from King Saul. Though Nabal detested the king as well, he did not consider these unsavory vagabonds as his allies. Yes, their presence had reduced the amount of criminal activity in the area, but he knew it was all pretense. He knew it was only a matter of time before they came looking for him to try to steal his wealth—just like all the others. That time had arrived. And it was on the eve of a feast day no less. How uncouth of them.

The ten messengers looked like warriors more than messengers, so Nabal surrounded himself with his bodyguard of twenty men to receive the visitors.

"Shalom be upon your house, Nabal of Maon," said the lead messenger. "My name is Joab, and this is my brother Abishai. We serve our lord, David ben Jesse." Abishai nodded respectfully, as did the nine others with them.

Nabal eyed them suspiciously. The leader named Joab had a nasty scar down his forehead and cheek that made him appear like a devious wolf.

Joab continued, "Our lord understands that you are shearing your sheep now in Carmel."

Nabal replied with sarcasm, "I can readily see your lord takes such dedicated interest in my property. So important is it to him that he sends his warriors instead of messengers."

"We are warriors, it is true," said Joab. "But we come in peace. We have watched over your shepherds for these past weeks and have done them no harm. Indeed, we have protected them from hostile outsiders, so that not a sheep has been taken."

Nabal knew exactly where this was going. He continued his sarcastic drawl, "What a privilege indeed is such peace. And what do I owe this son of Jesse for such unrequested protection?"

Joab said, "May my lord find favor in your eyes. For a feast day is upon us. He only asks whatever food and drink you may spare for your servants and your son, David."

"My *son*, no less," said Nabal. "And how many does this 'son' of mine employ in this protection business of his?"

"We are six hundred."

Nabal's countenance dropped. That was a lot of warriors. However, he had great trust in the two hundred mercenaries on his own payroll. They were mighty warriors as well, and they were itching for a chance to utilize the skills they had been trained and paid for. Besides, the mansion operated as a fortification, so it would not be a battlefield of one on one.

Joab could see Nabal's agitation, so he added, "We are accompanied by several prophets of Yahweh and a high priest."

Nabal thought, *So he thinks he can pretend to be less hostile and more holy, does he?* Nabal was not going to sit down and roll over for some young brigand's attempted extortion propped up by religious justification. He was not going to just give over his hard earned wealth to a gang of thugs.

Nabal hardened his stance and crowed, "Who is this 'son of Jesse' that he should demand of me such things? I did not ask him to 'protect' my shepherds or my land. But I do have a bodyguard I have hired to protect *me*."

Nabal's guard drew closer to him in response.

Abishai shook his head at the subtle threat. He could kill all twenty of these hired scrappers himself.

Suddenly, a woman's voice interrupted them all. "My lord, forgive my intrusion."

All eyes turned toward the most stunning woman any of them had seen in years, maybe in entire lifetimes. She wore a humble, hooded cloak of modesty, but it could not hide her radiant beauty, her thick red hair and piercing blue eyes.

"Ahem, Abigail," said Nabal, "should you not be cleaning out the sheep pen or some other duty?"

"Forgive me, my lord, but I have finished that chore and I came to tell you, when I overheard your conversation here."

Abishai and Joab were mesmerized at her every word and movement. She was so beautiful.

Abigail turned to Joab and Abishai, "Perhaps there is a third way out of this dilemma."

The brothers perked up with curiosity.

Nabal turned sour with offense.

"Would your lord, David, be willing to return my husband's kindness with a vow of chaste behavior and the blessing of a sacrifice by the high priest?"

Joab looked at Abishai who appeared to approve. But before he could respond, Nabal interrupted, "Please excuse my wife's intrusion. She speaks out of line with impertinence."

Joab glanced at Abigail, who dropped her head in shame.

Nabal continued, "Rather, ask your lord, 'my son,' if I should take the bread, water and meat out of the mouths of my servants who have earned it and give it to servants of those who have rebelled against their masters?"

Abishai shot a surprised look at Joab, wondering how he would respond. This disgusting, fat pig with an undeserved exemplary wife knew exactly who David was after all, and was now accusing him of insurrection.

Joab gritted his teeth. He knew this worm was not worthy of his wrath.

He said, "Very well, my distinguished host. I will relay your message to my lord. Though I suspect your wife's wise offer would be more acceptable."

He bowed. Nabal said, "My men will see you out to your horses." Nabal's twenty shadowed Joab and Abishai's party to their exit.

When they were alone, Nabal walked up to Abigail. She shrank back. She knew how he was going to respond. He was predictable. She never got used to it, but she knew what he was going to do.

He reared back and punched her in the face with his fist. She fell to the floor. He would never bother to backhand her. That was too restrained. He wanted her to feel pain, not mere insult. His only grace was his unwillingness to use his ringed hand, for that would have ripped up her face and made her repugnant to have to look at every day.

Since he was too fat to lean down for another hit, he merely kicked her twice in the ribs. Her arm was enough to shield her ribs, preventing the force from breaking any bones. He only bruised them, along with raising a welt on her arm.

"How dare you treat me with such disrespect," he hissed. "How many times do I have to tell you to keep your petty female mouth shut? Do I have to clamp it with a bit and bridle?"

Nabal had so frequently gotten himself in trouble with his greedy arrogance that Abigail often found herself saving his business or his life with her unique ability to soothe the offended parties with gracious diplomacy. The irony was that if she had kept her mouth shut, he would be dead by now, cut down by one of the many he had provoked with such impunity. Unfortunately, it also served to incite his self-loathing even more to be upstaged by the inferior sex.

"And another thing. What did you mean by demanding a vow of 'chaste behavior?' Were you mocking me?"

"No, my lord," she pleaded, "I merely meant to protect our maidservants and the women of the town from debauched outlaws."

"Is that what turns you on? You would like to be ravished by some strapping hard outlaw, wouldn't you? Is that what you like?" He pulled out his leather belt.

"Is that what you like?!" he yelled, and lashed her with it.

"No, my lord," she cried, trying unsuccessfully to protect her face from the stinging strap.

The sad irony was that Nabal's impotence was the fruit of his own debauched living and obesity, while Abigail had remained chaste. She wanted to honor her vows before Yahweh.

He spewed, "And then that line about a sacrifice by the high priest! Your sanctimonious piety makes me want to puke. You are no more holy than any of the harlots I know. And I must say, they were far more desirable and satisfying than you ever were."

After he had become impotent, she had to turn her eyes from his pursuits of ever-deepening depravity. She hated herself. No matter how untrue his accusations, his words nevertheless pummeled her worse than his fists. She had been given in an arranged marriage to the rich Nabal by her father, who had become mired in debt. Unfortunately, it was a world where a carefully weighed shekel counted more than love's amorous desire.

Her father's debt was forgiven, but his betrayal of Abigail could not be. She sought to be an honorable wife in such a painfully unjust situation, but she could barely take it any more. The thought of taking her own life had recently become a comfort.

He heaved with puffed up anger. "Get out of my sight."

They were the words she longed to hear. She got up and left his presence to dress her wounds.

CHAPTER 48

Mikael shadowed Saul on his journey back toward Gibeah from the wilderness of Maon where he had been hunting David. The archangel suspected Dagon, Asherah, and Ba'alzebul would be there in full force. He plotted a strategy of how he might withstand them. Humans were so unaware of the spiritual warfare in heaven that often accompanied the fleshly warfare on earth.

Two hundred strong escorted Saul on horseback in his northward passage. Their route passed through the Hinnom Valley, called Gehinnom, on the southwestern outskirts of Jerusalem.

Gehinnom was the territory of Molech.

Mikael kept out of sight on his own steed, high on the ridge above the valley, shadowing Saul. He pulled ahead of the party to reconnoiter the road ahead. He saw several tophets below, some with bronze images of Molech, others without, but all with the burning remains of sacrificed children. Hideous black smoke and the stench of burning flesh filled his nostrils and made him nauseous. It struck him as an odd coincidence that they would happen upon such an extensive display of evil at a time where he could do nothing to address it. His duty was to watch over Saul.

Then Mikael suddenly realized that this atrocity was not happenstance. Human sacrifice empowered Molech. And Saul was within the very lair of the monstrous god of the underworld.

Saul was galloping into a trap.

Mikael raced ahead to the end of the valley where he knew a narrow pass opened up to a plain leading north toward Gibeah.

It was the perfect location for an ambush.

• • • • •

The Maon forest stood a mile away from Nabal's hilltop residence, on the outskirts of Carmel. David had been stewing all day over the response he had received from Nabal. Joab and Abishai had told him of the insulting rejection and accusation of extortion from the corpulent rich man.

David did not like to think of himself as a common outlaw fleecing the innocent. How dare that fat slug make such accusations against God's Chosen Seed. How dare he!

David did not seek the Lord in prayer or with the ephod. He knew Nabal was right in his accusations of extortion. But he did not want to have to humble himself before such a proud and unworthy ingrate. It would only justify Nabal's selfish cruelty and abuse of privilege upon which he had built his entire estate.

David murmured to himself in a manner not unlike Saul's mad rambling, "I have guarded all that this ungrateful swine owns, and nothing has been lost or taken by my men. And what do I receive for my kindness? He returns evil for good. No, this creature must be punished for his insolence. He is an enemy of Yahweh."

David opened the curtain of his tent and shouted, "Benaiah!"

His captain was there in a moment. Benaiah could see David was ragged with bitterness and lack of sleep. His eyes were on fire.

"Prepare for an evening raid. Have four hundred men strap on their swords and suit up."

Joab and Abishai were close by and had arrived as well. Benaiah, said curiously, "My lord?"

David spit out, "By God, I am going to kill every male of this greedy Nabal's household by morning."

Joab and Abishai had no qualms with any order of David's. They were ready to obey.

Benaiah was not so hasty. "Are you sure of this, David?"

David looked at him with anger. "Are you now defying me as Nabal does?"

The accusation offended Benaiah. "I am not defying you, my lord. But I am questioning you. Have you inquired of Yahweh? What does he advise?"

"Benaiah," said David with resolve, "prepare my horse and draw four hundred armed men to raid Nabal's home."

Benaiah sighed with resignation. "We will be ready by moonrise."

David felt smugly confirmed, until Benaiah added, "Yahweh's will be done."

That aggravated David, but he knew he could not criticize or scold Benaiah without incriminating himself in the process. Instead, he pushed it out of his mind. *He* was Yahweh's Chosen Seed. His concern was for the injustice his own men experienced at the whim of this impudent Nabal.

Yes, that was what he was concerned about.

CHAPTER 49

Mikael knelt on the precipice and looked down one hundred feet below into the narrow gorge. Saul and his company of two hundred would have to squeeze through it before continuing their rapid journey north to Gibeah, in order to face the Philistine forces arraying against his capital city.

Saul's forces were still minutes away from the gorge. Mikael had little time to figure out what ambush, if any, was planned by the despicable underworld deity Molech for the king of Israel.

He spotted it.

At the bottom of the canyon, a hundred feet inward, a cadre of twenty priests of Molech hid behind boulders, armed with bows and arrows.

It struck Mikael as odd. Priests of Molech instead of soldiers? A mere twenty? Molech was not the sharpest tool in the workshop, but this strategy seemed below even Molech's stupidity.

Unless it was a diversion.

Just as he realized that, he heard the sound of running behind him. He turned in time to see Molech bearing down on him in a mad dash.

He tried to get up to face his adversary, but it was too late. The eight foot tall god hit him before Mikael could get his balance. He careened over the edge of the cliff.

Mikael was robust and agile. As he fell, he threw out his hands. He caught himself on a ledge a mere ten feet below.

He would not wait for the mole god to follow up his attack. Mikael used his muscular grip and sinewy legs to climb back up the ledge in seconds and bound back out onto the cliff top, ready for a fight.

But he was not ready for what he found before him.

Three gods stood beside Molech in battle position: Dagon with drawn sword, Asherah with javelin and shield, and Ba'alzebul with pummeling mace.

Four gods against a lone archangel.

He stood no chance.

• • • • •

David stopped with his four hundred warriors at the foot of the hill upon which Nabal's home rested. They were ready to ascend the mount and reap vengeance on Nabal.

A servant of the rich man's wife approached them. He begged David's indulgence to allow his master's wife an audience.

She came down the road on a donkey, followed by another servant in an onager-drawn wagon carrying cargo. She stopped and dismounted the donkey to approach David. He sat waiting atop his steed next to Benaiah, Joab, and Abishai.

Joab nodded to David. She was the wife.

David found her presence arresting. Even though cloaked in a nightly robe, he could see her flaming red hair in the moonlight and her piercing blue eyes when she stood before him.

David wondered why Joab did not tell him of this vision of beauty that now knelt before him in humility. Probably because he knew it would cloud David's thinking with curiosity. She had already begun to cloud his mind.

He got down off his horse to stand before her. She fell at his feet in the dirt. "My lord," she said, "allow me to speak."

"Please do," he said, as if in a trance. It was strange how the woman's beauty completely arrested David's emotional faculties. He instantly forgot all the wrath that had driven him to this very spot. Her beauty affected his fury as his music had affected Saul's madness.

She looked up at him. "Place upon me alone the guilt of my husband Nabal and his folly. He is a worthless man. And as Yahweh

242

lives, let all those who seek to do evil to my lord be as Nabal. You are free from bloodguilt should you choose to slay him. By my word, I believe this with all my soul. But I beg of you, please forgive the trespass of your servant. I have brought you a guilt offering."

She spoke with such breathless speed that David could not get a response in edgewise.

"On my wagon are two hundred loaves of bread, skins of wine, prepared sheep, with parched grain and clusters of raisins, as well as cakes of figs. Please give them to your men to eat and drink. For you are Yahweh's Chosen One. You fight Yahweh's battles and there is no evil in you. You are in the care of Yahweh. And when Yahweh has done to you my lord, according to all the good he has spoken concerning you, and when he has appointed you prince over Israel, may my lord suffer no pangs of guilt or cause of grief for having shed any blood without cause. And please, I beg of you, when Yahweh has dealt well with you, please remember your servant, and have mercy upon me."

She suddenly stopped her string of words. She noticed that he was chuckling with amusement.

David got out, "You are quite the talker, but you have not yet told me your name."

"My lord, I apologize," she said. "I am Abigail, wife of Nabal of Maon. I am your servant."

"Well, Abigail. You both amuse me and amaze me."

Now, in the moonlight, he noticed that she had a black eye and a welt on her cheek. He decided to wait to address that.

"How do you know of me? I pray not through the agency of spies."

"Oh no, good sir. I have learned from the visitation of Samuel the Seer to this city."

"I thank Yahweh he tilled the soil for my reception."

"It was truly saddening news to hear he had died within this last moon."

David froze in shock. "Samuel is dead?"

"You have not heard? They buried him in Ramah. I am truly sorry to bear the news to you, my lord."

A shroud of sadness fell over David. "I have been roaming the wilderness for too long. I am only too grateful to have heard it from such a pleasant and graceful soul as yourself."

"No, my lord. I am not as worthy as I appear to you."

"Did Nabal send you?"

"No. I came of my own accord. He is not aware of my actions."

David said, "What will he do when he becomes aware?"

She knew he was referring to her wounds.

"It is not my lord's concern."

David sighed and looked at her thoughtfully. It was hard not to stare, she was such a stunning visage of glory. It was a shame that such a worthless man as Nabal would abuse such a precious gift as this woman before him. She was a vessel of grace.

He said to her, "Blessed be Yahweh, the Elohim of Israel who sent you this day to me. And blessed be you, who have kept me from the bloodguilt of my own hands. Had you not run to me with your humility, truly by morning, there would not be left one male alive in all of Nabal's household."

Abigail began to weep. She alone could see that David's eyes had also teared up. For that single moment, they shared a lifetime of regret. Regret that Yahweh had not brought them together until it was too late for either of them to be together. Regret that he could not free her from her slavery. It was a moment that they would share only with each other, and could never speak of again.

David said, "I receive from you your gift. Go in peace to your house. I have heard your plea and I have granted your petition."

"My lord!" she exclaimed and began to kiss his feet. He pulled away from her, bent down, and out of earshot of his men, he whispered, "It is I who should be kissing your feet, for Yahweh has spoken to me through you when I would not listen to him in any other way. Go, my sister. Return to your husband and know that I will pray that he will be broken and repent of his mistreatment of such an excellent wife that he does not deserve."

She could not look at him. It hurt her more than Nabal's punch. She could only rush back to her donkey and run back up the hill to her prison of suffering.

When Abigail returned to her home, she entered the dining hall to find Nabal knocked out drunk at a table filled with the feast that David and his men should have been eating. She walked past him and went to her bedchamber to weep the night away.

The next morning, she entered the dining hall to find Nabal awakening from his previous night's stupor. His mouth and clothes were covered in his own vomit. He could not raise his fat body from the floor.

"Help me up, wench!" He spit out.

Abigail helped him up, gagging herself from the stench. Maybe she should end it all. What else could she see in her future but more of this same misery, only worse? Her encounter with David mocked her heart with the manly leader she could not have.

She no longer cared what Nabal did to her. She said, "I met David and his men at the foot of the hill last night. He is not a rogue as you claim."

Nabal grumbled, "Well he is no 'chosen one' as that dead seer called him." Then Nabal grew suspicious. "What was he doing at the foot of the hill?"

"He was approaching our home with four hundred men to slaughter you and all the males of your household. But I bribed him with a guilt offering for your offense."

Nabal's eyes went wide with shock. "Four hundred men? He was going to kill us all?"

"Not us all. Just you and the men of the household."

Nabal gasped. He stumbled and fell backward on a cushion. His left hand trembled from some physical malady. He could not speak. He could only gasp for air.

Abigail looked at him and thought he looked like he had turned to stone. In that instant, she knew that Yahweh was finally judging this evil man.

He didn't die. He just became like stone, staring up at the sky, breathing shallowly. His servants placed him on his bed and prayed for a hasty death.

CHAPTER 50

Mikael drew his sword. It was made of steel that had not been revealed to mankind yet, so it seemed like magic when it cut bronze and some iron weapons in two. An archangel with such powerful weaponry could take on a regiment of one hundred of the mightiest gibborim.

But the four beings standing before him on the ledge of a precipice were not going to be as easy to withstand. They were Watcher gods and each one singly was his equal.

Four times that power was overkill. With Ba'alzebul fully healed, it was more like five times overkill.

So why would they be here, instead of at the battle they were leading against Gibeah? His mind raced with confusion to find an answer.

Then it came to him. This was not the diversion, the battle of Gibeah was the diversion. The real goal was to capture Mikael himself, the prince of Israel.

Well, he thought, *they picked the wrong archangel to mess with. I have a chosen nation to protect.*

He pulled out his horn to call for help, but Ba'alzebul's mace smashed it out of his hands.

Dagon assaulted him with a barrage of sword slashes and strikes.

Mikael kept him at bay, but almost got stung by Asherah's javelin from the other side.

He dodged and kept moving. His Karabu training was his only hope. It was the heavenly battle technique of Yahweh's archangels developed to protect the Garden of Eden in primordial days. They had taught the human giant killers Enoch, Methuselah, Lamech, and Caleb the Way of Karabu, but now he would need to call upon his training to survive this ordeal.

He flipped, spun, and danced around the four attacking gods and their weapons. It frustrated the malevolent beings, which was to Mikael's advantage.

But archangels were still created beings. He began to grow tired. They were wearing him down.

Dagon's sword grazed Mikael's arm, cutting through his tunic.

He was not going to be able to keep it up. He would have to do something drastic.

Ba'alzebul moved in on Mikael.

The biggest, meanest, mightiest of the gods had been waiting for his opportune moment when Mikael was just weary enough, just worn enough, to be incapable of expecting the unexpected.

Ba'alzebul took the lead and pounded Mikael's sword with his mace and backed him up against the ledge.

Mikael looked down to the chasm floor. Saul and his forces made their way through the chasm below after slaughtering the priests of Molech. It wasn't a fair fight.

And neither was this fight. But Saul was safe. He had made it through and went north toward Gibeah.

But the gods were not here for Saul. They were here for Mikael.

Ba'alzebul suddenly threw down his mace and rushed Mikael like a bull goring its prey.

Mikael didn't register why, until Ba'alzebul hit him. The two of them launched off into space, plummeting toward the chasm floor two hundred feet below.

Angels and gods could not die. But they were not mere spirits. They were enfleshed spirits. While it was unique flesh that would heal miraculously, it was still flesh that could be hurt — as Ba'alzebul knew all too well from his own painful experience in the molten earth.

They hit the ground with a powerful thud and sank several feet into the dirt.

Every bone in Mikael's body was broken in the fall. He was paralyzed in excruciating pain.

Ba'alzebul had been on top of Mikael, so while he too would be somewhat incapacitated, it would not be as bad for him, having used Mikael's body as a cushion in the fall.

As Mikael slipped into a state of delirious pain, he knew that their goal had been to capture him this way. To ambush him and therefore make both Saul and David more vulnerable to human attack. But what did they plan for Mikael? He could not begin to imagine.

• • • • •

Ten days passed after the rich man Nabal had been struck by an attack in his internal organs when he learned about his deliverance from the hand of David by the word of his wife Abigail. At first, he had become like a stone. But he began to get well with each day. He had lost much of his strength and retained tremors in his hands. The left side of his body seemed weakened along with the left side of his face. But his bitter, ornery spirit remained, and even deepened. Through sheer will power, he was able to get up and limp around. Abigail sought to help him, but he berated her and insulted her with foul language. It was as if the sickness that was intended by God to humble him made him worse in his bitter resolve to defy Yahweh's Chosen One.

Abigail brought him food. He threw it in her face.

She tried to wash him and help him change clothes, but he pushed her away and cursed her.

On the tenth evening of his recuperation, Abigail brought him a pheasant to eat. He finally decided to consume some food and took out his knife to cut it up. He would not let her help him cut up the food, so it took him twice as long and he dropped as many pieces of the fowl on the floor as he placed in his mouth.

Finally, he stopped and glared at her, watching him. "What are you staring at? You think I am pathetic?"

"No, my lord."

"Where do you go at night as I lay here?"

"I retire to my bedchamber."

"No, you do not."

"Where else would I go, my lord? It is where I have always slept."

"You are sneaking down to that camp of brigands aren't you?"

"My lord?"

"I remember the look you gave that messenger of David. You wanted him, did you not?"

"You are my husband. I remain faithful."

"You are a faithless no-good slut and you are seeing him behind my back, are you not?"

"My lord, I am not."

"Come here, you whore." Nabal dropped his food and grabbed Abigail's neck with his greasy hands.

She choked and gasped for air.

"Admit it! Admit it, you harlot! You are unfaithful to me!"

She could not speak because his grip had fastened around her wind pipe. He did not have his usual strength, but it was still enough to strangle the life out of her.

Her hands desperately sought anything to use as a weapon to protect herself. She felt dizzy and on the verge of losing consciousness.

His screaming at her began to fade in her ears. She could only think of dying at the hands of this worthless scrap of human debris.

Then, her hand fortuitously fastened upon the knife he had been using to cut into his meat.

She swung upward with the blade. It sunk deep into his neck. She withdrew it to plunge it again.

But his grip loosened. His hands reached up to hold his neck wound that spurted blood faster than he could stop it.

She must have hit his artery.

He was not going to have the chance to hurt her ever again. She plunged the knife into his belly and slid the blade to the side like gutting a fish. His rolling fat was difficult to penetrate, but her blade had gone deep enough to open a cavity from which his bowels now spilled out onto the ground.

He fell over and groaned his last words, "You self-righteous bitch."

And he died.

She turned to see two manservants at the door. They had seen it all. They rushed to her side. One pulled her to safety and the other began to clean up the mess. They would make sure this would not become a scandal. The fat old hog deserved every ounce of pain, which was nowhere near the retribution for the lifetime of pain he had inflicted upon Abigail and the entire household.

But now he was finally gone. Abigail was free.

When David received word of Nabal's demise, he praised Yahweh for the merciful rescue of Abigail. He immediately sent for her to ask her hand in marriage.

Though she was a most desirable woman, and though they had been drawn to each other with intense attraction, it was still a political move for them both. For her, she would have the protection of a husband whom she was sure would be the next king. For him, he gained the wealth and resources of a rich, landowning widow, who was a high-ranking member of the clan that controlled the Hebron area, a target for his eventual proclamation of kingship.

In this world of blood and iron, romantic attraction was a luxury in the politics of kingdoms and dynasties. David was overwhelmed with gratitude to Yahweh for giving him far beyond what he deserved with this amazing woman he was about unite with in holy matrimony.

CHAPTER 51

David and Abigail performed a wedding ceremony as quickly as possible. But the particular formality of a celebration would not be so hurried. David's men had traveled long, fought hard, and suffered many losses for their leader. He wanted them to feel appreciated.

So Abigail set up a feast to last for several days at her home on the hilltop for the six hundred of David's company. She gave above and beyond what Nabal had withheld from David's request. There was much meat to fill their bellies, and much beer and wine to make their hearts glad. It was a welcome respite from the endless chase they had been engaged in, avoiding Saul's malevolent intent.

Late in the first evening, David and Abigail left for their first night together in the shepherd's quarters at the base of the hill. As strong as David's desire was to share their bodies, he felt a deeper necessity to first share their souls. She made him feel young again, almost innocent. But he also knew that she had suffered greatly under Nabal's abuse, and he wanted to treat her with the kindness and gentleness she had always deserved but had never known.

They sat just outside the quarters with the silent sheep sleeping in the field beneath the full moon. They could hear the distant sounds of his men enjoying themselves in the residence at the top of the hill.

David sighed, looking up at the sky, and said, "I miss those days, as a shepherd boy, with nothing but my staff and lyre. The quiet at night. The peace. Looking up at the vault of heaven and imagining what the waters above it looked like and what the heavenly temple above the waters was like."

"I would be bored," said Abigail. "And lonely. As much as I love the beauty of Yahweh's creation, I much prefer people."

"Ah, but that is where you are wrong," he said. "With Yahweh you are never alone."

"Then why did Yahweh say that Adam was alone when the two of them were in the Garden together?"

David thought for a moment. "I had never thought of that."

"Forgive me, my lord," she said. "I did not mean to offend you."

He looked over at her, surprised. His surprise melted when he saw her bruised face. She had been beaten down for so long by her worthless husband that she did not feel she could express herself without being reproached.

He touched her face with his fingertip—her precious, beautiful face. He wanted to feel the bruise so he could absorb it, take it away from her and onto himself, but he could not.

"You did not offend me, my lovely wife. You just blessed me. You made me wiser."

He could see her eyes tearing up. She had never been adored. The irony was that he adored her and appreciated her even more than he had his first wife Michal, now lost to him. Abigail was more mature, compared with Michal's youth. Abigail was a deeper, fuller woman because of her age—because of her suffering. David could see in her eyes that there were entire worlds to explore inside this wonderful woman of mystery. At the age of thirty, he had finally found someone he felt could understand him, could stand up to him, a woman who knew who she was, who could support him from strength instead of weakness, a woman instead of a girl. He had finally found his equal.

He could not ignore the painful marks on her face. He touched them again and said, "I will never hurt you."

Through her tears she responded, "I will never hurt you."

He said, "I will woo you. And I will tend you, like a loving shepherd, or like a bee that draws the honey from a flower. You are the most beautiful blossom I have ever had the privilege to experience in my entire life."

She returned his praise with a knowing smile, and said, "Well, then, woo me, why don't you, shepherd boy?"

David smiled back, held his lyre, and began to play a song — a very familiar song for him.

Hear, O daughter, and consider, and incline your ear:
forget your people and your father's house,
and the king will desire your beauty.
Since he is your lord, bow to him.
All glorious is the princess in her chamber...

He stopped playing right in the middle of the bridal hymn. It was the song he had used over the years to get what he wanted from women. He would play it and they would melt and become like clay in his hands. It was a trick he used to manipulate, and in the presence of this wise and goodly woman, he could no longer play it.

"Why did you stop?" she asked.

"I think there is a better song to sing."

He began to play. It was a song that united both of their hearts.

My God, my God, why have you forsaken me?
Why are you so far from saving me,
from the words of my groaning?
O my God, I cry by day, but you do not answer,
and by night, but I find no rest.
Yet you are holy, enthroned on the praises of Israel.
In you our fathers trusted;
they trusted, and you delivered them.
To you they cried and were rescued;
in you they trusted and were not put to shame.

It was not a song of seduction, but a song of suffering. It was in her suffering that he could touch her. For they had both felt the pangs of oppression, and yet the words were transcendent, pointing to something much higher, something beyond them.

For dogs encompass me;
a company of evildoers encircles me;
they have pierced my hands and feet—

I can count all my bones—
they stare and gloat over me;
they divide my garments among them,
    and for my clothing they cast lots.
But you, O Yahweh, do not be far off!
    O you my help, come quickly to my aid!
Deliver my soul from the sword,
    my precious life from the power of the dog!
Save me from the mouth of the lion!

It was not through the childish fun and shallow pleasures of youth that a man and woman would become one soul and plumb the depths of intimacy. It was through mutual pain and suffering. It was in sharing hope in the midst of pain that they touched the very presence of God.

You who fear Yahweh, praise him!
All you Seed of Jacob, glorify him,
    and stand in awe of him,
    all you Seed of Israel!
All the ends of the earth shall remember and turn to Yahweh,
    and all the families of the nations shall worship before
    you.
For kingship belongs to Yahweh,
    and he rules over the nations.

His music melted her heart. Not through manipulation or artifice, but through truth. Because the way to capture the heart of a woman of God was to be a man after God's own heart.

He kissed her, as he had never kissed a woman before.

CHAPTER 52

David's six hundred were a hearty lot. They were mighty gibborim warriors who fought hard and played harder. Many of them had been outlaws or rebellious men, so the combination of a wedding party with plenty of flowing wine and beer, carried the potential for getting out of control.

Up at Nabal's hilltop residence, now Abigail's, men sang songs, told battle stories, and competed in feats of strength with one another. Their rowdiness was held in check by some of the commanders of the Three and the Thirty who watched over the festivities like archangels.

Two of those watchers were Joab and Abishai, who refused to lose their wits or give in to their fleshly desires ever again, because of the secret guilt over their past betrayal. They remained sober and alert this evening, like a couple of sheep dogs.

Two drunken men began to brawl with weapons, so the brothers blindsided them both and knocked them into unconsciousness. They tied them up where they would awake the next morning to face their discipline.

Benaiah was not so guiltily disposed. He had had much to drink. But he did exercise restraint by stopping before he became too dizzy. He enjoyed the merriment that wine brought but was also determined to circumscribe that joy within the guidelines of Yahweh's moral law. Yahweh's good gifts were so easily abused to excess by the weakness that was humanity.

He scanned the crowd of drunken baboons, proud competitive peacocks and cawing crows. It seemed that fallen man so quickly degenerated into an animal in his behavior. Yet animals were not so foolish.

He saw a small group of men cheer loudly. They had just watched the Mouse, Jonathan ben Shimei, shoot his seventh arrow into a bulls eye the size of a sparrow. He really was an incredible marksman. But then Jonathan took his seventh drink and fell down to the ground, dead drunk, Benaiah smiled to himself. An incredible marksman who could hold his aim even when he could not hold his drink.

The Lion Men of Moab participated in the feast, eating their share of the meats and vegetables, but they seemed the only ones who did not drink. These half animals were the most disciplined of the entire regiment. Benaiah chuckled to himself at the irony. They had proven him the fool when they saved him from the Rephaim attack in the forest. He looked over them with respect, as he had come to know each of them by name.

Then something struck him. They weren't all there. He counted them. There were only eight of the eleven at the tables. The two who had saved him, Elzabad and Machbannai, along with a third, Jeremiah, were missing. He thought that maybe they were relieving themselves. He thought he should relieve himself.

Benaiah got up and stumbled out to the bushes. He breathed a sigh of relief as the pressure released and he realized his bladder had been quite full. He barely moved his sword in time to keep it from getting sprayed. Perhaps he did drink a bit too much.

He saw the bright moon and looked down upon the field at the bottom of the hill. He could see the shepherd quarters where David and Abigail were having much more fun than he was. He longed for a woman, a soft soul he could love and protect.

Something else caught his eye. He thought he saw three figures finding their way down the hill in crouched posture.

They had manes.

• • • • •

David and Abigail lay in each others' arms inside the shepherd's cottage on the floor. David felt undeserving of this amazing woman.

Abigail, finally, for the first time in her life, felt loved and accepted. For the first time in her life, she had experienced sexual love. She did not know such a thing could be. Her only knowledge of sex was the laborious and slavish use, at the hands of a selfish monster. But that was all gone and in the past. It could never be forgotten, but it could be covered. It had damaged her, but it could be redeemed. David had redeemed her, freed her from prison. He had tended her with care and had drawn honey from her petals as he had promised.

At first, she could not do it. Years of abuse had risen up from within and tore at her soul. Fear seized her, self-loathing. She even pushed David away reflexively.

But he understood what she faced and waited with patience. He whispered a lullaby of loving words that soothed her fears. He had a way with words, this one.

When she had finally given him permission, David had caressed her gently and had handled her like a lyre, plucking her strings with just the right pressure and creating music she had never heard before. So this was what it meant to be united with a real man, to share the pleasure of the marriage bed, with a man of Yahweh, no less! Yahweh made all things better. *All things*, especially sexual union. Yahweh was as much a part of their love together as he was a part of every blessing in her life. She had been so broken and abused. But now she saw hope for healing.

David's head jerked up. "Did you hear that?"

"Hear what?" she asked. She still swam in the delight of her afterglow.

David got up and walked to the window. A soft breeze blew upon his face. She smiled, looking upon his naked form in the moonlight, a taut and muscular body.

David turned from the window toward the door—and all Sheol broke loose.

The lattices of the window shattered with the incoming missile of an Ariel. He rolled to the floor, snapped out his massive claws and slammed them down toward Abigail's head.

David grabbed her feet and jerked her out of the way before the claws could make contact. They jammed into the floor boards and stuck. She screamed.

David pulled her up and pushed her behind him.

The cottage was small, only about twelve feet square. She was going to get hurt in the fray.

The Lion Man growled with anger. It was Elzabad.

The door to David's left burst inward off its hinges and slammed to the floor.

It was another Lion Man, Machbannai. He bared his fangs.

The other window lattices shattered inward as the third Lion Man, Jeremiah, leapt in and onto his feet.

David was outnumbered. He could take one of them, maybe hurt a second. But three of them in this small closed space was certain death.

His back was to the wall.

These Lion Men had fooled everyone by saving Benaiah's life, only to elicit the trust they needed to spring their long planned attack. They were the most clever of assassins.

The trio of assassins were surprised when Machbannai, at the door, was yanked backwards from behind—by Benaiah.

The other two Lion Men were thrown off. They had not anticipated discovery.

David saw his one opportunity and pulled Abigail to the door. He didn't know if there were other Lion Men outside, but if she stayed inside, she would surely die. With all his might, he threw her outside the doorway about six feet.

She landed with a thud and felt her rib bruised. But she knew David was getting her out of the way of the assassins. She got up and ran.

When David jumped outside the door, the two Lion Men followed. He stood before them vulnerable without a weapon. They too were without weapons. But they were like lions in the wilderness, well-equipped to vanquish their prey with muscle, tooth, and claw.

David saw Benaiah on the ground still wrestling with Machbannai. Ariels were extraordinarily strong and agile. David had once seen one of them take on a bear and win.

The other two circled David, claws extended, fangs bared, ready to pounce.

The sound of cracking bone turned everyone's heads. Benaiah's grappling hold had stayed strong. He had broken the neck of his adversary.

Benaiah was no bear. He was a behemoth.

Benaiah pushed the body off himself, drew his sword, and jumped to his feet.

He spit out, "Let us teach these pussy cats a lesson."

Benaiah tossed his sword to David, just as Jeremiah jumped. The Lion Man knocked the sword away as he tumbled into the dust. When the growling leonine warrior got to his feet, he stood over the sword.

Benaiah pulled his dagger.

Unfortunately for Benaiah and his one blade, Elzabad's two hands with claws was like facing a warrior with ten knives, and ten knives on his feet as back up.

Elzabad growled and charged him with claws extended. The growl exposed the Lion Man's teeth, resembling a mouthful of knives.

Elzabad swung his paws. Benaiah countered with his sweeping blade. They dodged and attacked each other in a synchronized dance of death. One false move would result in a slit throat or a gaping wound.

Benaiah could not keep up. He had been drinking too much earlier and his reflexes were slower than usual.

Two slices of the Lion Man's talons drew blood on his arm and chest.

Jeremiah did not pick up the blade. He wanted to kill the messiah king with his bare paws. He wanted to feel the flesh rip with his fingers, and taste the blood on his lips as the life left David's veins.

But David had much experience killing lions. And Jeremiah acted entirely predictably for one.

Jeremiah growled. He crouched low, muscles tightened, ready to bound upon his victim.

David saw the movements, planned his response.

When the Lion Man leapt, David ducked down and rolled beneath the flying assassin who landed in the dirt again.

David was still on the ground when Jeremiah gathered himself and immediately jumped toward David again.

Benaiah did not have a multitude of blades like his opponent. But his opponent could not throw his blades.

Benaiah saw the right moment and hurled his dagger at Elzabad when he was off balance.

It struck the Lion Man in his solar plexus, stunning him.

Before he could pull it out, Benaiah had launched into Elzabad, taking him down into the dirt.

Jeremiah jumped at David.

David snatched up the sword from the ground and rolled back around, thrusting the blade up at his flying predator.

The sword impaled the Lion Man through his gut.

He yelped and landed on David with a groan of deep pain, but he was not dead. He was close to David's face and had enough left in him for one last act. The Lion Man opened his mouth wide in order to rip out David's throat.

Before he could bite, another knife blade was embedded in his back from behind.

It was Abigail. She had found David's dagger in the cottage and used it against the beast to save her beloved.

The Lion Man was still alive and deadly. He swatted Abigail to the ground.

He turned back to David, whose arms were still pinned beneath him.

This was it. David's last stand. He had lost.

A blurred flurry of fur launched through the air and hit Jeremiah, knocking him off David and to the ground.

It was Ezer, the chief of the Lion Men.

Two other Lion Men were with him and they tore into Jeremiah's body with ferocious abandon.

David backed out of their way, disturbed by the gruesome sight.

The scene looked like a pride of hungry lions tearing into their prey, only it was one of their own. They were reaping judgment upon the assassin.

David crawled to Abigail and held onto her.

They turned and saw the other five Lion Men of Moab surrounding them.

Abigail gasped.

Joab's voice penetrated the night, "My lord, David!"

Everyone turned to see Joab and Abishai with a host of twenty men with drawn weapons.

David held up his hand to Joab. "NO!"

Joab and Abishai froze. They were about to attack the Lion Men.

But David knew he was no longer in danger.

Ezer slowly approached David, his figure covered in blood.

He stopped several feet from David and dropped to his knees.

"My lord," said Ezer. "Forgive me. I did not know we had traitors in our midst."

Joab thought it could be just another ploy.

David knew it was not. Ezer and his Lion Men had saved David from their own kindred. They were more loyal than half the mercenaries in David's band.

David smiled and placed his hand on Ezer's head and kissed him.

He said to Joab and the men, "We are safe."

Joab turned to the other warriors and said, "Let's get these bodies out of here and leave our lord alone with his lady."

Though she appreciated the gesture, Abigail was too traumatized to be able to enjoy the rest of the evening. She just wanted to be held in her husband's protective embrace and be told everything would be alright.

But everything was not alright.

Abigail whispered in dread, "David."

David looked over to see the third assassin lying over Benaiah's supine body like a sheet of death.

He crossed the space to Benaiah. Two others of Joab's group helped him lift the body of the Lion Man off David's savior.

Benaiah was covered in blood, but he was not dead. He was only groggy.

David saw the blade in Elzabad's gut.

The tumble had knocked Benaiah senseless. But he was back.

All he could muster was, "I told you so, my lord. But you did not take me seriously."

David smiled and hugged his beefy friend. "You did indeed, Benaiah. I will make it my duty to take your annoying advice more seriously in the future."

Benaiah grinned through bloody teeth. But he would never dare admit to David that he had been on the verge of drunkenness the entire fight.

It had almost cost him his king.

David was not satisfied to move on. He became serious again and stared at Benaiah as if he did not trust him. He said, "You fight with a fearlessness I have not seen in many. You do not care if you die."

"I do not, my lord," admitted Benaiah.

"I want to know why."

"I will not intrude on your wedding night, my lord and lady."

"You already have," said Abigail. "And now you have me as curious as my husband. I want to hear your story."

Benaiah stood dumbfounded.

• • • • •

"I lived in the Negeb near the border of Edom," said Benaiah. He sat uncomfortably in the cottage with David and Abigail beside him. The other warriors were already back up by the house on the hilltop. Abigail offered Benaiah some wine.

"No. I have had plenty for tonight, my lady," he replied with a wave of his hand. *More than plenty*, he thought.

"Relax, Benaiah," said Abigail. "Tonight, you are with friends."

Benaiah tried to relax, but she was stunningly beautiful, and no matter what they told him, he still felt like a child who walked in on his parents kissing and they pretended not to notice.

He journeyed on with some difficulty, "Edomite women are of course forbidden to our people."

Abigail brightened. She knew exactly where this was going. This *was* going to be an interesting story after all.

"I fell in love with one. Her name was…" his voice cracked with pain, "Imashtart."

Abigail's eyes began to tear slightly with empathy.

"Since my father was high priest, it did not help my cause, of course. It made it worse. I kept it a secret because I felt that the community was being intolerant and did not understand the Edomite people. That they hated them without cause and needed to be more open-minded."

Benaiah sighed. "It was just my own attempt to justify disobeying Yahweh's Law.

"One night, our tribe was attacked by the Edomites, and we lost more than half of the village. They knew the watchmen locations and the hour of changeover, all our strategic defenses."

Benaiah's long pause struck Abigail like a javelin. She and David knew what came next.

"Imashtart had told them."

A chill penetrated the bones of David and Abigail.

"At first I would not believe it. But I knew. And everywhere I went, everyone I saw looked at me as the fool whose heart betrayed their people and got their husband, wife, or child killed. I could not live under such guilt. That was when I cared no longer whether I lived or died. I set myself apart to the holiness that Yahweh demanded of our people. I left the village and became a wanderer—an outlaw."

He looked somberly at David. "That is why I do not trust foreigners, especially as allies."

David wondered what it would be like to be betrayed by his own beloved. Do we ever really know those we love? Do we not all have our dark secrets? Though Abigail was justified in killing Nabal, would that make her more capable of betrayal in the future?

"You are no outlaw," said David. "You are a man properly broken by Yahweh's Law. That is why you are my most trusted follower."

Abigail added, "The broken in spirit shall inherit the earth."

David mused over her statement. He could see that the wisdom of his new wife would be a wellspring of life to him. He was most blessed of men.

The heartbreak of Benaiah began to heal with the slightest of hope in the presence of this amazing woman whose very existence disproved the dark mistrust of women that shrouded his soul.

CHAPTER 53

Saul's battle against the five Philistine armies at Gibeah went surprisingly well for the mad king. He had returned in time to mount his forces. The Philistines seemed uncoordinated in their strategy and had fought half-heartedly as if they were without leadership. The Israelites were able to repel their invaders quite easily. Saul noticed that many of their enemy's iron weapons that lay in the battlefield had failed. It was usual for some weapons to break under the stress of combat, but there seemed more than usual this time. It had all the appearances to Saul of a miraculous victory. He wondered if maybe Yahweh had granted him favor again.

He quickly banished that mad thought from his mind. Yahweh could not possibly have changed his mind. David was still alive.

As quickly as he had arrived at Gibeah to finish his fight, just as quickly he returned to the south to hunt his ultimate nemesis, the son of Jesse.

He received intelligence that David was now hiding out in the wilderness of Ziph. So Saul took three thousand of his men and camped at the hill of Hachilah, which was beside the road on the east of Jeshimon. He sent several scouts out to reconnoiter the area and find David's men.

David caught those scouts and held them captive in the wilderness.

It was the midnight hour. Dark clouds obscured the moon. David stood with his leaders of Three and Thirty gathered around him. He looked troubled and weary. David had left Abigail at her residence to keep her safe until the day that he could return and bring her with him. He was lonely for her. It showed on his countenance. But then a resolve replaced that sadness.

He spoke to his men, "Who will go with me into the camp to Saul?"

The commanders were confused. Joab spoke up first, "What do you mean 'go to Saul?' Do you mean to make a treaty?"

"No," said David.

"Do you mean to assassinate him?" said Joab. "If so, you should leave that to us."

"No, I do not mean assassinate," said David. "We have been on the run from Saul for years. I want to prove to him that I am not his enemy. I will sneak in and take something personal of his and return to our camp. Then on the morrow, I will show him that I could have killed him, but did not. Perhaps then he will finally believe me."

"But you have already done that before," complained Joab. Joab referred to a previous time where they had been hiding out in a cave in the wilderness of Engedi. Saul had happened upon their hiding place without knowing it. He went into the cave to relieve himself. When he did, David cut off the corner of his robe in secret. When Saul left the cave, David followed him and showed Saul the piece of robe, proving his innocence and lack of hostility toward the king.

Joab completed his argument, "Saul bellowed with the tears of a crocodile until you turned your back. Then he sought you out again in the wilderness of Maon. He is a madman, my lord, and you know full well he is not to be trusted."

Abishai piped in. "I will go with you, David. I can pin him to the ground with my javelin. I will not need more than one thrust."

"No," said David. "No man can put his hand against Yahweh's anointed and be guiltless. We will enter his camp while everyone is asleep, and we will silently take his spear and the water jug at his head. We will return to our camp without waking them up. The next morning, Saul will surely see that I intend him no harm."

Joab would not shut up. "My lord, David. I must speak up. Your plan is a crazy one." The others nodded, but none were willing to use those frank words. "*You* are Yahweh's anointed messiah. Of all people, you should not be the one to endanger yourself with such outrageous plans. If you think you can sneak into the enemy camp and make your way to the center where Saul is and just slip out without waking a soul, I have to say that maybe you have gone as crazy as Saul."

David chuckled. "Joab, once again, I appreciate your candidness. And you are right. What I seek to do *is* crazy. But I am in a desperate situation that only faith can answer. I must do something that so clearly shows Yahweh's favor and defines my innocence, that even the most hard-hearted would have to accept it. If you really want to help out, Joab, then I suggest you get on your knees and pray that Saul's camp would be cast into a deep sleep."

David slapped Abishai on the back. "My mind is made up. Let us go, you and I, Abishai, and show these warriors who they are tangling with."

David and Abishai left the conference of the leaders. They slipped into Saul's camp while everyone slept, and took Saul's spear and jug of water from beside his head. Everyone was indeed in a deep sleep from Yahweh that allowed the two thieves to return to their own camp undiscovered.

The next morning, David assembled his men on the mountain opposite Hachilah, with a valley in between them. David shouted out to Saul's general of his forces, "Abner, wake up, you sluggard!"

From across the valley, he heard in response, "Who is this who calls my name?"

David yelled, "Who are you, Abner, son of Ner, that you have not kept watch over your king! For behold, last night, I was in your camp, and could have killed your king, but you did nothing to stop me!"

"Show yourself, villain!" yelled Abner.

David shouted, "Let me ask you a question, mighty Abner. Where is your lord's spear and jar of water that was at his head?"

There was no response from Saul's hill. David let him have time to discover it was gone. Then he shouted out, "Behold, my servant in the valley, returning the spear and jug of water that I took while you snored!"

David watched one of his men jogging across the valley to place the spear and jug halfway between the forces before returning. One of Saul's men ran to retrieve them.

Then Saul's voice bellowed across the valley. "Is this the voice of David, son of Jesse that I hear?"

David shouted, "It is my voice, my lord the king. Why do you pursue me? What evil is in my hands? The king of Israel has sought out a single flea like one who hunts a partridge in the mountains! If it is Yahweh who has stirred you against me, then may he accept my sacrifice. But if it is men or worse who have stirred you, then may they be cursed before Yahweh! My lord, the anointed king, I will never raise my hand against you!"

David stopped. There was silence for a moment.

Then Saul's cracking voice came across the valley. "I have sinned! Please forgive me, my son, David. I have acted foolishly in regard to you. Blessed be you, my son David! Please return, and I will return to you no more harm!"

Benaiah, Joab, and Abishai looked at David's face. The commanders awaited orders.

David looked at the ground painfully. "Joab, you were right. He cannot be trusted."

Joab felt vindicated, but he did not feel any better. Their prospects were still not hopeful.

David added, "And I am done running."

Now they were all confused. Was he going to turn himself in after all?

"What do you mean?" said Benaiah.

David continued without answering his question, "If I do not do this, I will perish one day by the hand of Saul."

Do what? they all thought.

"Gather the men. We are going to go to the one place that Saul will never follow me."

Joab blurted out, "Where is that, Sheol?"

CHAPTER 54

A few miles outside the city of Gath in a secret location in the hills, a band of fifty Gittite citizens and warriors congregated around a speaker. What marked these people out was not readily observable. They appeared to be normal Philistines from different sectors of life and did not stand out in any external way.

But they were rebels and subversives. They had been carefully sought out and vetted by the leader over years of careful covert deliberations. Some were regular citizens of Gath, more were disillusioned warriors. But they were all united in one commitment: they were secretly devoted to Yahweh, the god of Israel. If any of their neighbors found out about their beliefs, they would be handed over to the authorities, imprisoned, tortured, and executed. Apostasy was considered the highest treason against Dagon and his Philistine pentapolis.

Their leader was Ittai the Gittite. He had just explained to them how he had accomplished his sabotage against the Philistine armies. Ittai had been commissioned to forge some weapons for the previous united effort of the five cities in their battle at Gibeah against Israel. There are always a certain number of weapons that break or fail in battles. It was a normal statistic of fortune. But Ittai had deliberately smithed his weapons with a greater weakness so that a higher percentage of them would fail in battle, thus placing the soldiers at the mercy of their enemies and Ittai's secret allies, the Israelites. But he had to carefully plan it all out without getting caught. If too many weapons failed, word would get around and eventually lead back to him. So he tried to decrease the quality of his weapons just enough so that it would not be noticeable.

Evidently, it had not been noticed. One of the rebels, a member of the government, explained that the palace officials had still not become aware of his subterfuge. Ittai was safe for the time being.

They moved on to discuss their next issue on the agenda: a secret envoy.

One of them voiced the concern, "What you are asking of us, Ittai, is the highest risk we have taken yet."

"But necessary," he countered.

A warrior jumped in, "Whoever is in this envoy, if Israel does not believe them, they will execute them."

Another added, "Or worse, hand them back over to Achish, and we would be discovered. All of us, killed."

Ittai said, "We have counted that cost long ago."

"And what exactly are we to ask the Israelite army of rebels?"

Ittai said, "If their leader David is a messiah king. If he will bring redemption to the whole world, not merely Israel."

One of two new visitors to the group asked from behind his hooded cloak, "Do you mean for us to leave Gath and join the Israelites?"

"Exactly."

The other hooded visitor said, "But you do not know where this David and his men are hidden."

"We will seek them and we will find them," said Ittai with confidence. But he added for good measure, "We will pray for Yahweh to lead us to them."

"It is too late for that," said the first hooded visitor.

Ittai looked at him, confused. "What do you mean?"

The visitor gave a whistle call.

Suddenly, soldiers rose up, surrounding them entirely above the ridge. There were hundreds of them.

Some of the rebels gasped. A few women fainted. Warriors grabbed their weapons.

So this is it, thought Ittai. *We are finally found out. Now, we all die.* The two visitors had been brought by the government official. He had told Ittai they were safe. But they were plants of Achish, whose army now surrounded the rebels with arrows pointed at them from above.

The visitor barked out, "Hold your weapons, rebels! You do not stand a chance."

They circled around close to each other, looking up at the dark warriors above them, ready to rain down death.

The two visitors approached Ittai, who stood without concern. He was resigned to death anyway.

The lead visitor said with a casual calmness, "Ittai the Gittite. I was not aware you had done so much damage."

As the visitor came closer, Ittai planned what he would do. He would grab his dagger and leap upon the spy, and kill at least one of them before dying in a rainstorm of arrows. But he would get at least one of them.

The visitor was almost within jumping range. He continued, "Your prayers to find David are of no avail. And do you know why, Ittai the Gittite?"

"No," said Ittai snidely, "Tell me why." He was ready to pounce.

"Because David has found you."

Ittai paused. What did he mean David has found me?

The visitors pulled down their hoods for a better view.

The leader said, "I am David son of Jesse, and this is the captain of my guard, Benaiah from Kabzeel. These warriors you see about you on the ridge, they are my trusted gibborim."

Ittai's knees went weak.

David smiled. "And apparently, I have fifty more loyal followers to add to my forces."

Ittai fell to his knees. "My lord and king. We are but Philistines."

David lifted up Ittai's face. "Yahweh accepts any who repent and worship him from all tribes and nations."

The other rebels followed suit and bowed to the ground before their savior.

Ittai said, "We are servants of my lord. Command us and we will obey."

David turned and said to them all, "I want you all to return to your lives in Gath and the other cities."

"What will you do? We want to help you." said Ittai.

"I will come and join you."

"You will come to Gath?"

"Yes. I have been running from King Saul for too long, and I am weary. The only place he will not follow me is into Philistia. So into Gath I must go. You can help me by hiding me."

Ittai said, "I do not mean to be insolent, my lord, but Gath is the city of Goliath, the champion you defeated."

"Many years ago," said David.

"Gittites have never forgotten. They would hand you over to the king upon sight—if they did not tear you apart first. Achish is obsessed with conquering Israel. And there is a squad of assassins in Gath who are sworn to hunt you down. Gath is the one place you must not go."

"That is why I want to go there. I have a plan that may actually draw the interest of your king away from hanging me and onto harboring me."

Ittai could not possibly figure out what madness David was planning. He prayed that this Chosen Seed was indeed the messiah of life and not the angel of death.

CHAPTER 55

The city of Gath was the earliest Philistine settlement in Canaan. It had a large urban populace on one hundred and twenty-five square miles of land. As the furthest inland stronghold, nearest the Valley of the Terebinth, it maintained a strong siege system that made it impregnable to hostile forces. The walls were thirty feet high, surrounded by a man-made siege trench and an earthen embankment called a "berm" that made approach to the walls by besiegers extremely difficult. It was guarded by a threefold entrance gate to the city, watched over by a regiment of Gittite warriors.

All this fortification would be useless against the six figures who rode their horses to the city entrance. They would not be besieging the walls, and they would not be fighting the army of Gittites. They were simply nomadic travelers on a personal quest. They did not hide themselves, because they were not recognizable to any human inhabitants.

They were archangels.

Uriel, Gabriel, Raphael, Saraqael, Raguel, and Remiel walked their horses through the large Phoenician carved gates and into the city. They made no attempt to disguise themselves from the gods of the Philistines because they wanted the gods to know they had arrived.

They wanted a showdown.

They quartered their horses and found a tavern in which to gather, eat, and spread some gossip.

•••••

"What are we going to do?" cried Molech. He trembled with fear and wished he was back in the Hinnom Valley playing with his children.

"Shut your disgusting mouth, mole," spit Asherah. They stood in the large secret cavern carved out of the rock fifty feet beneath the temple of Dagon. Dagon and Ba'alzebul watched Asherah walk up to the rock wall where they had fastened Mikael's body. Or rather, where they had fastened the parts of Mikael's body.

When they had ambushed Mikael in the Valley of Hinnom, Ba'alzebul had fallen with him some two hundred feet to the valley floor where all Mikael's bones had been shattered. Ba'alzebul was also incapacitated in the fall, but because he used Mikael's body as a cushion, and because he had a much stronger bodily structure, he had healed more quickly and was ready for action.

But before Mikael could heal to move at all, they had him drawn and quartered. All four of his limbs were severed from his body, and he was beheaded. As an angel, he could not die, but this was surely a living hell as they pinned all his body parts spread out on the wall so he could look helplessly down upon them and their mockery.

Asherah looked into Mikael's eyes.

He could not respond verbally because his head was severed from his voice box and lungs, which were separated from each other by about six feet, like a sick spread-out puzzle. But he could watch her and hear their discussion.

Ba'alzebul said, "The only time all of them came together like this was to take back the body of Moses from Mastema."

Molech said, "I think they plan much more than retrieving the prince of Israel here. I think they came to bind us into the earth."

"Of course, you idiot," said Asherah.

"But why do they not hide themselves?" said Dagon.

Ba'alzebul said, "They want us to stand and fight."

"And why not?" said Asherah. "We are in our stronghold, we are empowered by the Philistines."

"We are confident," added Ba'alzebul. "Presumptuous. So we will be reckless."

"Exactly," said Asherah. "If they can deliver this blow to us now, they will control all of Canaan. Which we cannot allow. So we will run."

"Like cowards?" worried Dagon.

"Like insurgents," said Asherah. "Look at the Amalekites. They were almost wiped out. But their few roaming hordes have become a terror to the Israelites, because they cannot be targeted in a specific location. They hit and they run, and Israel has nowhere to respond or retaliate. In our fortified Philistine cities, the archangels know exactly where we are, and what we are doing in our temples. And they can come get us whenever they want. Because they know where we are. As they do this very moment."

The other gods nodded with understanding.

Asherah added, "It is time we become more mobile."

• • • • •

The cloudy, starless night hid well the six shadows that descended upon the temple of Dagon. The four guards were taken out easily and the six archangels slipped inside the large stone edifice of idolatry.

They made their way through the pillared hall with swords and battle axes drawn.

Within moments, they were through the sanctuary tunnel way and headed down into the cavern below the altar.

But the gods were gone.

"Deplorable," said Uriel, gazing upon the dismembered body parts of his brother archangel on the wall.

They carefully took down the arms, legs, torso and head of Mikael and reattached them like a human anatomy puzzle.

Uriel said, "Why would they have left all of him here for us to find and heal?" Uriel remembered all too terribly when he had been decapitated by Anu in the primeval city of Uruk. Anu had kept Uriel's head separated from his body so that the angel could not heal and fight them.

Gabriel said, "They must have wanted us to find him."

Raphael said, "But they did not want us to follow them, as we would have, had they taken part of his body." The angels had done so in the past when Ishtar had cut Gabriel in half and threw his legs into the Abyss.

"Which means we should follow them," said Uriel. "But where?"

It would take some time for his organic tissue to reconnect, including his voice box. But Mikael could not wait for that healing. His hand wrote out on the sandy floor, "Ashkelon."

CHAPTER 56

Ashkelon was the Philistine port city on the coast eighteen miles west-southwest from Gath. The gods Dagon, Asherah, Ba'alzebul and Molech arrived there early afternoon the next day. They knew the time was short before the archangels would find them.

Ashkelon was the oldest and largest seaport in Canaan. As one of the cities of the Philistine pentapolis, it supported a thriving import and export maritime trade. Its populace, about fifteen thousand people, lived on one hundred and fifty acres, surrounded by a mile and a half of brick wall fifty feet high and fifteen feet thick.

It was built on a large sandstone outcropping and included a large port. A long, manmade jetty about fifty feet wide and several hundred feet long functioned as a breakwater and housed a sea temple of Dagon on its outer edge. Departing and arriving ships could look upon the large, open-air rotunda encompassed by a ring of pillars and say their prayers to Dagon for protection on the seas or thanks for deliverance from the waves.

Inside that temple area, the four gods engaged in a sorcery ritual led by Asherah. She stood on the carcass of a lion and held two strangled ibexes, one in each hand. She wore large wings made of vulture's feathers on her back and a gem-laden horned headdress of deity. She was enacting her identity as "lord of the animals."

Asherah writhed and spoke forth incantations facing the sea that stretched out before her.

Behind her stood a five foot high golden "tree of life" that was an iconic metal casting of a trunk with eight branches, four on each side.

Dagon wore his fishy lower part for the ceremony. He achieved this by cutting the body of a large dolphin in half and sewing the tail over his legs. It was cumbersome and he wished he had never adopted the persona.

It had been a week since their narrow escape from the archangels at Gath, and it was time for their plan to unfold.

The gods were on the cusp of completing their ritual when the archangels hit them.

They had swum across the wharf area and slipped up the rocks to assault the gods from behind.

All seven burst in through the pillared open-air sanctuary, swords flashing.

The gods drew their weapons.

Dagon stuck his sword into his lower fishy half and cut it off with a swipe. He would not be hampered in battle.

Everyone paused for a moment. The four gods stood facing off against the seven archangels, each waiting for the other to make a move.

The mightiest of Yahweh's heavenly host were here to bind the Watcher gods who would be fighting for their eternities. This was going to be brutal.

An earthquake rattled the foundation of the temple. Everyone had to catch their balance. Dust and debris fell from the cracks in the stone above their heads.

Asherah and the gods smiled.

The archangels realized it had been no earthquake. That was an announcement of the arrival of something. Something very huge.

Something from the depths of the sea.

The water behind the gods suddenly exploded upward with the form of the seven headed sea dragon of chaos: Leviathan. It burst out of the water and leapt over the manmade jetty that housed the temple.

Mikael, now healed, joined his fellow archangels for the fight. He saw the huge four hundred foot long serpentine body fly past them through the air. It landed on the wharf side with a huge splash that drenched everyone in the temple. Its double tail followed, with a swipe at the architecture.

It smashed half the structure, wiping it into the water with the force. Gods and angels fell beneath the debris of the other half collapsing on top of them.

When the dust settled, pieces of stone began to move as the warriors of both sides pulled themselves out from under the ruins. Two of the angels, Remiel and Saraqael, had been pinned beneath too many tons of rocks to free themselves. It made the numbers more equal than they had anticipated. One of the gods, Asherah, had been swept into the water by the tidal wave of force that washed over them. Dagon was on the shoreline, picking himself up, bruised and battered, but in one piece.

Uriel and Gabriel, always synchronized with each other, immediately picked up their weapons and leapt down to the water's edge to engage Dagon.

Six heads erupted from the water with fangs flashing and mouths roaring. On the neck of one of them was Asherah, riding it like a steed. She pointed down at the approaching form of Mikael. The monster focused on the angel as a target. The sound of gurgling from deep within its bowels warned Mikael. He had been caught by this attack before, at the beach of Mount Sapan. He was not going to let it happen again. He dove behind a huge boulder as a stream of fire poured out from the dragon head and blackened the entire area of stone.

Another head reached down and Dagon leapt onto it, pulled away before Uriel and Gabriel could reach him.

Ba'alzebul and Molech dashed headlong at the seven heads. Ba'alzebul's muscular form launched an amazing thirty feet to catch one of the gaping jaws as it swung past the rocks of the beach. Molech was not so glorious. He could only make a good twenty feet. It was not enough to reach his target. He landed in the water in a belly flop.

Uriel and Gabriel could not help but look at each other, smirking.

One of the dragon heads reached down and picked Molech out of the water with its teeth and placed him on the back of another neck.

The head that Ba'alzebul had caught had a sword stuck in the roof of its mouth, the hilt sticking out of its head. It was Gabriel's sword, from their confrontation at Sapan generations earlier. Ba'alzebul pulled it from the creature's mouth and swung around to mount its neck. He raised the sword high in victory, as all seven heads plunged back into the deep, carrying its four riders away from the grasp of the angels.

Mikael stepped down to the shoreline to stand by Uriel and Gabriel as Raphael and Raguel helped the trapped angels get free from the rocks.

They looked out onto the frothing, swirling waters left behind by the exit of the gargantuan and its riders. There was no way the archangels could ever chase that chaos monster.

"You have to hand it to that Asherah," said Uriel. "She is one goddess with chutzpah, taking her chances with enchanting Leviathan."

Gabriel added, "And I thought Ashtart was gutsy."

"Ashtart cut your gut in half back at Mount Hermon," said Uriel wryly. "If I had not found your legs in the waters of the Abyss you would have been a paraplegic until the Resurrection."

Gabriel countered, "And I believe it was my trumpet call that saved your rear end against Ashtart's undead at the battle of Edrei."

"A trumpet call that you said yourself you learned from my use of it with the shades of Sheol," said Uriel.

Mikael interrupted, "Do we have to listen to your bickering until the end of days?"

The others joined them at the shoreline.

Mikael took command. "The gods are not cowards. They have escaped today, but they will return. We must be ready for them." He looked at Uriel and Gabriel. "You two squabblers try to gather intelligence on where they went. They will be much harder to catch if they become guerilla fighters."

Raguel said, "Mastema has left Assyria in the hands of another. I am needed there."

"And I at Babylon," said Remiel.

"Where did Mastema go?" asked Gabriel.

"To the Italian peninsula," said Raguel.

"That doesn't make any sense," complained Uriel. "That is a backwater of small Latin villages with undeveloped agriculture. There is no earthly power for him there."

"Maybe that is why he wants it," said Raphael, the angel who barely spoke. "He can build from the bottom up, and he can engage in his nefarious purposes unmolested for centuries."

Mikael said, "We need to focus on what is happening right now in front of us. I will return to Israel with Raphael. The Rephaim forces are building and the Sons of Rapha have not slackened their pace in hunting down the messiah king."

Saraqael said, "I am called to Syria. That will be Israel's next trouble, Mikael. They are amassing quite a strength up north."

"Well then," said Mikael, "let us call upon the name of Yahweh Elohim and ask for strength to face what is coming."

CHAPTER 57

David helped Ittai cast two bronze swords in his roundhouse smithery workshop. The first step was to create a mold from stone, carved with precision using stone and metal chisels. Two halves placed together with a hole at the top to pour in the molten liquid metal. These had already been created by Ittai.

The next step was to melt down the mixture of ninety percent copper and ten percent tin in a furnace forge. David pumped the bellows to keep the fire hot enough with a steady flow of air.

"Careful," said Ittai. "We do not want it too hot or we will spoil the strength of the final sword."

David lessened the bellows and continued their conversation, "By getting close to the king of Gath, I believe I can learn more about the plans and thinking of the Philistines, and therefore achieve the understanding of how to conquer them in the long run."

Ittai said, "I can help you with the mind of a Philistine. And my followers as well."

David remarked, "But you are not King Achish, the one I need to get close to."

"Indeed I am not," retorted Ittai. "And I will not kill you. But King Achish will."

With arms wrapped in leather to protect them from the heat, they pulled the white hot crucible from the coals with large tongs and carried it to the mold. The molten bronze for pouring filled it.

David tried to continue the discussion, but Ittai cut him off. "Shh!" interrupted Ittai. "The pour is crucial. We cannot spill it or allow impurities to get through. Keep your eyes out for pieces of charcoal or hardened metal."

David watched it closely.

The expertise of a blacksmith includes his ability to recognize the right color of the molten bronze to judge when it is ready to pour. Together, they poured the liquid metal into the hole at the top of the mold.

"Now, we let it cool," said Ittai. "And I attempt to cool you from your hotheaded folly."

David smiled. "As I was saying, here is what you may have missed. Achish wishes to conquer Israel, correct?"

"Yes."

"He would give anything to know the secrets of Saul's strategy, right?"

"Right."

"Well," said David, "He also knows that Saul hates me and wants to kill me. That makes me Saul's enemy. If Achish sees that we are both Saul's enemy, he may be willing to consider me his ally against Saul."

When the metal had cooled sufficiently, the mold was taken apart and the swords pulled out. They were then cooled by plunging them into a trough of water, which also made the metal harder and ready for action.

The hiss of the contact of the hot metal with the cool water was accompanied by a cloud of steam in David's face.

Ittai said, "Even so, you do not have the privilege of the time you would need to explain all this strategy to him before he kills you on sight."

"That is most likely true," said David. He thought it over.

Ittai added, "And Achish is not the only one who seeks you. There is a far more sinister force of evil in this city that will kill you long before you could even get into the presence of the king."

"Who?"

"They are called the Sons of Rapha. They are a military cult of Rephaim giants devoted to assassinating you. Goliath was the first, but there are five others."

"One of my swordsman, Sibbecai the Hushathite, killed one of them."

"So they already got close," said Ittai. "What did he look like?"

"He wielded two scimitars," answered David.

"That was Saph," said Ittai. "Four is less than five, but still certain death for you," said Ittai. He then told David about the history of the Sons of Rapha and who was in the cult and what he knew. He told him about Lahmi, the brother of Goliath and his lust for revenge. But he carefully left out his own identity and his attempt to join the guild all those years before.

Next, the edges and surface of the newly cast swords were filed down and sharpened with flint sharpening stones.

They each worked on one of the swords as they continued.

Ittai finally found the courage to ask, "David, do you believe there is the possibility of redemption for Rephaim?"

David thought for a moment. "Well, they are the result of the gods mating with human wives in the primeval ages and onward. So that would mean that they are demigods, right?"

"I suppose so," lied Ittai. He thought "demigod" sounded like such a grand and glorious identity of power. He felt more like he was ignoble and cursed.

David said, "Well then, that makes them half human. And whatever is human, Yahweh can redeem, I suppose."

"But the half that is divine," countered Ittai. "What of that?"

David thought some more. "I don't know, Ittai. But I do believe that Yahweh calls men from all nations to have faith and follow his law. So if a man—or a half man, half god—can obey Yahweh, then what of that?"

Ittai turned away to wash his blade off so that David could not see that his eyes were wet with hope he could not reveal.

Lastly, they wrapped leather around the hilts to create a good grip. Leather sheaths to carry the swords on belts were already made, waiting for the new weapons. The swords were finally ready to kill.

Ittai held up the two blades, now polished and ready. He handed them proudly to David. "You have done well, my lord. Thank you for taking interest in your lowly servant."

"Nonsense," said David. "You are my *loyal* servant." He lifted up one of the swords and appreciated it in the light they had. "And you have given me a loyal gift by forging these two swords from the remnant of the sword of Goliath. May they be used to cut down the rest of the Sons of Rapha as a symbol of Yahweh's glory and power."

Ittai thought of Lahmi and what a thing of beauty it would be to see him pierced with his own brother's sword. But then he turned somber and whispered painfully, "I was the one who forged this metal into the original sword for Goliath."

David looked at him with sympathy and said, "Well, I guess that proves evil can be redeemed."

Ittai felt a surge of emotion penetrate his soul.

David added, "So the original weapon of evil will be redeemed. I will use this reforged sword against the Sons of Rapha." David then placed his hand on Ittai's shoulder and handed the other sword to him. "I want you to have this one. May they both be used for such a grand and glorious purpose."

Ittai had no words to say. He took the sword and hugged it close to his chest with gratitude. *Yes, may they one day be used for such a grand and glorious purpose.*

David said, "I just thought of something. Remember that quandary of me not being able to come before King Achish without being immediately executed?"

"Yes."

"Do your people still believe that madness is the holy touch of the gods? A sacred protection?"

"Yes," said Ittai. "What exactly are you thinking?"

CHAPTER 58

The Gath marketplace square was full of Gittites. Every day at about this time, hundreds of farmers and craftsmen traded, stole, begged, borrowed, and gossiped in the square. Fisherman, blacksmiths, farmers, tanners, and all kinds of craftsmen engaged in their form of commerce and social gathering.

Today's society was rudely interrupted by a madman running through the square in nothing but a loin cloth, spittle dribbling down his beard, hair matted in wild animal-like display, skin blackened with dirt.

It was David. Though most would never recognize him, nor understand his importance.

He ran around slapping heads and growling like a wildcat, then howling like a wolf.

He jaunted up to the dais in the middle of the square. It was a large stone platform upon which sacrifices were made unto the gods, but also upon which public executions were exacted upon the criminals of Gath. A chopping stone for heads, and a wooden gallows for necks towered above the crowd like silent monuments of justice—or more precisely, entertainment, as the Philistine culture was a violent one.

David stood upon the chopping block and announced with a screaming frenzy, "I am David ben Jesse! King of Israel! Slayer of Goliath! King Achish cannot kill me! I rule the wilderness of Azazel! Bow down and worship me, all you Gittites!"

The citizens at first hardly listened to him. He got some laughs, and some rotten vegetables hit him on the chest and head, giving him an even more unpleasant odor to help his feigned madness seem more real.

David yelled, "I puke on the idols of Dagon, Ba'alzebul, and Asherah!" He stuck a finger down his throat to stimulate his gag reflex.

A stream of vomit burst out of his mouth upon the four horned altar stone. "Lord Achish is a patsy of his Lady! I am the king of Gath! Follow me, all you miserable flea-ridden Gittites! I am David ben Jesse, slayer of Goliath the Gittite! Bow before me!"

Ittai stood and watched David from one of the alleyways. He had helped coach him on how to act mad and what to say in order to get attention from the Gittites. But David had already learned much from his time with the tormented King Saul.

Ittai only hoped David would not be swarmed and lynched by an angry mob.

He looked up high at the top of a building where he saw Jonathan the Mouse poised with bow and arrow, ready to take out anyone who might try to harm David. Ittai had heard of the little man's sharpshooting reputation. He took an interest in Jonathan because he had reminded Ittai of himself. "Mouse" was about as derogatory a nickname as "runt," so they shared more in common than most others understood.

A few of the merchants reported the disturbance to some soldiers and soon a couple of guardsmen came to take David away. David squirmed helplessly as he was dragged out of the square.

Ittai and a few other well-placed secret insurgents shouted out at the soldiers as they passed, "That is David ben Jesse! I have seen him! He is the arch enemy of Lord Achish!"

The subterfuge worked. The soldiers took their captive to the palace.

Four soldiers dragged David in chains before the throne of Achish. David stared at them until he was dropped at the foot of the stairs before the throne. The guards did not leave him, but they released him. The chains around his neck, hands, and arms would not allow him any advantage.

David knew that Philistine Lords were technically not kings, but more like warlords in a confederation. But he noticed that they acted no different than kings and queens in their abuse of power, as well as their display of riches. Achish wore a gold-plated robe on his pudgy little body, and a silly looking golden miter on his head. His coregent, Bisha, was middle-aged, and dressed like a queen with a red velveteen satin dress, with plenty of jewels and heavy make up. She was attractive for her age, but had a malicious undertone to her presence. David saw her eyeing him.

To the poor citizens of such a feudal system, and to captives like David, the fine distinctions between monarchs and feudal warlords was irrelevant.

David stood proud and announced with a crazed look in his eye, "I am David ben Jesse, slayer of your champion oaf, Goliath, and the bane of King Saul. I am the ruler of the wilderness of Azazel." Then David howled like a wolf. He then let off a disgusting fart with humorous timing. It brought a smile to Achish's face.

David's play was not entirely insane. His madness did have meaning. The "howling" wilderness was considered the domain of chaos, where Azazel the goat demon and his fellow creatures of chaos resided. Centaurs, Lilith the demoness, and other goblins and chimeras would dance over the bones of dead soldiers and conquered cities. It was all connected to the image of chaos that David sought to impress upon Achish.

At that moment, three giants approached the throne and stood to the side of it.

Ishbi and Lahmi watched David closely. Though he was fifteen years older, much more ruggedly built and looking like a madman, Ishbi recognized something of the boy champion through the shaggy hair and beard. Lahmi could not place him in his memory. He assumed him an imposter. Runihura stood back. He was more superstitious.

Ishbi's familiar spirits exploded in his skull with a cacophony of hatred and violence. *Kill it! Destroy the Seed! Get away! Get away!*

David shuddered. He knew these had to be the Sons of Rapha that he had heard were after him. And here he was chained up like a piece of bait for them to chew on. He prayed silently to Yahweh and hoped that his plan would work.

Achish told the soldiers, "Take off those chains. This man is touched by the gods. He is sacred."

The soldiers obeyed. David made babbling noises and squeals of joy. He then ran around in a circle on all fours as if he was a wolf boy. He howled again. He sat down on the floor at the foot of the stairs, looking up at the Lord and Lady.

Ishbi said, "My Lord, you called us to see a madman?"

"Not just any madman," said Achish. "This is a very particular one. Someone you will be interested in, Lahmi. He is the one who killed your brother, Goliath."

Lahmi looked angrily at Achish, then at David. He couldn't believe it.

David could see Lahmi's reaction. He said, "I slew Goliath with a single stone in the forehead. Pow!"

Lahmi became agitated. This crazy little squirrel dared to speak of the mighty legend Goliath this way?

Then David said, "He called me a dog, so I pissed on his corpse like a dog." He barked and pulled up his tunic to take a pee on the floor. Considering he had felt the urge to pee earlier from his fright in the presence of these malevolent monsters, it was a convenient bit of drama.

It hit Lahmi like a brick. David's form and stature now became clear to him. He had watched the little desert rat relieve himself and cut off his brother's head. This crazed man crouching before them now was that young, vile enemy of the past now matured. Lahmi's rage boiled over and he started toward David.

"Lahmi, stop!" shouted Achish.

Lahmi did not listen to Achish. He kept pacing toward David, with eyes fixed to murder the vile little creature.

Achish commanded Ishbi, "Stop him, captain."

Ishbi grabbed Lahmi from behind, mere feet from David. He whispered with anger into Lahmi's ear, "Lahmi, obey your Lord."

Lahmi struggled. Ishbi held him tight.

Lahmi roared.

By now, David's fear had turned to faith. He ramped up his antics by mimicking the roar and running in another circle on all fours.

Bisha watched this exchange with great interest. She was affectionately intrigued by this little Hebrew. What if he had an evil spirit like his king Saul was alleged to be tormented by? She knew that Achish was superstitious enough to keep David alive, so she might actually get her chance yet to indulge in her illicit desires with an evil spirit.

Ishbi pulled Lahmi back out of the way, next to the throne. Lahmi growled to Achish, "That piece of dung killed our mightiest champion and defied our gods and your throne. How can you allow him to live and claim to be Lord?"

Achish said, "Our gods have seen fit to touch him with their sacred madness. I will seek Dagon's will in this matter. If you disobey me again, if you so much as put one hand on him, I will have you arrested and executed."

Achish looked down upon David, who now scratched himself like he had fleas. "Since our divinely filled captive thinks himself a dog, then we will keep him where he will feel safe—in a cage with the royal hounds."

CHAPTER 59

One hundred and thirty miles north of the coastal city of Ashkelon, the sister cities of Tyre and Sidon ruled the northern regions of Phoenicia. They were both port cities that were wealthy and cosmopolitan from merchant trading around the world. Both were cities of the goddess Asherah, but she favored Sidon with its larger temple and more loyal priesthood.

Unlike the patriarchal religions of Canaan, the Sidonian priesthood allowed female priests to serve alongside their male counterparts with equal authority. More deliciously, they also included many priests who dressed themselves as women. Others were women who dressed as men. Others sought an androgynous appearance without gender.

The goal was to defy Yahweh's distinctions within creation; male and female, adult and child, human and animal, god and human. But the most desirable object of pleasure to Asherah were the two high priestesses who were hermaphrodites, special creatures of the gods who were born as both male and female. Their extremely rare occurrence among humanity gave them worshipful status among the humans. But it also gave them special attention from the gods Asherah, Ba'alzebul, Dagon, and Molech.

Earlier, the four gods had exploded out of the sea onto the coastal shore of Sidon, released by their mount, Leviathan. The sea serpent, under the spell of Lady Asherah of the Sea, had helped them escape the archangels. It now returned to the depths of chaos in the waters of the Abyss. The gods made their way to the temple and put out a call to the local deities, Resheph and Qeteb, to join them in their plan.

When they were ready, they left the city on their trip eastward to the cosmic mountain of Hermon.

They had called an assembly of all the gods of Canaan.

CHAPTER 60

David jealously guarded his corner of the iron-barred dog cage. The large greyhounds lay down around each other at the other end. The cage was not tall enough for David to stand up, but he was comfortable enough to curl up in his corner. He had slept well through the night, and now it was time to hatch his plan.

He called out, "Guardsman, where am I? How did I get here?" A guard approached him. David said, "All I remember was the full moon and then I blacked out." The guard complained, "Crazy lunatic. The moon has passed."

David said, "I must speak to Lord Achish."

David was brought before Achish and Bisha at their breakfast table. They were seated on the floor with a display of freshly caught fish, fruits and vegetables before them. Achish was a bit of a slob when he ate, as he had stains and food pieces on his tunic front.

With his mouth full of plums, Achish said, "Son of Jesse, I am told you have a respite in your divine madness. Your mind has returned to you for the moment?"

"Yes, my lord," said David with a bow. "I wish to speak with you about something I suspect will be of great concern."

Bisha watched David with hungry eyes. This strapping, muscular Israelite before her looked very tasty. He had cleaned up, shaven and brushed his hair out. He seemed sane again. He was like an unblemished bull to Bisha—or better yet, an unblemished lamb—innocent and unspoiled. What a pleasure it would be to consume this one like a sacrifice. It would make her feel like a goddess.

She was feeling particularly divine because she had finally conquered one of her most difficult goals in bedding Ishbi ben Ob last night. He had been the last of the Sons of Rapha she had been trying to seduce. Since he did not desire women, she had to use blackmail on him. She told him Lord Achish was considering imprisoning Lahmi for his insubordination before the throne that day and that if Ishbi fornicated with Bisha, she would seek to persuade the Lord of Gath to withhold his judgment on the disrespectful Rapha.

Achish lifted a glass of wine to David, "You must be hungry. Please join us. Break your fast."

"Thank you, my Lord, but I am not hungry." Of course David was hungry. He just could not stomach eating a meal in fellowship with this disgusting swine and his despicable wife, who would not keep her eyes off David. He would eventually have to eat with them, if he was to fool Achish with his plan. But at this moment, he preferred the pangs of hunger.

"My Lord and Lady, it would be folly for me to ignore the fact that Israel is your ultimate enemy, King Saul, your most hated nemesis, and I, your worst insult and thorn in your side."

Achish smiled. "Ah, your reason *has* returned to you."

"Indeed, it has," replied David, "and with it, an offer for you that will result in great benefit to your strategy against Israel."

Bisha perked up with even more interest. She blurted out, "Do tell."

Achish gave her an annoyed glance, and said, "Yes, please, do tell."

David took a breath and said, "King Saul has spent great sums of money and much of his time chasing me around the wilderness and caves of the hill country. His madness has focused its attention on killing me as much as his desire to vanquish you."

"I have heard of his pursuit of you," said Achish.

"You and I have a common enemy in King Saul," said David. "You and I could be allies."

Bisha butted in, "Why does Saul want to kill you so badly? Are you this promised messiah king that threatens his reign?"

David could see she was the more cunning of the two. She was sniffing out David's real motives. He knew he had to throw her off with a half truth.

"My Lady," said David, "I have had several chances to kill King Saul and have deliberately refrained from doing so, because I believe that Saul is the messiah king of Israel, chosen by our god Yahweh, and anointed by our own holy Seer."

"But he considers you a threat to his reign," she repeated.

"I married his daughter and became closer than a brother to his eldest son, Jonathan, heir to the throne. The king became madly convinced I was conspiring to kill his son and steal the throne."

Bisha eyed him suspiciously, "Are you?"

"No," said David.

Bisha said, "Why not?" It was an accusation, as if to say that it would be hard to believe anyone having such righteous motives. She was taking over the discussion from Achish, flushing David out.

"Because, my Lady, I believe that if I were to touch Yahweh's anointed king, I would be cursed and under judgment."

"Hmmmm," she pondered. "That god of yours is a curious one. But how do we not know that you are pretending to get close to Lord Achish in order to kill him?"

"Yes," Achish finally jumped back in so he would not look too passive. "How can I know you are loyal to me?"

David said, "We have a common enemy. But I have worked closely with Saul. I know how he thinks and how he strategizes. I will give you intelligence on him that will enable *you* to have victory over him. I cannot kill him because of my belief in the curse. But what is that to you?"

"Nothing," said Achish quickly, with a smile. He also thought that as soon as he killed Saul, he would immediately kill David, to keep David from seeking the throne of Israel against him. Then all of Canaan would be his.

Achish added, "I find your offer enticing. You have proven yourself quite useful."

Bisha said dubiously, "I would like to add one condition of your loyalty."

"What is your wish, my Lady?" said David.

"I want you to fight for us. I want you to kill Israelites."

She saw David's face go taut. She was definitely trying to ferret him out. But he said, "I have prepared myself for such an eventuality, my Lady. And I have already decided that I will fight for you. I only ask that you allow me to gather my six hundred, who have been scattered from me, to form a combat unit. They will fight with me and for Lord Achish."

Bisha turned to Achish with overwrought deference. "My Lord Achish, forgive me for being forward, but before you grant a decision, may we talk in private?"

Achish turned to David. "Wait for us out in the hall with the guards."

"Yes, my lord." David left them.

Bisha waited until she was sure he was outside the door and out of hearing range. She spoke as if she was the Lord and Achish the Lady.

"Of course, you will accept his offer and be wary of ulterior motives. But I must warn you, I have spies who inform me that the Sons of Rapha are planning an assault on David." She was lying. She knew the plans of the Sons of Rapha because she just been with Ishbi ben Ob the night before. "Your best bet is to assign Ishbi and Runihura to head up two separate regiments in battle against Saul. Keep them out on the field of battle. That way, they will not be in town to plot against David."

"What about Lahmi?" said Achish. "What do you propose we do with him?"

"The insubordinate?" she said with contempt. "What do you think I would propose for the blood avenger of Goliath, who will not stop until your new ally is dead?"

• • • • •

Lahmi had just finished his morning exercises. He was exhausted and starving for a meal. He sweated heavily from his workout, so he walked about in his loin cloth to cool his body. He went into his kitchen, where he had left his partner from the night before.

But he was gone. Lahmi thought he might have gotten up to relieve himself, so Lahmi walked over to the latrine. It was empty. Not that he cared one whit for the moron. In fact, he would kick him out as soon as he could, because he tired of him.

He walked back out into the atrium, an open area about fifty feet square where he exercised. He ran into a regiment of twenty soldiers and the decorated General of Achish's forces, Phicol.

Lahmi stood in his bare loin cloth, vulnerable before the armed soldiers. Even so, they were visibly nervous to a man. Confronting a Son of Rapha, no matter their numbers and no matter how disadvantaged or surprised he might be, was a frightening prospect. That was why Phicol was there. As the most celebrated General of Achish's armed forces, Phicol commanded the respect and admiration of the entire Philistine pentapolis. If Lahmi resisted Phicol, it would spell certain exile or execution for him.

Phicol barked, "Lahmi of Gath, Lord Achish has ordered your arrest for insubordination to the throne and willful conspiracy. Will you surrender peacefully?"

Lahmi realized he had been betrayed by his partner. He stared into the eyes of Phicol with a smug smirk and held out his hands as if giving up his body as an offering.

• • • • •

Shortly after Lahmi was arrested and imprisoned, two of the three remaining Sons of Rapha, Ishbi and Runihura, were called before Lord Achish and Lady Bisha to accept a commission over three separate regiments of the Philistine armies of the pentapolis. They were told

Ekron and Gaza needed their leadership, so they would be split up and sent to these cities. They were also told that Lahmi had been arrested for insubordination and conspiracy against the crown. Obvious trumped-up charges to protect their new political alliance with the Hebrew scamp. Yes, the Sons of Rapha had their own spies within the palace as well.

Rather than react to Bisha's betrayal with hostility, Ishbi silently plotted his revenge against the Philistine queen. He would not let such minor inconveniences distract him from his ultimate responsibility before the gods: to continue to hunt down the Chosen Seed of Eve, David ben Jesse of Israel.

CHAPTER 61

That night, David was asleep in his bed chamber in the palace when he was awakened by a presence in his room. He turned over to find Lady Bisha standing with a small oil lamp in her hand, wearing a night gown. She was a mature woman that would otherwise be tempting to David, had her soul not been so rancid. She let down her hair and it fell to her shoulders. She shook it loose and stepped closer to him.

David rubbed the sleep out of his eyes. "Lady Bisha." He suspected that she had slipped unnoticed into his room through a secret passageway.

He sat up, wondering how he was going to escape. "Where is Lord Achish?"

"Do not be coy with me, David. I came to take what is mine."

He knew full well what she meant by that demand. He sighed.

She protested, "I made sure your request for the regiment of your men was granted by my husband. And I have protected you from death, by arresting Lahmi, your blood avenger, and ridding you of the Sons of Rapha."

"How did you do that?"

"I told Achish to split them up and place them in leadership over regiments in the other cities of the pentapolis."

David showed respect for her cunning manipulation with a nod and a raised brow.

She continued in her bribes, "You will see that I am your best ally in Philistia."

"I thank you, my lady. I am grateful for your help."

"Good. Now show me your gratitude." She moved up to him, inches away. He could feel her breath and smell her lotus perfume.

"I cannot betray my Lord Achish for his grace."

"Nonsense," she spit out. "Lord Achish is a fool. It is my grace that you are beholden to. And I want my compensation."

"I am afraid there is a higher grace yet to which I am beholden."

"Who?" she said with incredulity.

"My god, Yahweh."

It was his last resort and it worked. She backed away for a moment. He could breathe again.

"Ah yes, that evasive god of yours. I have been meaning to ask you about him."

"I will tell you anything you wish to know," he offered. Anything to turn away her aggression.

"Why is he so jealous and petty? His demand to exclusive worship is so —vainglorious. He is a megalomaniac."

David responded, "He is the creator of all things. He has the right to do and command whatever he pleases."

"Then why do the Israelites worship Ba'alzebul and Asherah throughout the land?"

"A serious moral failing of my people."

"Your leaders are no better, which reflects upon your god," she complained. "Your king is possessed by a demon. Even in your past, your deliverers were no more righteous than those from whom you were delivered. Samson fought against my people, yet he was no obedient Israelite. He frolicked quite eagerly with a Philistine woman." She stepped closer to David. The implication was obvious.

She concluded, "What kind of a god chooses such vile, hypocritical leaders to represent him? What kind of a god chooses such a pathetic and undeserving people to claim dominion over Canaan?"

David turned pensive. "I cannot deny what you say, my Lady. Yahweh indeed chooses unworthy vessels for his will." He was thinking of his own unworthiness as Yahweh's chosen messiah, yet to be inaugurated. All his sins were before him and he was ashamed of how he too was vile and hypocritical. "Sadly, I have seen all too often that the great are not the good, and the good are not the great."

When he spoke, Bisha did not realize that he was in fact speaking of himself. "Yahweh chooses what is foolish in the world to shame the wise. He chooses what is weak to shame the strong, and what is low and despised—the things that are not—to bring to nothing the things that are. The only thing I can offer you is that Yahweh did not choose Israel because she is more righteous than other nations. She is not. He chose her so that our faith in him may not rest in our own goodness, but in the power of Yahweh, who delivers us from our own evil."

Her look turned greedy again and she stepped closer to him. "Well, if your god enjoys using unfaithful hypocrites, then I am sure you will have no problem indulging in my little request, if it will help to glorify your god's greatness and goodness."

She grabbed him. He didn't know what to do.

Then it came to him.

He howled like a wolf.

He went mad again. That way, she would surely turn away in frustration.

But she did not turn away. Instead she breathed more heavily with desire and said, "Oh good. The demon is back. I badly want to copulate with a demon."

David could not believe his ears. This woman was thoroughly depraved. He shook himself free from her grip by shaking his entire body in a fake seizure. Then he jumped away, howled again, and bolted out the door of the bed chamber.

Bisha cursed him, picked up her gown, and fled back into her secret passageway.

CHAPTER 62

At nine thousand feet high, Mount Hermon was the highest peak in the Sirion mountain range at the northern edge of Canaan. It was twenty-five miles inland, over mountainous terrain from the city of Sidon. Its snow-peaked summit stood majestically over the surrounding forests and foothills. This cosmic mountain, where the gods assembled, had been the location of the original descent of the Sons of God in the primordial past when they rebelled from Yahweh's heavenly host and fell to earth.

It was at Hermon in the land of Bashan, "the place of the Serpent," that the two hundred rebels set up their supernatural fortress in the bowels of the mountain. From here, they engaged in their primeval plans of usurping Yahweh's authority, corrupting his creation, and violating his image. They proclaimed themselves gods over the people and began to mate with human women. Their offspring were the Nephilim, giants of old, demigods who would be considered the first of the Seed of the Serpent, Nachash.

Yahweh had most of the rebel Watchers bound into the earth, and drowned the land to stop the cancerous growth of this diabolical seed along with mankind's violence and idolatry. He saved Noah and his family to start over with a purely human bloodline from which to bring forth a new Seed, a messiah king, who would destroy the power of the Serpent and his Seed forever. Yahweh allotted the nations of sinful mankind and their territories to the rebellious Watcher gods. But he kept for himself the nation of Israel and claimed the land of Canaan as his allotted territory.

So long as the gods reigned over the land, there would be perpetual conflict between the Seed of Abraham and the Seed of the Serpent; a cosmic conflict of those who worshipped Yahweh versus those who defied him and worshipped other gods. And that clash of gods was about to intensify as an assembly of the gods convened within the cavernous interior of Mount Hermon.

The cavern was hundreds of feet in diameter with a large lake of black, flaming liquid in the middle: the entrance to the Abyss. Long stalagmites and stalactites filled the large subterranean area. They were covered with a phosphorescent moss that gave artificial light to the assembly hall. On the other side of the infernal black pitch lagoon were the thrones of Nergal and Ereshkigal, the god and goddess of the underworld, who guarded the entrance waters of the Abyss which led to Sheol.

Asherah, Ba'alzebul, Dagon, Molech, Resheph, and Qeteb had journeyed from Sidon to the mount of assembly. Marduk and Ishtar of Babylonia, Asshur of Assyria, Kumarbi of the Hittites, even Osiris and Horus from Egypt travelled their long distances to answer the urgent call for a council of the seventy gods over the seventy nations.

When Yahweh had sent the Great Flood and bound the Watcher gods into the earth and Tartarus, he left seventy of them to rule over the nations with their minions of fellow mal'akim. The lands were allotted at the Division of Tongues at Babel. This dispersion was supposed to keep mankind from ever again uniting in evil over the entire earth as they had under Nimrod the Mighty Hunter.

It had been generations since a call to council like this had been attempted. It was difficult for the gods to leave their territories in the hands of lesser deities in their absence. Power and idolatry left nations in unstable and precarious situations that could explode or collapse at any moment. The air of the council was one of impatience. The seventy were anxious to get back to their dominions and were angered at being inconvenienced.

There was only one significant entity who did not show up.

"Where in Sheol is Mastema?" griped Ba'alzebul, who had taken over the proceedings from Asherah and Dagon. It had not surprised anyone, as it was clear the bulky brute sought to return to his former glory as Elyon Ba'al, the Most High god over Canaan.

Asherah whispered to Dagon, "Wipe off that sour mug."

Dagon mumbled back, "How dare he take over like a pompous dictator. *I* am god of the Philistines and the Philistines are pre-eminent in Canaan. I should be…"

"You should shut your mouth," she interrupted him. "Alone, you have no chance against his power. If we are careful and wise, you and I can work together to undermine him."

Dagon gave her a surprised look. Did she just hint at conspiracy? Of course she did. Perhaps he was not so alone. Perhaps she and the brute were not conspiring against him after all.

Finally, Zeus from Greece, stepped out from the crowd and announced, "Mastema is on the west coast of Italy."

"He left Assyria? Why on earth?" said Ba'alzebul.

"He is working amongst the Etruscans and Latins," said Zeus.

Ba'alzebul could not understand the thinking. No one could. He complained, "Of what possible worth are those primitive savages, that he would neglect an urgent call to assembly? We are gathered to discuss the fact that the messiah king, the Seed of Eve, is alive in Canaan and poised to take reign and engage in all out war against the gods of Canaan. And Mastema is wasting his time with backwoods peasants and yokels?"

"That is the problem with you, Ba'alzebul," a voice boomed out from behind the crowd of divinities. A Watcher stepped out.

It was Mastema. "You are too shortsighted. You need a longer vision."

Mastema was a visually unimpressive looking god. Where Ba'alzebul bulged with muscles, Mastema looked scrawny in comparison. Where the storm god had a frightening, horned presence, Mastema was uncomely and unremarkably androgynous. Was he a scrawny male or an ugly female? It wasn't clear. What made

Mastema's aura so much more terrifying than Ba'alzebul's was his legal standing in the heavenly court. He was the Accuser who prosecuted cases against Yahweh and against his people. His legal acumen was so brilliant, he could outmaneuver any god before Yahweh's court except Yahweh himself. And in the end, knowledge of heavenly law was of far more earthly power than raw strength. So, no matter how much might Ba'alzebul could muster, Mastema would outrank him because of his mastery of the Law, and Yahweh ruled through Law.

Mastema stepped forward and took the stage from Ba'alzebul like a king taking it from a queen. The storm god backed down. He knew who had the greater authority here.

Mastema said, "Forgive my ignorance of the latest gossip, but where is this messiah king, David ben Jesse?"

Dagon blurted out, jockeying to be noticed, "With the Philistines at Gath. He has allied with them against Saul, who seeks to destroy them both."

"Do you not own Lady Bisha of Gath?" said Mastema.

Asherah jumped in, "Bisha is a slave of her passions. She won't seek to kill David because she is seeking to seduce him."

Mastema shook his head, then said, "What of the Sons of Rapha? Are they not an elite squad of assassins?"

"Disbanded by the Lord of Gath," said Ba'alzebul with an angry look at Dagon. "Achish is protecting David because he is using him in raids against the Israelites in the Negeb."

Dagon added, "The entire court of archangels sought to bind us at Gath, so we cannot return there."

It didn't take Mastema any time to think of it. He already knew the answer.

"Morons. Since David's rise to power is forestalled until Saul's fall, and David is now in Achish's confidence, the answer is obvious. Get Achish to fight against Saul with David helping him. Have Achish withdraw his forces from David in the battlefield. He will be killed by Saul's soldiers, and you kill Saul. The line of messiah Seed will die, and you can rename all of Israel 'Palestine.'" Palestine was the Latin pronunciation of Philistia.

Asherah added with a smirk, "Crushed by the mouth of the Serpent."

That drew Mastema's attention with a return smirk and nod. He said, "Well, you are not *all* buffoons."

Ba'alzebul's face went flush with offense. Dagon grinned.

Mastema added, "But beware, my divine imbeciles. The heavenly host will show up in full force. So you had better all be there, and you had better be in top form, or you will find yourself in a certain underworld dungeon that starts with a "T" and rhymes with Tartarus."

Molech's face scrunched up, trying to figure out the riddle. Asherah could see the poor sod was too dense to catch the obvious sarcasm.

Ba'alzebul puffed his chest out and tried to take command. "Who will stand with us to fight this infernal seed and his evil minions?"

The seventy silently weighed their options.

Asherah stepped in to add weight to the less than towering intellect of the Storm God. "If Canaan falls under this messianic seed, do not think the rest of you will be left alone. He will expand to the ends of the earth to steal all your allotted nations and throw all of you into Tartarus. If we do not stand together now, we will end up bound alone."

Slowly, the gods all raised their hands. All of them except Mastema, who Asherah and Ba'alzebul noticed had already slipped away from the assembly, no doubt to return to his futile pursuits in Italy.

Molech raised his hand, but secretly planned an excuse to return to Gehinnom to consume his child sacrifices in peace.

"Well, then," said Ba'alzebul, "let us get cracking. We have a war to prepare for."

CHAPTER 63

In recent months, Lord Achish had taken to imbibing of much wine and strong drink. He had the increasing dread that he was losing control. His desire to conquer Israel and gain the territory of the hill country for Philistia was growing ever elusive. His regiment of giant Rephaim warriors, now led by General Ishbi ben Ob, was gaining renown and becoming more independent. His wife, Lady Bisha, who had been a powerful political tool for his ambition, was becoming more flagrant with demanding her own intentions as well as indulgences.

He felt lost and without anchor in a churning sea of conflict. His response to the accumulation of pressure was to increase his consumption of alcohol. There was nothing more relieving of that pressure than the soothing flow of fermented drink pouring down his gullet and sloshing in his belly. It made him forget his troubles and numbed his dread, if just for a while.

He had finished his fourth goblet of wine when David responded to a call for an audience in his dining area. Achish lay on the pillows before the table. When he saw David, he lifted his goblet and said with a slight slur of speech, "David! My Hebrew spy. Enter, please and share some drink with me."

David saw that this was his opportunity to get what he wanted and maybe more. Achish was not senselessly drunk. He was more akin to slightly sloshed, but still mentally capable.

Most important of all, Bisha was not there to ruin everything.

David smiled and picked up another cup. Achish smiled and poured him some wine. David had to follow his slightly moving wine jar as it meandered to and fro.

David saluted Achish and took a drink. Achish belched in response, bringing a smirk to David's lips.

Achish pronounced, "You Hebrews are a contentious lot. You fight amongst yourselves almost as much as with your enemies."

David smiled, "I cannot argue with you there, my lord. We are the children of Jacob, a wrestler with Yahweh himself."

"King Saul is the first monarch to unite your people in four hundred years. And yet, there remains a division between Judah in the south and that of Israel in the north. Now, in your wanderings in the south, while on the run from Saul, you have been successful in garnering the favor of the Judahites, am I not correct?"

"Yes."

"That means that with you under my protection, Saul's kingdom is divided. So what is he thinking? Will he give up on Judah or fight for it? Will he fortify the heart of his stronghold in Gibeah? The Council of Five has appointed Gath as the vanguard of forces."

David toasted Achish's cup again and took a deep gulp. Or at least, pretended to, as Achish responded with his own swallow. Some wine dribbled down his beard. The drink had loosened the Philistine's lips enough for David to understand what he was thinking, even as Achish sought to understand what Saul was thinking.

Apparently, the overall strategy of the Philistines was to divide Israel. Philistia's location in the central south was prime opportunity to extend its grip directly inland from its coastal location. It could physically divide the territories held by Israel and weaken her. Gath was the furthest inland, so Achish was the key leader in achieving that expansion. David had to keep Achish from his own planned area of rule in the central highlands: Hebron and Jerusalem.

"My lord, Saul is impulsive. He reacts more than he plans." It was not entirely true. David knew that without Yahweh's guidance, Saul was desperate, but he was obsessive about his control, even to the point of his willingness to seek forbidden divination. "You Philistines are strong in the plains because of your iron chariots and heavy armor. But you are weak in the highlands where the Israelites are strong on foot with their lightweight armor."

Achish had stopped drinking and was trying hard to follow David's logic. His face scrunched in deep thought. His eyes looked into the distance. The wine had dulled his wits just enough to make him fail to see David's hidden agenda. But not enough to recognize the obvious. "Tell me something I do not know."

David continued, "I recommend a twofold strategy: leave the highlands of Judah and the desert of Negeb to me. I will secure your interests in that region. Instead of your forces attacking the interior, which will draw the fullness of Saul's forces into maximum conflict, I suggest you hit him on the periphery where you are strongest and he is weakest, on the flatlands of the Jezreel Valley up north."

Achish thought for a moment, then blurted out, "Brilliant!" Then he paused skeptically. "But that is quite a distance from our own stronghold."

"But it is flat plains all the way up the coast and inland to the city of Shunem. You could secure that whole region and therefore box Saul in from both north and south." David felt like the reverse of the Serpent in the Garden, leading the real serpent with his own whispering rhetoric.

Achish's mind was not as sharp as usual under the influence of wine, but it was not blunted completely. "How many Philistine forces will you require? That might split my own strength in half."

"None, my lord."

"None?" This was looking better every moment to Achish.

"I will not lie to you. Even though my men are rebels and dissidents from Saul, they are still Israelites, and they do not like fighting alongside Philistines. But they are loyal to me. So, if you give us our own city near the Negeb, and grant us a measure of independence, you need never fear an uprising. I will lead them in flash raids against Israelite clans in the far south to secure the desert territory.

That way, they can work out their enmity with rival tribes, without feeling as if they are fighting for you."

Achish moaned with agreement, but eyed him suspiciously. "You will be outside the pentapolis."

"But still inside Philistia," replied David.

"Autonomy," pondered Achish.

"Under your sovereignty," pandered David. "I will be at your beck and call. If Saul goes after me, Israel will be ripe for your taking. If he splits his forces against you and me, then you will still have an easy victory in the north."

Achish's face became deadpan still. David could not tell if he was still thinking it through or if the wine had finally overtaken him.

A smile suddenly spread over Achish's face and he said, "Excellent. If you keep this up, I may even appoint you to be my personal bodyguard."

"One thing at a time, my lord."

"Indeed. And the first thing is to get you settled. Tell your men to gather their families and move to the city of Ziklag. It is twenty miles south-west of Gath, on the outer reaches of Philistia in the Negeb. I will relocate the current inhabitants to Gaza and Ashkelon."

David bowed and left the cup on the table. "Lord Achish, you are too kind and too wise. I only hope to be worthy of your goodness and greatness."

David could flatter with the best of them. What he had planned for Achish was something quite different.

CHAPTER 64

David stood before his six hundred men, gathered in a small valley just outside the gates of Gath. Joab and Abishai stood with the Three and the Thirty behind David, along with prophets Nathan and Gad, as well as the high priest Abiathar, wearing his ephod.

David told them about their new home, the town of Ziklag, and their new mission of performing sorties and expeditions against the tribes of the Negeb, supported by their Lord Achish.

Some murmured in the crowd. David offered, "If there is any question in your minds, now is the time to air your concerns."

One of the men, a brigand with five of his comrades, shouted out, "David, we have followed you through battles with Saul in deserts and holes in the ground. We do not mind fighting with you against that tyrant and his minions. But you refuse to kill him. Now you want to pillage tribes of Judah? My comrades and I fear you are going as mad as King Saul."

Joab and Abishai drew their swords and stepped forward ready to slay the insolent brigand and his company of five. David held them back.

Joab spoke to David with hushed anger, "They have defied you, my lord."

"No," said David. "They are questioning me. And they have every right to. Because what I am asking of them is treason. *You* ought to have questioned me as much."

The brothers hung their heads. Their oath of devotion was to David, right or wrong. Was David claiming he was wrong?

David spoke to the rest of the gibborim along with the brigand. "Do you believe I am the promised messiah of Israel?" The men nodded their heads, some mumbled yes, and others shouted it.

David pulled Nathan, Abiathar, and Gad forward. "Do you believe I am receiving the word of Yahweh through the voice of his prophets and the ephod of the high priest?"

More "yeses" and nodding.

"Then I am asking you to trust me. You may not know the entire picture of the strategy that I and my leaders are planning. But you must trust me as you did in the battle of Keilah when you first fought against the Philistines. You were afraid and thought we would lose to them, but you trusted me, and Yahweh delivered the Philistines into our hands. And then you did not believe me when I said that Yahweh told me through the ephod that the city would turn around and betray us into the hands of Saul. But you trusted me anyway and we left, and averted sure disaster."

The warriors did not forget that episode. The quiet of the crowd illustrated a humbled agreement. The brigand and his men did not show such humility.

David continued, "I am asking you, trust me now as you trusted me then. Yahweh's will shall be revealed to you in time. But now, you must have faith that he will not lead you astray."

David had to keep his words vague enough in order to elicit his men's trust without revealing too much information for any spies Achish might have among them. He could not tell them what he planned. It was the universal bane of all generals in military strategy. The common fighter could only know his immediate goal in the battle. He could not be privy to the bigger picture plans of kings and generals. It would be too much upon him, and would jeopardize the mission if discovered by the enemy. The common fighter had to trust that however wrong a command may appear to be in the immediate, in the long term strategy, it may actually have the opposite meaning or result.

David concluded, "If any of you cannot abide such commands, then leave now, and I will not hold it against you. You have my word that you will receive your pay and you will not be harmed. Stand with me, and I promise you, all will come clear in Yahweh's time."

It was all he could offer them.

But it was still not enough for the brigand and his company of five men. They got on their horses and left the band of six hundred gibborim to their fate.

On the way out, they passed a group of about a hundred and fifty Gittite warriors approaching them. The gibborim were worried. Had they been betrayed? Had Lord Achish set a trap?

David saw that the leader of the squad was Ittai the Gittite. He led the dissident Gittites that David met earlier. Their numbers had grown.

They stopped and presented themselves formally to David. Ittai stepped forward and announced, "My lord David, anointed messiah king of Israel, please accept our force of Gittite warriors as your loyal followers. As Yahweh lives, and as my lord the promised king lives, wherever my lord David shall be, whether for death or for life, there also will your servants be. We will fight on your behalf and we will die on your behalf. Take us with you to Ziklag."

Benaiah cautioned David, "They are Philistines."

More murmuring in the group of leaders signaled agreement with Benaiah.

But David knew something the others did not. He turned to the rest of his men and announced, "Does anyone know any reason why we should not allow these circumcised warriors of Yahweh to join our forces?"

The gibborim muttered and buzzed with surprise. Circumcised warriors of Yahweh? Ittai must have led them in the Israelite sign of their covenant.

David shouted, "Neither do I! We welcome you, Ittai the Gittite and your number of faithful gibborim. Now, everyone go each to his own home and retrieve your families and possessions. We meet at Ziklag in a fortnight."

CHAPTER 65

Ittai felt great hope in his heart as he finished walking the street to his blacksmith forge. David had accepted him and his fellow Gittite warriors into the fold of his gibborim forces. He had secured the favor of Yahweh's promised messiah king. Maybe redemption *was* possible for a half breed after all.

He stopped at the door. The sound of crashing inside told him someone was breaking up his home. Invaders. He drew his sword. He was no coward. He would not try to sneak a peek or come in the back door. He was not afraid of death. He kicked open the door and burst into the room to face the danger fearlessly.

A woman's scream of surprise pierced the air. What Ittai had found inside was not danger, it was beauty.

Ummi was packing up boxes of tools to ready them for transport. He saw her own simple traveling pack at his feet.

"Ummi. What are you doing here?"

"I am packing up your tools for travel to Ziklag."

"How did you know I was moving to Ziklag?"

She smiled without words.

He said, "Did you follow me out to the valley?"

She said, "I follow you lots of places." She looked at him like a puppy fearful of punishment.

Ittai complained, "Well, that ruins my ability to detect spies."

She quipped, "Since you will not have me as wife, I have left my father and mother to become your servant."

He sighed. "Ummi, what am I going to do with you?"

"Feed me and house me. I will perform all the duties of a household servant for you, with none of the bothers of a wife."

"Ummi, you will not."

"I will."

"Are you disobeying me?"

"Does that mean I am your servant?"

He growled with frustration.

She picked up an awl on the table and moved toward the door as she spoke, "You were just accepted into the community of Israel by the messiah king himself, against all your fears of cursedness. And now you refuse to allow another cursed one the same grace you have been shown. Shame on you, Ittai."

He sighed again. It was all he could do, since he did not have much to argue with.

She stepped up to the door and pushed him aside. She backed up against the door and placed the awl at her earlobe against the door. The rite of bond servanthood was to puncture the earlobe with an awl into the door of the household of the master. It was a piercing of permanent devotion.

And it was painful.

He cried out, "Ummi, no!" He moved to try to stop her.

But it was too late.

She jammed the awl into the door and squealed with pain.

That sound pierced Ittai's soul with as much pain as she experienced. His love for her was so deep, he would take on himself anything that she would feel.

His hand lightly touched her ear, now bleeding down the door. He could not touch her to add any more pain.

Instead he dropped to the ground on his knees and bawled like a baby, clutching her skirt.

"I cannot," he cried.

"You can." She stayed still, the pain throbbing in her ear.

He said, "I cannot put you through the pain. I cannot give you a family."

"I do not want a family, Ittai of Gath. I want you. And the only pain I cannot bear to experience is the pain of a life without you. I would rather be your barren servant than a fertile queen in the house of a Philistine Lord."

He looked up at her. He knew she meant it. He felt the same way. In fact, he had resigned himself to a miserable existence, rather than put her through the pain of childlessness. He refused to reproduce because he was of Nephilim blood and he did not want to further the lineage of corruption.

He rose up from the floor. His crying had turned to sniffling. He put his hand on the awl and gently pulled it from her ear and the door.

She winced and whimpered. He winced and whimpered with her.

He put his lips to her bloody ear as if to heal it with his kiss, to taste the blood of her suffering.

He then whispered into her ear, "Ummi, my beloved, you shall never be my servant. Never. I will only accept you by my side as my wife. Will you have this miserable half-man as your husband?"

She looked up into his tear-stained red eyes and all the pain had gone away. She said, "You are a half-*angel*. And you are accepted by the messiah. I love you, Ittai of Gath, and I will follow you and your god to the depths of Sheol — as your wife."

They kissed.

And all the world fell away.

CHAPTER 66

David washed up and put on a new robe and tunic. Flowers put out by the servants spruced up his temporary domicile in Gath. The preparations were to accommodate two arriving travelers and their retinue before they left for Ziklag. Whether the two travelers would get along was what worried David most.

The travelers were his two wives, Abigail of Carmel and Ahinoam of Jezreel. He had a squad of his bodyguard collect them from their respective homes and accompany them to Gath. They were to meet with David there and journey with him to their new home in Ziklag.

The problem was that the wives had not met each other until this journey. Worse yet, they had not even *heard* of each other.

David had met Ahinoam at the city of Hebron, shortly after Michal had been taken from him by Saul and married to another man. He was lonely and on the run and feeling abandoned by Yahweh when he met Ahinoam.

Ahinoam worked with horses, so David met her when he housed his own in her stables. He immediately fell for her exotic charm and raven black hair. She was young and thin like Michal, and with a fiery temperament. He married her in secret and left her in Hebron when he traveled to deliver his family to Moab. She understood the danger of traveling with him while he was pursued by Saul, so she waited for him to send for her when the time was right.

Abigail had also waited to be sent for from Carmel when the time was right. And that time was now. Unfortunately, David had made a point never to discuss his previous marriage to Ahinoam with anyone, including Abigail. His commanding leaders knew of the union but did not speak of it. What their lord did not want to discuss was his own business. But they suspected that he was embarrassed by his impulsive desire to soothe the pain of losing Michal by so quickly replacing her with a woman of similar qualities. But judging by Ahinoam's beauty, they suspected his embarrassment was alleviated rather satisfactorily.

David rode to meet them at the gates of Gath upon their arrival. The women rode behind Joab and Abishai, and behind them, the party of twenty warriors.

Joab and Abishai approached David with stern faces and rolled their eyes simultaneously. They saluted David. Joab said, "My Lord, they are all yours. Abishai and I request a three day leave to rest from this most wearying journey."

There was something in their words that carried more than they were saying.

David said, "Granted," and they immediately gave looks of relief and galloped their horses like a getaway from a crime. They left David to watch Abigail and Ahinoam approaching him on their horses. He smiled and held his hands out in a welcome to the beauties bundled in desert robes for travel.

They had both pulled down their hoods and rode with stern postures. They looked forward frowning, without acknowledging David, and passed him by.

He gulped, knowing he was in trouble—big trouble. He dismissed the escort and chased after the women to lead them to their new home.

He rode before them and when they arrived at their new home, he helped Abigail dismount. Ahinoam didn't wait for him. She simply jumped down from her mount, and they followed him silently into the large, stone brick home, as servants took their luggage from the camel.

When the door had closed, they both turned to David with very angry faces.

He said, "Let me explain."

Abigail ignored David, looked at Ahinoam and said, "Shall we let our husband explain, wife number one?"

Ahinoam replied without looking at David, "I do not think so, wife number two. I am too weary from a long ride and in need of some rest."

David's countenance dropped. He did not know how he was going to fix this problem.

Ahinoam added, "But since we are two wives and not one, then we apparently will have to coordinate everything with each other, lest our husband get too confused with his appetite for multiple wives."

"Oh yes," said Abigail, still dripping with sarcasm. "Well, I can say as wife number *two*," she said the word "two" with great disdain, "I surely cannot share a bed with *our* husband at this time, since I am in the way of women. How about you, wife number one?"

Ahinoam responded with equal biting sarcasm, "I think I too am in the way of women, so I surely cannot share a bed with *our* husband." She said "our" with contempt.

They were clever, these two, as Yahweh himself forbade the marriage bed with a wife when she was in the way of women. It was uncleanness, and would result in a separation from the community.

Abigail said, "Perhaps he has a third wife we also do not know about, that he can visit to fulfill his needs, since we are no doubt not enough for him."

They both finally looked at David with wide eyes, expecting an answer, as if to say, "Well?"

David gulped. "There are no others."

"Other than Michal, that is," said Abigail.

"I told you about Michal," defended David. "And that is my marriage into the royal family. I told you, Saul took her away and had her remarried."

Ahinoam said, "Would you like the two of us to travel to Gibeah and try to get her back for you? We can persuade the king that two wives are just not enough for our hungry little husband, so gluttonous for wives is he."

Abigail jumped in, "Would you mind showing us our bedchamber, husband, and please find a good pillow to sleep on the floor because we have headaches of such ferocity that we simply must be left alone. No sharing of my bed tonight, and for Yahweh knows how long."

"Hmmm, yes," agreed Ahinoam, "No sharing my bed for a long, long time."

David sighed. He knew he could say nothing at this moment, so he silently led them to the bedchamber like a scolded puppy and gathered a pillow or two to sleep on the floor like the dog he had become in their eyes.

CHAPTER 67

In the morning, David had apologized to the two women several times over and promised that he would never treat them with such dishonesty ever again. Polygamy diluted the precious, exclusive unity of marriage. He tried to convince them that he was truly in love with the both of them, and he only hoped that he could prove that love over time.

"That would take a very *long* time," said Abigail.

"And *a lot* of proof," added Ahinoam.

They forgave him as best they could and tried to make the most of their situation, though they strangely still claimed to be in the way of women, and therefore unavailable to share his bed for some time.

On the day of their departure for Ziklag, Abigail pulled David aside to complain to him while Ahinoam prepared the horses.

"David, Ahinoam is very young and immature. She does not know how to keep a household. You need to tell her to stop treating the servants like they are horses. She gives them treats and allows them too much freedom. I am the eldest, and I require a certain amount of priority and deference. I am not being demanding. I am not asking to be the queen of Gath or anything. But she is like a child. She does not clean up after herself, and she has no manners."

David listened sincerely and tried to understand. But he had no idea what she was talking about. He did not believe she was lying, but he just did not see what she was referring to. Maybe some of it, but she seemed to remember enough details to choke an onager.

The next day, Ahinoam took him aside while Abigail went to market to get some food for the trip.

"David, Abigail is very old and set in her ways. She tries to control the household. You need to tell her to stop treating the servants as if they are captives of war. She does not reward them a bit, and allows them no freedom. I know I am the younger, but she is so demanding, she acts like the Queen of Gath. And she treats me like a child. She chases after me, picking up and clucking like an old hen. She is too fastidious and she has the manners of a grizzled war general."

David listened sincerely and tried to understand. It had started to become more clear to him that he was in store for a long and difficult polygamous marriage. It was hard enough to keep up with one woman's relational needs and peculiar mysteries. But two of them at odds with one another appeared to be an impossible task of unconquerable magnitude. He began to wonder if this was the chastising consequence of his own selfish choices. Yahweh was finally giving him his fill in order to teach him a lesson.

David's consolation was his lingering hope that once the two women had settled down a bit that they would forgive him. He prayed for harmony from Yahweh.

Still, the stress made him long for the exciting first love of his lost wife, Michal. How uncomplicated it had been with their young love. How easy everything seemed to work out with her. The pleasures, the simplicity, the fun of youth.

But that was all in the past for him now. He had to grow up into the leader Yahweh had promised he would be. He had to put behind him his childish ways of the past. He had to accept the responsibility of his own choices, as well as the calling of his god.

• • • • •

David rode ahead of his train of followers to Ziklag. Benaiah and his bodyguard of twenty gibborim accompanied him. They would scout the way to make sure there were no hostile tribes or enemy traps along the route. The twenty mile trek would take the six hundred warriors and their nine hundred family members two days because of the young and old traveling with them and carrying their entire households on the backs of camels and donkeys.

Abishai and Joab led the civilian train, Ittai and his Gittites picked up the rear. Jonathan ben Shimei rode with Ittai and Ummi. The Mouse had grown on the blacksmith. He had a witty tongue that compensated for his small size and made Ummi laugh. But Ittai had also seen himself in the little warrior, who gave his soul to the cause with everything he had, and always seemed to surprise those around him because they maintained such low expectations for him.

Though Ittai looked tall to other Israelites at about five foot, eight inches, he was actually a dwarf by the nine foot giant standards of most Rephaim. So he never called Jonathan "Mouse," as the others did. It reminded him too much of his own insulting nickname, "Runt." Instead, he trained Jonathan in fighting tactics and building muscle. But Jonathan's skill with a bow was so superior to others, Ittai made sure his apprentice focused on keeping that talent sharpened and ready. Ittai thought to himself, *One day, they will no longer call him Mouse, they will call him Hawk for his sharpshooting skill.*

Jonathan interrupted Ittai's thoughts, "I cannot wait to kill my first giant."

Ittai looked at him. "It is not a game, Jonathan. Rephaim are not like animals we hunt. They are the Seed of the Serpent."

"Is that not what you are training me to understand?"

"Yes. You must know your enemy before you can overcome them. Inside and out."

Jonathan sighed. "It is clear I will never be of enough physical prowess to vanquish one. And if I could not hit their head, I doubt an entire quiver of my little arrows could drop one."

"Unless you hit them in the right spots."

Jonathan considered his words.

Ittai added, "Know them inside and out, and you have the key to their downfall."

Jonathan looked over at Ummi who had been listening the entire ride. "Is that how you engineered Ittai's downfall, Ummi? You know him inside and out?"

Ummi smiled. "Inside and out."

Ittai looked at his beloved and they shared a loving smile.

•••••

David and his men arrived at the empty town on the first night. Achish had already cleared it out of its original inhabitants to make room for David and his people.

They set up tents just outside the perimeter of the city and waited for their countrymen to catch up with them before entering the city as a whole community.

After a good meal of quail and wine, David retired to his tent to get his rest for the evening. But shortly before midnight, he heard the sound of a party arriving on horseback. They were greeted by David's guards and allowed entrance to the camp. It must have been someone from their group running ahead. Since he was not alerted, David knew it was not an emergency or alarm from attack.

A sole figure approached his tent with a lamp. He could see it was clearly a woman in cloaked garb. He got excited. It was one of his wives. But which one? After a lonely week, were they already beginning to compete for his attention? This one was the first. She was the most aggressive.

Was it Abigail, staking her claim as the eldest?

Was it Ahinoam rushing to get the first kiss because of the hungrier desire of youth?

He cared not whoever it was. He loved them both.

She pulled down her hood and his heart sank.

It was Lady Bisha.

She pushed him inside his tent and closed the flap behind her. She was breathing heavily.

"My lady. What brings you this evening?"

She stared at him with ravenous eyes. "Well, aren't you the wild stud, with your two mares?"

He said, "Lady Bisha, you should not be here."

"No?" she said. "I think I should be. How is your new arrangement working out for your marriages? I understand twice the women results in twice the dissatisfaction."

"How would you know…" he began to ask.

She answered him before he could finish asking, "I am queen of Gath, David. I have my spies. But I don't have everything I want."

He sighed. She whispered, "I want to make you an offer, my love-starved liege."

He swallowed.

She stepped closer to him like a panther on the hunt. "You and I both know that marriage is an agreement for political or other purposes. And you and I both know that duty and obligation strangle the romance out of the relationship of husband and wife, or in your case, *wives*. Familiarity, propriety, and all the petty squabbles and demands of lawfully wedded women."

She dripped with spite for the law. But he could not deny that there was truth to what she was saying.

"I offer you freedom from all of that," she continued, "and the opportunity to abandon your moral scruples to the wind. I offer you complete and absolute submission. I, Bisha, the Lady queen of Gath, will lay down my power and will do anything you want. *Anything*. I will be your slave. I will let you hurt me. You would have complete control of me with no consequences and no shame. I swear to you, David. Anything you desire."

He looked at her. "Anything?"

"Anything—*and everything*," she repeated.

"Complete obedience?"

"Absolute. As unto a god."

"Good," he said. "Then I command you to return to Gath this very moment."

Her eyes went wide with shock. She thought she had finally conquered him, but she had only walked into her own trap.

Her face wrinkled in anger.

"Am I hurting you now?" he asked. "You wanted to be hurt."

She did not answer. She could not answer. It was a stab of righteousness in her gut.

He said, "No consequences—my lady. As you promised. Complete and absolute submission. I am still a servant of Gath, performing raids on the Negeb for Lord Achish."

She tramped out without a final word.

She finally knew she could not have him.

So she would destroy him.

CHAPTER 68

The prison of Gath was not built for giants. So Lahmi the Rephaim was manacled to the wall of his isolated cell by his arms, with his legs double bound with thick rope, and his waist chained to a boulder. He was not as concerned about his bindings and how to get out of them as much as he was about fleeing the city, once he escaped the dungeon. He could easily be hunted down by Gath's finest warriors. Then he would have to kill some of his brothers in arms, which he deeply wanted to avoid. But Lord Achish would undoubtedly send some Rephaim to make the catch more certain.

Lahmi's thoughts were interrupted by a servant bringing gruel to eat. The servant was let in and brought the bucket up to the bound Rephaim, and ladled the slop into his mouth to eat. It was hard to tell if it was food or garbage, but he needed his strength.

Then the servant pulled back her cloaked hood. It was Lady Bisha in disguise.

"What are you doing here?" he whispered. "I had assumed it was you who ordered my imprisonment."

It *was* Bisha who ordered his imprisonment. But that did not suit her interests any longer. She concocted a new story. "Do not be such a fool. Achish wanted to protect his investment in conquering Saul. You have your own imbecilic behavior to blame. Had you kept your childish temper to yourself, you would be out hunting David right now instead of stewing in your own excrement."

Lahmi felt duly chastised. She was right after all. He had used every trick in the book to rationalize to himself his idiotic outburst. A thousand scenarios had gone through his head with a thousand different ways of giving Achish a piece of his mind as he imagined strangling the life out of him. Languishing in a dungeon tended to do that to a prisoner.

She was wrong about one thing, though. Stewing in his own self-deception was far more miserable than stewing in his own excrement.

She gave him some more to eat and continued, "I am here to give you a chance to fulfill your vengeance, if you do not ruin it again for yourself."

"I am listening," he whispered.

She said, "I have made clandestine contact with an Amalekite clan in the south. They are sending a small squad to break you out and will help you to kill David. He now resides in Ziklag."

"When? What am I to look for?"

They were interrupted by an angry guard opening the door and stomping in, complaining, "If you are going to talk and not eat, then take the gruel and be gone with you."

Bisha pulled up her hood so she would not be noticed.

She said in a scraggly voice, "Yes, my lord."

Lahmi watched her walk away with the bucket. He was desperate to know what was coming, but he could not lose Bisha's cover. The guard jerked her away without saying a word.

It was late into the night when Lahmi awakened with a start. Everything was silent, but his Nephilim sixth sense could tell something was afoot.

He heard the sound of muffled thuds and dragging bodies. He knew the guards must have been asleep at this point, so they were probably all taken by surprise.

The dungeon door opened.

It was not an Amalekite that came through, but a Gittite, one of the guards. He dragged the corpse of an Amalekite by the hair and dropped him within Lahmi's sight at his feet. The Amalekite's savage painted face was bashed in like a bloody pulp.

"So, it looks like you have some vicious desert rats as your friends. Five of them tried to kill us to free you."

Another Gittite guard stepped in, limping with a wound from the fight.

A third Gittite entered, dragging another dead Amalekite to drop him on the floor.

The first guard said, "They are all dead. Killed a few of my comrades. And that gives me the chance to do what I have wanted to do for a long time: kill you and make it look like it was an accident of our brawl."

The Gittite did not need to draw his sword, he already carried it in his hand.

Lahmi stared at the man with shock. "Why do you want to kill me?"

"For murdering my son, you unholy abomination."

Lahmi could not possibly know who the guard was or who his son was. Lahmi could not remember how many young men he abused or how many of them had died in his violent hands. There were dozens—buried and forgotten by him. As an elite Son of Rapha he was legally untouchable in such debauchery.

But it was inevitable one of them would come back to find him. He just never expected it would be at such an inopportune moment. His arms were chained to the wall, his legs bound fast in rope and a boulder chained to his waist.

The first guard thrust his sword toward Lahmi's throat.

Lahmi dodged his head just in time.

The sword lodged between two of the stones in the wall behind him.

Lahmi yanked with all his might on his right chained arm.

The anchor for the chain ripped out of the wall and flew like a sling, hitting the guard in the gut, breaking his ribs.

He dropped to the floor, leaving the sword stuck in the wall.

It had been his one surprise tactic. Lahmi had been preparing for a few days by loosening the anchor. The chains and manacles were made to retain normal men, not giants of extraordinary strength.

He reached up to grab the sword. But the second guard launched at him with a battle axe.

Lahmi had to release the sword and roll out of the way.

The battle axe came down and hit the sword, snapping it in two, leaving half the blade in the wall. The sword was useless.

Lahmi rolled to his stomach, his left hand still chained to the wall.

He looked back to locate the second guard and swung his hand backward.

The chain, weighted by the anchor, wrapped around the guard's neck, and the anchor plate dug into his head, crushing it instantly.

The guard fell to the floor.

The chain had wrapped and embedded in the corpse. He could not shake it from the body. It turned Lahmi's only possible weapon into a dead weight.

The third guard held a javelin toward Lahmi. But he stood defensively, not ready to attack.

The first guard yelled at him, while grabbing his throbbing ribs, "Give me the javelin, you fool!"

He ran over to grab the weapon.

Lahmi swiped his roped legs and tripped the first guard onto his face on the ground.

Lahmi yanked the chain in his right hand and it snapped off the head of the guard it was wrapped around.

He whirled it around and caught the javelin on the shaft, wrapping around it tight.

He yanked and the guard fell forward right into Lahmi's grip. The fool had not let go of the weapon.

Lahmi pounded his fist onto the fool's head.

Lahmi's legs were still roped tight, he was entangled in two dead bodies, and the chain to the boulder would not let him move any further.

He looked up to see the first guard picking up the battle axe.

Lahmi searched for an option, and saw the broken blade piece in the mortar above his head. He grabbed it and pulled it out, hands bleeding from the sharp edges.

The first guard raised his axe high above Lahmi.

Lahmi threw the sword blade and caught the first guard right in the throat.

He fell backward to the floor.

Lahmi grabbed the javelin blade, snapped it off the staff and cut off the ropes on his legs.

Then, he pulled with all his might, using his legs to counterweight against the wall and yanked the other anchored chain from the stone.

He was free enough to reach the dead bodies of the guards. He found the keys to free himself from the boulder and manacles.

He gathered a dagger and two swords from the other dead warriors in the hallway. He sighed. If this was the Amalekites breaking him out, he had a thing or two to teach those incompetent barbarians. He made his way out of the dungeon.

• • • • •

When Lahmi reached the forest outside Gath on foot, he was met by a raiding party of fifty Amalekites. Five of them were giants. They were painted for war with camouflage. They had crazed eyes. They twitched and spasmed their muscles as if they were being afflicted or manipulated by spirits. Lahmi had always considered them too bizarre to deal with, but now that they were aiding him through Bisha's political machinations, he decided to take advantage of their offer.

The leader of the tribe greeted Lahmi. He patterned himself after the memory of the infamous Agag in every way, including his dress and name.

"Greetings, gibborim. I am Agag the Second. Your brother's greatness has not been forgotten by my people. We seek a common goal: the destruction of the Seed of Abraham." His eyes and neck twitched.

Lahmi was familiar with the original Agag. Though it was not unusual in the world for royalty to take on previous names in honor of their lineage or greatness, Lahmi thought it lessened the king's own glory to mimic another rather than to carve out one's own destiny. But they did share in common a hatred for the Israelites and their abominable presence in Canaan, as well as a desire for revenge upon the murderers of their kinsmen.

"From the river to the sea," said Lahmi. By "river" he meant the Jordan River. "I will fight until these Hebrews are driven into the jaws of Leviathan."

"Into the jaws of Leviathan," repeated Agag. "Let us go. A search party is already after you."

Strange, thought Lahmi, *Agag's voice sounded like it became another person.*

Lahmi turned to see a party of fifty gibborim on horseback and ten Rephaim on foot leaving the gates of Gath.

The Amalekites and Lahmi disappeared into the foliage of the forest on their way to their camp, miles in the southern Negeb.

CHAPTER 69

The tribe of Amalek camped on the north side of the Besor Brook about fifteen miles south of Ziklag. This was an outlier military post as the other few Amalekite tribes were across the brook, deeper in the Negeb.

Joab and Abishai had scouted out the camp. They told David the population of three hundred were all warriors, so David took a contingent of four hundred of his own with him.

Jonathan the Mouse had wanted so badly to help David kill Amalekites that when he wasn't chosen for the raiding party, he caused a ruckus of complaint. David had to punish him with incarceration. Ittai stayed and watched over his apprentice, teaching him the finer points of obedience to their commander.

David watched from his vantage point on the ridge, overlooking the encampment of Amalekites. The desert tribe performed their worship of Azazel, the satyr goat god of the desert, the realm of chaos, while the sun set behind them on the orange horizon.

They beat drums with a chaotic pulse and danced around as a group. If dancing was what you could call their frenzied and jittering jumping and shaking. Howls filled the air from the participants, signaling their abandonment to forces beyond them.

"Siyyim and iyyim," said Benaiah next to David. "The howling demons of the desert wasteland. It appears their entire tribe is inhabited with them. They are evil spirits that dance destruction upon the graves of the dead."

"This is not going to be easy," said Abishai. "They are stronger by such possession. Harder to kill."

Without taking his eyes off the ritual below, David said, "Then we will kill them harder."

Night fell. In the camp of Amalek, the warriors quieted down and rested from their ritual dance and feast. Some gorged themselves, which was providential for David and his band of three hundred gibborim. Bellies full of meat would make them more sluggish in combat. David's men concealed themselves on the periphery of the camp in the bushes and gullies.

When David blew his war horn, they rose and attacked the Amalekite camp as one man.

They rushed their opponents, catching many off guard. By the time the Amalekites had gathered to arms, David's warriors had swept into camp and were cutting, stabbing and slicing their way to a quick victory.

But the Amalekites were possessed by a legion of evil spirits.

They howled and fought with fury. The noise pierced the eardrums of the Israelites. It caused some of them to falter. The Amalekites pushed back, gaining ground.

Benaiah and the bodyguards fought next to David. Amalekites ran at them like crazy, screaming banshees.

Benaiah cut off the arm of one, but he kept attacking. He cut off the other arm, and the Amalekite still kept coming. He thrust him through the gut and the cannibal tried to bite him, until he finally dropped. Benaiah withdrew his blade.

Abishai was near him. He shouted out, "I told you this would not be easy."

"Five!" yelled Joab. "You are getting behind, Abishai!"

Joab and Abishai were competitive even on the field as they sought to keep up with one another in terms of body count.

Abishai joined his brother and increased his ferocity to catch up.

The demonic Amalekites howled and fought like a pack of hyenas mad for blood.

But these were David's finest warriors, his gibborim, his mighty men. They cut through the sons of Amalek like wheat. It just took a little longer for the harvest, because they were not typical enemy combatants.

When the dust settled, they had slaughtered the Amalekites to a man.

David looked out across the Besor Brook, with his commanders by his side. "Now, we gather all the booty, animals, gold and silver, and we bring it to Achish as our first of many raids on 'Israelite' settlements."

Benaiah, Abishai and the others smiled with understanding. He never intended to kill his people after all. It was all a pretense.

David added, "No survivors, no evidence."

• • • • •

David and an entourage of fifty men arrived at Gath with their wagon loads of booty from the several raids they had made in the Negeb on the Amalekites and other Canaanite tribes. They were ushered into the Lord and Lady's presence to examine the loot.

"Impressive," said Achish. "Do you not agree, my lady?"

Bisha looked over the spoils seized by David from a raid on Israelite tribes. But she did not look at the gold and silver so much as the jars and containers that carried the gold and silver.

She said, "Hmmmm," with a kind of detachment that made David grateful she was no longer eyeing him as a prize of her battle.

She said, "How many raids did you say these spoils are from?"

David answered, "Three. All of them were Israelite settlements in the Negeb: Judahites, Jerahmeelites and Kennites."

She picked through a pile of stolen garments. "Have you encountered any hostile forces in the desert? Bands of outlaws? Giants?" She deliberately avoided using the word 'Amalekite' so as not to lead him.

"No, my lady," replied David. "But I expect them eventually. We will be equipped to deal with them."

"You kill them all, do you?" she queried, looking at some jewelry.

"The Israelites? Yes," David answered. "If word were to get out that I am against my countrymen, it would jeopardize our strategy."

"And your reputation," she added, looking accusingly at David. "Nobody likes a traitor, do they?"

"No, my lady." He stared right back at her. "The only thing worse than a traitor who betrays their own is a usurper who seeks to take what is not their own."

Bisha tightened. She knew he was directing her accusations right back at her, and Achish had no clue what was going on, the ignoramus.

"Perhaps that is why we get along," she said. "The house of Achish and the house of David have a common enemy and a common ethic. Unlike, say, the Amalekites who seem to have nothing in common with anyone."

David stiffened. Could she tell? Was she hinting to him that she knew what he was doing?

She continued, "Who knows but that one day, our gods may find common ground, that we might finally have shalom."

She deliberately used the Hebrew word for "peace." David thought to himself, *We have nothing in common, you slave of Dagon. And one day, I will impale you on a pike and kill every last Philistine as my god commands.*

Finally, Achish joined the conversation. He had been musing this whole time, considering an option that he now decided upon. "David, I want to appoint you captain of my bodyguard."

Bisha looked with shock at her husband. "What are you talking about? He is in Ziklag. He cannot be the captain of your bodyguard from such a distance."

David chimed in, "Lord Achish, it would be an honor, but Lady Bisha is right. It would divide your interests."

"Not in the least," said Achish. "I am going to follow David's counsel and invade Saul's northernmost region in the Jezreel Valley. It is a perfect battlefield for our chariots. David can guard me in the battle against King Saul and when we have vanquished the Israelite king, David can return to his duty in Ziklag."

Finally, thought David. *My opportunity has arrived. I must feign disinterest.* He said, "Can you not use the Sons of Rapha?"

"No. I have other plans for them. You and your men can go with me into the battle. It will no doubt draw Saul himself out into the open."

"Yes," Bisha jumped in, eyes locked on David. "Since David has displayed such skill at killing Israelites, this would provide for him even more opportunity for us to see what he can do."

Achish looked eagerly to David for his response. David took a deep breath as if considering his choice. Then he said, "Very well. I will go out with you. And you shall know what your servant can do. I will retrieve my men from Ziklag."

They had no idea what David was about to do. No one, with the possible exception of Bisha.

• • • • •

After David left for Ziklag, Bisha called upon her Amalekite spy, Arkos, and met with him in secret in the queen's privy.

Earlier, when she had examined the spoils from David's alleged victories over Israelite tribes, she had noticed a contradictory witness to his claims. She was quite familiar with the decorations and fashions of the various inhabitants of Canaan. She could see that the garments and pottery David had seized were clearly Amalekite, not Israelite. She had figured out that he was lying about his battles to Achish. He was not killing Israelites. He was killing Amalekites and other desert tribes. David had not betrayed his people after all. He was on course to betray

Achish. Lahmi must attack David when he returns to Ziklag and kill him before he has a chance to move north to the battle against Saul.

She handed a sealed scroll to Arkos and whispered, "Take this to Lahmi in the westernmost tribe of Amalek, across the Besor Brook. It is of life and death importance. Do not fail me."

"Yes, my lady," said Arkos, and left immediately.

CHAPTER 70

By the time Arkos the messenger reached the Amalekite tribe where Lahmi was hiding out, it was too late to catch David at Ziklag. David had quickly gathered all six hundred of his fighting men and left the town to join Lord Achish at Aphek with the rest of the Philistine forces. He would need his full force for what he planned to do.

Unfortunately for Arkos, he was captured by one of David's own scouts on his return to Bisha.

Unfortunately for David, Arkos told the scout only that he was on his way to report David's movements to Bisha.

• • • • •

The armies of the Philistine pentapolis had assembled with Achish and his Gittites at Aphek, thirty miles south of the Valley of Jezreel. Saul's forces were staged at the spring of Jezreel near the eastern edge of the valley near Mount Gilboa.

The Philistines mustered to prepare for their final march through the Carmel pass into the valley. The Lords of the other four cities had arrived with their forces of two thousand apiece, for a total of ten thousand armed Philistines. They were Dothan of Ekron, Tarhunda of Gaza, Mutallu of Ashdod, and Suwardata of Ashkelon. Ishbi and Runihura led two battalions of several hundred Rephaim total.

Dagon, Ba'alzebul, and Asherah scouted ahead to find out how many of the heavenly host would be fighting on behalf of Israel and King Saul.

What they found shocked them.

"There is not a single archangel or member of the host guarding Saul," said Ba'alzebul, as the three of them gazed down from Mount Gilboa upon Saul's army and the surrounding area.

"Where are they?" asked Dagon.

"How should I know?" spit Ba'alzebul.

"You are the emerging leader in this campaign," said Dagon with a bit of sarcasm in his voice. He relished the idea of Ba'alzebul making a tactical fool of himself. He may be a mighty storm god, but the strategies of war required more mental power than mere muscle-bound brawn.

Asherah was not distracted by their squabbling. She stared out toward Gilboa and said, "Has the entire ascendancy of David to the throne been a mere ploy?"

Dagon added, "An alternate scheme of Yahweh."

• • • • •

Down by the spring of Jezreel, Saul's encampment of six thousand prepared for combat; sharpening their swords, practicing their battle moves, and praying to Yahweh. A messenger had arrived with intelligence on the Philistine forces.

"Curses!" exclaimed Saul. "It keeps getting worse. Now David is fighting with the Philistines *against* me? Yahweh mocks me."

"No, father," said Jonathan. "I do not believe it." He and his two other brothers, Abinadab and Malchi-shua, were with Saul's advisors. They were leading regiments of Israelite warriors for the battle.

Jonathan had not been in contact with David for a long time. But he knew David's heart. He knew he would never lift a hand against Saul. He had multiple opportunities to do so through the years and never once seized upon it. No, Jonathan did not believe David would fight against Israel, no matter what it may have appeared to the eyes of others.

Jonathan added, "I beg of you, father, consult the Urim and Thummim. Find out what Yahweh's will is in this matter."

Saul barked back, "You fool! Yahweh has not spoken to me in many years. The Urim and Thummim, the prophets, and my dreams are all mute. I have given up on them long ago. How often do I have to tell you? I am godforsaken!"

Jonathan and the other ten advisors cringed. They hoped that Saul was not about to explode into a rage again. The evil spirit in him could do so at any given moment. They tried not to aggravate him.

Saul looked out onto the valley before them. "The Philistines will be here on the morrow. We do not stand a chance against their chariots. Tell the men we are moving position to the heights of Mount Gilboa."

• • • • •

David and his gibborim marched behind Achish's forces at Aphek. His hopes had finally found opportunity. Achish was leading the Philistine armies into battle against Saul.

But Saul was Yahweh's anointed, and David would never forget that. He had successfully fooled Achish into thinking he had been killing Israelites in the Negeb, when in fact he had been killing Amalekites, Geshurites and Girzites. He had built trust with Achish to the point where the foolish Lord had exclaimed that he wanted David to be his bodyguard for life. David knew Lady Bisha was skeptical of his loyalty, but he had Achish in his hands.

As David marched with Benaiah by his side and his commanders of the Thirty and the Three, he mused over his plans for the battle. As Achish's bodyguard, David and his men would stay near the rear of the battle guarding Achish and therefore not confronting Israelites directly. But if and when the fighting got closer to Achish, David would find his opportunity to skewer Achish with his sword or javelin, just in time for Israelites to see and report back to Saul his deed of loyalty to the throne. The betrayal would no doubt turn the tide of war and secure Saul's victory over the Philistines. Saul may have been oppressed by an evil spirit, and out to kill David, but Achish was herem, cursed by Yahweh to total destruction.

Damn Achish to Sheol, thought David.

• • • • •

"Are you trying to damn me to Sheol?" complained Achish in the tent of Lords.

A general council of the five Lords of the Philistine pentapolis had been called. Several of them had noticed David and his men marching behind Achish's forces and had demanded to know what the Hebrews were doing in his army. Ishbi and Runihura were in the meeting as well.

Dothan of Ekron said, "This David is the man of whom it was said, 'Saul has slain his thousands, David, his ten thousands.'"

"It is a woman's song," said Achish. "Female sentiment."

"And it was a woman's song about Jael who nailed the tent peg into Sisera's skull that gave Israel victory over the Canaanites." Lady Bisha had just entered the tent. "I believe we are all familiar with that 'female sentiment.'" Her contempt was biting.

Achish resisted her. "Since he deserted to me from King Saul, I have found no fault in him to this very day. He has killed hundreds if not thousands of Israelites for me to prove his devotion."

"He has killed Amalekite tribes and told you the spoils were Israelite," countered Bisha.

The statement took Achish by surprise. She had been keeping the revelation for just the right moment.

Bisha continued, "My lord and love, I know Amalekite fashions and decorations when I see them on garments, jewelry and pottery. The spoils David brought you were *not* Israelite. David is a liar."

Achish floundered in confusion. "Why did you not tell me, if you thought this?"

"I tried, my Lord. But you would not listen." The other Lords of the pentapolis could not possibly know that she was the liar. She was so seductively believable in her beautiful queenly outfit. It distracted the minds of the Lords in her favor.

She summed it up with firm conviction, "My Lord Achish, I believe the Israelite David plans to kill you in battle. It is a brilliant long-planned conspiracy."

Achish said, "But why did he not kill me all this year? He had plenty of chances in close proximity to me."

Bisha countered, "But not in the sight of his king, before whom he seeks to justify himself as true believer."

Ishbi jumped in. "As a leader of the Sons of Rapha, I concur with Lady Bisha's assessment. I ask for the Lords' permission to arrest this traitor immediately and execute him."

"You will do no such thing!" yelled Achish. "This is speculation. Until I have had a better chance to examine the claims and evidence, David remains under my protective custody."

Dothan spoke again. "Nevertheless, Achish, you must accept the fact that there are enough witnesses that this Israelite is too questionable to risk putting your life in his hands."

Bisha started reconsidering whether the potential death of Achish may be desirable after all.

Tarhunda of Gaza added, "His presence jeopardizes the mission. We cannot allow it."

"I prayed to Asherah and received a vision," interrupted Bisha. The men all looked at her. "If you lead David on, you can sally him forth into battle. Then withdraw your forces and allow him to be slaughtered by Saul, whom you then slaughter. You can crush this Seed of Abraham and his messianic pretender with one stone to the forehead."

The ironic imagery she evoked was not missed by any of them.

"It is too risky," complained Mutallu of Ashdod.

"I agree with Mutallu," said Suwardata of Ashkelon. "We do not even know if David will advance against his own people. If he does not, you remain in jeopardy, Achish."

Tarhunda added, "We *all* remain in jeopardy with that possible traitor behind our lines."

"He is not a traitor!" yelled Achish.

Dothan spoke calmly, "The council has already decided, Achish. Send David back to Ziklag. He shall not go down with us to battle."

"You decided this before I arrived here?" said Achish crestfallen.

"Achish," said Dothan, "this matter is too close to you. We had to."

Achish gave a look of betrayal at Bisha and then the others. He sighed and said the formal acknowledgement, "So be the wisdom of the council."

The five Lords responded, "So be the wisdom of the council."

Achish began to plot the murder of Bisha.

• • • • •

Ishbi and Runihura led a guard accompanying Achish back to David's regiment. Achish demanded that his escort wait outside David's tent as Achish told him the news. Ishbi and Runihura kept their Lord in visible sight through the tent entrance. It was all they could do to keep from attacking the enemy target protected by their king.

"What have I done?" said David. "What have you found in your servant from the day I entered your service until now, that I may not go and fight against the enemies of my lord the king?"

"Nothing," replied Achish. "I have found nothing wrong in you from the day of your coming to me to this very day. I told them as much. You have been honest and I trust you with my life."

"But the Lords of the Philistines do not. Why?"

"David, please return peaceably to Ziklag and I will meet with you after this campaign."

David would not stop. "What do they think I am going to do, turn on you and kill you in the battle? After all this time I have shown my loyalty? That is ridiculous!"

It was exactly what he planned to do. In the midst of battle, he was going to thrust a javelin through the pudgy gut of this Yahweh-hating pile of excrement.

Achish said, "You are as blameless in my sight as an angel."

The angel of death, thought David.

But David said, "My heart is grieved," as he thought, *That my plans for bringing Yahweh victory are now delayed.*

The glaring distrust of the Rephaim giants outside the tent ensured that David could not get away with an assassination at this moment.

Achish said, "It would be best if you depart early in the morning, as soon as there is light. We do not want you to draw attention."

"I will do as you say, my lord," said David. "Though all doubt my loyalty and devotion, yet I remain allegiant to my Lord." He thought, *To my Lord Yahweh, that is.*

Achish embraced David and whispered, "You have been like a son to me."

David thought, *I am no son of a serpent.*

Then he said, "May my lord live, till next we meet."

He thought, *That I may strike you down still.*

CHAPTER 71

Saul approached a cave in the foothills of Endor, within a few miles of his encamped army on Mount Gilboa. He would have called the close proximity a miraculous provision, but since Yahweh had forsaken him, he could only consider it luck. The person he was visiting was the Ob of Endor, whom he had visited years ago.

Since Saul had captured the area from the Philistines, he had outlawed all necromancy and sorcery under pain of death. So the Ob had abandoned her original home in the city of Endor and found this cave in the foothills from which she could continue her work without arrest.

For that reason, Saul disguised himself in a common cloak and hood with a mere two soldiers to guard him, also dressed as commoners to avoid detection. It would not do well for the king's reputation to visit an Ob in direct defiance of his own law. But it was doubly dangerous because the Philistines were mustering at Shunem which lay in between Endor and Gilboa. If Saul was captured, it would end the war between the two nations in favor of the Philistines.

He paid an informant to lead him to the location before which he now stood. It was a small hidden opening in the rocks, leading into a grotto that was set up for the Ob's practice. A small fire burned at the mouth of the space, and scattered incense sensors gave off their lofty smoke. The scent immediately made Saul a bit light-headed.

A figure came out of the smoky curtain of incense: the Ob. She was the same beautiful young woman with brunette hair and reptilian slivered pupils. This time, he noticed something new about her. Her forehead appeared to have serpent-like scales that blended down into the smooth pale skin of her face. Saul could not tell if they were tattooed or real scales. He crouched his shoulders and pulled his hood tighter so she could not recognize him from his past visit. If she discovered his true identity, she would think he was there to execute her and he might lose his opportunity to do what he came for. He changed his voice to sound like a scruffy old man.

"Ob," he croaked. "Divine for me by a spirit and bring up for me whomever I shall name to you." He threw a bag of coins at her feet.

She didn't pick it up. She stared at him skeptically. She spoke with the hiss of a snake.

"Surely you know what Saul has done. He has cut off the mediums and the necromancers from the land."

Saul said, "Saul is not here to know, now is he?"

"Are you laying a trap for my life?" she asked.

He said, "As Yahweh lives, no punishment shall come upon you for this exchange. We will not speak of it outside of this cave."

She stared at him in stone silence for what seemed like minutes. Saul's eyes adjusted to the low light and he could finally see the serpentine shadows slithering around them in the dark. He knew that she could call upon her "servants" to attack if she felt endangered.

The Ob was no idiot. She knew these men were in disguise. They were not normal men. That they swore upon the name of the Hebrew god meant they were Israelites, which did not bode well.

On the other hand, the Philistines were encamped between her cave outside Endor and Saul's forces on Mount Gilboa, so the likelihood of their king surviving the next few days was slim anyway. He would most likely not survive to continue persecuting her.

She picked up the bag of coins and finally spoke, "Who shall I bring up for you?"

Saul smiled with satisfaction hidden in the shadow of his hood. "Samuel the Israelite Seer."

The Ob tilted her head with curiosity at the request. She reached over, grabbed a shovel and pick that was against the wall, and threw them at Saul's feet with the same kind of disdain that the bag of coins had been thrown down at her feet.

"Dig a pit," she said. "Six feet deep."

Saul turned to his two companions, who picked up the tools and began to dig. The Ob knew this old man was not who he appeared to be. He was some kind of leader.

The men finished the pit. The Ob had them slaughter a black pig as before and placed its body at the edge of the pit as a sacrifice. She dropped some burning logs from her fire into the pit along with some incense. The smoke rose and filled the room.

She placed some foodstuffs and wine at the pit's edge to call up the spirit with offerings to consume. She also threw a piece of Saul's silver into the pit, as part of the conjuring.

The Ob ritually rubbed salve on her face. Its glistening in the firelight gave her already unearthly look an added ghostly aura.

She gave Saul a dagger to cut his palm, as they had done years before. He cupped his hand so she could not see the previous scar and recognize him. He then squeezed his blood into the burning hole. She chanted under her breath the whole time.

Her body started twitching and convulsing. Saul's body started twitching in like manner. She noticed it and immediately knew this old man was inhabited by a spirit. She sensed a familiarity but could not place it. So she concentrated on the ritual.

Her usual routine was to call up her familiar spirits, who would then masquerade as whatever loved one the client of the Ob had asked for. As spirits they had access to some secret knowledge. But they were not Yahweh. They did not have all-knowing powers. They also used some information gleaned by the questions asked by the Ob of the client beforehand.

The Ob went into a trance of swaying before finally crying out, "I call forth the spirit of Samuel the Israelite Seer! Samuel, come forth!"

She twitched some more. Saul twitched some more.

She saw it before Saul or his men could. She stepped back in fright. It was not one of her familiar spirits.

It was Samuel the Seer.

The evidence finally came clear to her; the familiar spirit in the old man, his leader status, his disguise. This was not an old man with her. She turned to him angrily. "You have deceived me. You are King Saul!"

Saul was increasingly losing control of his muscular movements. But he could still speak. He said, "Do not be afraid. Please, just tell me what you see."

She said, "I see an elohim coming up out of the earth. An old man wrapped in a robe."

Saul threw back his hood and bowed to the ground in homage. The other two men followed suit.

Slowly, they looked up.

And everyone saw the image in the flames. It was shadowy, and just as she had described him, an old man in a diviner-prophet's robe. It was Samuel.

The spirit spoke with fiery indignance, "Why have you disturbed me by bringing me up?"

"Forgive me, Samuel," replied Saul. "But I had no other recourse. The Philistines are at war with me, and Yahweh has forsaken me. He answers me no more through prophets, dreams or Urim. I summoned you to tell me what I should do."

The spirit remained perturbed. "You are still the fool I left you as. Yahweh has become your enemy and you think I, his prophet, would not also be? You have deserved everything I prophesied. Yahweh has torn the kingdom from your hands and has given it to David."

"But why?" interrupted Saul. "What have I done to deserve his wrath?"

"SILENCE! You fool. How often have I told you? Yahweh has done this to you because you did not carry out his wrath against the Amalekites."

Saul trembled uncontrollably.

"Moreover, Yahweh will give you and Israel over into the hands of the Philistines and tomorrow, you and your sons shall be with me."

"No! No!" cried Saul. "No! No! NO! NO!"

The spirit of Samuel faded into the ground.

Saul started convulsing. Guttural sounds came from his throat. It was like something inside him was trying to come out. It *was* something inside him trying to come out: Nimrod. In the face of such sure doom, even the evil spirit would have nothing to do with Saul.

Saul's body flopped around like a fish out of water sucking air. The two men tried to hold him down. But suddenly an ear-piercing screech came out of Saul's gullet. It was not his own. It was the bellowing of the mighty evil spirit of Nimrod being ripped from his host to return to Sheol where he belonged.

Saul went limp. The spirit was gone.

As Saul came back to consciousness, the Ob became desperate to protect herself. While Saul was still shaking off his dizzy confusion, she blurted out, "Behold, your servant has obeyed you. I have taken my life in my hand and have listened to what you have said to me. Remember the obedience of your servant and the covenant you cut with me."

"What difference does it make, hag?" said Saul. "Have you not been listening?"

Saul felt a strange sense of loss. He had just been released from an evil spirit that had taunted him for many years. But after being rejected by Yahweh and his prophets, and his entire family, even such a spirit was a kind of comfort. He had counseled with it, and he had developed a relationship with it. It had become his only companion in a world of rejection.

But now, it too was gone, with all its rage and hatred and manipulation. But it was gone. And he was now more alone than ever in a vast void of emptiness. At least possession by an evil spirit meant he was considered of some value to someone. Now, he was of no value at all. All hopes for greatness and glory had evaporated into nothing. Now, if Samuel's prophesy was correct, and he always was, Saul was about to face the total oblivion of Sheol.

But Saul could not begin to explain this feeling of despair to anyone. So he said simply, "I need some food and rest and we will be on our way."

CHAPTER 72

Samuel was not the only one summoned to the cave at Endor that evening. After Saul had left to return to his camp, Ba'alzebul, Asherah, Dagon, and Resheph and Qeteb arrived at the Ob's residence. Several miles away, in the camp of the Philistines, they had heard the demonic scream of Nimrod leaving Saul and knew something significant had occurred that could affect the outcome of their plans.

The Ob nearly fainted at their entrance. She had endured the most difficult night of her life, and now it had become the most frightening. Why were the mighty Canaanite gods of storm, sea, pestilence and plague visiting her? What was this confluence of supernatural warfare that was going on?

She told them what had happened with Saul and Samuel.

Asherah thought out loud to the group, "So that is why there is no heavenly host at this battle. David has left and Saul is to be killed."

Ba'alzebul said, "David will be king."

Dagon said, "Shall we go after David?"

"No," said Asherah. "That is exactly where the heavenly host will be."

Dagon said, "But can we not bring the fight with us? The assembly will be here soon."

Resheph spoke up. "The assembly will not be coming."

The others looked at Resheph with surprise. Qeteb stepped closer to him as a team and said, "They appointed us as ambassadors to convey intelligence to the assembly. They said if David was not here, they would not show up for battle."

"Spies!" spit Dagon.

"Not spies," said Resheph. "Messengers."

"Spies," repeated Dagon.

Dagon stepped closer in hostility. The two tightened their stance, looked at Ba'alzebul to see what the mighty storm god might do. They were afraid of him alone. The others, they could handle.

Asherah shouted, "Dagon, stop puffing your chest! They are right. It is entirely reasonable for the assembly to appoint messengers, and we are not the most objectively reliable in this scenario." She knew they would only lessen their chances of victory if they created a rift of hostility within the assembly and became divided. She had to maintain the illusion of unity and subordination.

"Tell the assembly," said Asherah, "that we affirm their plans to call off the fight, and will notify them of any future opportunities to kill the messiah king."

Ba'alzebul watched her closely. He knew exactly what she was doing and had thought of the same thing himself. They were becoming quite united in their ability to strategize.

"I have a better idea," said Ba'alzebul. "Tell them the three of us will fight to protect Saul. It will be our contribution to thwart Yahweh's plans and keep the messiah from rising."

"Brilliant," Asherah smiled. "Deliciously brilliant." Protecting Yahweh's currently anointed king would be the opposite of what the heavenly host expected of the gods. It would place the archangels in the unenviable position of having to fight on behalf of the Philistines.

Dagon was completely frustrated that his rule of the Philistine dominion in Canaan was being co-opted by these two glory-seekers. He would not speak up, he just boiled with bile.

Then Asherah looked at him and winked. Ba'alzebul had not seen it. She must have been acknowledging that their conspiracy against Ba'alzebul was still on.

Resheph and Qeteb took their leave to return to Mount Hermon.

The gods suddenly became aware that they had become completely engrossed in their discussion. They had forgotten that the Ob was listening to them the entire time.

Asherah stepped up to her. The Ob stepped back frightened. Asherah assured her with a smile as she stooped down to her knee to look her in the face. She stroked the human's face and said, "My dear Ob, you have been so helpful to us. Allow me to show our gratitude for your loyalty."

The Ob relaxed.

Asherah snapped her neck and threw her body in the flames of the bonfire. She said as she walked out of the cave, "We cannot afford a single leak of our plan."

Ba'alzebul commanded, "Gods, prepare for battle."

CHAPTER 73

On the third day of their return, David and his men were within miles of Ziklag when they saw a plume of smoke rising in the distance from where their town was. Panic filled David and they raced the rest of the way to their destination.

They made record time. They broke over the ridge and saw the razed and pillaged ruins of their town before them. Many of the homes were already burnt to the ground, others smashed to pieces. Ziklag had been raided.

David screamed out as they closed the distance to the city limits. The six hundred warriors raced through the rubble and flames to find their families. No one was there. It was a ghost town. The few old men that remained told David they had been attacked by a tribe of Amalekites one day earlier. The attackers had ridden south, toward the Besor Brook, with the Israelite families as captives; all the wives, sons, and daughters.

"But they did not kill any of them," said one of the four old men that stood before David and his generals.

Relief flooded all the commanders.

Ittai teared up with the hope of his Ummi being spared. But if she was touched, or hurt, he feared he would go berserk and lose all constraint in a bloodbath of Amalekite carnage.

For David, Ahinoam and Abigail were alive. *Thank Yahweh they were alive.*

"Is there anything else you can tell us?" said David.

One of the other old men spoke up, "They were led by a Rephaim Gittite. Over eight feet tall. Red hair."

Ittai stepped forward. "How do you know he was a Gittite?"

"I know the armor used by Gittites. Much as your own."

Ittai said, "What was his weapon?"

"A scimitar," replied the old man. That was not as common. But it was the signature of the Sons of Rapha.

"Was he right or left handed?"

The old man thought for a moment. "Left handed."

Ittai turned to David. "That is Lahmi, brother of Goliath. When he escaped from Gath's dungeon, he must have ended up with the Amalekites."

David gritted his teeth with vengeance. That son of Belial was going to pay for this evil. His older brother got it quick and easy. This one, he would make suffer.

At that moment, the generals noticed that the other warriors were drawing near with anger.

One of them cried out, "What has happened to our families?"

David yelled out to the lot of them, "Amalekites have taken them hostage! But they are not dead!"

Another one shouted, "Our families as slaves and breeders for Amalekite scum!"

A mutinous rumble went through the crowd.

Someone else bellowed, "If we had not been licking Philistine toes, we would have been here and this never would have happened!"

The crowd became more restless.

Someone yelled, "We should stone the man responsible for this!"

Shouts of agreement rose up.

David's generals tightened their circle around him.

Benaiah drew his sword and stepped in front of David.

Ittai pulled a battle axe. The Mouse nocked an arrow. They were ready to defend their lord against mutiny.

David moved out from behind his protectors and quieted the crowd down.

He proclaimed with courage, "Men of Israel! You are right to be distraught and bitter! For I am distraught and bitter at losing my family as well! I do not blame you! I share your wounds!"

David turned to his generals and found Abiathar the high priest standing to their side. He gestured him to approach.

As Abiathar stood next to David, he proclaimed, "Mighty gibborim of Yahweh! I will waste no time in consulting the will of Yahweh for our families this very moment!"

"Right here?" said Abiathar. "Right now, in front of them all?"

"Right here in front of them all," repeated David. He knew that the only way to stop the rising mutiny was to do something drastic. He needed something that would impress each and every one of them with obligation before Yahweh, and break the spirit of rebellion. Using the ephod was a sacred private endeavor that usually happened within the priestly tent. Only in times of community tradition and influence such as a coronation would it be used publicly to induce unanimity. The result was a holy fear that swept through the masses as they stood before the very tangible visible expression of Yahweh's will. David needed that now, or he would find himself stoned to death by the mob.

He told Abiathar to prepare the ephod. One of the other priests scrambled and brought the ephod forward to place on the high priest.

The crowd of warriors knelt in the dust before the scene. David then cried out, "Oh Yahweh, I inquire of you, shall I pursue after this band of Amalekites? Shall we overtake them?"

The crowd had gone silent.

The high priest drew the lots and David had his answer. He raised the affirmative lot up to the crowd and pronounced, "Thus saith Yahweh, the Lord of Hosts! Pursue the Amalekites and you shall overtake them and rescue your families!"

The mutinous attitude turned to righteous faith and the six hundred cheered with a war cry.

David yelled, "Mount up, oh Men of God!"

The gibborim gathered for war.

CHAPTER 74

War already raged in the north on Mount Gilboa. Saul's forces had taken the heights, so the Philistines could not use their chariots. Saul was outnumbered two to one, but the Israelites were superior fighters in the hills. They had perfected the art through generations of disadvantage on the plains.

But numbers were still numbers, and the Philistines pressed the Israelites upward under sheer power.

Samuel's curse and prophecy had changed Saul. Rather than cowering in fear of his destiny, he had resigned himself to his fate. He realized that if he was going to die, he was going to die, and there was nothing he could do to stop it any longer. He was tired of fighting Yahweh after thirty years and had given up all hope in his heart. He decided that he would die in a blaze of greatness and glory and try to achieve some heroic deed in his death.

He engaged the Philistines head-on near the forefront of battle, with his armor-bearer fearfully following him into peril. To his soldiers, it was insanity. But they had grown used to Saul's momentary lapses of reason over the years and considered it one more crazy, desperate act by their crazy, desperate king.

Jonathan did not accept it though. He fought near his father to keep an eye upon him. After all the years of abuse and contempt, Jonathan remained loyal to his father. He did so with an accurate and efficient use of the bow. With his string-launched missiles, he kept many at bay, preventing them from getting within striking range of his father.

Saul's bodyguard was not up to the task of adequately defending their king. They were quickly winnowed down under the flashing heat of iron against bronze. Israelite weapons had gotten better over the years, but Philistine smithery was still superior, and it seemed that David had drawn all the best gibborim to himself.

Saul felt his time arriving as Philistine warriors pushed closer to him in the fray. He was fairly skilled with his sword. But he was very old now, about seventy years of age, and both speed and skill had deteriorated with that age. He turned to his armor-bearer and switched to javelins.

A fresh wave of Philistines started for Saul. He breathed a sigh of relief that it would finally be all over. Jonathan moved to his aid, nocking, aiming and releasing arrows one after another. He even pulled arrows from dead bodies to unleash them back upon the Philistines.

It would be of little help. There were just too many of them.

Suddenly, three warriors, about eight feet tall bounded into the clash.

Saul and Jonathan thought at first that they were Rephaim who would surely kill them both.

But they were not.

They began to fight on Saul's behalf!

They stopped the flood of warriors like a dam. One of them was huge and muscular. He bludgeoned and smashed dozens with a deftly handled mace. The second was less impressive, but used a battle net and, strangely, a trident to skewer and impale dozens of others. The third was a female warrior. She was built as a battle maiden should be, and she cut through Philistines with her sword effortlessly.

There was only one thing that Saul and Jonathan thought they could be: archangels. But why? After years of rejection, after divine prophecy of sure destruction through his prophet Samuel, why would Yahweh change his mind and send archangels to protect him? Had his favor changed? Was there hope finally in this last moment turn of events? And why did one of them have horns like a bull?

There was no time to fiddle with such time-consuming questions. Saul and Jonathan fought for their lives behind these saviors, these wonderful heavenly saviors.

On the Philistine side, a counter force of three paladin warriors appeared, of equal strength and skill, though smaller of size to Saul's rescuers. They did not kill Israelite warriors, but avoided them on their way toward the three savior archangels. These, Saul believed were the territorial demons of Philistia, evil spirits embodied in flesh to fight the archangels and bring death and destruction upon the Seed of Abraham.

They were in fact the archangels Saraqael, Raguel, and Remiel. They had come to make sure that Yahweh's will was carried out in full. They exploded with force upon the gods Ba'alzebul, Dagon, and Asherah, who were protecting Saul.

CHAPTER 75

David and his men had arrived at the Besor Brook on their expedition against the Amalekites. They had run at full force, and some of the men were exhausted. David decided to keep two hundred of them at the brook, with Ittai and several other commanders to watch over them.

That meant the Mouse would have to stay behind again with Ittai. He fumed with anger.

Ittai complained to David apart from the others, "My lord, you must not do this. You must bring me with you."

"I *must* not do anything," said David. "*You* are *my* subject."

"But I have known Lahmi since we were children. I know how he thinks, how he fights. You need me to defeat him. Do not steal from me my one opportunity for revenge."

David looked compassionately upon Ittai. Of all his warriors, he was among the most trustworthy and devoted. Even more than Abishai and Joab, if that were possible. But he could see Ittai's weakness. He could see it in his eyes and in the words that gave him away.

"That is why I am not taking you, Ittai. You are crippled by your need for revenge. But 'Vengeance is mine,' saith Yahweh."

Ittai's face went red with fury. He held it back and gritted his teeth, but he did not respond, because he knew David was right.

David put his hand on Ittai's shoulder in camaraderie. "My dear Ittai. I do not speak from the lofty heights of perfected holiness. I too have been ravished by vengeance. I too have failed to understand its fine distinction of separation from justice. It is only because I have seen the damage of my own vengeance that I am keeping you from this fight. You are not ready. Pray and beseech your Adonai, Yahweh, for understanding."

"It is not fair." The voice came from the Mouse, who had snuck up on them in discussion. "I have been waiting to kill giants forever. My lord, I can take down this one you seek with my arrows before he even gets near you."

David glared at Jonathan. "Not now, Mouse. I have not the time for your squeaking."

David turned away to organize his forces.

Jonathan was stunned, humiliated. David had never called him that before. Only the other warriors ever did. He must have pushed his commander too far. Now he got angry with his own stupid pride.

Ittai said to him, "I guess we both have more in common than just our size. We have to accept Yahweh's choice and Yahweh's timing for our lives."

"What do you mean, *our* size?" said Jonathan. "You are not small."

"That depends on what standard you are using," replied Ittai to a curious look on Jonathan's face. "Never mind. It is a long story," he concluded.

Still, Jonathan wondered if he would ever get to kill one of those evil serpentine no-good giant freaks.

And that was why Ittai knew he could not tell Jonathan his real identity.

• • • • •

The Israelite warriors had found an Egyptian servant left for dead in the desert by the Amalekites who led David to the location of the enemy. David and his generals climbed a hill overlooking a vast plain of desert below them.

The Amalekites were spread out upon the plain, feasting and celebrating their recent spoils from Ziklag, as well as several other Judean and Philistine towns.

Benaiah pointed out the corral built at the center of the camp, where the seven hundred Israelite captives and a few hundred others were kept. Because the Amalekites were cannibals, they often ate their hostages, but David knew Lahmi would not have allowed it until he drew David into his trap.

Abishai whispered to David, "There appears to be about fifteen hundred of them. And a squad of a dozen giants." A squad of giants was like a small army in and of itself.

David had only four hundred men.

But David's men were gibborim warriors, many of whom had performed amazing feats of valor on behalf of Yahweh and his messiah seed. Besides Benaiah's mighty deeds against the Egyptian Rephaim and the Lion Men of Moab, Abishai had first won his name by conquering three hundred men with his javelin. The chief of the Three, Jashobeam, wielded a spear against three hundred men at one time and came out victor as well. He swore it was eight hundred, but most thought he was just trying to one up Abishai. The second of the Three, Eleazar, as well as another gibbor, Shammah, both single-handedly held separate plots of ground against entire battalions of Philistines. Eleazar's fighting was so fierce, his hand had frozen to the hilt of his sword as if the weapon was an extension of his very arm. Yet of all of these leaders, Joab, was the fiercest and most ruthless. And he was looking for his opportunity at mass slaughter to prove his worth to his lord.

Fifteen hundred bloodthirsty, savage Amalekite cannibals against four hundred Mighty Men of David.

"Easy odds," murmured Joab.

• • • • •

King Agag sank his teeth into the hip bone of a human carcass.

Lahmi sat next to him, holding back his disgust for these barbaric brutes. Their manners were despicable, their dress was juvenile with its animal skins and horn pieces, and their body piercing practices were simply foolish. Ears, cheeks, nipples and other body parts were pierced with metal rings and rods that just made it easier for an enemy to grab or maneuver in a fight. Even their war paint was primitive by the more sophisticated Philistine standards of artistry. They looked like children who splashed mud and chalk on their faces rather than warriors inspiring terror with frightening designs.

Lahmi got up and returned to the squad of giants set apart from the others. Rephaim felt superior to normal warriors and tended to separate unto themselves. They ate goat meat. Lahmi had given up human flesh because he had discovered the madness disease that seemed to plague cannibals and drive them to wild displays of screaming and fits. The Amalekites thought it empowered them with the vital life force of their victims, but it really just turned them into deteriorating maniacs.

Lahmi kept an eye to the horizon. He knew David would arrive soon in search of his captured people. Lahmi did not want to be caught unawares with a belly too full of meat and a mind too dulled by much wine.

No, vengeance was his drink. It empowered him with constant bitter readiness.

The moon was obstructed by a cloudy sky and visibility was low. Lahmi thought to himself, *This is a dangerous night. These stupid boors are all drunk on alcohol and delirious with the strange weed they burned in censers around the camp.*

Though he was ostensibly one of several leaders under Agag, he in fact manipulated Agag like a puppet. He thought to himself, *Tomorrow, I will tighten the reins. I will take over more outward control and slap these buffoons into shape with my Rephaim. They have no idea who they are about to face. They have no...*

The sound of a war horn broke the darkness. At first, it blended into the loud music and chaotic drums leading the celebration. Nobody paid it any attention.

Lahmi recognized it. It was an Israelite horn of war. He threw down his goblet and yelled at Agag, "We are under attack!" He ordered his giants beside him, "Rise up, Rephaim."

It took a moment for Agag to realize Lahmi was right. Lahmi and his squad of giants were already up, strapping swords on backs and hefting shields and javelins.

Agag yelled to his trumpeter to call to arms.

Lahmi heard the pounding music stop and saw the confusion around him. The Amalekite horn bellowed through the camp. He barked a command to his warriors and ran to his tent to gather a most precious weapon he had saved for this very moment: Goliath's javelin. He had taken it from his dead brother's headless corpse in the Valley of the Terebinth and had saved it, with the intention of using it to impale Goliath's own murderer: David ben Jesse of Israel. *That puny Hebrew rodent will bleed out with my javelin piercing his belly.*

Lahmi snatched up the javelin. He dashed from his tent, and scanned the landscape to see from which direction they were being attacked. But he could see no charging force, no battle line approaching. He only saw strikes from all around, as if the Israelites had surrounded the camp and were attacking from every side, squeezing in. It seemed like it was a large force. Had they conspired with Philistines? Lahmi looked for the fiercest concentration of fighting, guessing that David would be the most protected in battle.

He found it and marched with deliberation toward the action.

• • • • •

The reason it seemed as if the Israelites had a large force was because they had spread out their four hundred in number around the entire camp. When the war horn sounded, they attacked from every side. There were a few men in small fighting squads, but the impact of a simultaneous invasion from all sides had an overwhelming effect. It caused panic in the ranks of the Amalekites.

David had counted on that panic, coupled with the Amalekites' diminished capacity from celebrating, to help even out the odds. But with gibborim like Abishai, Benaiah, Joab, Jashobeam and others beside him, those odds were now in his favor.

They cut through the desert camp with a fury. Abishai and Joab went to protect the captives. Jashobeam and Eleazar led squads to torch the tents. Only Benaiah and the Guard fought with David as he pushed his way toward the center.

The battle went quickly and decisively in David's favor. Amalekites were running, jumping on their camels and trying to escape.

Through the smoke and flames, the mad screams and scattered confusion, David noticed a sole figure at a distance of a hundred feet, a giant walking his way, unscathed by the battle, intent on a mission. He cut down Israelites without even looking at them. He was in fact looking at David.

It was Lahmi.

In an instant, David suddenly knew it was a mistake to have left Ittai back at the brook.

His attention was diverted by ten attacking Amalekites, screaming with madness and wielding swords, axes and maces. Benaiah and he met them with skilled technique, superior to their enemy's demonic insanity.

Lahmi stopped seventy-five feet away from David and set his javelin loop for a throw.

David finished off two Amalekites. He turned and saw the javelin already in the air flying towards him with mighty speed. In the darkness, he could not judge its distance or speed well and did not have enough time to dodge it.

It was going to skewer him.

Benaiah's leaping figure intercepted the javelin in mid-air, mere feet from David's body. He tumbled to the ground snapping the javelin in two with a roll to his feet.

David looked back up to see the figure of Lahmi curse him and then bolt off into the darkness of the desert with other Amalekites on their camels. Lahmi knew his chances were slim at closing the distance and getting a strike in on David before being overwhelmed by the host of gibborim around him.

David was about to order a chase, when the dozen Rephaim broke through the smoke with all their senses locked as one onto David.

Benaiah, Abishai, Joab and the other gibborim responded by lining up in front of David.

The giants attacked. On their way toward their target, they ran over warriors, both friend and foe, without even noticing them. Their skill and speed were frightening.

They hit the line of David's gibborim. These warriors, who had taken down hundreds of men in single battles and thousands over their lifetime were taxed to their utmost of skill and energy to keep these twelve giants at bay. It was the most ruthless fighting David had yet seen. And it caused him to wonder how impossible it might be to confront an army of them.

But his mighty men rose up that night with supernatural vigor. They not only held the giants at bay, they ended up slaughtering every last one of them. No one was going to touch their anointed messiah.

David looked out into the darkness where Lahmi had fled, and he knew the giant would be back one day. He only hoped he would be ready for him.

CHAPTER 76

Saul had run out of steam. He had switched to a battle axe earlier, but his arm felt heavy as lead. He could swing no more. Jonathan's bow was empty. The armor-bearer was out of arrows. The fight between the three guardian angels and the three demons from hell continued unabated. But the demons were pressing in. The fighting all around Saul dizzied him. Jonathan pulled his sword and held his own against the onslaught.

Mount Gilboa had turned into a mountain of death.

Earlier, dark storm clouds had gathered overhead. Now thunder cracked the sky, and it began to rain.

Asherah had faced off against Remiel, who was relentless with a battle axe. She matched him stride for stride. When the first drops of rain struck her, she thought to herself, *Just like Yahweh, the cowardly cheater.*

Since before the time of the Great Deluge, she and her fellow gods had been created with a weakness in water. Their supernatural strength would become as mere humans when submerged. By making it rain on this Jezreel Valley battle, Yahweh was tipping the scales in his favor.

By the time the gods were drenched in the rain, they had begun to falter. All of them could feel it. Even Ba'alzebul's mighty brawn had lessened to a mere mortal's. Saraqael began to push him back. Dagon's arms tired with the use of his trident against Raguel. Asherah felt every hit of Remiel's sword jar her muscles.

The hill had turned into a pile of slippery mud. Jonathan slipped and fell into the muck. It gave his opponent the opportunity to thrust his sword into Jonathan's gut. He screamed out.

Saul howled, "Jonathan!"

He picked up a javelin with a superhuman burst of energy and thrust it into the Philistine attacker.

Then he was by Jonathan's side. The armor-bearer shielded them for the moment.

"Father," Jonathan grimaced. Saul saw his blood pumping out and mixing with the rain in the mud. Jonathan was pale. Saul placed his hand on the wound. He knew it was the end.

"My son. What have I done? What have I done?"

Saul looked into Jonathan's eyes and knew in that moment that he was about to lose everything: his life, his sons, his kingdom, his legacy. He was being cast off to the uttermost. Deep within him a black rage welled up. *It is all Yahweh's fault. He has done this to me. He has cursed me. He has caused this evil. I was a great man. He took my glory because he was a jealous, selfish tyrant.*

Jonathan whimpered, "Father, Yahweh is just," and he died in his arms.

Saul set him down with a steel heart. *Yahweh is just? Yahweh is just?* After all that Jonathan had been through, and now, the end of the Saulide bloodline, and the words on Jonathan's dying lips were, "Yahweh is just?" Absurd. Preposterous. His son had died a deluded fanatic.

Saul stood up to scream into the black, stormy sky, "CURSE YOU! DAMN YOU TO SHEOL!"

Though the spirit of Nimrod had long since departed from Saul, he retained a kind of madness. The only one with power to damn a creature to Sheol was Yahweh. So an attempt to curse Yahweh was the kind of irrational bellow that could only come from a mind and heart ravaged with the madness of unmitigated pride. It was pride that was the elemental sin of mankind. And pride unchecked became an obsession to control that would always end in the frustration of unfulfilled self-deification. Though he tried, man could not be God.

At that moment, Saul looked up into the sky. He saw a flurry of Philistine arrows raining down upon them.

Asherah and the gods knew they had failed. They braced themselves for impact.

A thousand arrows peppered the area, piercing men and god alike. The angels were hit. The gods were hit. Saul was hit. His armor-bearer had used his shield to protect himself instead.

Saul fell to the ground with three shafts in him. He lay in the muck next to his son's body.

The gods pulled out the arrows from their bodies like annoying pins and needles. They knew they had lost. So they turned from the battle and ran off, leaving the angels to nurse their own wounds.

A new wave of Philistines approached Saul. They would be there in moments.

Saul looked up at his armor-bearer and grunted, "Draw your sword and thrust it through me, lest these uncircumcised Philistines treat me with dishonor."

The armor-bearer stood agape with fear. He fell to his knees weeping. "I cannot, my lord. I cannot bring myself to it."

Saul whimpered, "Forsaken by everyone."

He picked up his own weapon, placed it at his gut and fell on his sword.

The Philistines came upon them. The armor-bearer looked up and followed his king by falling on his own sword.

The reign of Saul had ended.

CHAPTER 77

The town of Ziklag had been repopulated with the hostages rescued from the Amalekites. David and his four hundred men slaughtered eleven hundred of their enemies. Four hundred of them had escaped on their camels, and along with them, Lahmi of Gath.

But now they had their work cut out for them in rebuilding the ruins of their town. It would take many months to repair what evil had destroyed in one day.

Ittai stared out into the hazy desert terrain. He was on duty as watch-guard of the town's perimeter. David had felt foolish because of his decision to leave Ittai out of the raid on the Amalekites. He had almost been killed because of it. He told Ittai he would never let that happen again.

Ittai's attention was piqued by the sight of a single man on a horse approaching the city. He appeared to be half dead, in ragged clothes and almost falling off his mount.

Ittai rushed out to meet the visitor with a squad of gibborim.

• • • • •

"I am the son of a sojourner," said the man in tattered garments. He knelt before David in the leader's war tent, surrounded by his trusted commanders.

"My name is Namiaza. In my travels, I happened upon the aftermath of a battle at Gilboa between the Philistines and Israel."

David gestured to some servants, who brought forward some wine for the messenger. Namiaza's eyes went wide and he gobbled up the bread, nearly choking on it, spilling the wine as he guzzled it desperately.

Abishai and Joab looked askance at David, who sighed in thoughtfulness. "Tell me what you saw, Namiaza."

Namiaza spoke with his mouth full of food. "The Israelite forces have scattered. Many are fallen and dead. Saul and his three eldest sons are dead."

A sea of heads turned to look at David. He closed his eyes with pained heart. His whisper was only heard by Benaiah. "Jonathan."

Namiaza continued, "The Philistines found the bodies of King Saul and his three sons. They cut off Saul's head, hung his body and his son's bodies on the walls of Beth-shan, stripped his armor and hung it in a temple of Ashtaroth."

Idol of shame, thought David.

He looked back up at the traveller. "How do you know this?"

Namiaza took another gulp of food. "I travelled through Jabesh-gilead. And some of their valiant men had taken the bodies down from the walls of Beth-shan. They burned the bodies and buried them under the tamarisk tree in Jabesh."

Silence permeated David's men. It was a holy silence of respect. The world had just changed and the implications were far reaching.

"But I have not told you the most important part," said Namiaza.

David looked at him with curiosity.

"You see, I had travelled through the battlefield before the Philistines had plundered it. And I had happened upon Saul, still alive, and leaning on his spear."

David could not believe what he was hearing. All ears waited to hear what happened next.

Namiaza continued, "He called out for me to kill him before the Philistines were upon him, because he was already dying with some arrows in his body. I quickly recognized him as the king, and so I obeyed him, to protect him from the abuses of the Philistines."

Terror filled David's face. He slowly reached up and grabbed his outer robe and ripped it. The other leaders followed him, ripping theirs as well in the traditional manner of grief.

Namiaza reached into a sack he had with him. Benaiah and others reached for their swords in defensive reaction.

But it was not a weapon that Namiaza pulled from the sack. It was a golden crown and an armband, the royal emblems of Saul.

Namiaza approached David and knelt before him, handing him the crown and armband. He said, "My lord, how the mighty have fallen."

He had hoped that since David would be the new king, maybe he would appoint Namiaza to some important position with wealth and prestige for his honorable obedience to the king and for producing the king's crown.

He had counted wrong.

David's eyes thinned in anger. "How is it you were not afraid to raise your hand in destruction against Yahweh's anointed one?"

Namiaza's eyes filled with terror. "But I obeyed the king! And I brought the crown to you."

David looked away from him and said, "Execute this blasphemer."

Joab had been waiting for this very moment before all the others. He stepped out, drew his sword, and cut down Namiaza.

David looked back upon the corpse and said without mercy, "Your blood be upon your own head. For you have testified against yourself when you said, 'I have killed Yahweh's anointed.'"

Two men dragged the body away. David said to his men, "Tonight, we will fast. Have everyone meet in the town square for a lamentation."

• • • • •

That night in the town square, David sang a lamentation he had written in honor of King Saul and his son Jonathan.

"Your glory, O Israel, is slain on your high places!
How the mighty have fallen!
Tell it not in Gath,
publish it not in the streets of Ashkelon,

lest the daughters of the Philistines rejoice,
lest the daughters of the uncircumcised exult.
"You mountains of Gilboa,
let there be no dew or rain upon you,
nor fields of offerings!
For there the shield of the mighty was defiled,
the shield of Saul, not anointed with oil.
"From the blood of the slain,
from the fat of the mighty,
the bow of Jonathan turned not back,
and the sword of Saul returned not empty.
"How the mighty have fallen
in the midst of the battle!
"Jonathan lies slain on your high places.
I am distressed for you, my brother Jonathan;
very pleasant have you been to me;
your love to me was extraordinary,
surpassing the love of women.
"How the mighty have fallen,
and the weapons of war perished!"

After the lamentation, David looked out upon the people gathered around him. They were weeping for their king and for Israel, their people. He wept for his brother, Jonathan. The only man he had ever known who was without guile. He was the only man David could ever trust without reservation, because he was the only man who willingly gave up a kingdom for the glory of Yahweh.

His was a faith that had changed David. Beside Jonathan's true, unwavering belief, David's passionate ups and downs felt like so much juvenile insincerity. Yahweh had described David as a man after his own heart, and yet, David knew deep down that Jonathan was more worthy of that designation. He could only conclude that Yahweh brought things into being for his purposes. What Yahweh declared, he would create and make it so. David prayed that he would one day become what Yahweh had proclaimed him to be.

He quieted them down and announced, "I have consulted the ephod of Yahweh!"

The crowd waited to hear what the will of Yahweh was.

"We will go up to Hebron. And there, I will be crowned king of Judah!"

The crowd leapt with cheers.

After all these years of running and fighting, the time had finally come.

Someone yelled out, and the crowd chanted, "The king is dead! Long live the king! Saul is dead! Long live King David!"

CHAPTER 78

David looked out upon the city of Jerusalem before him. His forces were arrayed for a triumphal entry through the gates. He had conquered the city and was making his official entry to establish his kingship and rule from the city as his new capital.

So much had happened since he had been anointed king of Judah at Hebron. Now, he was about to be crowned as king of both Judah and Israel in this new city, dubbed, "The City of David." This would be the new capital from which he would rule a united kingdom of Judah in the south and Israel in the north.

The first thing he had done upon conquering and naming his City of David was to find a hill just outside the northern walls where he buried the skull of Goliath of Gath deep in the rocks of the earth. It was a symbolic ceremony of remembrance. That rocky ridge he named "Golgotha," for "place of the skull."

A company of minstrels and women dancers led the procession through the gates of the city. Women waved long, flowing, silken banners to the sounds of timbrel, lyre and tambourine. Other women sang songs of victory and kingship. Citizens laid palm leaves and branches on the ground as a ritual carpet of entry.

Benaiah sat ever-presently beside David, still the king's chief counselor, and head of his bodyguard of Cherethites and Pelethites that followed the king's entourage.

Joab rode at the forefront of the king's escort with his brother Abishai next to him. Abishai was still chief of the Thirty, but Joab had finally surpassed him after years of competitive attempts to outperform his older brother. Joab was now Chief General Commander of all of David's armed forces.

He had won this distinction by accepting David's offer for a competition. The armies of Israel had besieged Jerusalem's walls, but could not penetrate them to conquer the Jebusite inhabitants. So David offered the position of General Commander to anyone who would lead a strike force into Jerusalem using the underground water shaft. Joab volunteered first and led Judah to victory. It was Joab's fearless leadership that led to the very triumphal entry that entered Jerusalem right now.

Behind the Cherethites and Pelethites were a contingent of David's gibborim, his finest warriors who performed amazing feats of daring in battle and defense of the king. Many were in his original band of outlaws when he was on the run from Saul's murderous pursuit.

In the back of the train were the chained captive Jebusite leaders led on foot through the streets of the city for humiliation of the vanquished and exaltation of the vanquisher. They would be executed when the king was enthroned as the final display of power over the principalities and authorities.

The chariots of Elohim are twice ten thousand,
  thousands upon thousands;
Adonai is among them;
  Sinai is now in the sanctuary.
You ascended on high,
  leading a host of captives in your train
  and receiving gifts among men,
even among the rebellious,
  that Yahweh Elohim may dwell there.

There were five acts to the king's enthronement and coronation. First, the procession arrived at the palace steps where David stepped off his carriage and stood on the steps before the people. It was a small Jebusite palace and would have to be rebuilt soon with the aid of David's ally, the Phoenician King Hiram of Tyre. But that would have to wait.

The court prophets and priests surrounded David on the top of the steps. David's eyes met with his close confidant, Nathan the prophet, who had been with him from the earliest days before Samuel's school of prophets had been slaughtered by the Rephaim. They shared a bond of honesty that David treasured in a court full of sycophants. The high priest Abiathar approached David. He had also been with David from the early days after escaping Saul's murder of the priests of Nob. These men had been through much pain and violence together.

Abiathar placed a golden crown upon David's head. This was the very crown retrieved by Namiaza from Saul's dead body on Gilboa. It was a crown with a bloody past of betrayal and dishonor that David would now seek to redeem with his rule.

He was also handed the "testimony," a large scroll that contained the words of Yahweh's Law handed down through Moses. He was charged with the obligation to uphold that holy code in his personal conduct as well as his governance of the nation. In Israel, the king was not above the law. All men were subject and accountable under Yahweh's kingly rule, especially the monarch. He kissed the scroll and held it high to the cheers of the crowd.

He glanced over at his wives, who stood to the side on the steps. He now had seven of them. When he became king of Judah at Hebron, he brought his two wives Abigail and Ahinoam with him. But while there, he married four others and began to have sons and daughters. He sired six of them at Hebron alone. It was a weakness that Nathan said would be the ruin of him: he loved women. As king he justified the need for a well-populated royal family and diplomatic ties with allies. But Nathan warned him it would be a habit that would assuredly be adopted with less restraint by his sons.

David's biggest heartbreak stood with the six other women: Michal. During the recent civil war with Ishbaal, Saul's son and claimant to the throne of Israel, David had negotiated the return of Michal to his household. Though she was his first love and wife of his youth, she had been stolen from David by Saul and unlawfully married to another man. Nevertheless, it had been some ten years since she had been so unjustly treated by her father, and she had learned to adjust to her new life and even love her new husband.

When she was returned to David, her husband, Palti son of Laish, followed her, weeping for miles. Her return to a distant and changed David with her own changed heart was bad enough. But to become one of seven in a harem of wives was devastating to her heart as it was to all their hearts. Now, she could not stop longing for the singular devotion of her second husband Palti, who worshipped her and treated her like a queen. Now, she was treated with the others like a pet.

It was the universal curse of polygamy, an institution that favored the interests of men in a patriarchal society. It reduced women to breeders and objects of male taste. A different wife for each night of the week or for each whim of desire for variety. When a relational problem arose with one wife, he would simply avoid that one by moving on to another until things settled down. It was a way for the husband to skirt the responsibility of relational holiness and sacrifice. It bred male selfishness and destroyed the one flesh unity that Yahweh had originally designed for marriage. While there was no explicit command forbidding polygamy by Yahweh in the Law David now held in his hand, it certainly defied the original definition of marriage in the Pentateuch, and worked against every intention of the heart of his God.

Michal was now trapped in it like her other six sisters were. She suffered from bouts of sadness that rendered her morose and led to sleeping more hours than was healthy. She also sought more comfort praying in the arms of Asherah, her goddess.

Abigail dealt with the plural status differently. By virtue of her age, she became a kind of older sister to the others, encouraging them to be strong in the face of adversity and to see their value to Yahweh in spite of a devalued harem status. Because of her harsh treatment at the hands of her previous husband, Nabal, she had become a survivor. Though she was older, without the nubile and innocent nature of the younger wives, David was still drawn to her most because of her strength and how she carried herself with such royal dignity. She knew Yahweh valued her, regardless of her social status or value to the king. She did not seek the praise of man but the praise of Yahweh, and ironically, that made her more desirable to the king. To David, the notion of a strong and virtuous, queenly woman willingly submitting herself to him was far more desirable than the young and simpleminded following him out of the weakness of their youthful will.

The second act of enthronement and coronation was the anointing, also performed by Abiathar. David bowed before him and he withdrew a horn of oil, which he poured down over David's head. This act indicated that the king was Yahweh's chosen one, the messiah of the nation.

The third act was the proclamation of the anointed king and the people's response of clapping and acclamation, "Long live the king! Long live the king!"

With my holy oil I have anointed him,
so that my hand shall be established with him;
I will crush his foes before him
and strike down those who hate him.
My faithfulness and my steadfast love shall be with him,
and in my name shall his horn be exalted.
And I will make him the firstborn,
the highest of the kings of the earth.
I will establish his Seed forever
and his throne as the days of the heavens.

For the fourth act of the enthronement and coronation, the gathered throng of royalty and palace staff proceeded inside to the palace, where they seated David as king on the throne. An enthronement hymn was sung by the minstrels that marked his assumption of power.

> *"I have set my King*
>   *on Zion, my holy hill."*
> *I will tell of the decree:*
> *Yahweh said to me, "You are my Son;*
>   *today I have begotten you.*
> *Ask of me, and I will make the nations your heritage,*
>   *and the ends of the earth your possession."*

David's heart melted with the recognition of his own unworthiness to be seated on such a holy throne of Yahweh's Chosen Seed. He reflected upon the past twenty years since Samuel the Seer first anointed him. He had been so young back then—too young. He never forgot the words of the Seer over him as the oil dripped down his face as it did this day. "I anoint you, David, son of Jesse by the authority of Yahweh, elohim of Israel."

He could see now what Yahweh was doing; taking the youngest runt of a litter out of an insignificant family in an unimportant town, giving him the faith to face and defeat the titanic champion of Yahweh's worst enemy with a mere stone, inciting Israel's own mad king to hunt him down for years as an outlaw, and forcing him to live for a time in the lair of the dragon itself, all while waiting over twenty years to fulfill a promise. It was to show Yahweh's greatness and goodness in the face of David's own weakness. Yahweh had forced David to be broken, so that he would have to trust in Yahweh and not his own strength. He would have to seek Yahweh's righteousness in a thoroughly depraved world.

But he could see now how he had failed to live up to that trust. As he sat in this holy position of honor, his sins flooded his memory as if raised by the Adversary of the Divine Council: his allowance of the idolatry of his first wife, Michal, ignored for the sake of his passions; his tolerance of wickedness within his warrior ranks for the sake of a better fighting force; his extortion of Nabal's wealth in the name of "protection"; his rationalization of his regal polygamy to cover his insatiable hunger for women; and possibly worst of all, his harsh temper that led to excessive violence far beyond Yahweh's "eye for an eye" justice. He would never attain the goodness of his god for which he was called. He was a man of bloodshed and it had changed him so deeply and thoroughly from that young shepherd boy who played a lyre and wooed the girls of his village. Yet, in some ways, he had merely become a more sophisticated adult version of that same passionate, intemperate fool that he had been as a youth, with his spiritual highs and earthly lows, at war within himself.

With all these memories of his moral failures and fleshly excesses, he felt like a fraud. He did not deserve this throne. Jonathan of the house of Saul did, and he had lived the faith required for it. David had sought greatness over goodness, but saw how the good were rarely the great and the great were rarely the good. Jonathan had chosen goodness over greatness.

But Jonathan was dead. And Yahweh had chosen David, not because of David's righteousness, but because of Yahweh's own mysterious purposes. Just as he had chosen Abraham out of pagan Ur, dim-witted Isaac over Ishmael, and the deceiver Jacob over Esau. Yahweh seemed to enjoy using the foolish things of the world to confound the wise, the weak and worthless things to shame the strong, and the low and despised, the things that were nothing, to bring to nothing the things that were. God used sinners and their evil to accomplish his good. But he also redeemed them and made them good.

For I know my transgressions,
and my sin is ever before me.

Against you, you only, have I sinned
and done what is evil in your sight.
Purge me with hyssop, and I shall be clean;
wash me, and I shall be whiter than snow.
Create in me a clean heart, O Elohim,
and renew a right spirit within me.
Cast me not away from your presence,
and take not your Holy Spirit from me.
Restore to me the joy of your salvation,
and uphold me with a willing spirit...
For you will not delight in sacrifice, or I would give it;
you will not be pleased with a burnt offering.
The sacrifices of Elohim are a broken spirit;
a broken and contrite heart, O Elohim,
you will not despise.

The fifth and last act of the enthronement ritual had the king receive the high officials of the state, who declared their fealty to his throne and to the kingship of Yahweh Elohim over all the earth. As each member knelt before him, David reminisced over their impact on his ascendancy to kingship over the years.

Benaiah, son of Jehoiada of Kabzeel, bent his knee and pledged his heart and soul to the king. This Judahite from the desert was his most trusted warrior. He had the kind of holy devotion that reminded David of Jonathan. He had saved David's life from the Lion Men of Moab and the Egyptian giant who sought his head. He had an obsessive mistrust of non-Israelites and all things foreign, which made him a harsh taskmaster of the Cherethite and Pelethite bodyguard under his command. He had purified the ranks of soldiers, but David worried that his rigid righteousness was so excessive that he failed to understand faith and how it played into a convert's identity.

And David knew that Benaiah was driven by his guilt for having been betrayed by his Edomite lover in his past. Though he was a thoroughly devoted man of Yahweh, he had yet to discover a faith somewhere between complete suspicion of man's evil and naïve trust in man as the image of Yahweh.

The brothers Joab and Abishai, sons of Zeruiah, bowed the knee with their fealty to David. These two brothers from the very start had been the most fierce and ruthless in their devotion to David. They were competitive, trying to outdo each other in everything, whether deeds of greatness or acts of loyalty. Unlike Benaiah or Nathan the prophet, who challenged David all the time regarding his own obedience to Yahweh's Law, these two were unquestioning in their own obedience to their earthly lord. Which actually disturbed David. For men who did not question their king by a higher law were men who could do much evil should their king become lawless. Without a loyalty to something higher than the king or the state, what would stop them from disobeying a god for the sake of their king? They tended to act in the name of the king before receiving royal approval, which caused David much trouble. And they seemed to have a secret between them, an oath of some kind that hid their past, hinted at by the scar on Joab's face. It was as if their display of loyalty was an energetic attempt to redeem themselves from some shame they would never speak of.

When David first became king of Judah, a civil war had been initiated by Saul's General Commander, Abner, by crowning Saul's son Ishbaal as king over Israel. Many battles for superiority ensued between Judah and Israel as the house of David and the house of Saul. Abner eventually deserted Ishbaal for David. Ishbaal was killed, resulting in David being the one king over all the tribes of the land. But in the course of these events, Abner had killed the youngest brother of Abishai and Joab. The brothers refused to believe Abner's loyalty, and killed him in revenge for their brother's death. David was so vexed that he cursed the house of the two brothers with perpetual sickness and violence. But he would not execute them. They had become so critical to his success and greatness that he overlooked their lack of goodness. David had succumbed to favoritism and it haunted him.

When Ittai the Gittite bowed before David, the king considered him an ironic contrast with the two brothers before him. Ittai's past was thoroughly confessed to David in all its excruciating detail. Ittai's honesty and repentance made him as trusted as Benaiah. David had given Ittai command of a squad of six hundred Philistines who had joined David from Gath. They were affectionately referred to as the Gittite Brigade.

The real tragedy was the Gittite's own inability to believe he could be redeemed. He regretted the miserable accident of his birth as a Philistine. He showed more faith in Yahweh than any in all of Israel, and yet, his presumed identity as a Rephaim born of Nephilim blood caused him to have returning grief and doubts of his own atonement. Despite this unjustified fear, he had given up everything to follow Yahweh, even the joy of offspring with his beloved wife Ummi in order to stop his cursed bloodline. What more could illustrate the faith of a redeemed Seed of Abraham, and not the cursed Seed of the Serpent? Ittai's mother was the Rapha, not his father, and the seed came from the father. Ittai's genealogy was not everything he had first thought it was. What David did not tell Ittai was how much he had learned from the doubt-wracked Ittai about true believing faith.

The rest of the Gibborim commanders and other ministers of state pledged their lives to the king in order. It was a long and torturous affair where David barely managed to stay awake. But when it was done, he felt a new surge of excitement. The coronation and enthronement was followed by a feast, where he would finally get a chance to play his lyre again with the musicians before the court. He had gotten much out of practice over the years of running and hiding and fighting. He had written during this time of painful anxiety, but did not have the opportunity to play his instruments. Now that he was ensconced in the throne, he had every intention of getting back to playing the music that soothed his soul and filled his difficult life with shalom, the peace of wholeness.

> *Clap your hands, all peoples!*
> *Shout to Elohim with loud songs of joy!*
> *For Yahweh, the Most High, is to be feared,*
> *a great king over all the earth.*
> *He subdued peoples under us,*
> *and nations under our feet.*
> *He chose our heritage for us,*
> *the pride of Jacob whom he loves. Selah*
> *Elohim has gone up with a shout,*
> *Yahweh with the sound of a trumpet.*
> *Sing praises to Elohim, sing praises!*
> *Sing praises to our King, sing praises!*
> *For Elohim is the King of all the earth;*
> *sing praises with a psalm!*
> *Elohim reigns over the nations;*
> *Elohim sits on his holy throne.*
> *The princes of the peoples gather*
> *as the people of the Elohim of Abraham.*
> *For the shields of the earth belong to Elohim;*
> *he is highly exalted!*

David would have a hard time enjoying the celebration, because his next plan preoccupied his thoughts. It would be a bold move that would require spending much money and the enlistment of the pagan king Hiram of Tyre to help him.

CHAPTER 79

Phoenician laborers, carpenters, and stone masons filled the streets of the City of David. Large logs of cedar from the forests of Lebanon were carted to a work area along with quarried stones to build the palace of King David. The city of Tyre was known throughout the world for its master craftsmen and architectural artistry. Their buildings were the finest in all of Canaan, so David wanted the very best of designs for his own palace residence.

It was a perfectly political agreement between the two kingdoms. Hiram of Tyre wanted safe trade route access to Anatolia in the north, Mesopotamia in the west, and Egypt in the south; David wanted quality Phoenician craftsmanship and access to the greatest port of sea trade in all of Canaan. The Phoenicians worshipped Asherah and Ba'al and other deities, but artistic design was not in itself evil. Yahweh did not curse the creativity of the idolaters. Though morally corrupt, the Sea People were still imagers of Yahweh with their artistic imagination. An aesthetic style was only evil when it was used for evil purposes. But it was morally sanctified when used for righteous purposes.

David had been overseeing the day's construction when he received scouts from the surrounding area. They told him a gigantic force of Philistines was amassing just outside the Valley of the Rephaim.

He knew this day would come. He knew that once he established a united kingdom of Judah and Israel, those monsters of Dagon would eventually mount an offensive to try to wipe him out before he could fortify and expand that rule. They wanted to invade his kingdom before he invaded theirs.

He called for an immediate war counsel.

• • • • •

The Lords of the Philistines had chosen the Valley of the Terebinth as their gathering point to muster armed forces for a march on Jerusalem. They had chosen this site as a symbolic launching point because of its historical notoriety as the location of Goliath's defeat at the hands of David a generation earlier. They were going to reverse that infamy with an all-out assault on Israel's king and her new capital and they were going to feed the vultures in that same valley on the corpses of King David and his Hebrews.

All five cities of the pentapolis lent six thousand soldiers to the effort, for a total of thirty thousand Philistine warriors that converged just outside the city of Gath. Lord Achish of Gath was again appointed General Commander because of his previous success with destroying King Saul's forces. The five Lords met in the war council tent to discuss their stratagem with the Sons of Rapha, Ishbi ben Ob and Runihura. They looked over a map of the area.

Achish pointed to the map. "We will traverse the Valley of the Rephaim to Jerusalem, twenty-five miles. The brook is dried up because it is summer, so we will not have to deal with that inconvenience."

"Whose forces will lead the attack?" asked a dubious Dothan of Ekron.

"Yours," said Achish.

"Why?"

"Because I had decided that whichever Lord asked first must be the most anxious to fight Hebrews, and therefore deserved the honor of first kill."

The opposite was the case. Dothan cursed himself for speaking up so hastily. He was vying for his own soldiers' safety, but to admit such would be considered weakness or worse, cowardice, so Dothan tried to hide his miserable frown.

But Dothan still had questions. "What about the Sons of Rapha? Their stature makes them more capable of scaling the walls of

Jerusalem and their power makes them capable of wiping out the Hebrews before they even get their armor on."

"No," said Achish. "You know full well that casualties are high for scaling attacks. Your men will build battering rams to break through the walls. *Then* we will send our Rephaim forces through the breach. Ishbi, what are your numbers?"

"Six hundred troops," said Ishbi. It was an ironic reflection of David's six hundred gibborim. He added, "And our secret weapon."

He and Runihura smiled. Everyone knew the secret weapon was Argaz, their fifteen foot tall, twelve hundred pound colossus killing machine, held back for just the right moment of mass terror followed by mass devastation.

What Ishbi did not say was that he, Runihura, and Argaz had remained true to the original pact of the Sons of Rapha to assassinate the messiah King David. They had been disbanded years before by Achish when he had accepted David as an ally. When David became king of Judah in Hebron, Achish left him alone, as long as he remained at war with the northern Hebrews of Israel. A house divided could not long stand. Let the Hebrews kill each other to prepare the way for Philistine dominance.

It was too much for Achish's pride to admit that David had lied about killing Israelite tribes in the Negeb when he was at Ziklag. And then came the dirty Hebrew's bid to unite Judah and Israel from Jerusalem. If Achish reconstituted the Sons of Rapha, it would be tacit admittance of his failure. Besides, he wanted to conquer this messiah king through the command of his armed forces, not allow these pompous giant braggarts to steal his glory.

The Sons of Rapha, on the other hand, were going to lead their Rephaim forces in battle to hunt David down and kill him. They saw this as their last stand, and they were determined to accomplish their blood oath at any cost. They were even prepared to kill their own if their own got in the way.

Brian Godawa

• • • • •

The assembly of seventy gods gathered in the divine council room at Mount Hermon. Zeus led the deliberations from the throne before the black lake of the Abyss.

"Mastema refused to come this time, so he sent me in his stead," said the impatient father of the Greek gods. "He said you wasted his time with your last scheme years ago on Mount Gilboa regarding King Saul. And I am inclined to agree with him."

Mumblings of agreement went throughout the seventy.

Ba'alzebul stood angrily with his horns held high, next to Asherah, Dagon, and a slinking, duplicitous Molech. He returned the impatience with impertinence. "We were deserted by our fellow council members without fair warning."

Grumbling turned to insult in the crowd.

Asherah touched Ba'alzebul's arm to restrain him, and jumped in. "My dear, divine comrades, I think that what Ba'alzebul is trying to say with a rather inappropriate attitude"—Ba'alzebul stared at her, betrayed—"is that the three of us were not able to keep King Saul alive, but with all your help, we could have. And that is why we need the support and involvement of the entire divine council for this task which is surely as significant and as difficult as anything we have attempted before."

Osiris from Egypt knew the plans of the Philistines because they were still allies of Egyptian rule. He got to the point. "The Philistines are amassing for battle against the Israelites and you want us to join the battle?"

"No," said Asherah.

Osiris and the others were thrown.

She continued, "We want you to help us capture Yahweh-of-Hosts-who-sits-enthroned-upon-the-Cherubim."

A moment of silence swept over everyone as they considered the shocking words.

That descriptive phrase about the ark was a reference to the fact that it was effectively an earthly symbol of Yahweh's throne in heaven, and as such it had spiritual unity with that heavenly seat. When the ark was in the Holy of Holies in the Tabernacle of Yahweh, he would meet with Moses as a king would meet with his subjects sitting upon his throne. Since Yahweh was not physical or visible, it could only be symbolic, but it was no less real. Yahweh no longer spoke to man face to face as he did with Moses, but the ark remained the holy seat upon which Yahweh was enthroned on earth as god of Israel. Capturing the ark would be a crime of infinite offense against the infinite Creator by his fallen heavenly host.

Marduk of Babylonia clarified, "The Israelite ark of the covenant has been stored at Kiriath-jearim unmolested for the past twenty years."

"Yes," said Asherah. "That past dreadful incident of the tumors and diseases has stuck in the minds of the Philistines like a lion's claw. So the ark sits virtually unattended because everyone is simply too afraid to go near it."

Zeus said, "I do not think we would fare any better if we tried to confiscate it."

Asherah looked at Ba'alzebul with a gesture for him to resume with more calm. It was, after all, his plan.

He said, "You are correct, mighty Zeus. But I beg the indulgence of the assembly to hear us out." *Mighty Zeus, my rear end,* thought Ba'alzebul. *I could wipe the floor of this cavern with that golden Greek oaf.* He hated having to show respect to other deities when *he* was the mightiest of them all. Except for that snake, Mastema.

Dagon jumped in, trying to grab some credit. "According to *our* plan, Yahweh would never expect us to try to capture the ark, and that is why he has not guarded it more cautiously...."

Ba'alzebul jerked Dagon forcefully back behind him and took the floor again. "But once our plan is discovered, we will need this entire assembly with us to fend off the response sure to follow."

Asherah added, "For this to work, we must have all of you with us — unlike at Mount Gilboa. If you do not show up, we will fail." She licked her lips and added with spicy delight, "But if you do show, the Seed of the Serpent will crush the Seed of Abraham."

The council members brightened with smiles and agreement. They were hungry to hear the details.

Zeus said, "I think I know where you are leading with this. You Philistine gods are quite the masters of strategy. I am impressed."

Idiots, thought Asherah. *Now I know why Ashtart was unwelcomed by this pantheon of divine imbeciles.*

"As king of the Philistine gods," said Dagon trying to steal the credit again, "I salute you, magnificent Zeus, for your insight."

Asherah rolled her eyes at the undisguised flattery.

Zeus said, "If what I am thinking is your plan, your Sea People may end up ruling Canaan after all."

Dagon lifted his chin high with prowess.

No, thought Ba'alzebul. *I will rule Canaan after all.*

CHAPTER 80

The Philistine forces filled the Valley of the Rephaim on the way to their destination. They favored the flat terrain of valleys because of their heavy reliance upon their iron chariots and heavy armaments. They were separated into three main divisions, with chariots first, then the cavalry, and finally, infantry. The infantry had divisions of pike men, javelins and a few archers in the rear. At the back of all the forces, the five Lords, led by Achish, rode in their war chariots, guarded by Rephaim who ran along beside them. Behind them, a contingent of priests carted their idols with them, stone and wooden images of Dagon, Asherah, and Ba'alzebul. These images would even be sheltered in their own tents for rest during travel.

Israelite farming villages along the valley floor were razed and their occupants taken captive and horribly abused. The Philistines trampled and destroyed everything without concern, from homes and businesses to herds and agriculture. The Israelites had developed ingenious techniques of farming the steep slopes that turned otherwise unusable hills into rich farming terraces. All of it was pillaged and plundered. A once fertile valley was left a wasteland in their wake.

Achish looked up at the steep walls of the Sorek Gorge that they now passed through. It would be a perfect place to ambush them from above, so they had scouts at the top of the cliffs, reconnoitering to warn them.

He smiled to himself at the thought of their war campaign. It was perfect. They had the numbers. They had the time. While they besieged the city of Jerusalem, they would simultaneously create a barrier between the northern and southern trade routes, keeping the Israelites divided and cut off from supplies. The longer King David stayed behind his walls, the worse the state of his entire nation.

High above the marching armies of thousands, six scouts jogged ahead, making sure the way was clear for the Philistine Lords.

But they were not Philistine scouts. They were archangels who had surreptitiously killed the Philistine scouts and donned their clothes and armaments.

One of the scouts, Uriel in disguise, approached Mikael as he waved the clear sign to the Philistine commanders below.

"Mikael, I have bad news. The reason why we cannot find Dagon, Ba'alzebul and the others is because there was an assembly of the gods at Hermon. And they have constituted an army of the Seventy and all their minions."

"All seventy?" asked Mikael, deeply concerned.

"All seventy," repeated Uriel.

"We have not seen such a display of force since the War of Gods and Men."

"Do you think they could be trying it again?" said Uriel.

"What is their direction?" said Mikael.

"South through the Jordan Valley."

Mikael thought through the various motives of such a plan. "The only reason for such an extreme act would be for an extreme prize. Like when they tried to capture the Tree of Life in Eden."

Uriel suggested, "Are they on their way here to support the Philistines?"

Mikael thought for a moment. Terror swept his face. "Jabesh-gilead is in the Jordan Valley."

Uriel said, "They are going to try to steal the ark of the covenant!"

Mikael signaled across the chasm to the other three disguised archangels, then barked to Uriel, "Alert the others up ahead. We are going to need an army of the heavenly host."

• • • • •

David had consulted the ephod through Abiathar to discern Yahweh's will on how to respond to the Philistine approach. He consulted with his commanders and they quickly prepared for their defense.

David said to his Three and Thirty, gathered around him, "The Philistines are no doubt prepared for a long siege. What is our intelligence on their numbers?"

"My scouts say about thirty thousand," said Abishai. "And their entire two Rephaim regiments of giants, six hundred."

David asked Joab, "How many standing forces do we have available at this short notice?"

"About ten thousand," said Joab.

David's throat went dry.

Joab added, "If I had two weeks, I could match their thirty thousand from all the tribes."

"We do not have two weeks," said David. "We have two days."

Joab said, "We can send for reinforcements and wait behind the walls for them to arrive."

Benaiah said, "They will be expecting that. They'll have the entire region guarded to catch spies."

David said, "They are also expecting and preparing for a siege. So, we will give them a battle in the valley instead. A pre-emptive strike."

"Yes, my lord," said Joab. "Brilliant stratagem."

David said, "Save your praise for Yahweh, Joab. I got it from him."

David turned to Benaiah, "Set up an assassination squad for the Sons of Rapha. It is time the hunted becomes the hunter." Benaiah smiled.

David found his favorite Philistine. "Ittai, I need a Gittite. Someone who still has connections at Gath and can pass through their detection into the palace."

Ittai said, "Yes, my lord. May I ask what for?"

David said, "I have more than a war to settle this day. I have old scores."

CHAPTER 81

Achish could see the City of David about a mile in the distance as the sun rose behind them in the east. They had stopped to receive intelligence from their scouts and to prepare for their first strike. Israelite chariots and infantry could be seen camped outside the walls, spread out wide, ready to meet the invaders.

"So they have chosen to meet us in the valley after all," said Dothan of Ekron. "Fools."

Achish said to the commanders of hundreds and thousands, "Prepare your forces for our first wave attack."

The commanders bowed and left the Lords.

Achish leaned toward the Rephaim, Ishbi and Runihura, standing near him. He whispered up at them, "I am no idiot. I know ever since I broke up the Sons of Rapha, you have remained devoted to your sacred blood oath." Ishbi and Runihura looked down at him, listening with rapt attention.

Achish continued, "We all want King David's head on a pike. So let us work in unison rather than at odds. Fair enough?"

The giants gave each other a side glance of acknowledgement, then slight nods of approval.

"Fair enough."

Achish sighed. Though he and the four other Lords of the pentapolis carried the weight and power of Philistia behind them, he knew in the depth of his being that these giants were an independent clan of solidarity, a river of fury and chaos held back by the slenderest thread of civilization, just waiting to be unleashed with the words of their leaders, the Sons of Rapha. He knew that he did not have much choice but to seek peace with them through compromise.

Achish turned to his high priest and said, "Let us give an offering to the images of Dagon and Ba'alzebul for our victory."

• • • • •

The small town of Kiriath-jearim rested in the foothills of the Jordan Valley in a wooded area nine miles north of Jerusalem. Its name meant "city of the woods," as it was surrounded by a small forest. Today, it was a haunted forest underneath a cloudy dark sky, and filled with a misty fog.

Three eight foot tall dark, cloaked figures walked the empty streets of the waking village. They were far from the marketplace, where merchants were already setting up fish, bread, and vegetables for sale. Ba'alzebul, Dagon, and Asherah sought for a particular house. In one street behind them lay the dead bodies of several villagers. Ba'alzebul dragged one survivor in the dirt, delirious, almost dead.

They stopped at a cul de sac of several homes. Ba'alzebul turned and leaned over the dragged villager. "Which one?"

The villager could barely raise his hand to point. His tongue had been cut out so he could not scream. He began to pass out. Ba'alzebul dropped him in the dust as the three of them approached the house of Abinadab.

Dagon said, "It doesn't make much sense. Why store such a significant relic in such an insignificant town of yokels, and without angelic protection?"

Asherah replied, "He didn't protect his box when the Philistines stole it either. Yahweh is vainglorious. He likes to elevate his greatness by stressing the humility of his servants. The conceited pig."

Ba'alzebul growled, "We will humble him. We will take his ark and we will slaughter this entire town of his worthless servants."

Suddenly, six figures stepped out from the alley to bar the threshold of the house of Abinadab.

"There is your angelic protection," hissed Asherah.

They drew their weapons.

Before them stood the six archangels: Uriel, Gabriel, Raphael, Saraqael, Raguel, and Remiel.

They drew their swords.

A lone villager stepped outside, saw them all, and shrieked. She ran back into her house, bolting the door. Others would be out soon. There was not much time before the entire town would be awake.

Uriel spoke to the gods, "Looking for something, divine burglars?"

Gabriel said, "We have been dying to bind you cowards since you ran away at Gath."

Uriel had to have the last joke. "Sorry, no sea dragons out here."

But then the gods did something the angels did not expect.

They turned tail and ran.

Uriel, Gabriel, and Raphael took off after them. The other three stayed behind.

They chased the three gods toward the perimeter of the city. Uriel saw the forest up ahead and shouted, "We'll lose them in the woods!"

As they breached the forest's edge, Gabriel yelled, "Worse than that, dear brother!"

The three archangels ran headlong into an ambush of seventy gods and thousands of spiritual minions, hidden in the foggy mist of the trees.

CHAPTER 82

The benefits of having lived among the Philistines for over a year finally became useful for David. He had been in close to the inner workings of Gath and its Lord Achish. He had learned how both king and soldier thought, and what were their strengths and weaknesses in battle. That knowledge could make the difference against these odds.

That, and Yahweh on his side.

The strength of the Philistine war machine was the chariot, and they had hundreds of them, backed by hundreds of cavalry. The Philistine chariot was ironclad with heavy wheels and drawn by two horses. Like the Hittites, they had three riders: a driver, a shield bearer, and a spearman, with two long spears for each. They were made for short range combat and hand to hand fighting. They were heavy and they were slow.

The Israelite chariot on the other hand was lighter, like the Egyptian war cart, and was built for speed. They had two riders, one with a bow and some javelins. They could dash around, avoid the slower chariots and strike from a distance. But they only had a few dozen, along with a few hundred cavalry.

In order for David to have a fighting chance with chariot warfare, he would have to engage in a pre-emptive strike to keep the Philistine chariots from being able to charge their ranks. If they charged with a lightning strike, they could do much damage.

So the Israelite forces, led by Joab, left the walls of the City of David and attacked the Philistines in the valley at morning sunrise.

David had organized his units according to skills within the various tribes. His heavy armored pike men of Judah and Naphtali were shock troops that created a wall of impenetrable power to back up their chariots. But behind them, the infamous Benjaminites, who, since the days of the Judges, had perfected the art of slinging launched stones at their foes. And the archers of Zebulun and Simeon brought up the rear with composite bows that were accurate at over a hundred yards. The Philistines lacked the bow, which would be their weakness in this pitched battle.

There was one soldier conspicuously absent this day from the ranks of the Israelite archers: The Mouse, Jonathan ben Shimei. Finally, after all these years, David had chosen him for his own squad of warriors and their secret operation. Though the Mouse was now twenty-six years old and well-trained by his mentor, Ittai, he was still a tiny four-foot-nine pipsqueak compared to his warrior brothers. But he had proven himself in his proficiency with the bow, and David needed that proficiency now more than ever.

When the chariots and cavalry clashed on the field, the smaller forces of the Israelites dashed and dodged and slung arrows into the frustrated Philistine tortoises. The few Israelite riders that got too close were crushed by iron and spear, but the others retreated—covered by a massive wave of Israelite slung stones and arrows that covered the Philistine chariots and the soldiers behind them with a blanket of death.

Like the Israelites, the Philistine ranks had also been organized by skills and tactics. The Gazans used a particularly gruesome ploy that terrorized their enemies. Instead of using traditional shields against the volley of stones and missiles launched against them, they used captive Israelite prisoners as human shields instead.

Thousands of arrows and rocks launched by the Israelites pierced and pounded hundreds of their fellow countrymen to death, placed in the way by the Philistines. It was a barbaric act of unusual cruelty that struck fear into the hearts of the Israelite warriors when they realized what had happened. It made them feel as if they just killed their own civilian innocents. Of course, they did not kill them, the Philistines killed them by using them as shields, but the psychological effect was still powerful, no matter how unjust and evil it was.

The Gazans dropped the dead Israelites at their feet and the Ashkelon soldiers launched their own bizarre counteroffensive. The lines opened up and a slew of dozens of *children without weapons* ran toward the Israelite enemy, screaming in high pitched voices. Because they were teenaged and unarmed, the Israelites hesitated to kill them. They froze in confusion.

All of the boys and girls running at them had their bodies covered in large bulging bags of liquid. It made them look like a battalion of obese juveniles, screaming, waddling, and bouncing toward them.

Some Philistine arrows hit the corpulent adolescents from behind. But they did not puncture flesh. Instead, they broke open the bags of black pitch that oozed out in a trail following the running children.

The screaming children ran into the ranks of the frontline Israelites without trying to fight anyone.

The soldiers gathered around the children, but did not hurt them. They were children, for Yahweh's sake.

What kind of people would willingly send their own sons and daughters like this into the fray of a battle?

Everything became clear when a volley of fire arrows launched from the Philistine ranks hit the puddles of pitch that had leaked onto the ground. The fire travelled all the way to the bulging children and ignited them on fire.

They burst into flames, and became screaming fireballs that killed nearby Israelites. They became a wall of fire that hindered the Israelite warriors, scattering them.

The only words that could describe these poor creatures were child suicide soldiers.

The Philistine spearmen then engaged the Israelites, pushing them back. But the fires that had broken the ranks of the Israelites, now hindered the advance of the Philistines.

Back in the ranks of the Philistine army, Ishbi and Runihura stood upon a war wagon searching the Israelite forces for a sign of King David. The Rephaim were holding back to make a blitz strike for the anointed messiah as soon as he was targeted.

But he was nowhere to be seen. They saw someone else leading the troops, but did not know who he was.

What is more, they could see that the Israelite army was not deep. They were spread out wide to look like more than they were.

They were only a few thousand.

And now they started to pull back and retreat toward the city.

Where was their king?

As the Philistines marched after the retreating Israelites, the sound of their footsteps echoed off the tops of the trees of the balsam forest to their right. Their heavy artillery and armor precluded their use of the forest in any way.

The forest environment camouflaged seven thousand light infantry Israelites, led by King David. They had been hiding out in the foliage, waiting for their cue and this was it. A cue given by Yahweh himself. David thought to himself that the echo of the marching troops in the treetops sounded like Yahweh's heavenly host marching above them on David's behalf.

No war horn was blown, no command shouted. They followed their messiah out of the concealment, like a silent force of wasps with stingers drawn and ready.

They descended upon the rear of the advancing army.

They took the Philistines entirely by surprise, and the five Lords entirely unprotected.

Another warrior hid in the forest, just out of sight of David's raiding party. He was an eight and a half foot tall, five hundred pound giant Rephaim, leading a small battalion of a dozen Amalekite guerillas. He had been hunting David for years, seething with the bile of vengeance, and he was determined to avoid the combat mistake he made the last time.

It was Lahmi of Gath.

CHAPTER 83

When the three archangels followed their quarry into the dark misty forest outside Kiriath-jearim, they knew full well what they were entering—and they were prepared.

When they hit the foggy foliage, Gabriel blew his war horn, and the angels immediately engaged the enemy.

The first wave of gods fought the archangels with the furor of those fighting for their eternities. If any of them should be wounded and bound into the earth or Tartarus, they would remain captive until the judgment.

All of them were frightened by the prospect.

Zeus, Marduk, Horus, Shiva, and Odin struck the three angels with lightning bolts, mace, talons, six-armed swords, and staff.

The angels held their ground, dodging, parlaying, and striking back, blow for blow. These angels were not merely messengers and ministering spirits, they were Karabu, trained in the heavenly art of warfare.

Despite their strength and skill, there was no way in heaven and earth that the archangels had a fighting chance alone against seventy gods and their supporting minions.

There were thousands of the enemy.

But the angels were not alone.

At the sound of Gabriel's horn, tens of thousands of heavenly host entered the forest from the backside and descended upon their supernatural foes in battle.

The forest became alive with the unseen clash of spiritual warfare.

The three angels guarding the house of Abinadab saw the townspeople running in the streets at the strange sounds in the woods. They all looked out into the misty forest but could see nothing through the ethereal fog. The townspeople could only imagine what must be going on in the invisible world around them.

Inside that bewitched forest, the Seventy saw the host of heaven descending upon them. Before the approaching Sons of God could meet their seventy rebellious brothers and properly engage them, the gods made a break for it and ran away. Just as the Philistine deities had done earlier in the town.

It didn't make sense to the archangels. Why would they give up so quickly and easily?

They had no time to think.

Uriel saw the huge body and horns of Ba'alzebul. He was getting away with Dagon and Asherah.

He yelled and his two brothers followed him.

As the gods fled the forest, Ba'alzebul saw that the three angels were locked in on them like lions on blood. He cast a knowing look to Asherah, on the other side of Dagon.

Ba'alzebul and Asherah drew their swords and simultaneously swung low, slicing through the ankle tendons of Dagon between them.

He screamed in agony and tumbled to the ground in a pile of pain. His two betrayers raced onward back to Mount Hermon and safety.

The three angels came upon Dagon and stopped to bind him.

Gabriel kept his eye on the gods. "They are too fast. We will not be able to catch them."

"Cockroaches scurrying from the light," said Uriel, staring daggers into Dagon's fearful face. "At least we'll bind one son of Belial."

Dagon clutched his ankles writhing in agony. He bellowed in a voice that could be heard for miles, "CURSE YOU BA'ALZEBUL AND ASHERAH! DAMN YOU TO TARTARUS!"

"Oh, they will make it to Tartarus eventually," said Uriel. "And then you can play dice with them there until the judgment."

Raphael grabbed his hands and bound him with the material from his armband. It was thin, white and indestructible hair from the Cherubim that surrounded Yahweh Elohim's throne chariot in the heavenlies. It was the only material that the gods could not escape. It still held many of the original two hundred rebels bound in the depths of the earth from the time of the Deluge.

Dagon would not be getting out of this binding.

Gabriel said, "Nothing like being given up as a sacrifice to save others, is it, Dagon? Or should I call you by your true name, Kestarel?"

Dagon hissed, "You only have me because I was betrayed, godlickers."

Asherah had led Dagon to believe that they would betray Ba'alzebul to the angels. Dagon boiled with anger at her double-cross. He had been the target all along. He should have seen it. Now they could split Canaan between the two of them as king and queen.

"Which strikes me as odd," said Uriel. "What was the point of this exercise in futility? Did you really think you had a chance at capturing the ark of Yahweh?"

Dagon laughed. "You fools. Asherah was right. You are such easy targets."

"Yeah," said Uriel, "we do not have your depraved minds to think your perverted thoughts after you. But I'll bite the bait. What are we missing?"

Raphael was already figuring it out.

Dagon said, "We were not here to fight. Or steal the ark. We knew that if we showed up in force you would equal us with all your most high forces—to stop us from capturing your silly little god throne."

Raphael, who rarely spoke, said it. "The archangels and the heavenly host drawn here leaves the messiah unprotected against the Philistines and the Sons of Rapha."

"What a genius you are," mocked Dagon. He mumbled, "Simpletons."

Uriel blurted out, "We have to get back to the Valley of the Rephaim."

Gabriel halted him. "But we have to bury this brigand."

"We cannot make it back in time," countered Raphael.

"You are already too late," cackled Dagon.

• • • • •

When David's stealth forces hit the rear guard of the Philistine army, the Lords of the pentapolis became easy targets. Their royal war chariots had running guards of four giants each, but many of them went down in a wave of arrows, led by the marksman, the Mouse and his mighty bow.

Three Lords died instantly, Tarhunda of Gaza, Suwardata of Ashkelon and Mutallu of Ashdod.

Dothan of Ekron was severely wounded.

Only Achish survived intact. But he panicked.

He screamed like a woman, pushed his driver off his chariot, took the reins himself and trampled over his own soldiers getting away from the battlefield.

David saw the cowardly king drive his horses into the tree line ahead of them. Achish jumped off, running away into the forest.

Lahmi saw David from a distance. He aimed his loop javelin for a throw, and launched it. The special loop released the missile with an extra strong force that increased its speed fivefold.

David raced after Achish, with Benaiah and their armor-bearers by their sides.

Lahmi's javelin hit a soldier where David had been a second before. Lahmi cursed at his second miss against the messiah in two battles. It would not happen again.

Lahmi sprinted after David into the forest.

Ittai saw his childhood friend and lifelong enemy, Lahmi, through the fighting.

Ittai and his armor-bearer, Elhanan, sprinted after him.

The Philistine forces were now without leadership. They were pinched in front and behind by the Israelites.

Chaos erupted.

But Rephaim thrive on chaos, so the regiments of giants leapt into action.

Abishai met the attacking giants with a strike force he had put together of several hundred of the finest gibborim. They pounded each other in a clash of unrelenting fury between giant and Israelite.

Abishai cut down giants on his way to his target: Ishbi ben Ob, the prized leader of the Sons of Rapha.

Abishai could see a whirlwind of demonic spirits around the giant as he fought. It was as if the supernatural evil that accompanied this beast had become visible to the naked eye. They added a level of terror to an already terrible and frightening warrior. He was covered by the enchantment of sorcery.

Abishai didn't care. He was covered by Yahweh, the creator of spirits.

Achish ran like a scared pig through the underbrush of the forest. He kept tripping and falling and picking himself up, a bungling and pathetic mess. Then the chubby leader ran headlong into a tree and knocked himself to the ground, dizzy and seeing stars.

When David and Benaiah came upon him, they noticed Achish had soiled his battle skirt and was crawling on the ground like a wounded rat trying to get away.

Benaiah stood back with their armor-bearers.

Achish looked up at David and cried out, "You traitor! You double dealing spy! I trusted you! I let you into my palace, and you betrayed me!"

"You betrayed yourself, fool. Philistia is an abomination of desolation, and you expect me to be loyal to you? To double cross my countrymen? To betray my anointed king? To blaspheme my god?"

"I should have listened to Bisha! I should have killed you when I had the chance."

"*I* should have killed Bisha when I had the chance," said David. "But be aware O king, that you will see her today where you are both going."

"You think you are so holy and pure, you Hebrews." said the king. "But you are no different than your enemies. You kill women and children, you annihilate and enslave. Your god demands exclusive worship, yet he is just one among many who seek power over territory with violence."

David replied, "There is a difference between us, Achish. You worship demons. But Yahweh is the Creator of all things. You defied him, and now you blame him for your evil."

David raised his sword to Achish. "You are a Seed of the Serpent. You will bite the heel of Yahweh's people no more."

Then, with a determined resolve and a mighty stroke, David brought down his weapon on the neck of the debauched Philistine. Achish's lifeless head tumbled aside and landed facing skyward; his final expression of horror a trophy in David's heart.

• • • • •

Twenty miles away, in the royal palace of Gath, the Gittite spy sent by Ittai stepped out of Lady Bisha's bed chamber. He wiped blood from his dagger and made his way to the city gates.

Inside the chamber, Lady Bisha lay in a spreading pool of her own blood, her intestines spilled out on the floor beside her. In her last moments, all she could worry about was how bad she would look when they found her. Her hair was a mess and she had not gotten the chance to put on her makeup for the day.

She couldn't go out this way. It wasn't fair. It wasn't right. She was Lady of Gath. She deserved better.

Blood all over her new dress.

I should have killed that Hebrew, she thought as her life slipped into the oblivion of Sheol.

But David was wrong about her reunion with her Lord. They would not be seeing each other ever again. They would be seeing nothing but the eternal worm, utter darkness, piercing shrieks, and the wailing and gnashing of teeth.

• • • • •

On the Jerusalem side of the Valley of the Rephaim, Joab held the Philistines at bay. The giants began to push back, when Joab implemented the next plan of action.

He and David had studied the tactics of warfare used by Joshua to defeat the giants of Canaan in the conquest. They had read in the *Book of the Wars of Yahweh* how Joshua had overcome Og of Bashan. How they had built large composite bows the size of two or three men, laid on their side and operated by several soldiers. The large size of the bolts could take down giants.

Joab rolled up a dozen of these newly crafted huge bows, and they aimed above the heads of the normal soldiers at the giants in their midst. They released large bolts that found their large targets, skewering two or three giants at a time.

A contingent of giants charged the bows and scattered the Israelites, smashing the large devices to smithereens.

But the damage had been done. Casualties were high for the Rephaim.

That is when the Lion Men of Moab mobilized their offensive. Eight sharp-in-tooth, long-in-claw, lion-maned hybrids armed to the teeth with iron pounced. This clash between Rephaim and Ariels would not end well for either side. They ripped each other to shreds. Within the hour, the last of several hundred giants were bleeding in pieces on the valley floor—but so were eight mighty Lion Men who gave their lives in a heroic last stand for the King of Israel.

From this came the saying of these warriors of Gad and Moab, "The least was a match for a hundred men and the greatest for a thousand."

At the rear of the battle, Abishai and his gibborim slaughtered their giant enemies. The Rephaim numbers dwindled in the face of the Israelite warriors, as they had with the Lion Men. Six hundred had become one hundred. The gibborim had been commissioned to fight until every last Rapha was dead. It was like hacking up a den of snakes.

When Joshua first conquered the Promised Land and decimated the Seed of the Serpent, he had left Philistia alone. He had cut off the Anakim from the hill country, from Hebron and Debir, and Anab. There were no giants left in all the land. They were all devoted to destruction along with their cities. Only in Gaza, Gath, and Ashdod did some Rephaim remain, left by the withholding of Joshua's hand. These Serpent Seed were the descendants of that remnant of giants.

But the time had come for the messiah king and his forces to complete the task started by Joshua. The only problem was, the Rephaim remnant turned the tables on their vanquishers.

Two things happened at once that broke the surge of Israelite victory. First, Ishbi ben Ob yelled the name "Argaz" with a thundering voice, and second, he pulled out a special weapon he had saved for this very occasion.

The weapon was the ten foot long whip sword nicknamed Rahab that he had confiscated from Ittai's smithery many years ago. He had been practicing with it for some time and could wield it with efficiency. Its blade was a flexible indestructible metal that, under the strength of a giant's arm became a fan blade of mass death.

He swung Rahab and sliced dozens of Israelite soldiers in pieces, with ease. The demonic spirits around him howled with shrieks that pierced the ear drums of all around.

The Israelite forces backed away, bleeding and dazed.

The ground rumbled under the footsteps of a new arrival: a fifteen foot tall, twelve hundred pound colossus named Argaz. He wore nothing except sandals, bronze grieves, and a bronze helmet. His bubbling decrepit flesh was so hideous, it frightened the Israelites just to look at him. His face looked like a skull with barely enough skin on it for a covering. His eyes were bulging orbs, his teeth, a perpetual skeletal grin. He looked like a monster ascending from the bowels of Sheol. He used a mace to bludgeon dozens of Israelites to death as they stumbled over one another trying to escape the frightening sight.

He was a Rephaim storm god.

Combined with Runihura, who now swung his javelin with deadly force, this giant trinity became an unstoppable force.

And they pushed their way toward the forest, in the direction of King David.

CHAPTER 84

David, Benaiah, and their armor-bearers did not see the huge log that soared in the air at them from behind. They only heard the sound of leaves and branches being broken from the velocity of something that made them turn.

It was too late. The log was about three feet in diameter and about six feet long, a rotted husk that broke into pieces when it struck them.

Benaiah's armor-bearer was killed, Benaiah, left unconscious under the wood debris.

David awakened just as a huge hand grabbed the scruff of his neck and dragged him like captured game into a large clearing.

He was thrown down into the grass and lost his breath.

He looked up into the raging face of Lahmi of Gath.

"You despicable little Hebrew. I have been waiting for this moment for too many years." In his hand was his large, signature scimitar dripping with the blood of a hundred Israelites. "I will finish what my brother started. And I will desecrate your corpse with my seed."

He raised the sword to cleave David's body in two.

Just then, a blur hit him broadside, tackling him to the ground in a tangle of arms and legs. It was Ittai the Gittite. The sword broke from Lahmi's grip.

Ittai tumbled through the grass and roots with Lahmi, grappling for control. He was much smaller, at only six feet to Lahmi's eight plus. But Ittai had mighty strength, and he had bested Lahmi enough in the past to make this fight equal—and deadly.

David crawled over to his armor-bearer, who had come to and knelt up to give him his sword.

Ishbi spotted the movement. His chance had come to achieve his goal. He snapped the serpentine blade through the air, aiming to cut off the left arm of King David.

The blade struck its target. The amputated limb fell to the ground. Another strike and his right leg was sliced from his body.

Ishbi saw the king's dismembered figure fall to the ground bleeding out.

Ishbi yelled with victory, raising Rahab's handle high in his hand.

But it was premature.

He had mistakenly killed the king's armor-bearer, *not* the king.

David stood up from where the body of his armor-bearer lay and brandished his sword against the titan.

His puny little sword.

Two other giants, Runihura and the enormous Argaz, stepped into the clearing and stood beside Ishbi to face down David. The three towered above him and they all shared one single goal: to kill the Chosen Seed, messiah of Israel.

Ittai and Lahmi wrestled for dominance. Ittai got Lahmi in a headlock. He spoke through the strain. "We were brothers, Lahmi."

The giant muttered with gritted teeth, "We were never brothers."

Ittai grunted, "We fought together. We overcame death." He meant the plague they both survived when they were but children and forever friends.

Lahmi hissed and tried to pull out, but he could not. "You were always weak," he spit out.

Ittai knew he wasn't referring to physical strength, but moral constitution. Ittai had always been hindered by petty concerns of right and wrong. Lahmi wanted to win and dominate.

"You could never be a Son of Rapha."

"I don't want to be a Son of Rapha," Ittai growled. "I am a son of Abraham."

Lahmi said, "This ends today—Runt."

Ittai burned at the old insulting nickname. It brought back painful memories of rejection and unrequited respect.

He squeezed to make Lahmi pass out. Instead, Lahmi suddenly stood up, carrying Ittai on his back, and slammed him into a tree.

Ittai lost his breath.

A second slam and Ittai lost his grip. He fell to his rear on the ground, his head spinning, ribs bruised and cracked.

Lahmi moved away from him. He reached in his belt and pulled out a socket axe.

He drew back to throw it into Ittai's chest.

He heard Ittai's armor-bearer yell out.

He saw a sword flying through the air—and plunging blade-first into the ground in front of Ittai, who reached out and pulled the blade up to defend.

Lahmi turned his aim to throw the axe at the armor-bearer.

Ittai screamed, "ELHANAN!" But it was too late.

The axe struck Elhanan deep in his shoulder, dropping him to the ground.

Lahmi turned back to Ittai and picked up his scimitar right from the ground at his feet.

Ittai prayed to the Lord of Hosts, "Yahweh, use this sword, forged from the metal of Goliath's own blade against his brother."

Lahmi lunged.

David stared down the three giants about to slaughter him; Ishbi, Runihura, and the gigantic Argaz. It was all he could do to keep from staring at the gargantuan, a frightening monstrosity that looked like a tower of ugliness and evil. *How could that thing be killed?* He needed to stay focused.

What he wouldn't give right now for a sling and three smooth stones.

Instead what he got was three gibborim giant-slayers with weapons drawn and in full attack: Abishai, armed with a glaive, had followed his prey into the clearing; the newly conscious Benaiah stood up next to David; and last but not least, the Mouse, that tiny little bowman with the tireless spirit, carrying two full quivers of arrows.

But there was a fourth surprise that made everyone pause with shock—a miraculous surprise. David's dismembered armor-bearer stood up, with both arm and leg reattached. And he wielded a sword against Ishbi.

It was Mikael, Prince of Israel, guardian of King David. He had disguised himself to become one of David's armor-bearers at Jerusalem.

And he was done hiding. He muttered, "I am getting really tired of being cut to pieces."

David said simply, "Glad you are on my side."

Mikael retorted, "Here to protect you."

Benaiah complained, "Hey, what about me? Am I not adequate...?"

Before Benaiah could finish his question, Ishbi swung Rahab at Mikael, trying to cut him in half again. But Mikael was ready this time.

He was the only fighter present who could take on this special weapon, forged of heavenly metal in the furnace of God's mountain, and stolen by this thieving spawn of the Serpent.

Mikael was going to take it back.

He pulled David down and the blade swung inches over their heads. Mikael then flipped, twisted, and dove the warrior moves of Karabu as Ishbi swung and snapped at him.

Ishbi's blade could not touch this dancing, darting archangel. And his demons were howling mad. Their frenzy created a vortex of supernatural storm around him.

Metal struck metal with rapid succession like lightning strikes. The clashing blades of angel and giant caused a shower of sparks that started fires in the brush all around them.

The giant's arm became tired.

Mikael found his moment and stuck his steel sword in the air to catch the serpentine blade. It wrapped around his own and he gave a yank with all his might. It jerked out of Ishbi's hands and flew into the brush.

David could only think of one thing as he saw Mikael's moves: poetry. His movements flowed like a song. He was a living, moving psalm—an imprecatory psalm of judgment.

Contend, O Yahweh, with those who contend with me;
fight against those who fight against me!
Take hold of shield and buckler
and rise for my help!
Draw the spear and javelin
against my pursuers!

Let them be like chaff before the wind,
with the angel of Yahweh driving them away!
Let their way be dark and slippery,
with the angel of Yahweh pursuing them!

Then my tongue shall tell of your righteousness
and of your praise all the day long.

Meanwhile, Benaiah matched Runihura staff for staff. Benaiah was at a disadvantage, being dizzy from being knocked unconscious. But this was the warrior who fought another giant with a concussion and killed two Lion Men while drunk. The Egyptian didn't stand a chance.

The flames spread through the fighting arena, creating pockets of fire that the fighters had to avoid.

> *They say, "Come, let us wipe them out as a nation;*
> *   let the name of Israel be remembered no more!"*
> *O my Elohim, make them like whirling dust,*
> *   like chaff before the wind.*
> *As fire consumes the forest,*
> *   as the flame sets the mountains ablaze,*
> *let them perish in disgrace,*
> *   that they may know that you alone,*
> *whose name is Yahweh,*
> *   are the Most High over all the earth.*

Because of Jonathan's small stature, no one ever believed he could face a Rephaim giant. Now, after all the years of complaining about David holding him back, the Mouse faced off against Argaz, the behemoth, largest of the Sons of Rapha. Jonathan was small and speedy, while Argaz's size made him slow and lumbering. And Jonathan wasn't affected by the creature's frightening look either. It only made it easier to attack.

Jonathan sprinted around Argaz, dodging his swinging mace, while emptying two quivers of arrows into the giant's hide. They were annoying and insignificant pin pricks that the giant would snap off immediately from his over-scarred flesh.

The most deadly target for Jonathan, the Rapha's head, was unfortunately protected by his bronze helmet, so the Israelite peppered his opponent's body with two dozen pin pricks, all around his frame, making Argaz more furious than ever.

Your arrows are sharp
in the heart of the king's enemies;
the peoples fall under you.
Your throne, O Elohim, is forever and ever.

The moment after Mikael had disarmed Ishbi of his serpentine whip sword, he shouted for Abishai, who stepped in and barked, "Leave some glory for the rest of us, archangel!"

Mikael grabbed David and said, "Let us get you out of here."

Abishai wielded a glaive, a pole-arm weapon that affixed an eviscerating large blade to the end of a long pole. He swung it around like a fan blade and faced down the giant, who drew his scimitar with bravado.

"Well, if it isn't my favorite Hebrew traitor. I have you to thank for the tasty prophets of Ramah."

Abishai's jaw went tight. So this was the demon monger who skinned all those holy men of Israel. And he was able to do so because of my indiscretion with the Qedesha.

Ishbi's sarcasm turned to taunt, "Get out of my way, Asherah lover, I have a messiah to gut."

Abishai faltered at the remark. His spiritual betrayal had almost caused the death of his king. And now this uncovering of his secret almost caused his own death, as it distracted his defense against Ishbi's slashing scimitar.

Abishai fell to the ground. He rolled just before the descending curved blade could cleave him in two.

But he was up again, all his senses regained.

This battle would be his redemption.

In more ways than one, this giant must die for Abishai to live.

O Elohim, you know my folly;
  the wrongs I have done are not hidden from you.
Let not those who hope in you be put to shame through me,
  O Adonai, Lord Yahweh of hosts;
let not those who seek you be brought to dishonor through me.
I have become a stranger to my brothers,
  an alien to my mother's sons.
Deliver me
  from sinking in the mire;
let me be delivered from my enemies
  and from the deep waters.
Let not the flood sweep over me,
  or the deep swallow me up,
  or the pit close its mouth over me.

Ittai and Lahmi exchanged blows with their swords. Lahmi pushed Ittai to the edge of the clearing. The curve of his scimitar's blade gave Lahmi an added advantage over Ittai's straight sword. He used his blade to hook his adversary's weapon in its curve and spin it out of his hands onto the ground.

Ittai was weaponless.

He backed up into the woods, dodging Lahmi's thrusts and swipes. They had become a relentless flurry of madness that chopped down saplings and branches around Ittai like mere kindling. This also created a maze of dangerously sharp protruding branches that Ittai had to avoid in the tangle of combat.

Lahmi was not going to stop until his enemy was cut to bloody ribbons.

Ittai saw the blind rage and took his opportunity. He backed up against a tree.

Lahmi swung hard and wide.

Ittai ducked and the scimitar embedded in the tree behind Ittai. But it was not a sapling. It was old and thick. Lahmi's blade was stuck deep.

Ittai threw himself into the giant's chest and shoved him away from his weapon.

The two of them launched backwards and Lahmi hit a tree with a grunt of pain.

Lahmi's eyes went wide with shock.

Ittai felt his adversary's grip release him.

Ittai backed up to see what had happened.

He had unknowingly shoved Lahmi right into the jagged limb of a large broken tree branch cut by Lahmi's own blade. It jutted out from Lahmi's chest, along with his blood pooling on the ground below him.

Ittai should not have been horrified, but he was. Even though this childhood friend had become a monster, even though Lahmi had sought to cut him down and assassinate Ittai's messiah king, he still was shocked and horrified at his old friend's fate.

Lahmi's rage cooled as his face turned pale and his breathing labored. Suddenly his look melted into one of familiarity—and regret.

Ittai saw wetness in the impaled giant's eye. He croaked out, "Ittai."

Suddenly, all the hatred and venom had been drained from this serpent's fangs.

"Ittai," he gurgled again looking down at Ittai's belt.

Ittai looked and realized what he meant. Ittai had forgotten that he still had his dagger. Lahmi was asking for a quick death, an honorable death.

Ittai pulled the dagger and snapped it up to Lahmi's throat, ready to cut. Lahmi groaned with agony. Every movement of his body brought intense pain from his impaled wound.

Lahmi looked pleadingly into Ittai's eyes. Ittai tightened his grip. He gritted his teeth.

But he could not do it.

As much as it was his moral right to do so, Ittai felt that this last act between the two of them would seal a hatred he had sought to turn from all his life. He would not finish what Yahweh had started. He would let Yahweh's judgment take its own course. "Vengeance is mine," saith Yahweh.

Ittai shook his head just slightly and wiped the tears that were starting down his own face. The dagger dropped at Lahmi's feet.

Ittai slowly, sadly, walked back over to draw the scimitar from the tree and return to the clearing.

Lahmi gritted his teeth in agony and his knees buckled. His weight broke the branch impaling him, and he fell to the forest floor—where the dagger lay.

In a last ditch burst of strength, Lahmi picked up the dagger.

Ittai had his back to Lahmi. He did not see it coming.

The sounds of battle in the clearing had covered Lahmi's movements.

Lahmi lunged at Ittai's back.

But he stopped with a last gasp as a sword penetrated his heart from behind, next to the broken limb.

Ittai turned in surprise.

Lahmi dropped to the ground to reveal a bloody, wounded Elhanan behind him.

Elhanan had brought Ittai's sword from the clearing. It was the sword forged from the sword metal of Goliath, the defeated foe of young David the Anointed One, the Chosen Seed, The Messiah King.

Now it ended the life of the dead dragon's wicked brother.

Elhanan collapsed to the ground.

If a man does not repent, Elohim will whet his sword;
Behold, the wicked man conceives evil
His mischief returns upon his own head,
*   and on his own skull his violence descends.*

425

I will sing praise to the name of Yahweh, the Most High.

The burning brush fires struck fear into the heart of the gargantuan Argaz. Memories of his immolation caused hesitation that little Jonathan noticed. Was this his chance?

The fear brought a surge of energy into Argaz. He was a Rephaim warrior, and he had had enough of this pesky little Hebrew mosquito and his stings. He stampeded through a fire, singeing his feet and legs without concern.

Jonathan had stopped his darting dodges from the giant's clutches. His back was up against a wall of fire. He had one last shot.

As Argaz descended upon him, Jonathan nocked his last arrow, aimed, and released.

It hit his target, the giant's grisly left eye.

But it did not go in deep enough to reach the brain.

And Argaz was pumped up.

He did not slow down. He ripped the arrow out, pulling his left eye with it, and tossed it behind him.

That was it. Jonathan was out of arrows and had nowhere to go.

Argaz was upon him.

He grabbed the little archer in his huge six-fingered hand.

He began to squeeze. Would he pop him like a pus filled wound?

Then Argaz became dizzy.

He held Jonathan up to his good eye. He wanted to see this bothersome creature before biting off its head. Who was this gnat that could have inflicted so much damage upon the mighty Argaz?

He was nothing. He was a gasping little mouse that could barely survive the tight hold of the giant's grip.

Then Argaz stopped. His thoughts went foggy. Everything swirled and blurred.

Jonathan grinned through crushing pain.

He had done it.

His pestering little pin pricks had all been carefully aimed at precise points of Argaz's grotesque anatomy. The giant's naked musculature made easy target for Jonathan's aim. Know your enemy inside and out, Ittai had told him years ago. So Jonathan had learned where all the vital organs in the body were. He had targeted those spots with his expert precision. He had so punctured the Rapha's lungs, heart, kidneys, liver, and abdomen that the accumulative effect had finally taken its toll. Argaz's life had bled out of his vital organs.

Argaz dropped Jonathan. His good eye rolled up in his head, and he fell dead on his face, right into the flames. The stench of the giant's burning flesh was both ironic and sweet in the nostrils of his conqueror, the mighty, tiny Jonathan the Mouse.

Yahweh finally finished the judgment of fire he had begun on the monster all those years ago.

> *He has bent and readied his bow;*
> *he has prepared for him his deadly weapons,*
> > *making his arrows fiery shafts.*
> *The righteous will rejoice when he sees the vengeance;*
> > *he will bathe his feet in the blood of the wicked.*
> *Mankind will say,*
> > *"Surely there is a reward for the righteous;*
> > *surely there is an Elohim who judges on earth."*

This was no time to rest in my victory, thought Jonathan. He quickly pulled one of the whole arrows from Argaz's scarred lower back and nocked it on his bowstring, aiming at Runihura who was being pushed backward by Benaiah's handling of his staff.

He released and the arrow hit the Egyptian right in the neck. It was not a kill shot, but it was enough of a wound to make Runihura drop his guard at the sharpness of pain.

Benaiah saw the opportunity and spun his own staff around the Egyptian's javelin, disarming him.

He then knocked the giant to the ground with a series of rapid hits.

He grabbed Runihura's own javelin and thrust it into the fallen giant's heart. Runihura grunted with surprise and pain as he died beneath his own spear.

Benaiah glared over at Jonathan, a good twenty feet away and shouted, "I had him! I did not need your help!"

Jonathan shrugged sorry.

The fires had grown out of control. The entire clearing was surrounded by engulfing flames. Ittai could not get back to his comrades through the circle of fire, so he carried the body of Elhanan with him out to the valley.

The other warriors in the clearing panicked. Would Yahweh allow them to die in the fires of judgment? Jonathan and Benaiah looked for a way out through the wall of fire, but there was none.

Their victories were in vain.

But they had failed to look overhead, where large storm clouds had gathered.

Thunder drew their attention above and it started to rain. Sheets of it, poured down upon them with lifesaving hope. The true God of storm, Yahweh, had come upon a swift cloud to Philistia, and he opened the floodgates of heaven with his voice of seven thunders.

Ishbi was still in combat with Abishai when he realized that he alone was left, that David was gone, and that the rain was dousing the fires around him.

So he turned around and ran through the smoldering brush, back toward the valley.

Back toward David.

• • • • •

David looked out upon the carnage drenched in the falling rain. The fighting armies were gone. All that was left were the dead. Corpses of Philistines, Rephaim, and Israelites heaped upon one another carpeted the valley.

David faltered. Benaiah and Mikael held him up. A few Israelite soldiers had been picking through the bodies, killing any survivors of the enemy.

One of them bowed before David and said, "My lord the Philistine forces were decimated. They split apart and ran away, into the north and west. They are being chased down by Joab as we speak."

"We must catch them," said David. "I must lead my forces."

"Joab will do just fine," said Benaiah, now beside him. "My lord the king should return to Jerusalem."

"But I am their king."

"Exactly," said Benaiah. "And that is why you should no longer go out with us to battle, lest you quench the lamp of Israel."

David looked at him as if he had been insulted. But Benaiah held firm. Mikael nodded in agreement. David knew his chief bodyguard was right. He was getting too old, and the assassins had come too close. If he kept going out to war, he would only give his enemies more opportunities to finally achieve their vile serpentine goal of extinguishing the Chosen Seed.

David pulled away from Benaiah like a child unwilling to accept what he was told. He trod through the muck and the flesh. Small rivers of blood and water formed swirling reddish pools of death everywhere.

David stepped over bodies, looking all around him at the horrifying results of war. Of course, he had done what he had to do. Yahweh himself had led him to wipe out the Philistines and their Rephaim, and devote to destruction the Geshurites, the Girzites, and the Amalekites. In the heat of battle, there was no time to philosophize or contemplate the eternal meaning of it all.

But now, in this graveyard of slaughter, as the pouring rain drenched the sea of slain in its heavenly baptism of silent cleansing, he came face to face with the tragedy of his own being. He had become a man of much bloodshed. It had changed him, and he would never be the same. He could never go back. He knew in that moment that his kingdom would never see the shalom of Yahweh over the land. It would take another king, one of his sons, to build a kingdom of peace upon this kingdom of blood.

He saw a contingent of Rephaim dead strewn about. Their large carcasses were intertwined with the bodies of hairy opponents: Lion Men of Moab. It was a mass butchery.

The accompanying soldier muttered, "The Lion Men fought well. The last of the Rephaim were annihilated. They are no more."

They are no more, thought David. *At what price?* He reached down and pulled some hair out of the face of one of the Lion Men. He squeezed his eyes tight with the pain of recognition. It was Ezer, their chief. He had been one of those who rescued David from his own countrymen when they attempted assassination. Rain pelted his silent, peaceful sleep, the sleep of the dead.

David stood back up. The piles and piles of bodies seemed to go on forever. He could not see the end of them through the pouring rain. He could not see where the death would end and new life could begin.

> *Save me, O Elohim!*
> *For the waters have come up to my neck.*
> *I sink in deep mire,*
> *where there is no foothold;*
> *I have come into deep waters,*
> *and the flood sweeps over me.*
> *I am weary with my crying out;*
> *my throat is parched.*

My eyes grow dim
with waiting for my Elohim.

More in number than the hairs of my head
are those who hate me without cause;
mighty are those who would destroy me,
Let heaven and earth praise him,
the seas and everything that moves in them.
For Elohim will save Zion
and build up the cities of Judah,
and people shall dwell there and possess it;
the seed of his servants shall inherit it,
and those who love his name shall dwell in it.

"DAVID!" The voice of Benaiah brought him out of his rumination.

He looked up to see a figure running at him full tilt from out of the forest with scimitar raised over his head. In the rain, David could not see who it was.

He only saw it was a giant.

Benaiah and Mikael were too far away to protect him.

David had lain his sword down by Ezer and forgot to pick it up.

Twenty feet, and the giant would be upon him.

Ishbi had silently run through the forest knowing stealth was his last chance. As he broke the clearing, he saw the two warriors to his right and the single man in royal robe among the bodies. The voices in his head screamed "MESSIAH! MESSIAH!"

He sprinted with all his might and raised his scimitar to cleave his victim in two. His demonic spirits circled him like a hurricane of furious hate.

But suddenly, something wrapped around his neck from behind.

A flexible metal blade.

As Ishbi made his final launch at David, the wrath of Rahab yanked backward. Ishbi's body lurched forward, but his head launched backward, sliced from his body by the heavenly sword. The sound of supernatural howling filled the air as Ishbi's headless corpse landed in the muck with a splash. It slid forward to a stop just feet from David.

He looked up to see a panting Abishai drop the whip sword and then kneel in the mud catching his breath.

Mikael was by David's side in a flash. Benaiah helped Abishai up and found their way to the king.

The body of Ishbi ben Ob quivered and jerked with the final spasms of death as the evil spirits left it in search of some other host.

It was a sacred moment of silence for them all.

But then…

"Abishai," said David. "Your brother Joab will no doubt be very jealous of this mighty deed. I do not know if that one can ever be topped."

Abishai replied, "You can be sure my lord that he will never hear the end of it."

They smiled. They had to find some hope, some life in the midst of all this death.

Ittai and Jonathan came from the woods and joined them.

They each threw a giant's head at the feet of David.

David said with curiosity, "And who vanquished that colossus?" He figured the large charred black skull was that of Argaz.

"I did, my lord," said Jonathan.

David looked at him with surprise.

Ittai added, "And he helped take down Runihura as well."

Benaiah snapped, "I already had him. He butted in, is what he did."

David smiled, reached over and tussled Jonathan's hair as one would a younger brother. Jonathan hated it when he did that.

David said, "I do believe my little nephew here may have outdone us all, my legend included." The men all chuckled.

Jonathan demurred, "No, my king. Your youthful defeat of Goliath was much more."

"The Serpent's head," added Ittai. "We merely finished off the tail."

"A thrashing powerful tail at that," said David.

Abishai whispered to Jonathan, "The chronicles of Israel will probably not record the details of your victory because you are not the king. But *we* will never forget."

David added, "Jonathan, I was wrong. You have proven yourself a mighty gibborim, a giant slayer." He looked at the others like a father would his children and concluded, "And I think you finally warrant the end of the nickname Mouse. Do you not agree, warriors?"

They smiled and nodded.

Ittai said, "I think we should call him Hawk from now on." The others agreed and Jonathan the Hawk grinned from ear to ear.

The men suddenly noticed Mikael looking up onto the ridge above them. The rain was starting to clear, but all they could see were six paladin warriors on horses staring down at them like solemn harbingers of death.

Benaiah and the others drew their weapons.

"Philistine scouts? Assassins?" wondered Ittai aloud.

"Neither," said Mikael. "They are my comrades. Late as usual."

Benaiah looked at Mikael. "We could have used their help."

Mikael said with a knowing smile, "They were helping us."

"How?" said Benaiah.

"You would not believe me if I told you," grinned Mikael.

CHAPTER 85

The sounds of festive music filled the streets of Jerusalem. Shouts of joy mixed with timbrel, lyre and horns. A parade of women led a procession through the city with dancing streamers that flowed around them like billows of smoky trails.

Trumpets announced a military parade of triumph. The ark had entered the City of David.

Behind the ark, at the end of the procession, pairs of oxen dragged statues of gods captured from the Philistines. Images of Dagon, Ba'alzebul, and Asherah ground their faces in the dust before being cast from the heights into the valley below where they were pulverized to pieces.

After the slaughter of the Philistines at the Valley of the Rephaim, David chased the enemy all the way from Gibeon to Gezer. He then performed a mopping up operation in taking Gath and her surrounding cities. After all the generations of warfare with the Philistines, David, the messiah king of Israel, had finally vanquished the Philistines and eliminated the last of the giants of the land.

David thought to bring the ark out of hiding and into Jerusalem. But when he sent a team of men to retrieve the ark with a cart and oxen, a terrible incident occurred that shook David to the core of his soul. The cart had been traveling on the road for some time when it hit a bumpy location and the ark began to fall. When one of the men reached out to stop it, he was struck dead by Yahweh at that very spot.

At first David was angry with Yahweh. Why would he do such a thing? Why would he smite someone who was trying to protect his own covenantal monument?

But then he became full of fear when the prophet Nathan told him that Yahweh's holiness was completely disregarded and David should be glad Yahweh did not smite him as well.

Yahweh had always commanded that only the Levites should transport the ark on the poles as they would transport a king's throne. So the cart was an insult. But Yahweh had also said that no man should touch it because it was emblematic of Yahweh's holy presence with Israel—Yahweh who is seated enthroned above the Cherubim.

Touching the ark was not a mere attempt to rescue it from damage, it was a final act in a long string of acts of disobedience that violated Yahweh's holy commands. Nathan said the road to Sheol was paved with good intentions of individuals who sought to follow Yahweh on their own terms.

But Yahweh was not so to be trifled with. He was Creator and King, but he was also Judge of all the earth.

So David concluded that he was not worthy of having the ark with him. He immediately sent it to the house of Obed-Edom the Gittite near Kiriath-jearim, a man he had met when he was at Gath. He had been one of Ittai's converts.

The ark stayed there for three months until David finally called upon the Levites to bring it properly to the city as he should first have done. They had even performed a sacrifice of ox and fattened animal after it had gone six steps. This time, David would do it right. This time, he would honor Yahweh's greatness and goodness with the holy respect and awe he deserved.

David followed the ark, leaping and dancing with the dancers before Yahweh, wearing a mere linen ephod. He followed the ark up to its temporary home in a special tent on the elevated high place above the city overlooking his own palace.

He offered sacrifices and offerings and distributed cakes of bread and raisin with meat to all the people gathered around. The joyous occasion was concluded with a concert of praise unto Yahweh.

Arise, O Yahweh and go to your resting place,
you and the ark of your might.

Let your priests be clothed with righteousness,
and let your saints shout for joy.
For the sake of your servant David,
do not turn away the face of your anointed one.

David returned to his house that evening to bless his household and hopefully bless his bed with one of his wives' companionship—or maybe two if *he* was blessed. All this worship of Yahweh did not make him tired, it energized him. It roused his hunger for the earthly side of his relationship with Yahweh. Being fruitful and multiplying to fill the earth was one command of Yahweh's he found the easiest and most desirable to obey. He smiled to himself.

As he approached the entrance to his palace, he was met by Michal on the steps. He could see she was not in a pleasant mood. She had not seemed to be interested in him at all since he had gotten her back from Saul's illegal remarriage of her to another man. She had seemed bitter and hard.

Her words were sarcastic. "How the king honored himself today in the celebration of Yahweh's ark."

"What do you mean, Michal?"

Her venom was thick. "Uncovering yourself before the eyes of your female servants."

It took David by surprise. "What?"

"Like some kind of vulgar, shameless pervert."

"It was before Yahweh that I danced. The ephod is a symbol of his communication with me."

Her bitterness of years would not give way. "You do everything for your own glory."

David knew he had to become firm with her childish insolence. "Yahweh chose me above your father and above all his house to appoint me as leader of Israel. So I will celebrate before Yahweh, and I will make myself even more contemptible before your eyes if it means honoring my Creator."

She stared at him silently, eyes unforgiving.

"Michal, despite all my sins, and they are many, your unforgiveness is not against me. It is against Yahweh. It has soured you and I would not doubt that it has soured your womb to lack a child in the House of David."

Michal's eyes went wide with shock. "How dare you! May Asherah prove you wrong with her fecundity!"

She left him in a huff, planning her next sacrifice to the goddess. *And I'm bringing those teraphim back into the household.*

David watched her stomp away. A painful tear flowed down his cheek. She had been the wife of his youth. They had discovered life and love together. It had been so simple at the start. But as his life became more complicated, he made more mistakes and hurt more people. He had not treated her as he should. But he did not know how to fix that now.

Maybe she was right. Maybe he had lived more for his own glory than he had thought. Maybe he was fooling himself and others with humble claims of unworthiness, while actually seeking the greatness and glory of the world.

The words "House of David" echoed in his mind. He looked up at his palace, his "house." It was a grand and glorious work of Phoenician architectural expertise. House of David was a term of the lineage of royalty that encompassed all his many sons. It was entirely legitimate, and yet it now mocked him.

House of David.

What of the House of Yahweh? He had a myriad of Sons of God or Bene Elohim, who surrounded his throne and carried out his sovereign will. But why did he not have a temple on earth that connected to his temple in heaven? Why was the very artifact of his presence, the ark of the covenant, residing in a mere tent while David lived in a glorious house of cedar?

Maybe Michal was right. Maybe David did do everything for his own glory and not the glory of Yahweh.

He needed to speak to Nathan the prophet right away. He was the only one he knew who would tell him the honest truth from Yahweh's own mouth to David's ears.

CHAPTER 86

Nathan stood in the firelight of David's writing room. Scrolls and manuscripts were strewn about with lyres, flutes and other instruments that David would practice with. It was the one room where he could be alone to play his music and concentrate on writing songs when he had the time. As king he did not have much time for this anymore, so he spent most of it trying to put to parchment what he had written when he was younger.

Nathan had first thought David's idea of building a house for the ark to be just fine. He had told him to do whatever was in his heart, for Yahweh was with him.

But then Nathan got a word from Yahweh, and learned it was not quite that simple.

He said to David, "Thus saith Yahweh: Would you build me a house to dwell in? I have not lived in a house since the day I brought up the people of Israel out of Egypt to this very day. I have been moving about in a tent for my dwelling. Not once did I ever demand the judges who ruled Israel build me a house of cedar."

David sat looking into the flames of the hearth. These times of chastising always hurt, but he knew it was for his good. And he wanted to honor Yahweh with all his heart.

Nathan continued with Yahweh's words for him, "I have been with you wherever you went and have cut off all your enemies from before you. I will make your name great, like the name of the great ones of the earth. And I will appoint a place for my people Israel, so that they may dwell in their own place and be disturbed no more."

David's eyes glistened with wetness as he continued to stare into the flames. They reminded him of the fires of purification.

The words of Yahweh are pure words,
  like silver refined in a furnace on the ground,
  purified seven times.
You, O Yahweh, will keep them.

Nathan continued, "I will give you rest from all your enemies. Moreover, Yahweh declares that Yahweh will make *you* a house."

The prophet's words pierced through the crackling of flames. Even David's desire to build a house for Yahweh was presumptuous. He had much to learn yet of humility.

"When your days are fulfilled and you lie down with your fathers, I will raise up your seed after you, and I will establish his kingdom. He shall build a house for my name, and I will establish the throne of his kingdom forever. I will be to him a father, and he shall be to me a son. My steadfast love will not depart from him. And your house and your kingdom shall be made sure forever before me. Your throne shall be established forever."

By the time Nathan finished, David was weeping with repentance. He reached for a quill and papyrus amongst his implements. He had been inspired to write. The words pounded in his head and would not leave him alone.

He scribbled them down.

I have set Yahweh always before me;
  because he is at my right hand, I shall not be shaken.
Therefore my heart is glad, and my whole being rejoices;
  my flesh also dwells secure.
For you will not abandon my soul to Sheol,
  or let your holy one see corruption.

Yahweh says to Adonai, my Lord:
  "Sit at my right hand,
    until I make your enemies your footstool."
Yahweh sends forth from Zion
  your mighty scepter.
    Rule in the midst of your enemies!
Yahweh has sworn
  and will not change his mind,
"You are a priest forever
  after the order of Melchizedek."

He sat back on his bench and contemplated the lyrics he wrote. They were words of prophet, priest, and king. He knew in his heart that no matter which of his sons should rule after him, and no matter how righteous they were, they would all die as all men died. But who was this "holy one" who would not see corruption? Who could have an eternal throne, who could sit at the omnipotent right hand of Yahweh, but Yahweh himself? What mortal being could be like Melchizedek, with no beginning or end? Could a Son of David be a Bene Elohim, a Son of God?

For the next book in this story timeline get *Jezebel: Harlot Queen of Israel*. Though it is in the Chronicles of the Watchers series, it is the next one you want to get. This is because Chronicles of the Watchers is interwoven with Chronicles of the Nephilim to fill in the gaps of the storyline of the Nephilim series.

If you liked this book, then please help me out by writing an honest review of it on Amazon. That is one of the best ways to say thank you to me as an author. It really does help my exposure and status as an author. It's really easy. In the Customer Reviews section, there is a little box that says "Write a customer review." They guide you easily through the process. Thanks! — *Brian Godawa*

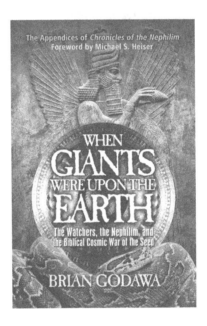

APPENDIX
GOLIATH WAS NOT ALONE

David Ascendant tells the story of a league of giant assassins who seek to kill King David during his reign as the ruler of Israel. Goliath is only one of them, and when his brother Lahmi, another giant, discovers David killed his sibling, he sets out to kill the Israelite leader for both revenge and to stop the messiah king from securing victory over the Philistines and ownership over all of Canaan.

As much as I admit creative license in my adaptation of Scriptural story, my goal for the entire saga *Chronicles of the Nephilim* is to faithfully retell those stories of the Bible that touch on the giants and the War of the Seed as expressed in Genesis 3:15 through God's curse upon the Serpent: "I will put enmity between you and the woman, and between your offspring [Seed] and her offspring [Seed]; he shall bruise your head, and you shall bruise his heel."

My goal has been to bring to light all these Biblical references to giants (ala, *Chronicles of the Nephilim*) that hint at that cosmic war of principalities and powers against the Biblical God, Yahweh and his victorious Messiah. My standard for deciding which stories to tell was only those that had explicit or implicit references to the Nephilim giants and their progeny in the Bible. Admittedly, Scriptural references to the giants are sparse, but they are significant and seem to hint at this War of the Seed that I have been writing about.

In *Noah Primeval* and *Enoch Primordial*, I retold the story of the Flood based on Genesis 6 and the book of 1 Enoch that the New Testament uses as source material. In *Gilgamesh Immortal*, I retold the pagan myth about a giant king as a prelude or origin story of the Biblical uber-villain, Nimrod. Then in *Abraham Allegiant*, I expanded on that villain and his building of the Tower of Babel and how it wove into the Divine Council worldview of God allotting territory to fallen Watchers. These were the same Watchers who sought to use the giants as the "Seed of the Serpent" to corrupt the earth and destroy the bloodline of God's people and his Messiah. The giant clans are referenced in Genesis 14 and the Watcher/human copulation is hinted at in the Sodom and Gomorrah episode in Genesis 19. Abraham settled right near the city of Kiriath-arba, later called Hebron (Gen. 13:18). Kiriath-arba was the city of King Arba, forefather of the Anakim giants that Joshua would battle (Josh. 14:15, 15:13). That is a subtle but critical theological fact that is easily overlooked by less rigorous Bible study. The Sons of Anak and the Sons of Abraham had a history together that went back to Arba and Abraham, their forefathers. Or in other words, the Seed of the Serpent and the Seed of Eve.

In *Joshua Valiant* and *Caleb Vigilant*, I retold the conquest of the Promised Land, where the Bible indicates a deliberate targeting of giant clans by Joshua for eradication (Joshua 11:21-22). We even read about specific giants in Scripture who were mighty opponents of this campaign, such as the Rephaim giant king Og of Bashan (Deut. 3:1-11), and the Anakim giant warriors; Ahiman, Sheshai, and Talmai (Num. 13:22; Josh. 15:14; Judges 1:10). Again, we are not told the details of these giant warriors, so I filled in between the lines of Scripture with story that would be consistent with those lines, making those apparently random historical "factoids" more meaningful in the big picture of God's plans. I connected the dots that our western Christian bias might miss because of our lack of ancient Near Eastern Jewish context.

As much as I assume there had to be giants in Canaan during the time of the book of Judges, none are actually mentioned in that Biblical tome, so my saga must jump from the story of Joshua's conquest of Canaan to the next Scriptural occurrence of giants, which is in the life of David.

Goliath and Giants Galore

In King David's story there are five passages that contain giants in the narrative. The most famous one is 1 Samuel 17 that tells the story of Goliath. In fact, that story is so famous, it seems that some Christians think he's the only giant in the Bible! Others say he wasn't much of a giant at all. That's because there are textual problems with the sources we have for the English text of the Old Testament.

In 1 Samuel 17:4, Goliath is described as being "6 cubits and a span." Scholarly consensus describes the "cubit" as being approximately 18 inches, measured by the distance between an average man's elbow and forefinger. A "span" is about half of that length, which is about the distance of an outstretched hand, or 9 inches. So by these standards, Goliath's "6 cubits and a span" was about 9 feet, 9 inches tall.

But there is a problem with that measurement. The 6 1/2 cubit dimension is taken from the Hebrew Masoretic Texts (MT), which are not always the most reliable in their transmission history. Some scholars point out that the Septuagint (LXX), the Dead Sea Scrolls (DSS), and Josephus after them describe Goliath at only "4 cubits and a span," which would make him more like 6 feet, 9 inches tall. According to archeological estimates of discovered remains in Canaan, the average Jew was about 5 feet, 6 inches tall.[1] This shorter version of Goliath would still be a tall man compared to the average ancient Jew, but not at all the supernatural monstrosity of 9 feet, 9 inches tall.

---

[1] G. Ernest Wright, "Troglodytes and Giants in Palestine," *Journal of Biblical Literature* 57:3 (Sept 1938): 305-309.

But scholar Clyde Billington has pointed out that the DSS and Josephus took their cue from the LXX, which was translated in Egypt. Egypt's royal cubit was consistently at 20.65 inches.[2] It is entirely reasonable that the LXX translators would adjust the Biblical numbers to coincide with their own definitions of measurement. Using the Egyptian cubit would make Goliath's height from the LXX come out to 7 feet 9 inches, not as tall as the MT, but a giant nonetheless.

A further complication arises when one considers the fact that Moses had been raised and educated as royalty in Egypt. So he and the Exodus Israelites no doubt used the Egyptian royal cubit in their measurements. The question then is whether or not the *original* Hebrew text translated that cubit measurement to the smaller Mesopotamian/Levantine cubit.

There is an indication in other Biblical texts of the awareness of this cubit difference. The writer of the Chronicles (written much later in Israel's history during the exile) makes this distinction when describing the dimensions of Solomon's temple. He writes, "the length, in cubits *of the old standard*, was sixty cubits, and the breadth twenty cubits" (2 Chron. 3:3). Ezekiel describing the measurements of the temple in his vision also makes this distinction of cubit difference when he writes, "the altar by cubits (the cubit being a cubit and a handbreadth)" (Ezek. 43:13). He later calls this a "long cubit" (Ezek. 41:8). So these parentheticals written by authors around the time of the exile indicate that during that time, there was still an awareness of the older longer Egyptian cubit as if they had been still using it up until that date.[3]

---

[2] Clyde E. Billington, "Goliath and The Exodus Giants: How Tall Were They?" *JETS*, 50/3 (September 2007) 489-508.
[3] Conservative scholars claim that Moses wrote the Pentateuch during the time of the Exodus, so that would most likely mean that the older longer cubit was used in those texts. Critical scholars claim that Moses did not write the Pentateuch, but that it was mostly written and/or compiled during the time of the Exile which would mean they most likely used the newer shorter cubit in the Pentateuch, but then made some reference to that older cubit in Chronicles and Ezekiel to remind their readers of the changeover.

If we apply this longer cubit measurement to Goliath's 9 cubits and a span, we get a height of about 10 1/2 feet tall![4] Remember Og of Bashan, whose bed was 9 cubits long? (Deut. 3:11). That would make his bed approximately 15 1/2 feet long and Og about 13 to 14 feet tall.[5] And the Egyptian warrior that was killed by Benaiah (1 Chron. 11:23) 8 feet 6 inches tall.

Whichever way one measures a cubit, Goliath was a giant. But that is not the only controversy surrounding that rabid Rephaim Gittite of old.

In 2 Samuel 21 we read a description of several giant warriors who were killed by David's Mighty Men (*gibborim*). But verse 19 is a disturbing sentence that seems to contradict David's slaying of Goliath. It says, "And there was again war with the Philistines at Gob, and Elhanan the son of Jaare-oregim, the Bethlehemite, struck down Goliath the Gittite, the shaft of whose spear was like a weaver's beam."

Well, who was it that killed Goliath, then? Was it David or Elhanan? Critical scholars use this single difficult text to justify constructing a complex conspiracy theory that David didn't exist and that Elhanan killed Goliath, but the Jewish writer then attributed it to a fictional "David" but forgot to make that change in this passage.

On the other side of desperate conspiracy theories are desperate hyper-literalist harmonizers who conclude that either Elhanan was another name for David or that there was a second Goliath of Gath who was killed by a different warrior later than David. But the lack of a David/Elhanan connection anywhere else in the Bible and the clear coincidence of redundant language about Goliath are no less biased in their attempts to harmonize.

---

[4] If this is the case, then the Septuagint translators misunderstood the cubit of the Hebrew text as being the smaller cubit, when in fact it was the larger Egyptian cubit. They would then be translating the number incorrectly downward.

[5] The longer cubit however is most likely not being used in reference to Og's height since the text says it is measuring "according to the common cubit" as opposed to the royal cubit.

Desperate conspiracies and harmonies aside, the problem needs a reasonable answer. And there is one. 1 Chronicles 20:4-8 is a rewrite of the same historical information in 2 Sam. 21:16-22. They are passages that have clearly used the same source with some modifications. They talk about the same Israelite warriors killing the same giants. But there are some slight differences. And the biggest difference is where the Chronicler addresses that sentence about Elhanan's victory over the giant. Here are the two passages after one another to make the point:

> 2 Samuel 21:19
> [19] And there was again war with the Philistines at Gob, and Elhanan the son of Jaare-oregim, the Bethlehemite, struck down Goliath the Gittite, the shaft of whose spear was like a weaver's beam.

> 1 Chronicles 20:5
> [5] And there was again war with the Philistines, and Elhanan the son of Jair struck down Lahmi the brother of Goliath the Gittite, the shaft of whose spear was like a weaver's beam.

1 Chronicles 20 says that Elhanan struck down *Lahmi, the brother of Goliath*, not Goliath! So was it Elhanan or David? Did they kill Goliath or his brother Lahmi?

In short, the answer is quite simply that 2 Samuel 21 is the problematic text as the result of scribal error. Michael Heiser, a Biblical language scholar, explains the forensic anatomy of the scribal mishap. He looks at the Hebrew behind the texts and shows how the Hebrew words for "son of Jaare-oregim, the Bethlemite," (1 Sam.) and "Lahmi the brother of" (1 Chron.) contain very similar Hebrew constructions that show the writer of 2 Samuel confusing the word for weaver (oregim) and adding it to Jair, and then misconstruing the Hebrew word for Lahmi as meaning Bethlehemite. The writer of 2 Samuel had a defective text and tried to fix it. In so doing, he created the problem that we now have.

Heiser's conclusion:

> The solution to the contradiction between 2 Sam 21:19 and 1 Chr 20:5 is recognizing that 2 Sam 21:19 is a defective reading since it is the result of a scribe's sincere effort to cope with a problematic manuscript…1 Chr 20:5 should be used to correct 2 Sam 21:19. David killed Goliath as 1 Samuel 17 says, and Elhanan killed Lahmi, the brother of Goliath.[6]

The Other Five

There are two other passages in 1 Chronicles, with parallel passages in 2 Samuel that explain the giants defeated by David and his Mighty Men. I will only reproduce the 1 Chronicles passages and fill out the facts with additional information from 2 Samuel.

> 1 Chronicles 11:22–23
> [22] And Benaiah the son of Jehoiada was a valiant man of Kabzeel… And he struck down an Egyptian, a man of great stature, five cubits tall. [7 1/2 to 8 1/2 feet] The Egyptian had in his hand a spear like a weaver's beam, but Benaiah went down to him with a staff and snatched the spear out of the Egyptian's hand and killed him with his own spear.

---

[6] Michael Hesier, "Clash of the Manuscripts: Goliath & the Hebrew Text of the Old Testament," *Bible Study Magazine* May/Jun2009, Vol. 1 Issue 4, p33; http://biblestudymagazine.com/interactive/goliath/#

1 Chronicles 20:4–8

[4] And after this there arose war with the Philistines at Gezer. Then Sibbecai the Hushathite struck down Sippai [Saph - 2 Sam. 21:18], who was one of the descendants of the giants, and the Philistines were subdued. [5] And there was again war with the Philistines, and Elhanan the son of Jair struck down Lahmi the brother of Goliath the Gittite, the shaft of whose spear was like a weaver's beam. [6] And there was again war at Gath, where there was a man of great stature, who had six fingers on each hand and six toes on each foot, twenty-four in number, and he also was descended from the giants. [7] And when he taunted Israel, Jonathan the son of Shimea, David's brother, struck him down. [8] These were descended from the giants in Gath, and they fell by the hand of David and by the hand of his servants.

2 Samuel 21:16–22

[16] And Ishbi-benob, one of the descendants of the giants, whose spear weighed three hundred shekels of bronze, and who was armed with a new sword, thought to kill David. [17] But Abishai the son of Zeruiah came to his aid and attacked the Philistine and killed him.

So in all, we have five giants being killed by David's men. 1) Benaiah killed an Egyptian giant, 2) Sibbecai killed the giant Sippai [Saph], 3) Elhanan killed the giant Lahmi, brother of Goliath, 4) Jonathan killed an unnamed giant, and 5) Abishai killed Ishbi-benob the giant.

But these are not mere chronicling of random deaths of a few tall bad guys. There is meaning and deliberation behind these facts. There is deliberate intent by the author to link these giants to the Nephilim of Genesis 6 whose diabolical plan was thwarted by God with the Flood.

Firstly, they are all summarized in the same paragraph, indicating a theological purpose behind combining them together. Secondly, except for the Egyptian, they are all Philistines fighting Israel. In Deut. 3:1-11 we read that Joshua killed Og of Bashan, the last of the Rephaim giants. Then in Joshua 11:21-22 we read that Joshua deliberately sought out the Anakim giants in Canaan and cut them off everywhere in the hill country. But then it gives this qualification: "There was none of the Anakim left in the land of the people of Israel. Only in Gaza, in Gath, and in Ashdod did some remain."

So, some giants were left by Joshua – in the land of Philistia. The very cities from which came the giants David would fight, including Goliath. It was almost as if God was deliberately keeping the last of the giants in order to finally destroy them through his messianic king. They were the leftover giants from Joshua's conquest, and they were linked back to the evil Nephilim before the flood (Num. 13:32-33).

And there is strong indication that the giants were trying to kill David specifically as well. Ishbi-benob is said to explicitly have been trying to kill David (2 Sam. 21:16); another one "taunted Israel" (1Chron 20:7), the same phrasing used of Goliath; and of course, Lahmi, Goliath's brother, would no doubt have revenge against the slayer of his sibling on his mind. But there is still more to this picture.

The English phrase used of the giants in these passages is that they were "descendants of the giants." It is used three times in 1 Chron. 20 and four times in 2 Sam. 21. The authors go out of their way to stress these warriors as connected to that special group of giants that were theologically tied to the Nephilim of Genesis 6.

Brian Godawa

Excursus on Connecting the Nephilim giants of Genesis 6 to the Rephaim giants of King David's Time

1) The Nephilim offspring of the fallen angelic "Sons of God" were part of God's reason for judgment.

Genesis 6:1–4
The Nephilim were on the earth in those days, and also afterward, when the sons of God came in to the daughters of man and they bore children to them. These were the mighty men who were of old, the men of renown.

Genesis 6:11–13
[11] Now the earth was corrupt in God's sight, and the earth was filled with violence. [12] And God saw the earth, and behold, it was corrupt, for all flesh had corrupted their way on the earth. [13] And God said to Noah, "I have determined to make an end of all flesh, for the earth is filled with violence through them. Behold, I will destroy them with the earth.

2) The Anakim giant clans that Joshua was to eradicate were theologically connected to the cursed Nephilim before the Flood.

Numbers 13:32–33 (ESV)
[32] So they brought to the people of Israel a bad report of the land that they had spied out, saying, "The land, through which we have gone to spy it out, is a land that devours its inhabitants, and all the people that we saw in it are of great height. [33] And there we saw the Nephilim (the sons of Anak, who come from the Nephilim), and we seemed to ourselves like grasshoppers, and so we seemed to them."

3) The giant clans were all considered Rephaim in a generic sense. Rephaim can be the catch-all term for all giant warriors.

Deuteronomy 2:10–11
[10] (The Emim formerly lived there [in Moab], a people great and many, and tall as the Anakim. [11] Like the Anakim they are also counted as Rephaim, but the Moabites call them Emim.

Deuteronomy 2:20–21
[20] (It [Ammon] is also counted as a land of Rephaim. Rephaim formerly lived there—but the Ammonites call them Zamzummim— [21] a people great and many, and tall as the Anakim.

4) The Philistine "Descendants of Giants" ("Sons of Rapha") in David's time were considered descendants or devotees of those

452

> ## cursed Rephaim/Anakim that Joshua had left alive in Philistia (Joshua 11:).
>
> Joshua 11:21–22
> [21] And Joshua came at that time and cut off the Anakim from the hill country, from Hebron, from Debir, from Anab, and from all the hill country of Judah, and from all the hill country of Israel. Joshua devoted them to destruction with their cities. [22] There was none of the Anakim left in the land of the people of Israel. Only in Gaza, in Gath, and in Ashdod did some remain.
>
> 2 Samuel 21:22
> These four [giants warriors] were descended from the giants in Gath, and they fell by the hand of David and by the hand of his servants.

This narrative theological thread of giants from the Nephilim of Noah's day to the Rephaim of David's time conspires to imply a deliberate summary of climactic conflict between the titan Seed of the Serpent in Canaan and the Seed of Abraham from Eve.

But a closer look at the original Hebrew behind the translation "descendants of the giants" in 1 Samuel and 1 Chronicles reveals much more then merely being linked to those oversized warriors left alive by Joshua in Philistia.

Biblical scholar Conrad E. L'Heureux examines this Hebrew phrase, *yalid ha rapha*, that translates as "descendants of the giants." He explains that the word *rapha*, is the specific word for the Rephaim giants and warriors in the Bible. But the word *yalid*, "never refers to genealogical lineage. Rather, the *yalid* was a person of slave status and dedicated to the deity who was head of the social unit into which he was admitted by a consecration."[7]

Because the discoveries of Ugarit shed light on the Rephaim as deified dead giant warriors,[8] this religious devotion indicates that the

---

[7] Conrad E. L'Heureux "The yelîdê hārāpā': A Cultic Association of Warriors," *Bulletin of the American Schools of Oriental Research*, No. 221,(Feb., 1976), pp. 83-85.
[8] See Brian Godawa, *Enoch Primordial* Appendix on the Rephaim,(Los Angeles, CA, Embedded Pictures Publishing, 2012), pp 364-366.

"descendants of the giants" is really more the giant "devotees of Rapha." L'Heureux concludes that this was probably some kind of reference to an elite fighting force religiously bound to their Rephaim code. What was that code? Was it to hunt down and destroy the Seed of Eve, the messianic king?

He then points out that of the eight times that the Bible speaks of the location of battle called "Valley of the Rephaim," five of them are in these narratives of the Philistines fighting Israel in that valley. This brings him to suggest that "Valley of the Rephaim" may simply be an anachronism that was used in the stories about where that name came from. They called it Valley of the Rephaim because that valley is where David's army defeated these Philistine elite fighting forces.

Thus, the origin of my elite corps of giants in *David Ascendant* called the *Yalid ha Rapha* or the "Sons of Rapha," bound by oath to their own Seed (of the Serpent) to destroy the Seed of Eve, David.

Were Agag and Saul Giants?

Agag. In 1 Samuel 15 we read that King Saul defeated the Amalekites, ancient enemies of the Israelites. God tells Saul in verse 15 to "devote to destruction, all that they have. Do not spare them, but kill both man and woman, child and infant, ox and sheep, camel and donkey." This was the language of *herem* (devotion to destruction) used for Joshua's conquest of Canaan's Nephilim infestation. It was not used for all of Israel's enemies, only the specific clans that God was focusing on, and those clans all had Nephilim or giants in them.[9]

While 1 Samuel does not tell us that Agag was a giant, there is some indication that he could have been and that the Amalekites also had giants in their midst.

Their history goes all the way back to Genesis 14 and the Giant Wars in the days of Abraham. In that passage, Chedorlaomer leads his

---

[9] See Appendix B "The Nephilim," *Noah Primeval* (Los Angeles, Embedded Pictures, 2012), 304-322.

alliance of four Mesopotamian kings to wipe out specific giant clans in Canaan. The list of giant clans they take out are the Rephaim, Zuzim, Emim, Horites and Amorites. In *Abraham Allegiant* I explained this campaign and how Abraham fit in with it. But for our purposes now, suffice it to say that mentioned within that list of giant clans is one more people group: The Amalekites.

Though it is not stated explicitly that the Amalekites were a giant clan, it is implied by its inclusion in the list of all the other giant clans. In the Zohar, a 13th century Jewish mystical text, there is a clear reference to the Amalekites as giants among the Nephilim, Anakim, and Rephaim.[10] The Arabs also have legends about Ad, the son of Amalek, being a giant.[11]

Some scholars think that this Genesis 14 reference is just an anachronism in the Bible text, and that the Amalekites did not come in history until later. Genesis 36:12 states that Amalek came later as a son of Esau, father of the Edomites, a tribe that Israel was commanded by God *not* to fight (Deut. 2:4-6). But there is a problem here. When the Israelites encounter the Amalekites in the desert during the Exodus, God says, "I will utterly blot out the memory of Amalek from under heaven...The LORD will have war with Amalek from generation to generation" (Ex. 17:15-16). After Israel had taken the Promised Land for an inheritance, God told them again, "You shall blot out the memory of Amalek from under heaven; you shall not forget" (Deut. 25:19). Again, the holy war language used against the Nephilim in Canaan.

---

[10] Special thanks to Doug Van Dorn for this bit of research. *Beresheet A,* 20.224, "There are five races of mixed multitude. These are the Nefilim (fallen), the Giborim (mighty), the Anakim (giants), the Refaim (shades) and the Amalekim." Van Dorn, Douglas (2013-01-21). *Giants: Sons of the Gods* (Kindle Locations 2629-2631). Waters of Creation. Kindle Edition. It is important to note however that the Zohar is of questionable origin, so it represents a much later tradition than is preferable for our ancient research.

[11] "A tradition told in the famous Al-Khitat, a history of Egyptian lore compiled by al-Maqrizi (1364-1442 AD), recounts the teaching of one master Ibrahim bin Wasif Shah (d. 1203 AD) who said that King Adim (Ad) was, 'A violent and proud prince, tall in stature.'" Van Dorn, *Giants* (Kindle Locations 2605-2608).

So either Genesis 36 is an anachronism and a contradiction or there are two separate lines of Amalekites, one from Esau and one from this earlier giant clan in Abraham's time. Balaam's prophecy, just before the conquest of the Promised Land, seems to blend both clans into one. It indicates that "Amalek was the first among the nations, but its end is utter destruction" (Num. 24:20), thus favoring the earlier Genesis 14 existence. But it also links Amalek to Edom, the favored nation of Seir in verse 18, favoring the Esau lineage. The problem is that the prophecy from God himself then declares that Edom shall be dispossessed by Israel. Why would God change his mind and dispossess the tribe he was protecting? Maybe there was some kind of mixing of two Amalekite clans into one under the name of Amalek. And that people group had giants.[12]

Saul. One more literary reference hints at Agag being a giant. In Balaam's prophecy just quoted, Israel is predicted to overcome her enemies in Canaan.

> Numbers 24:6–8 (NASB95)
> [6] [Israel is planted] like cedars beside the waters. [7] "Water will flow from his buckets, And his seed *will be* by many waters, And his king shall be higher than Agag, And his kingdom shall be exalted... He will devour the nations *who are* his adversaries, And will crush their bones in pieces.

This Scripture uses the language of the giants in an ironic application to Israel. The cedar tree, used in reference to the giants of Canaan (Amos 2:9), is now used of Israel; the nations of giants that

---

[12] Like Edom, Moab and Ammon were to be left alone by the Israelites in their conquest because of their descendancy from Lot, Abraham's nephew (Deut. 2:9, 19). But then King David conquers all three of these peoples for his kingdom; Edom, Moab and Ammon (2 Sam. 8; 10). It was as if God was saving their ultimate dispossession for his messiah king.

"devoured its inhabitants" (Num. 13:32), would be devoured (same Hebrew word) by Israel instead. Like a giant, Israel would crush the bones of his enemies. The seed motif is brought up that reminds us of the Seed of Eve versus the Seed of the Serpent (Gen. 3:15). And then we read that Israel's king shall be "higher than Agag."

This reference to height is an obvious metaphor for glory and exaltation of David's house. But of course it also hints at Agag's own stature being a defining trait. An interesting textual gloss appears in some of the Septuagint manuscripts that render Agag as "Gog" or "Og."[13] We've seen Og before: The last of the Rephaim giants in the Transjordan during Israel's approach to Canaan.

Another literary linkage seems to be occurring in the Biblical text. 1 Samuel goes out of its way to point out that Saul was "taller than any of the people from his shoulders upward" (1 Sam. 9:2; 10:23). This would make him at least 6 1/2 to 7 feet tall. Could he have been of Nephilim seed? Verse 2 also says, "There was not a man among the people of Israel more handsome than he." It was customary to describe kings in glorious language as exemplary physical and spiritual specimens to justify their royalty.[14] This description of Saul is used to make a point later that God does not look upon the outward appearance like man does, but upon the heart (1 Sam. 16:7). However, as Bible commentator Bergen points out, it is not a coincidence that "Saul is the only Israelite specifically noted in the Bible as being tall; elsewhere it was only Israel's enemies [the giants] whose height was noted (cf. Num. 13:33; Deut. 1:28; 2:10; 9:2; 1 Sam. 17:4). Israel had asked for a

---

[13] "There shall come a man out of his seed, and he shall rule over many nations; and the kingdom of Gog (or "Og") shall be exalted, and his kingdom shall be increased." Lancelot Charles Lee Brenton, *The Septuagint Version of the Old Testament: English Translation* (London: Samuel Bagster and Sons, 1870), Nu 24:7. For the Og version, see John William Wevers, ed., *Numeri, vol. III, 1, Vetus Testamentum Graecum. Auctoritate Academiae Scientiarum Gottingensis Editum* (Göttingen: Vandenhoeck & Ruprecht, 1982), 289.

[14] John H. Walton, *Zondervan Illustrated Bible Backgrounds Commentary (Old Testament): Joshua, Judges, Ruth, 1 & 2 Samuel, vol. 2* (Grand Rapids, MI: Zondervan, 2009), 311.

king 'like all the other nations' (8:20), and the Lord was giving them the desires of their heart, even down to the physical details!"[15]

So Saul is likened to the giants of Israel's enemies. This is not to say that he was a Nephilim, but certainly the writer is making a theological comparison with Saul to Israel's enemies. But with Saul at close to 7 feet of height, no doubt some Israelites gossiped to one another about the possibility of such a thing. A double irony occurs in that Saul, the giant's equal, does not kill Israel's perpetual enemy the Amalekite king (a giant?), but David, the ruddy and small youth, does kill Goliath the Rephaim giant who embodied the last of the Serpentine Seed in the Promised Land.

What this all means is that Israel's first encounter with giants may have been when they battled the Amalekites in the exodus (Ex. 17:8-16); Saul may have defiantly failed to kill the Serpentine Seed of Amalek, which resulted in his cursing by God; and David may have faced those giants when he all but wiped them out at Ziklag in 1 Samuel 30, resulting in their ultimate decline.

Yet One More Giant

But there's one more giant hiding out between the lines of sacred writ. The Septuagint (LXX), an earlier Greek translation of the Old Testament that Jesus and the apostles quoted as authoritative, contains additional information about one other giant that was left out in the Masoretic text, or later Hebrew version of the Old Testament.[16]

In 2 Samuel 21, the Gibeonites demand that David release to them all of Saul's sons as justice for their oppression by Saul. David hands over six of them to be hanged by the Gibeonites. But David spared Mephibosheth, because of his oath of loyalty to the crippled son of Saul. One of the mothers, Rizpah, asks for the remains of the victims

---

[15] Robert D. Bergen, *1, 2 Samuel*, vol. 7, The New American Commentary (Nashville: Broadman & Holman Publishers, 1996), 121.
[16] Special thanks to Douglas Van Dorn for this discovery.

and spreads out a sackcloth to mourn over them and protect them from the vultures.

The LXX then adds this gloss:

> 2 Samuel 21:11 (LXX)
> [11] And it was told David what Rizpah the daughter of Aia the concubine of Saul had done, and they were faint and Dan the son of Joah of the descendant of the giants overtook them.[17]

Apparently, Dan ben Joah, was a giant. The text is not clear as to who was faint or what it means that Dan "overtook them." Overtook who or what? The *bones*, or the *scavengers* that Rizpah was keeping from the bones? It would not make sense for Dan to overtake the scavengers of the bones, because giants are always in a negative disposition toward Israel in the Bible. Dan would not care to protect Israelite bones. If it was the bones that Dan overtook or "captured" as other translations have it, then David would have had to fight the giant to get them back because in verse 21, David gathers those bones with the bones of Saul and Jonathan to bury them all.[18]

Interestingly, the name Dan has a nefarious heritage in Biblical tradition. He was described in Genesis 49:17 as "a serpent in the way, a viper by the path, that bites the horse's heels so that the rider falls backward." This serpentine connection rings ominously familiar with the Genesis 3:15 prophetic curse on the Serpent's Seed biting the heels

---

[17] Lancelot Charles Lee Brenton, *The Septuagint Version of the Old Testament: English Translation* (London: Samuel Bagster and Sons, 1870), 2 Kgdms 21:11.

[18] David scholar McCarter suggests "overtook them" may be translated "captured them," as in capturing the bones of the Saulides. (P. Kyle McCarter Jr, *II Samuel: a New Translation with Introduction, Notes, and Commentary, vol. 9, Anchor Yale Bible* (New Haven; London: Yale University Press, 2008), 440.) The Lexham LXX translates that phrase as "took them down," as if to mean that the giant took down the remains of the six hanged descendants of Saul in order for the Gibeonites to release them to Rizpah. But in the Bible, giants are never in a positive disposition toward Israel, so this is most likely not the best translation. Randall Tan and David A. deSilva, Logos Bible Software, *The Lexham Greek-English Interlinear Septuagint* (Logos Bible Software, 2009), 2 Kgdms 21:11–12.

of Eve's Seed. Is it mere coincidence that the tribe of Dan lost their apportioned land in Canaan (Josh. 19:47), leading them to take the territory of the city Laish (Judg. 18) in the far north of Bashan, "place of the serpent," in the foothills of Mount Hermon, the location of the Watchers' fall and the pagan community of Banias that worshipped Azazel?[19]

The text also says that this giant Dan was from the "descendants of the giants." The Greek for this phrase in the LXX is *apoganon ton giganton*, the same Greek translation of the *Yalid ha Rapha* warrior cult of the other four giants in 2 Samuel 21:22 (LXX): "These four were descended from the giants (*apoganoi ton giganton*) in Gath."[20]

Like the other five giants spoken of in 1 and 2 Samuel, we have no personal details spelled out for us beyond the statements of fact. So the storyline of these giants in *David Ascendant* is speculative conjecture, but surely consistent with the explicit facts and implicit connections of the text.

Giant Weapons

Goliath's armor is among the most studied in the Old Testament. The reason for this is because it is the most descriptive of all passages about a soldier's armor anywhere in the entire corpus. It reads like a Homeric description of the heroic warrior in Greece.

> 1 Samuel 17:5–7
> [5] He had a helmet of bronze on his head, and he was armed with a coat of mail, and the weight of the coat was five thousand shekels of bronze [126 pounds]. [6] And he had bronze armor on his legs, and a javelin of

[19] Brian Godawa, Appendix, *Joshua Valiant*, (Los Angeles, CA: Embedded Pictures Publishing, 2013), 322. See also, Judd H. Burton, *Interview With the Giant: Ethnohistorical Notes on the Nephilim* (Burton Beyond Press, 2009) 20.
[20] Randall Tan and David A. deSilva, Logos Bible Software, *The Lexham Greek-English Interlinear Septuagint* (Logos Bible Software, 2009), 2 Kgdms 21:11, 22.

bronze slung between his shoulders. [7]The shaft of his spear was like a weaver's beam, and his spear's head weighed six hundred shekels of iron [16 pounds]. And his shield-bearer went before him.

Though the Philistines most likely consisted of Mycenaean and other Sea Peoples who had migrated to Canaan from the Aegean, they nevertheless were highly adaptive and built their own culture through assimilation of others. Thus, scholars indicate that Goliath's armor was not distinctly Mycenaean Greek or even uniquely Philistine but rather a kind of conglomeration of different styles.

His helmet was not the typical feathered headdress of the Philistines, but rather a bronze covering more akin to Greek or Assyrian protection.[21] His bronze cuirass of armored scales was also unlike Aegean style armor, but more like Egyptian styled scales like that seen on Pharaoh Shishak's tenth century engravings.[22] His bronze shin greaves were Greek and his shield bearer before him apparently was carrying a full-bodied shield rather than the small round one of the Philistines and other Sea Peoples. Goliath was a Philistine, but his Rephaim background and his distinct armor indicates he was most likely indigenous to the region, making him either a Canaanite convert or conscript of his Philistine rulers.

In the English translation it says that Goliath had a "javelin of bronze slung between his shoulders." Citing similar language in the War Scroll at Qumran's Dead Sea Scrolls, recent scholars have more accurately translated that phrase as referring to a bronze scimitar sword (curved blade), not the javelin.[23]

---

[21] David Tsumura, *The First Book of Samuel, The New International Commentary on the Old Testament* (Grand Rapids, MI: Wm. B. Eerdmans Publishing Co., 2007), 442.
[22] Yigal Yadin, *The Art of Warfare in Biblical Lands*, 2 vols. (New York: McGraw-Hill, 1963), I, pp. 196–97; II, p. 354.
[23] Ralph W. Klein, *1 Samuel, vol. 10, Word Biblical Commentary* (Dallas: Word, Incorporated, 1998), 176.

Another translation clarified by many scholars is that the shaft of Goliath's spear being "like a weaver's beam" is more accurately a likeness of the shape rather than the size of his dart. A well known form of javelin used in both Egypt and Greece included a loop or leash attached to the missile that could be flung by the fingers of the soldier to facilitate a throw of up to three times the normal velocity and distance.[24] This looped leash is very similar to what the heddle rod on a weaver's beam looks like, thus indicating it as a new weapon in the eyes of the Israelites.

And that "weaver's beam" javelin is the exact same description used of the weapon of another giant, the unnamed Egyptian Rapha (1 Chron. 20:5, 11:23). These giants are linked together by their elite guild connection as well as the weapons they use.

Goliath's iron spearhead weighed 16 pounds. Ishbi-benob's bronze spearhead weighed 7.5 pounds, since bronze is a lighter metal. Ishbi-benob is also described as carrying a "new sword," in 2 Sam. 21:16. But as commentator Robert Bergen points out, the Hebrew word for "sword" is not actually in the text, making the phrase a reference to an unnamed weapon unknown to the writer. Translators assumed it was a sword, but we don't know for sure.[25] Thus, the strange new weapon Ishbi-benob carries in *David Ascendant*. Strange for the Israelites, but not for readers of previous *Chronicles of the Nephilim*

Lastly, the unnamed giant killed by Jonathan in 2 Sam. 21:20 and 1 Chron. 20:6 is described as having six fingers on each hand and six toes on each foot. This is the only place in the Bible where a giant is described with polydactylism, but its genetic connection to the other giants is a strong possibility. While some may not think extra digits on hands and feet are a weapon, they certainly increase the gripping power extent of hands while adding wider balancing skill for feet that are no

---

[24] Yadin, Y. 1955. "Goliath's javelin and the menor `orgim", *PEQ* 87:58-69
[25] Robert D. Bergen, *1, 2 Samuel, vol. 7, The New American Commentary* (Nashville: Broadman & Holman Publishers, 1996), 448.

doubt advantageous in battle. This is the origin of the polydactylism of the giants as read in *Chronicles of the Nephilim*.

The descriptions of the giants and their weapons mentioned in Chronicles and Samuel indicates obvious ties between Goliath and the elite members of the giant warrior guild, the *yalid ha rapha*. And these giants are strongly implied to be part of a deliberate plan on the part of the Seed of the Serpent at war with the Seed of Eve: God's people, king, and messiah.

Lion Men of Moab

Another strange warrior breed shows up in *David Ascendant*: Lion Men of Moab called *ariels*. They are effectively werewolves – but more like werelions.

In 2 Sam. 23:20 Benaiah, a valiant warrior, strikes down "two *ariels* of Moab." The word "ariel" is a transliteration because scholars are not sure what it means. The King James and Young's Bibles translate these opponents of Benaiah as "lion-like men of Moab," which captures the strangeness of the creatures but fails to express the religious or supernatural connotation of the word.

Some translators translate the phrase "*ariels* of Moab" as "sons of Ariel of Moab" after the unlikely LXX Greek translation,[26] or "lion-like heroes of Moab." But there is no Hebrew word for "sons of" in the sentence, no indication of *ariel* being a personal name, and no Hebrew word for warrior used in the sentence. The Hebrew word for mighty warrior, *gibborim*, is used frequently throughout David's narrative and that word is not here. The text says "two *ariels* of Moab."

---

[26] "Although the LXX interferes seriously in the text, presupposing a double haplography in the Hebrew text, this reading points into the right direction. As a matter of fact NKH Hiph'il in the historical books never means to strike upon an object (cf. also E. Jenni, ErIs 24 [1993] 114–118), but to strike down, i.e. to kill somebody... Consequently, Ariel here designates some kind of person, best translated as 'lion of God': S. Münger, "Ariel," ed. Karel van der Toorn, Bob Becking, and Pieter W. van der Horst, *Dictionary of Deities and Demons in the Bible* (Leiden; Boston; Köln; Grand Rapids, MI; Cambridge: Brill; Eerdmans, 1999), 88–89.

Some suggest it may be a reference to killing two lions. But the very next sentence states that Benaiah, the killer of the *ariels*, then killed a lion in a pit.

> 2 Samuel 23:20
> And Benaiah the son of Jehoiada was a valiant man of Kabzeel, a doer of great deeds. He struck down two ariels of Moab. He also went down and struck down a lion in a pit on a day when snow had fallen.

The Hebrew word for "lion" is not *ariel*, but *aryeh*. Adding the suffix "el" to the word adds a religious dimension of meaning that transcends mere lions. This is why Hebrew lexicons explain the most likely meaning as "lion of god."[27] El was not merely a name used of Yahweh in the Bible, it was the name of the figurehead deity of the Canaanite pantheon as well as a general reference to deity in Mesopotamia.[28]

In 1 Chronicles, some additional warriors from Gad join David when he is at Ziklag, and they are described exactly like *ariels* as "lion-faced warriors" with preternatural skills:

> 1 Chronicles 12:8
> From the Gadites there went over to David at the stronghold in the wilderness mighty and experienced warriors, expert with shield and spear, whose faces were like the faces of lions and who were swift as gazelles upon the mountains:

[27] Francis Brown, Samuel Rolles Driver and Charles Augustus Briggs, *Enhanced Brown-Driver-Briggs Hebrew and English Lexicon*, electronic ed., 72 (Oak Harbor, WA: Logos Research Systems, 2000).
[28] W. Herrmann, "El," ed. Karel van der Toorn, Bob Becking, and Pieter W. van der Horst, Dictionary of Deities and Demons in the Bible (Leiden; Boston; Köln; Grand Rapids, MI; Cambridge: Brill; Eerdmans, 1999), 275.

Though animal-like skills is a common metaphor used to describe extraordinary warrior skills, having faces like the faces of lions could mean more in light of the existence of these *ariels,* or Lion Men of Moab. Since the tribal location of Gad was precisely all the land of Moab across the Jordan, I decided to make the Gadite lion-faced men be those very Lion Men of Moab who converted to Israel and joined David. Two of these hybrid warriors then become the two traitors who face down Benaiah.

Psalm 57 was written when David was on the run and hiding out in a cave from Saul's bounty hunters. Verse 4 says, "My soul is in the midst of lions; I lie down amid fiery beasts— the children of man, whose teeth are spears and arrows, whose tongues are sharp swords." Though a surface reading of this text appears to be an obvious figurative expression of David's enemies, scholar B. Mazar suggests it may be a reference to a mercenary military corps of archers whose emblem was the lion-goddess.[29] Could they have come from Moab?

So what if these *ariels* are hybrid creatures reminiscent of the Watchers' miscegenation in Genesis 6? What if they are elite warriors with hairy bodies and lion-like faces that only one of David's own *gibborim* Mighty Men could slay? After all, the exploits of those Mighty Men in the passages we have been looking at are supernatural slayings of giants and hundreds of soldiers by single warriors. If these *ariels* were mere warriors, then the feat accomplished by Benaiah in slaying them would be the only one in the entire passage that was banal and without significance.

These *ariels* were something more than men, maybe something supernatural.

The ancient understanding of *ariel* as a lion-like hybrid humanoid finds support in a later Nag Hammadi text that speaks of a gnostic deity,

---

[29] B. Mazar, "The Military Élite of King David," *Vetus Testamentum*, Vol. 13, Fasc. 3 (Jul., 1963), 312.

Yaldabaoth, who was an *ariel* (spelled slightly different): "Ariael is what the perfect call him, for he was like a lion."[30]

The Dictionary of Deities and Demons in the Bible says of this possible religious mythical interpretation of *ariel*:

> This interpretation could be supported by a recently found bronze-silver figurine from Tell Abū el-Kharaz in Transjordan representing, according to the excavator's opinion a male lion-faced warrior(-god?), which can be viewed, because of its appearance and its attributes, as a male pendant.[31]

The author then reveals that the word *ariel* shows up in the Mesha Stele, a Moabite stone inscription not too long after the time of King David.[32] These are the very Moabites from which 2 Samuel says the *ariels* come. The line of text in question could be translated, "the lion figure [*ariel*] of their beloved (god)' which was dragged before Chemosh after the fall of the Israelite city."[33]

Bible scholar B. Mazar notes this Mesha Stele connection and adds that the word *ariel* became a synonym for the lion-headed cherubim at the base of kingly thrones.[34]

---

[30] James McConkey Robinson, Richard Smith and Coptic Gnostic Library Project, *The Nag Hammadi Library in English*, 4th rev. ed., 173 (Leiden; New York: E. J. Brill, 1996).

[31] S. Münger, "Ariel," ed. Karel van der Toorn, Bob Becking, and Pieter W. van der Horst, *Dictionary of Deities and Demons in the Bible* (Leiden; Boston; Köln; Grand Rapids, MI; Cambridge: Brill; Eerdmans, 1999), 89. Münger refers to the *Annual of the Department of Antiquities of Jordan* (P. M. Fischer, *ADAJ* 40 [1996] 101–110, esp. 103–104 with figs. 3a-b).

[32] 850 B.C.

[33] S. Münger, *DDD*, 89. Pritchard's *Ancient Near Eastern Texts Relating to the Old Testament* translates *ariel* as the name of the king of the city, and Hallo's Context of Scripture translates it as the more unlikely object, *fire hearth*. James Bennett Pritchard, ed., *The Ancient Near East an Anthology of Texts and Pictures, 3rd ed. with Supplement* (Princeton: Princeton University Press, 1969), 320; William W. Hallo and K. Lawson Younger, *Context of Scripture* (Leiden; Boston: Brill, 2000), 137.

[34] B. Mazar, "The Military Élite of King David," *Vetus Testamentum*, Vol. 13, Fasc. 3 (Jul., 1963), pp. 316.

So in *David Ascendant*, I created a special unit of these Ariels, lion-headed warriors of Moab, to explore that supernatural dimension with imagination that fit the thread of the cosmic War of the Seed.

The ancient Book of Jasher was a source text for both Joshua and David's stories (Josh. 10:13, 2 Sam. 1:18). The extant version we have of the Book of Jasher, though dubitable, tells of two different stories that contain hybrid creatures that may be similar to the lion-men of Moab or the satyrs of Panias. In Jasher 36:29-35 we read of Anah, one of the sons of Seir the Horite, (remember the Seirites' connection to satyrs) during the days of Abraham. There is a large storm that the writer says caused a group of about 120 "great and terrible animals" to come out of the forest by the seashore to be witnessed by Anah feeding his asses.

> Jasher 36:29-35
> And those animals, from their middle downward, were in the shape of the children of men, and from their middle upward, some had the likeness of bears, and some the likeness of the keephas, with tails behind them from between their shoulders reaching down to the earth, like the tails of the ducheephath, and these animals came and mounted and rode upon these asses, and led them away, and they went away unto this day.[35]

Another chapter in Jasher tells the story during the youth of Balaam son of Beor, about a strange animal that was devouring the cattle of the people of Chittim. A man named Zepho went in search of this creature and...

---

[35] Johnson, Ken (2012-01-09). *Ancient Book Of Jasher* (p. 129). Kindle Edition.

Jasher 61:15

he came into the cave and he looked and behold, a large animal was devouring the ox; from the middle upward it resembled a man, and from the middle downward it resembled an animal, and Zepho rose up against the animal and slew it with his swords.[36]

Were these creatures just legends or were they genetic hybrid remnants of the miscegenation of the Watchers?

Dagon and Asherah

Two new gods take the stage in *David Ascendant* that were not in previous Chronicles: Dagon and Asherah. These are both mysterious deities about whom not much is revealed in the Old Testament or in ancient extra-Biblical sources beyond their names and few details.

Dagon. In the Bible, Dagon is described as the chief god of the Philistines. The story of Samson's death in Judges 16 takes place in the temple of Dagon, god of the Philistines. In 1 Chron. 10:10 the Philistines are said to have hung the decapitated head of King Saul in a temple of Dagon at Beth-shan. 1 Sam. 5 tells the story of Philistines capturing the ark of the covenant and placing it in the temple of Dagon in Ashdod. Two mornings in a row, the statue of Dagon was found flat on its face before the ark, the second time, with its head and hands "cut off." Severing hands and heads was a common tactic of ancient Near Eastern powers, both Mesopotamian and Canaanite.[37] This supernatural "power encounter" between Yahweh and Dagon becomes then a spiritual polemic of warfare and conquest between gods. But beyond these mentions, nothing more is revealed in the Old Testament.

---

[36] Johnson, *Book Of Jasher* (p. 223).
[37] Steve A. Wiggins, "Old Testament Dagan in the Light of Ugarit," *Vetus Testamentum*, Vol. 43, Fasc. 2 (Apr., 1993), 370.

The meaning of the name Dagon is uncertain. Early scholarly interpreters argued that it came from the Hebrew word for "fish," thus one tradition depicts him as a hybrid deity with the upper torso of a man and the lower bottom of a fish. The 1 Samuel passage describing the lower part of the Dagon statue has been interpreted by some as "his fishy part." Later scholars argued the name Dagon came from the Hebrew word for "grain," thus another tradition understands him as a god of fertility or grain. Still others have argued Dagon was a storm god, whose name came from the Arabic word for cloudy rain.[38] No scholarly consensus has been reached on these interpretations, though the earlier ones have fallen out of favor.[39]

Dagon had a strong presence in Mesopotamia and Syria primarily as a storm god, spelled *Dagan,* and likened to the Babylonian weather god Enlil.[40] The Syrians included Dagon in their pantheon at Ugarit, which was in Syria, but nowhere in Canaan. The Canaanite champion deity Ba'al is described throughout the Ugaritic texts as the "Son of Dagon" which made him an outsider to the family of gods ruled over by the high god El and his wife, Athirat (Asherah), the Mother of the Gods.[41]

But since the Philistines were known for adapting customs and gods from their newly conquered lands it is entirely possible that Dagon was imported from Philistine contact with Syria and adapted to the interests of the coastal Sea People.[42] Because of this syncretistic

---

[38] T. C. Mitchell, "Dagon," ed. Geoffrey W. Bromiley, *The International Standard Bible Encyclopedia,* Revised (Wm. B. Eerdmans, 1979–1988), 851; Lowell K. Handy, "Dagon (Deity)," ed. David Noel Freedman, *The Anchor Yale Bible Dictionary* (New York: Doubleday, 1992), 2.

[39] It is now thought by some that Dagon as a fish-man may have been etiologically influenced by Atargatis, a mermaid goddess of nearby Philistine Ashkelon and by the Sumerian fish-man god Odakon as interpreted by the Babylonian historian Berossus. Frank J.. Montalbano, "Canaanite Dagon: Origin, Nature," *Catholic Biblical Quarterly,* 13 no 4 O 1951, p 395.

[40] Montalbano "Canaanite Dagon," p 381-397.

[41] Mark S. Smith, *The Ugaritic Baal Cycle: Introduction with Text, Translation and Commentary of KTU 1.1-1.2, vol. 1* (Leiden; New York; Köln: E.J. Brill, 1994), 293.

[42] Wiggins, "Old Testament Dagan," 372.

worldview of the Philistines, I combined all three of the major interpretations of Dagon into one in *David Ascendant* as a hybrid fish-man who is a god of both storm and grain. And this is not too different from the nature of the Babylonian Marduk and the Canaanite Ba'al, who were also both gods of storm and vegetation.

Asherah. The name Asherah appears 40 times in the Bible (plural: *Asherim, Asheroth, Ashtaroth*). Some of those instances refer directly to the goddess herself (Judg. 3:7; 1 Kgs. 14:13, 18:19; 2 Kgs. 21:7, 23:4) and many others refer to a wooden cult object used in worship to symbolize the goddess (Deut. 16:21; Judg. 6:25-30; 2 Kgs. 18:4; Isa. 17:8; Jer. 17:2). From the time of Judges on into the monarchy and the Josianic reforms, The Asherah poles or sacred pillars are often spoken of in close connection with altars of Ba'al (Judg. 6:25; 1 Kgs. 16:33; 2 Kgs. 17:16; 21:3), which hints at a theological connection between this unseemly pair of idols that exercised an ongoing apostasizing influence on Israel throughout her history. Archeological discoveries of inscriptions in Israel have even confirmed the attempt of Israelites to syncretize Asherah into their religion as Yahweh's consort (Deut. 16:21-22).[43]

Asherah appears extensively in the Ugaritic texts from Ras Shamra. There, she is referred to as *Athirat*. John Day points out that as consort of the high god of the pantheon El, she is called "mother of the gods," whose divine offspring are called the "seventy sons of Athirat." He then concludes, "There is a direct line of connection between this concept and the later Jewish idea of the seventy guardian angels of the nations (see 1 Enoch 89:59; 90:22-25; Tg. Ps.-J. on Deut 32:8)."[44]

She is a goddess of fertility and connected to sacred prostitution (2 Kgs. 23:7). She is also linked with the host of heaven (2 Kgs. 17:16;

---

[43] John Day, "Asherah in the Hebrew Bible and Northwest Semitic Literature," *Journal of Biblical Literature*, Vol. 105, No. 3 (Sep., 1986), 391-92. While the Scriptures are replete with many calls to Israelites to repent from worshipping Ba'al and Asherah, there is no Biblical indication that Israel ever worshipped Dagon, the god of the Philistines.
[44] John Day, "Asherah in the Hebrew Bible," 387.

21:3; 23:4), which are acknowledged as deities (Job 38:7), thus supporting her moniker the "mother of the gods."

Here is what the *International Standard Bible Encyclopedia* says of Asherah in the Ugaritic texts:

> In the *Râs* Shamrah texts Asherah is the consort of El, the supreme god. She is mentioned as "creatress of the gods" and as "Lady Asherah of the sea," titles that are given to the most important goddess of the pantheon. In the Ugaritic Keret text Asherah is said to have a shrine in Tyre, which would indicate her supremacy there also. She is the adversary of Baal... As the role of Baal grows in importance and overshadows that of El, Asherah's interest seems to shift more toward Baal. When a house is to be built for Baal, he and Anat, his sister-consort, bribe Asherah with gold and silver in order to persuade her to intervene for them before El, a mission she gladly undertakes. Again, in a myth stemming from the Late Bronze Age, Asherah attempts to seduce Baal.[45]

The Asherah as a wooden cultic object has several explanations without a clear conclusion. The Septuagint translates the word Asherah as "groves" of trees. Thus some earlier scholars argued they were literal groves of trees. But as Day explains, "the OT often refers to the making of Asherim (1 Kgs 14:15; 16:33; 2 Kgs 17:16;21:3, 7; 2 Chr 33:3) and also of the building (1 Kgs 14:23) and erection (2 Kgs 17:10) of Asherim, which does not seem appropriate for trees."[46] He concludes that the most widely held view is that the Asherim were wooden poles

---

[45] K. G. Jung, "Asherah," ed. Geoffrey W. Bromiley, *The International Standard Bible Encyclopedia, Revised* (Wm. B. Eerdmans, 1979–1988), 317–318.
[46] John Day, "Asherah in the Hebrew Bible," 402.

sacred to the goddess Asherah. But how they functioned and exactly what they looked like, no evidence can be found.

For additional Biblical, historical and mythical research related to this novel, go to www.ChroniclesoftheNephilim.com under the menu listing, "Scholarly Research."

If you liked this book, then please help me out by writing an honest review of it on Amazon. That is one of the best ways to say thank you to me as an author. It really does help my exposure and status as an author. It's really easy. In the Customer Reviews section, there is a little box that says "Write a customer review." They guide you easily through the process. Thanks! — *Brian Godawa*

GREAT OFFERS BY BRIAN GODAWA

CHRONICLES OF THE APOCALYPSE

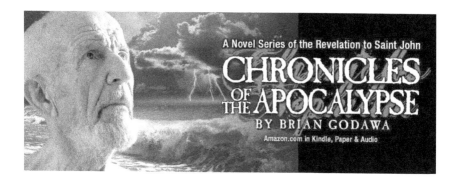

A Novel Series About the Book of Revelation & the End Times. A Fresh Biblical View.

www.Godawa.com

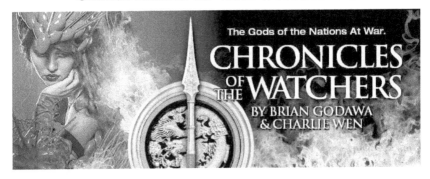

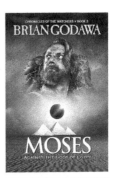
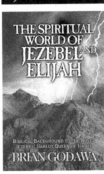
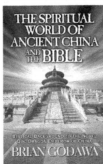
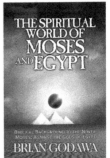

VIDEO LECTURES

The Book of Enoch: Scripture, Heresy or What?

This lecture by Brian Godawa will be an introduction to the ancient book of 1Enoch, its content, its history, its affirmation in the New Testament, and its acceptance and rejection by the Christian Church. What is the Book of Enoch? Where did it come from? Why isn't it in the Bible? How does the Book of Enoch compare with the Bible?

Available on video.

Chronicles of the Nephilim: The Ancient Biblical Story

Watchers, Nephilim, and the Divine Council of the Sons of God. In this dvd video lecture, Brian Godawa explores the Scriptures behind this transformative storyline that inspired his best-selling Biblical novel series Chronicles of the Nephilim.

Available on video.

To download these lectures and other books and products by Brian Godawa, just go to the STORE at:

www.Godawa.com

GOD AGAINST THE GODS

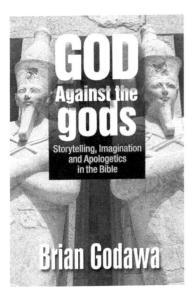

How God Captures the Imagination

Brian Godawa, Hollywood screenwriter and best-selling novelist, explores the nature of imagination in the Bible. You will learn how God subverts pagan religions by appropriating their imagery and creativity, and redeeming them within a Biblical worldview. Improve your imagination in your approach to glorifying God and defending the faith.

Demonizing the Pagan Gods
God verbally attacked his opponents, pagans and their gods, using sarcasm, mockery, name-calling.

Old Testament Storytelling Apologetics
Israel shared creative images with their pagan neighbors: The sea dragon of chaos and the storm god. The Bible invests them with new meaning.

Biblical Creation and Storytelling
Creation stories in the ancient Near East and the Bible both express a primeval battle of deity to create order out of chaos. But how do they differ?

The Universe in Ancient Imagination
A detailed comparison and contrast of the Biblical picture of the universe with the ancient pagan one. What's the difference?

New Testament Storytelling Apologetics
Paul's sermon to the pagans on Mars Hill is an example of subversion: Communicating the Gospel in terms of a pagan narrative with a view toward replacing their worldview.

Imagination in Prophecy & Apocalypse
God uses imaginative descriptions of future events to deliberately obscure his message while simultaneously showing the true meaning and purpose behind history.

An Apologetic of Biblical Horror
Learn how God uses horror in the Bible as a tool to communicate spiritual, moral and social truth in the context of repentance from sin and redemptive victory over evil.

For More Info
www.Godawa.com

THE IMAGINATION OF GOD

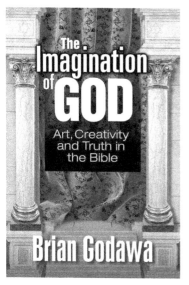

Art, Creativity and Truth in the Bible

In his refreshing and challenging book, Godawa helps you break free from the spiritual suffocation of heady faith. Without negating the importance of reason and doctrine, Godawa challenges you to move from understanding the Bible "literally" to "literarily" by exploring the poetry, parables and metaphors found in God's Word. Weaving historical insight, pop culture and personal narrative throughout, Godawa reveals the importance God places on imagination and creativity in the Scriptures, and provides a Biblical foundation for Christians to pursue imagination, beauty, wonder and mystery in their faith.

This book was previously released with the title, *Word Pictures: Knowing God Through Story and Imagination.*

Endorsements:

"Brian Godawa is that rare breed—a philosopher/artist—who opens our eyes to the aesthetic dimension of spirituality. Cogently argued and fun to read, Godawa shows convincingly that God interacts with us as whole persons, not only through didactic teaching but also through metaphor, symbol, and sacrament."

— Nancy R. Pearcey,
Author, *Total Truth: Liberating Christianity from its Cultural Captivity*

"A spirited and balanced defense of the imagination as a potential conveyer of truth. There is a lot of good literary theory in the book, as well as an autobiographical story line. The thoroughness of research makes the book a triumph of scholarship as well."

— Leland Ryken, Clyde S. Kilby Professor of English, Wheaton College, Illinois
Author, *The Christian Imagination: The Practice of Faith in Literature & Writing.*

For More Info
www.Godawa.com

ABOUT THE AUTHOR

Brian Godawa is the screenwriter for the award-winning feature film, *To End All Wars,* starring Kiefer Sutherland. It was awarded the Commander in Chief Medal of Service, Honor and Pride by the Veterans of Foreign Wars, won the first Heartland Film Festival by storm, and showcased the Cannes Film Festival Cinema for Peace.

He also co-wrote *Alleged*, starring Brian Dennehy as Clarence Darrow and Fred Thompson as William Jennings Bryan. He previously adapted to film the best-selling supernatural thriller novel *The Visitation* by author Frank Peretti for Ralph Winter (*X-Men, Wolverine*), and wrote and directed *Wall of Separation,* a PBS documentary, and *Lines That Divide*, a documentary on stem cell research.

Mr. Godawa's scripts have won multiple awards in respected screenplay competitions, and his articles on movies and philosophy have been published around the world. He has traveled around the United States teaching on movies, worldviews, and culture to colleges, churches and community groups.

His popular book, *Hollywood Worldviews: Watching Films with Wisdom and Discernment* (InterVarsity Press) is used as a textbook in schools around the country. His novel series, the saga *Chronicles of the Nephilim* is in the Top 10 of Biblical Fiction on Amazon and is an imaginative retelling of Biblical stories of the Nephilim giants, the secret plan of the fallen Watchers, and the War of the Seed of the Serpent with the Seed of Eve. The sequel series, *Chronicles of the Apocalypse* tells the story of the Apostle John's book of Revelation, and *Chronicles of the Watchers* recounts true history through the Watcher paradigm.

Find out more about his other books, lecture tapes and dvds for sale at his website www.godawa.com.

BLANK PAGE

BLANK PAGE

BLANK PAGE

BLANK PAGE

BLANK PAGE

BLANK PAGE

BLANK PAGE

BLANK PAGE

BLANK PAGE

BLANK PAGE

BLANK PAGE

Printed in the USA
CPSIA information can be obtained
at www.ICGtesting.com
LVHW022240250324
775504LV00040B/1115

9 780991 143467